Praise for

THE INSPECTOR RAMIREZ SERIES

"Peggy Blair writes like an author possessed, with story-telling skills that make her a must-read writer beyond the mystery genre."

—*The Hamilton Spectator*

"Blair's prose is evocative, nary a word amiss."

—*The Vancouver Sun*

"An affecting series. Even if impoverished and politically oppressed Havana presents unique burdens, Ramirez is not without a sense of humour as he goes about his clever sleuthing."

—*Toronto Star*

"This series . . . continues to be a delight."

—*The Chronicle Herald*

"Blair invests Havana geography (with its decaying buildings and rusting American cars) with new vigor by focusing not only on photo-worthy street scenes but also on the complex lives of the people who live inside the broken buildings."

—*Booklist*

"Ramirez is a wonderful guide—hiding nothing but hoping we'll look past the poverty, hardship and political corruption to see the beauty and humanity of his battered city."

—*The New York Times*

"Great sensitivity and a well-timed sense of humor."

—*Kirkus Reviews*

ALSO BY PEGGY BLAIR

Hungry Ghosts
The Poisoned Pawn
The Beggar's Opera

UMBRELLA MAN

PEGGY BLAIR

Published by Simon & Schuster

New York   London   Toronto   Sydney   New Delhi

SIMON &
SCHUSTER
CANADA

Simon & Schuster Canada
A Division of Simon & Schuster, Inc.
166 King Street East, Suite 300
Toronto, Ontario M5A 1J3

This Simon & Schuster Canada edition June 2016

SIMON & SCHUSTER CANADA and colophon are registered trademarks
of Simon & Schuster, Inc.

For information about special discounts for bulk purchases,
please contact Simon & Schuster Special Sales at 1-800-268-3216
or CustomerService@simonandschuster.ca.

Manufactured in the United States of America

10 9 8 7 6 5 4 3 2 1

Library and Archives Canada Cataloguing in Publication

Blair, Peggy J. (Peggy Janice), 1955–, author

        Umbrella man/ Peggy Blair.
Issued in print and electronic formats.
978-1-4767-5796-4 (paperback).—ISBN 978-1-4767-5797-1 (ebook)
        I. Title.

PS8603.L316U45 2016   C813'.6   C2015-908144-0
                                        C2015-908145-9

ISBN 978-1-4767-5796-4
ISBN 978-1-4767-5797-1 (ebook)

TO IAN RANKIN, WITH THANKS

A murder is abstract. You pull the trigger and after that you do not understand anything that happens.

—Jean-Paul Sartre

UMBRELLA MAN

1

An old black woman sat on the curb beside Ramirez's small blue car. She lifted her head as he approached, fixing her dark eyes on his. He couldn't tell from her expression if she was sad or angry.

Inspector Ricardo Ramirez eased himself onto the curb beside her. "Your grandmother," Mama Loa said, in her soft Creole accent, "she come to see me last night. She say the gods don't like that you gave back your gift."

Although Ramirez's long-deceased slave grandmother was Yoruba, and Mama Loa was Vodun, both adhered to Santería, a mix of Catholicism and African animism. They both believed the dead were everywhere, and that they visited their dreams.

"Have you found a new home yet?" Ramirez asked the old woman uneasily, changing the subject. The last time he'd seen Mama Loa, he had given her a thick braid of gold chain, one of the many seized items that never quite found their way into the police exhibit room. The chain was valuable enough on the black market to pay for at least a few months' accommodation for the old woman and her strays.

"Not yet," Mama Loa said, shaking her head. Her long grey dreadlocks bounced on her shoulders. "The government still looking for a place for us, I guess. I got a new goddaughter waiting to move in with me. But Nevara say she don't want to wait no more. She say some Russian's going to pay her to go to work for him instead."

Her goddaughters, Mama Loa called them. Prostitutes. *Jineteras* who had no safe place to live when they wanted to get off the streets. They found a sort of refuge with her, or at least they had, until the apartment building she'd lived in was declared too dangerous for habitation, which in Havana was saying something.

A bureaucratically displaced person like Mama Loa had few options. She'd ended up living in a shack made from scavenged wood in a shanty town on the outskirts of the city. The Isle of Dust, locals called it. That's about all that was left of their hopes once they landed there, thought Ramirez—ashes and dust.

"Believe me, I appreciate everything you done for us." Mama Loa glanced at him sideways. The whites of her eyes were bright against her ebony skin. "I know you think I'm crazy. But I always speak the truth."

Ramirez tried not to smile at her unabashed honesty. "I've never doubted that for a moment, Mama Loa."

"It's not your fault you don't know the way. Your grandmother, she say she warned you to never make the gods angry."

"I'm sorry to hear you had such frightening dreams." Ramirez shifted from one foot to the other. How could she possibly know about his grandmother's warning, or what he'd done to rid himself of his visions? Had Mama Loa followed him to the beach that afternoon in March, watched him scrape a shallow hole in the hot sand?

He'd burned heaven money he'd purchased at a Chinatown kiosk—paper bills in ridiculously high denominations. The vendor had laughed and called it hell money. The irony hadn't escaped him—that he'd found himself pleading with ancient gods to convince ghosts he wasn't sure existed either, to leave him alone so his life could return to normal. But afterwards, the spirits that haunted him had vanished. Had they ever been real?

Ramirez's beloved grandmother had died when he was ten. On her deathbed, she'd warned that he would see ghosts, his gift as the eldest son. But his mother quickly disavowed him of that notion: his grandmother had been sick. She had dementia; she didn't always know what she was saying.

Eventually, as time passed without him seeing any ghosts, young Ricky reluctantly came to accept that his grandmother had made it up. After all, she'd also told him fanciful stories of lost pirate ships and giant squid, of huge octopuses that waged deadly underwater battles by gripping poisonous blue jellyfish in their tentacles as weapons.

But then he joined the Cuban National Revolutionary Police, or PNR, and, as soon as he was promoted to homicides, the murder victims of his unsolved files began to haunt him. He'd begged the gods to take them away, that hot day in March, and now the ghosts were gone. Ramirez had since managed to persuade himself that the apparitions were simply hallucinations, products of stress, too much work, too little sleep.

As for how the ghosts so often knew things that Ramirez himself didn't know, his friend Hector Apiro once described how the human brain could retain information without being aware of it. "A German suffers a head injury one night and wakes up speaking Welsh," Apiro had chortled, bobbing his large head, "a language he claims he's never heard before, and an excruciatingly difficult one at that. And yet he must have encountered it somewhere, because suddenly he's fluent. The brain is a complex repository, Ricardo—the biggest library in the world."

That's all the ghosts were, Ramirez decided. Buried memories.

Subconscious tricks. People he'd encountered somewhere and forgotten. Nothing to do with an absurd, superstitious prayer to the
orishas on a stifling hot day or a dying woman's vivid imagination.

Suddenly embarrassed, he glanced at his watch and stood up.
The light fabric of his pants clung to his legs. He tried to straighten
the creases.

"You'll have to excuse me, Mama Loa. My wife and I have plans
to go to a movie this afternoon. She'll be annoyed if I'm late. And
trust me, even the gods don't want to see Francesca angry." He
smiled, but Mama Loa's face remained stern.

"I know you don't believe me yet," she said, "but you will."
She pointed a long, nicotine-stained finger towards the heavens.
A jetliner was passing high overhead; it left a brushstroke of white
against the intense blue sky. "The sky gods aren't happy with you.
Those people up there who fly in the clouds? Some of them are
going to die."

2

Elizardo Ramos Avilo parked his bright yellow coco-taxi in the shade of a royal palm tree. The cab—a round fibreglass shell mounted on a three-wheeled moped—was open at the front and sides with a cut-out rear window to let in the breeze. Even so, the plastic seats were hot. So was the *chica* in tight little shorts and a skimpy top shimmying towards him down Paseo del Prado, past the tourists and the old men playing dominoes in the shade of the boulevard's trees. She wriggled her hips to the rhumba music that drifted from cafés, the blasts of Carlos Santana from car radios.

"Hey, *linda*," he called out, "you wanna ride, sweetheart?"

He was still grinning when his vehicle rocked sideways as an *extranjero* clambered in the back and tossed a handful of pesos his way. "You speak English?" the man said.

"Sure, dude." Elizardo reached down to pick up the bills, astonished to find a hundred CUCs, or convertible pesos. The usual fare was five, and even that was generous in a country where most people lived on less than the equivalent of ten or fifteen dollars a month. He ran his fingers over the tourist currency, hardly believing his good luck.

"Then drive. Fast." The passenger pointed towards the Malecón. He slapped the back of Elizardo's seat. "Fucking *go!*"

"Okay, okay," said Elizardo.

Turistas, he thought. Why the rush? It was a beautiful day: deep-blue sky, only a few thin clouds, a slight breeze. Why not relax? Besides, the speed limit in Havana was fifty kilometres, and there were *policías* on almost every corner. He couldn't afford to pay a hefty fine, not even for a big fare like this.

He strapped on his black helmet and started the ignition. He pulled the coco-taxi around and headed north, towards the Malecón.

"This way," the man urged, as they approached the intersection of El Prado and the famous seaway. He gestured west, in the direction of Vedado. "I need to get back to my hotel."

Elizardo checked the two round mirrors that poked up like tiny periscopes on either side of his cab. The squat little taxis were so low to the ground that buses and trucks couldn't easily see them, and they had no protective bumpers. Coco-taxi drivers had to be alert to avoid accidents; if they hit another vehicle, the odds weren't in their favour.

A red car suddenly pulled up behind them—too close for comfort. Elizardo turned his head, shouting to be heard above the *put-put-put* of his motor. "Hey, *acere*, give us a little room, man."

The driver held an arm out the window and waved at Elizardo to pull over.

Elizardo was offended. He had a high-paying passenger in a hurry, and it wasn't a police car. Why should he stop? He shouted at the driver to change lanes if he wanted to pass and kept going. Then he heard a loud *crack*, and the fibreglass shell of his taxi shattered.

"*Yob tvoyu mat*," his passenger screamed in Russian. Fuck your mother.

Something whizzed past his head and Elizardo ducked. "Jesus," he shouted, crossing himself with his right hand. "He's shooting at us." He hit the throttle hard and jerked the handlebars to the right, swerving across two lanes of traffic. The red car stayed right on his tail. Angry horns barked; worn brake pads screamed as a *carro* skidded sideways to avoid a collision. Elizardo's coco-taxi clipped the front wheel of a bicycle rickshaw. The bici-taxi almost tipped over as the coco-taxi jumped the curb.

"*¿Que coño?*" the driver bellowed, waving his fist. What the fuck? "You're on the sidewalk!"

"Sorry," Elizardo yelled back.

"Keep going," his passenger shouted, leaning forward. "Don't let him catch up!"

Elizardo narrowly missed hitting a decades-old Chevy as he raced down the pitted limestone sidewalk next to the seawall. He steered the moped between tourists, hustlers, and street musicians, who scattered to get out of his way.

A young *policía* dove to the side as the vehicles almost ran him down. "Hey, you!" he shrieked. "Stop!" He grabbed for his police radio and began to run after them. Two other foot patrolmen quickly joined the chase.

The red car pulled beside Elizardo's vehicle, forcing him towards the stone wall of the Malecón. As soon as Elizardo was trapped, the red car rammed his cab hard.

The coco-taxi careened crazily. Two of its three tires lifted off the ground; it took all of Elizardo's strength to keep it upright. Then the red car butted it again.

The little cab spun like a top before it wobbled into the path of a heavily loaded truck. The impact knocked the coco-taxi over and stopped the truck cold. Hundreds of watermelons tumbled from the truck's tailgate, scattering fragments of green shell and pink flesh as they bounced and smashed along the seaway.

The coco-taxi rolled like a billiard ball before it finally came to rest on its side.

Elizardo crawled out. He tried pulling his passenger from the debris, but the man was firmly stuck. Blood trickled down the man's forehead.

Elizardo saw the driver's door of the red car open; he heard it slam shut. "I'm sorry," he whispered, tears filling his eyes at his cowardice. He scrambled on his hands and knees behind the melon truck, leaving his injured passenger behind. The truck driver remained in his cab, too dazed to move.

Seconds passed before Elizardo dared to peek beneath the truck's chassis. All he could see were sharp-toed boots as the driver approached the wreckage of Elizardo's livelihood. But when the driver squatted down, Elizardo's eyes fixed on his small black gun.

"I thought it was you," the gunman said in Russian.

"*Potselui mou zhopy*," the passenger responded angrily. Kiss my ass.

The gunman rifled casually through the passenger's clothing as the man struggled to get free. He pulled a flat booklet from the man's pants pocket and flipped it open before slipping it into his own. "*Nu vse, tebe pizda*," the gunman said and shrugged. Elizardo understood the words: That's it; you're fucking dead.

"Fuck," said Elizardo. He looked over his shoulder. There were always *policías* lounging on every street corner. Where were they today? Sirens throbbed in the distance. He saw the three foot patrolmen running towards them—getting closer—but they were still at least two blocks away.

Elizardo watched, stunned, as the gunman pressed his gun to the temple of the best-paying passenger he'd ever had in his short life and pulled the trigger.

3

The lineup snaked down Avenida and all around the block. People spilled over the sidewalk and onto the street. Cinemagoers queued as if lining up for the monthly ration of black beans instead of a Sunday matinee.

A handful of policemen stood on the street, closely watching the *cola*. Sometimes, crowds surged when the theatre doors opened. On occasion, people were injured.

"Open the doors!" someone yelled. Others in the lineup whooped and cheered.

"Are you sure you want to take a chance on waiting?" Ramirez asked Francesca. He craned his head to count the people ahead of them, calculating how many seats there were in the Cine Acapulco's auditorium and their odds of getting in.

"I'm sure we can find something to do at home if we have to," Francesca squeezed his arm and grinned. "After all, we don't have to pick up the children until late this evening. But we so seldom go out, Ricardo. Let's wait and see if we get lucky."

"Well," said Ramirez, leaning in to her, "I certainly like the backup plan. It sounds as if I'll get lucky either way." He kissed the side of his wife's neck, almost hoping the *cola* proved to be too long.

The manager opened the glass doors to the flat-roofed brick building and the crowd pushed slowly forward. Once they'd squeezed inside, Ramirez bought two tickets. They cost four pesos, the equivalent of around twenty cents. Ramirez wondered how many tourists in the line with them were aware they would be charged CUCs and pay almost twenty times as much to see the same show.

They made their way through the foyer, admiring its giant mirrors and ornate wood panelling. The screening room was a huge auditorium with an old projector and faded screen.

Most of the cinemas in Havana had been shuttered or demolished after the revolution. Most of those that remained were hot and stuffy like this one, and the seats were hard; it was the reason Cubans nicknamed their equally uncomfortable buses "Saturday movies." Nonetheless, people were addicted. Supply and demand, thought Ramirez. They always want what they can't easily have.

They found seats near the back of the room just as the first reel unwound. Ramirez sat back, enjoying the warmth of Francesca's hand resting against his thigh. He let go of thoughts of Mama Loa and her unnerving prophecy and began to relax.

The Lives of Others was set in Communist East Germany. A Stasi agent, Wiesler, was assigned to monitor a playwright named Dreyman. Ramirez and Francesca watched, fascinated, as Wiesler and his team meticulously planted listening devices throughout Dreyman's apartment.

It could be called *Our Life*, Ramirez thought. He hadn't yet told Francesca that their own apartment had been bugged by the Ministry of the Interior eight months before. Manuel Flores, a criminal profiler, acting on the minister's orders, had hoped to find something incriminating to use against Ramirez. Instead, when Ramirez discovered the listening devices, he'd left them in place so he could misdirect his eaves-droppers while he sorted out what to do. He'd used them, in fact, to trap Dr. Flores into confessing he'd conspired with the American CIA.

But now that Flores was in custody in Mazorra, Ramirez's some-what rocky relationship with the minister had regained equilibrium. Ramirez once again reported to General de Soto, the head of the Havana Division of the National Revolutionary Police, instead of directly to the politician.

Ramirez genuinely liked the general, who had once been a de-tective himself, and not having to deal directly with the minister relieved some of the political pressure on Ramirez and his unit. It helped as well that Havana had not experienced a homicide in months. Ramirez now spent his evenings kicking a soccer ball with his son, Edel, in the park across the street from their apartment and reading bedtime stories to his little girl, Estella.

Ramirez wasn't sure if the lull in murders was the reason his ghosts had vanished, but when his visions disappeared so had his resolve to tell Francesca about them. She had no idea he'd ever seen them, or how frequently. She'd always thought she and Ramirez were alone when all too often they weren't.

Right now, he thought, if his ghosts were still around, it would be typical for one of them to be seated nearby, nodding to him, per-haps pointing to something in the movie that might help him solve his or her murder.

They'd show up in his car, his apartment, his office, and at his crime scenes. Most never spoke, only gestured, and since Ramirez wasn't particularly good at charades, he frequently misunderstood what they wanted to tell him. They were polite and considerate about personal boundaries—all he had to do was give them a meaningful glance and they would shrug apologetically and leave. His bedroom was usually off limits, as was the bathroom, although not the one down the hall from the Major Crimes Unit, Havana Division.

But he hadn't known how to tell Francesca that their apartment was often haunted by people who had been stabbed, strangled, beaten, or drowned. It would anger her, he knew, the idea of silent strangers wandering around their home—even more than the notion that he'd lost his mind.

Ramirez had been raised a Catholic. He wasn't sure if he had ever believed in Santería, despite his Yoruba grandmother telling him stories of gods so flawed they were practically human. He hadn't completely believed in the supernatural even when he was seeing ghosts; for years, he thought he had inherited his grandmother's rare form of Lewy Body dementia. Then Hector Apiro found her autopsy records and said she'd died of natural causes.

But like most Cubans, Ramirez hedged his bets. You didn't have to believe in God to believe in ghosts, did you? Or believe in ghosts to believe in gods? It was a philosophical debate he could save for Apiro's morgue. It was the kind of discussion he would find interesting.

But he'd never told Apiro. In fact, the only person he'd ever told about his ghosts was Manuel Flores, because Flores was a psychiatrist as well as a criminal profiler, and Flores had used that information against him. Ramirez no longer had the courage to tell anyone his secret. Not his wife. And certainly not his best friend.

"I can't believe that it was illegal in East Germany to own a typewriter," Francesca said, as they strolled back to his car after the movie, holding hands. It was late afternoon. A light breeze ruffled Francesca's short skirt. Ramirez was flattered by the number of men he saw admiring her legs. She ignored the catcalls and hisses, but he knew that she was pleased too.

"Maybe it wasn't," he said. "It could have been a plot device. Perhaps the red ribbon was supposed to be a metaphor for censorship."

Francesca nodded thoughtfully. "I like that Wiesler removed it before the Stasi arrived, though. He tried to protect Dreyman, even though Dreyman was the person he was supposed to be investigating."

"I worry about that sometimes," Ramirez said. "Becoming like Wiesler. Overly sympathetic to my quarry. Losing my objectivity."

"That's a funny way to think of suspects, Ricardo," Francesca said. "As prey." She smiled and squeezed his fingers. "Poor Wiesler. He did the right thing and got caught. Now he has to spend the rest of his career steaming open envelopes in a dark little room. I'm so glad we don't live in a country where we have to worry about someone watching our every move."

Ramirez did nothing to relieve his wife of her innocence. "Don't worry. It could never happen here—there's a shortage of typewriters."

Francesca chuckled. "I loved how Dreyman's piano sonata changed the way Wiesler thought about the world," she said, as Ramirez opened the passenger door for her. She slid onto her seat. "Oh my goodness, that's hot."

Ramirez walked to the other side of the car and pulled on the driver's door. He left it open for a moment, hoping to cool the interior. He finally climbed in, squirming as the heated vinyl burned through the light fabric of his clothing. "Lenin once said that if he had listened to Beethoven's *Appassionata* a little longer, he might never have finished the revolution."

"Too bad Fidel didn't listen to Beethoven. Maybe we'd have at least one theatre that still had air conditioning."

Ramirez smiled at his wife's subversiveness. As he put the key in the ignition his cell phone rang. "Just a minute, *cariño*." He took the call, frowning as he heard the news.

"I'll have to drop you off with my parents," he told Francesca. "There's been a car accident on the Malecón."

"That doesn't usually involve Major Crimes, does it?"

Ramirez shook his head. His unit mostly dealt with homicides. "No. But Hector wants me there. There must be something about it that's unusual. I'll try not to be long. We can always leave the children with my parents some other night. The only thing going on this week is the trade fair, and nothing ever happens there."

But as it turned out, Ramirez was wrong.

4

Inspector Ramirez parked his Chinese mini-car behind the row of white police cruisers that blocked the six lanes of the Malecón to traffic. Their blue lights winked like a string of Christmas lights. He got out, slamming the rusted car door to secure it, and stood for a moment, surveying the scene.

The decrepit buildings on the other side of the seaway were little more than facades, the wrought-iron lampposts in front of them the only evidence of the restoration transforming Old Havana into a tourist destination.

A bright yellow coco-taxi lay on its side next to the sidewalk, its fibreglass body cracked in pieces like an eggshell. A dozen or so blue-uniformed policemen gathered in clusters, waiting for instructions. Two patrolmen stood about thirty feet apart in the middle of the road, measuring a thick black skid mark with a long grey tape.

Hundreds of smashed watermelons littered the cracked asphalt.

A white-coated technician was sweeping away fragments with a wooden broom, as screeching gulls circled above.

An old truck was parked a few hundred yards from the remnants of the coco-taxi, its tailgate down and bed empty, the hood crushed like an empty pop can. A morose-looking man leaned against the seawall, massaging his forehead with one gnarled hand. From the man's weathered complexion and sad expression, Ramirez assumed the broken melons were his.

Detective Fernando Espinoza stood on the sidewalk, making notes as he spoke to a man who gripped a motorcycle helmet in both hands. Ramirez guessed it was the coco-taxi driver; they were required by law to wear helmets.

A white technical services van was parked beside them. Between the truck and the shattered coco-taxi, Hector Apiro kneeled beside a man's body that was stretched out on a black plastic tarp. Ramirez glanced from side to side but saw no sign of the man's ghost.

Ramirez nodded to Detective Espinoza and walked over. Apiro worked part-time as the pathologist on call to the Major Crimes Unit. He suffered from—or, more accurately, lived with—achondroplasia. Dwarfism was a genetic condition, he'd explained to Ramirez, but he couldn't trace it in his case to any particular family member. He'd been adopted and knew nothing about his parents. His size startled most people. His head and hands were unusually large, while his legs and arms were abnormally short. His intellect and his generosity, however, were huge.

"Who's going to pay for all of this?" Ramirez heard the coco-taxi driver say to Espinoza.

"It could be worse, Señor," the young detective replied. "We could charge you with speeding."

"*Hola*, Hector," Ramirez said to his closest friend. "What do we have here? I don't usually get called to come to a collision."

The deceased was a large man, Ramirez noted, white, perhaps in his late thirties. He wore a tailored dark grey suit that looked foreign, perhaps European. His hair was cropped close to his skull.

The pathologist looked up and smiled. "Good afternoon, Ricardo. It's more like an execution, I'm afraid. This man was shot at extremely close range. There's gunshot residue around the entry wound. That means the gunman held his weapon right up against the victim's temple when he pulled the trigger." He lifted the dead man's head and gently turned it to show Ramirez the damage. Ramirez crouched to get a better look.

"It's a hard contact wound," Apiro said. "You can tell by the abrasion ring, here." He pointed with a gloved finger to a dark circle on the victim's temple. "That's the imprint of the barrel. The fact that the contusion is round indicates he held the gun perpendicular to the head; otherwise, the defect would be shaped like a teardrop. If you can find the gun, this mark might help identify it. But the pressure may have created a seal between the muzzle and the victim's skin. That can stop combustion gases from escaping. There may not be any tattooing."

Ramirez understood Apiro's verbal shorthand. When a gun was fired at short range, gunpowder was forced into the skin at a high velocity and left a spray of marks, called *tattooing*, on the shooter's hand. But if the gun was pressed tightly enough against the victim's skin, the combustion left its mark on the victim instead.

Ramirez frowned. In all his years of investigating homicides, he had never seen an execution-style killing. Shootings were rare at the best of times. There were only a few thousand guns on the island, most of them improvised from common household materials or smuggled in; occasionally, one or two floated around the black market.

But finding ammunition could be tricky. Even military exercises usually involved unloaded weapons. With little to no military budget for ammunition, the army assigned soldiers who once fought in Angola and Ethiopia to repair sewers and dig up fields.

"Do we know who he is?" Ramirez asked.

Apiro shook his large head. "No ID. Only a wallet full of kooks." *Kooks* was slang for the convertible pesos, or CUCs, which foreigners were required to use. It was illegal for Cubans to exchange them; they had their own nearly worthless currency. "I'll take fingerprints once we get the body to the morgue."

"The coco-taxi driver's name is Elizardo Ramos," said Fernando Espinoza as he joined them. Ramirez stood up. "Señor Ramos thinks the victim was Russian," Espinoza continued. "He's picked up a few words from his passengers over the years, mostly swear words. He heard the shooter speak Russian too."

Espinoza flipped through the pages of his notebook, running his finger beneath the lines as he summarized what the witness had said. "Señor Ramos picked up his fare at the corner of the Malecón and Prado at approximately fifteen forty-five. A red Peugeot started chasing them when they turned west onto the seaway. He thinks the shooter fired at his cab a couple of times, because the shell fractured, but he never heard any actual gunfire, not even when the gunman shot the victim. None of the other witnesses heard any shots either."

"A silencer?"

Espinoza shook his head. "Señor Ramos saw the gun. It was small and snub-nosed. Black. Nothing was attached to the muzzle. By the way, a foot patrolman, Officer Pacheco, observed most of the chase. He says the vehicles almost hit him when they drove down the sidewalk. He ran after them for blocks. The shooter's car sped off just as he caught up. It had maroon plates—he recorded a partial number. I've called it in already. The first letter was a *T*."

Ramirez nodded slowly. "A tourist rental," he said. All vehicles in Cuba had coloured plates to indicate if they were government or privately owned. Sometimes the plates flagged the status of the person driving them. The ones on rental cars were maroon, with a *T* for *tourist*. "Can anyone identify the shooter?"

"No. They all said it happened too fast. Señor Ramos hid behind the truck as soon as the driver got out. He looked under it a few times, but he only saw the lower part of the shooter's body. He says the shooter bent down and rifled through the victim's clothes. He took something from the victim's left pants pocket before he killed him. It was burgundy or dark red. Señor Ramos isn't sure but says it looked like a passport."

Ramirez nodded. EU passports were burgundy, as were Lebanese passports and those from the UK. But so were Russian ones.

It troubled Ramirez that the gunman had searched for identification before he pulled the trigger. "I hope this wasn't a contract killing," he said. He looked over his shoulder, half-expecting to see the dead man materialize to offer him silent clues about his executioner. For the first time since his ghosts disappeared, Ramirez wondered if he'd made the right decision when he banished them.

Natasha Delgado, the only female detective in his unit, jogged over. "Patrol's found an abandoned vehicle. It's red, with signs of damage to the front fender and hood. It was left running on a numbered *calle* in Vedado. The keys are in the ignition but the licence plates are gone."

"That must be the one," said Espinoza. "Why leave it running?"

"Maybe he was hoping someone would steal it," said Delgado.

"I think this man is a professional," Ramirez said. "He probably thought it would take us longer to find out it was a rental if he removed the plates. And it would have, if not for that foot patrolman, Pacheco. The shooter also checked the victim's identification. I think he wanted to be sure he had the right man before he pulled the trigger."

Ramirez turned to Delgado. "Natasha, get one of the patrolmen to take you over to the abandoned car. Find the serial number and run it through the motor vehicle registry. I want to know which agency rented it, who they rented it to, and when. See if the rental clerk remembers anything about the transaction. Ask if they have a security camera."

Delgado bobbed her head and quickly walked back to the group of patrolmen to negotiate a ride. At this time of year, even police cars were low on fuel—favours would be exchanged.

"I'll send one of my technicians with them to dust the car for prints before it's towed to the compound," Apiro said. He stood up painfully. Ramirez had observed him limping more often recently. His condition caused his joints to be sore, but there was almost no aspirin to be found because of the trade embargo, and little to relieve his discomfort.

"When will you do the autopsy?" Ramirez asked.

"Tomorrow morning at eight. I have another one scheduled tonight: an old woman they brought to the hospital morgue a few hours ago. I think she died of natural causes, but because of the advanced state of decomposition, the hospital wants to be sure." As well as working part-time on call for Major Crimes, and seeing plastic surgery patients occasionally, Apiro had recently returned to shifts at the emergency room to make a little extra money. Ramirez thought it was because Maria Vasquez had moved in with him; she far out-earned Apiro, and the small doctor had his pride.

"We need to identify this man as soon as possible," said Ramirez. He thought for a moment. "Fernando, I want you to accompany the body to the morgue. After the technicians have cleaned him up, get a photograph and take a copy around to the hotels."

Ramirez knew that finding an unidentified guest by checking with each hotel was a long shot—hundreds of thousands of tourists visited Havana every year—but for the moment that was all they had to work with. "Get Patrol to help you. Russia, the EU countries, Lebanon, they all have burgundy passports. Let's check with their embassies. Maybe someone will know who he is."

"What about the British consulate?" said Espinoza. "UK passports are burgundy."

"Yes," Ramirez nodded. "There, too."

"The people you show the photograph to will need to use their imagination, Detective Espinoza," said Apiro. "A high-velocity shot to the head like this distorts the features. It stretches the skin on impact. It has almost the effect of a facelift. He may have been a decade older than he looks."

Ramirez studied the crumbling buildings on the opposite side of the Malecón, searching for video cameras. There were at least two on every city block, monitored by Cuban Intelligence officers. Most *habaneros*, including his wife, conducted their daily lives unaware of the full extent of the surveillance.

He made a mental note to find out if there were any cameras nearby that might have captured some of the chase.

"Let's get a copy of that photograph to the airport as well," he instructed Espinoza. "If this man was a foreigner, he had to come through Customs."

Espinoza scribbled in his notebook. "I forgot to mention, Inspector," he said. "The shooter said something in Russian before he shot the victim. Señor Ramos wasn't sure if he heard it correctly." He flipped through the pages until he found the entry. He pronounced the words phonetically.

"Interesting," said Apiro. He raised his thick grey eyebrows. He had studied plastic surgery in Moscow and spoke Russian fluently. "It means, 'You should have stayed dead.'"

5

Dan Yaworsky was surprised that the Captain had chosen this dump as their meeting place. The motel was a shack on the outskirts of Washington, DC. It was so rundown that it looked like a set from *Psycho.*

His shoes kept sticking to the cracked linoleum in the bathroom. He sure wasn't about to take them off. He half-expected to see blood running down the drain when he pulled aside the stained shower curtain. He checked baseboards, lights, and switches with a radio frequency detector. Cockroaches scuttled away as he swept beneath the sagging bed. Satisfied there were no bugs besides them, Yaworsky opened the front door to let the Captain in.

Everyone in Special Ops called the older man the Captain. He had been a submarine warfare specialist—some kind of cryptologist—until they'd decommissioned his sub.

The older man had a bottle of Jack Daniel's tucked under one arm. He looked around the cramped space purposefully, then walked over to the battered chest of drawers. A tray with two smudged water glasses sat on top. He pulled the paper cover from one, twisted the cap off the bottle, and poured himself a drink. He held the bottle, waggling it in the air, inviting Yaworsky to join him. The amber liquid caught the light. Yaworsky nodded, wondering why they were there.

The Captain filled a second glass and handed it to Yaworsky. Then he strode to the window and shut the curtains tightly. He seated himself in one of two shabby chairs and gestured to Yaworsky to sit down.

Before he did, Yaworsky picked up both paper covers and tucked them in his jacket pocket. He reminded himself to wipe down all the smooth surfaces before they left, including the doorknobs.

The Captain tipped his tumbler from side to side, letting the bourbon varnish the walls of the glass. Probably to disinfect it, thought Yaworsky. It wasn't a bad idea; he did the same.

"Now, Dan, I'm sure you know all about Lourdes," said the Captain. "The listening post, I mean. Not the place that's supposed to have all the miracles."

"The one in Cuba? Sure."

Lourdes had been Russia's central processing facility for electronic espionage. It had been the most valuable tool in the Russian spy network until Putin closed it in 2001. Yaworsky recalled that Raúl Castro once told a group of Mexican journalists that almost all of Russia's strategic intelligence was routed through it.

"Vladimir Putin shut it down after President Bush said we would never deploy our missile defence systems in Eastern Europe," Yaworsky said.

That was the same year Yaworsky had started in Special Ops, only a few months after Ana Montes, the senior Cuban analyst in Defence Intelligence, was charged with treason.

"That's the one," the Captain said. He took a drink from his glass. Yaworsky waited, remembering his training. *People don't like silence; they fill it up with words.*

"I sometimes think Putin was happy to let the damn thing go," the Captain mused. "It was their largest SIGINT site." The term stood for signals intelligence, the gathering of information by intercepting signals. "But it cost them almost two hundred million a year to rent, and they weren't getting shit except disinformation, mostly from our unit. Castro was sure pissed off, though, when two thousand Russian intelligence officers up and left without any notice."

Fibre optics had changed the spying game and rendered the post obsolete. Information was no longer carried by microwave and satellite communications. Digital cell phones were often encrypted; it wasn't as easy to grab emails as before.

Even so, Yaworsky recalled, the closure had come as a huge surprise to the Cuban government. The Russians had told them the listening post would be permanent. And Cuba needed the money. Seven thousand Soviets had already abandoned the country following the collapse of the Soviet Union, leaving behind only their Ladas and Gazas and thirty billion dollars of loans they somehow expected to be repaid.

"Castro said that was the end of Cuba's military ties with Russia," Yaworsky said.

The Captain nodded. "And it was, right up until George Bush started talking about setting up defence missile shields in Poland and the Czech Republic."

The Captain shook his head as if he couldn't imagine anything more stupid. Not President Bush *doing* it, but announcing it to the press. Putin was furious, Yaworsky remembered. He'd called Bush a liar. Just a month or two ago, he'd equated Bush's plans with the Cuban missile crisis of 1962—or, as Cubans called it, the October Crisis—when the U.S. and the Soviet Union went mano-a-mano and almost started a nuclear war.

"In the past couple of months," the Captain said ruefully, "Russia's been warming up to Cuba faster than a hooker in the back of a police car."

"So I've heard," said Yaworsky. "Igor Sechin, the Russian deputy prime minister, visited Havana three times this year. There's scuttle that Putin could start refuelling Russian military jets on Cuban air-bases, maybe go so far as to reopen Lourdes, now that they've closed their listening post in Yemen. There are even rumours he could send warships to Cuba."

Of course, Russia denied them. "We regard these sorts of reports from anonymous sources as nothing more than disinformation," a Russian defence ministry spokesman was quoted as saying in the press. Well, if it was, thought Yaworsky, it was one of the rare times when the disinformation didn't originate from *his* section.

The Captain smiled slightly. "If Putin sends warships down there, the State Department will issue a statement saying we're not too concerned, but believe me, we are. Putin's making noises about moving some of his nuclear missiles to Cuba, too. We can't let that happen. Not with Fidel Castro finally out of the picture."

Fidel Castro was recovering from a mysterious illness; his brother Raúl was acting president.

"Do you think Cuba would accept them?" Yaworsky said doubt-fully. "Surely they don't want another missile crisis?"

The Captain shrugged. "They aren't happy about our new bases in Colombia. And they don't much like the way we've handled Luis Posada."

Yaworsky agreed. Luis Posada Carriles was to Cubans what Osama bin Laden was to Americans. But a Texas judge had dropped all the charges against Posada in April. Not that the charges were the ones the Cubans had hoped for. No bombing, no conspiracy: just entering the country illegally. His lawyer had smiled all the way through the trial.

The older man leaned forward, holding the bourbon bottle in the air again as he raised one eyebrow. Yaworsky nodded but hoped the liquor wouldn't loosen his tongue. *A chatterbox is a spy's treasure.*

The Captain topped up their drinks. Then he pulled a Cuban

cigar from his jacket pocket and patted his pants, looking for a match. "Once we take out Raúl Castro, that whole dictatorship will collapse like a Havana flophouse."

Startled, Yaworsky took to his feet.

"You mean, kill him?" he said. "But how? The CIA has tried to assassinate Fidel hundreds of times. The former head of Cuban security wrote a whole book about it. Nothing worked."

He fumbled for his lighter as if he'd planned to get up all along. He held the flame under the end of the Captain's cigar until it caught, then sat down again. The blue smoke hung in a cloud in the small room, adding to his feeling of claustrophobia. The Captain seemed oblivious, but then again, he was more accustomed to tight spaces.

The Captain tipped his glass one way, then the other, watching the liquid roll from side to side. Yaworsky had the sense he was being assessed, but he wasn't sure why.

"Now that's where you're wrong," said the Captain, but he didn't elaborate. "Raúl Castro is going to be at the Havana International Trade Fair on Tuesday night. Ramón Castro is getting an award from the Florida Ranchers' Association at twenty-one hundred hours. Raúl plans to be there to say a few words in support of his brother. You know how lengthy those Castro boys' speeches can be—it's the best window of opportunity we'll ever have. I want you in Havana to handle the op."

"What does the director say about all of this?" Yaworsky asked as his heart began to tap dance.

"He doesn't know," the Captain said. "Remember why Special Ops was created?" He put his empty glass down hard on the table, as if to emphasize his point. "Plausible deniability."

"Has anyone thought about who will succeed Raúl? How do we know the new leader won't just go ahead and let Putin do whatever he wants?"

"Probably Marcelo Diaz Linares," said the Captain.

"But Major Diaz is a technocrat. He's not the type to turn Putin down."

"Then José Ramón Fernandez Alvarez. He's Castro's number two. We trained him."

"Fernandez is in his late seventies," said Yaworsky, shaking his head firmly. "And he's loyal to the Castros; I've seen his case file. Besides, he used his CIA training to defeat U.S. troops at the Bay of Pigs."

The Captain stubbed out his cigar impatiently in the ashtray. "It doesn't matter who it is. It will have a destabilizing effect on Cuba to have both Castros gone; that's the goal. You can work with us, or . . ." He shrugged.

Yaworsky didn't need to hear the alternative. Never get promoted. Never be trusted. Find himself transferred to some shithole in the Balkans.

He nodded slowly. It would mean he might finally get to do the job he'd spent years preparing for. The risks were extremely high and could be fatal if he got caught. "How will I get there?" he asked, his mouth suddenly dry.

It was illegal for Americans to fly to Cuba directly from the United States and far too dangerous for Yaworsky to travel on his own passport. And, while there was the American military base at Guantánamo Bay, the Cactus Curtain between it and the rest of Cuba was eighteen miles of barbed wire, trenches, and land mines. The two sides were linked by only one road. Both sides had armed checkpoints.

"Not to worry," the Captain smiled. "That's all been taken care of. You're booked on a charter out of New York; the paperwork's already done. You should be in Havana in time for dinner. I knew you'd want to be part of this." He stood up and patted Yaworsky on the shoulder. "Now you be careful down there. Our agent's been in deep cover so long, he sometimes forgets he's one of ours."

6

After at least an hour spent navigating the telephone maze of Cuban Intelligence, Inspector Ramirez was finally transferred to Lieutenant Juan Ortiz, the officer in charge of video surveillance. Ramirez told Ortiz what he needed.

"I'm sorry, Inspector, I can't turn over any tapes to you unless someone with Cuban Intelligence was involved in the shooting. *No está autorizado.*" It is not authorized. This was the polite refusal provided by all Cuban bureaucrats to almost all requests to do their jobs.

Ramirez frowned. "But if one of your officers was involved in the shooting, there would be no need for us to see the tapes; the Intelligence directorate would handle the investigation."

"That's correct."

"So what you're really saying is that Cuban Intelligence won't share its videotapes with us even if there's a police investigation that requires them."

"I would not like to say that, Inspector. There could be exceptions."

Ramirez noted that Lieutenant Ortiz hadn't named any, leaving him to guess. "Is one of them a warrant?" He could almost see Ortiz vigorously shaking his head on the other end of the line.

"No. We would claim national security."

Ramirez sighed. "Based on what?"

"I can't answer that for you, Inspector, because I haven't seen the warrant or the tapes." Ramirez felt the urge to throttle him. "That is, if we have any tapes, which of course I can't verify without seeing them."

Ramirez thought for a moment. "Why don't you take a look for them, then? If you determine that there aren't any that solves our problem. And, if there are, but there's nothing relevant on them, that would get us around this whole issue."

"I would, Inspector Ramirez," Ortiz said, "except you've already confirmed that this incident has nothing to do with Cuban Intelligence. Therefore there is no reason for me to watch the tapes. *No está autorizado.*"

Ramirez hung up the phone, frustrated, as always, with the convoluted nature of the bureaucracy. But that simply meant finding creative ways to work around it. He was thinking about how to do that when Detective Natasha Delgado appeared in his doorway.

"I managed to track down the rental agency for the Peugeot," she said. "The gunman picked it up four days ago from Havanautos in Terminal Three. He paid with cash, convertible pesos. He gave them an American driver's licence. The name on it was William Tattenbaum. I checked with Aduana"—the Customs office—"and there is no *tarjeta del turista* issued under that name, and no special licence." The *tarjeta del turista* was a tourist card, a requirement for entry. "We dusted the rental application for prints, but there were only smudges, nothing useful. The rental clerk didn't bother to check the photograph on the licence against the passport the suspect provided, and the toner in their photocopier was so low, the picture is impossible to make out. The street address is illegible on the driver's licence, but the city is Shakespeare, New Mexico."

"An American?" said Ramirez. "That's unusual."

Very few Americans ever came to Cuba. In the 1960s, a squadron of American bombers painted to look like Cuban planes and flown by CIA-backed Cuban exiles had bombed airports on the island as part of the Bay of Pigs invasion. Castro banned all flights from the United States soon after. The U.S. government then reciprocated, making it illegal for Americans to fly directly to Cuba. It wasn't until the 1990s that charter flights were allowed to fly from New York City and Miami to Havana, but *americanos* required special licences that were easy to track. Besides, everything about the victim suggested he was Russian. It was a puzzle. "Are there any video cameras at the rental agency?"

"One above the counter, but it hasn't worked for years."

That was disappointing but not surprising. "Is there a description of the person who leased the car?"

"The clerk says he rents out over a hundred cars a day and all the *extranjeros* look the same. Sunburned." She made a face.

Ramirez sat back and folded his hands behind his head. "If the shooter was Russian," he mused out loud, "why would he use an American driver's licence? Being American draws attention."

Delgado shrugged. "There are dozens of Americans in town for the trade fair. He may know that we don't have access to American databases to verify it one way or another. Besides, just because someone speaks Russian doesn't mean they are Russian and vice versa. I have dual citizenship, and I can't speak a word."

"Good point," said Ramirez. He looked at Delgado and smiled. Thousands of Cubans had taken advantage of Russian scholarships. Many got married in Moscow and brought their spouses back to Cuba, although some returned to Russia when the Soviet Union disintegrated. Natasha Delgado's father had been Russian; he was one of those who stayed.

"Well, let's hope we have better luck with Interpol," Ramirez said. "I have a feeling the only way we're going to find our shooter is once we identify his victim."

The phone on Ramirez's desk rang. "Excuse me," he said to Delgado, picking up the receiver. She bowed slightly and left.

"I know it's almost dinnertime, Ricardo, but if you can, I think you should come to the morgue," said Apiro. "We removed the victim's clothes for processing and found something interesting. Can you bring a roll of film with you? I managed to take a few photographs for Detective Espinoza, but I've completely run out."

"I'm on my way," said Ramirez, standing up and reaching for his jacket. "I'll stop in the exhibit room and see what I can find."

———

The shooting victim's bruised body rested on the metal gurney that Hector Apiro used for autopsies. A proper table had run-off areas to collect blood and other fluids; Apiro made use of metal buckets.

Ramirez hung his jacket on a hook on the wall beside the door. He climbed into a pair of the white overalls visitors were required to wear in the pathologist's workspace. Opera music played softly in the background. It was one of Apiro's passions, one that he and Ramirez shared, the original basis of their long-standing friendship.

Apiro stood at the counter, folding a faded white sheet for laundering and sterilization. Ramirez handed him the roll of film. "I'm glad you were able to find one," Apiro said, smiling. "*Gracias.*" Apiro had long since accepted that thievery was part of his job.

The police exhibit room acted as an unofficial warehouse for the Major Crimes Unit. Items seized from tourists, particularly batteries and film, were quickly repurposed. It provided a generally reliable source of toys, rum, and foreign currency as well. Ramirez had even seen a dusty bottle of vodka during his scavenger hunt, although he didn't expect it would be there for long. Ever since Raúl Castro had assumed his brother's role, there had been cuts to the *libreta*, the ration card. The vodka could be exchanged with a neighbour for a bag of potatoes, maybe a small piece of beef. For a moment, Ramirez regretted not taking the bottle himself.

Apiro loaded the new film into the camera and fiddled with it for a minute, adjusting the settings. He handed Ramirez the camera while he positioned his three-rung stepladder beside the gurney. He clambered up the first two rungs and moved the overhead gooseneck lamp so it shone directly on the dead man's torso. The lamp had a long neck to compensate for Apiro's small size. "Here, Ricardo, take a look." Apiro inclined his large head towards the body.

Ramirez approached the corpse tentatively, in case it moved, although none of his ghosts had ever entered Apiro's private sanctuary. Ramirez often thought the dead were as uncomfortable at the idea of watching their dismemberment as he was.

"Some of these look newer than others," Apiro said. "The colours are brighter. Over time, tattoos fade."

Ramirez raised his eyebrows. What he'd at first thought were bruises were exquisitely detailed designs. Roses adorned the corpse's chest with splashes of red; barbed wire coiled around each ankle. There were bells on both his feet; stars on his knees. An epaulette hugged one shoulder; a snarling cheetah circled his forearm.

"He has a sailing ship tattooed between his shoulders. It covers almost his entire back. Maybe you can put on some gloves, Ricardo, and help me turn him over?"

Ramirez pulled on a pair of thin latex gloves and they rolled the cadaver onto its stomach, so he could see the design. Apiro took several photographs before they returned the corpse to its original position.

"You know, I've seen tattoos like this before," Apiro said. He hopped down from his stepladder and seated himself on its lowest rung. "When I was studying reconstructive plastic surgery in Moscow. There was a man who came to our clinic who wanted his removed. He said he got them in prison, but he was highly secretive about the details. I warned him I wouldn't be able to make them completely disappear and there could be scars, and he decided not to proceed. I spoke to a colleague at the hospital about it later. He explained that former prisoners were often afraid that if they tried to remove their tattoos and were left scarred, it might look as if their tattoos were taken off by other inmates because they hadn't earned them. That could get them killed."

"That seems a little extreme," said Ramirez. "Just because of tattoos?"

"The Romans used to tattoo their mercenaries to prevent desertions," said Apiro, shrugging his narrow shoulders.

Ramirez pulled over a wooden stool, his way of ensuring that he and Apiro were on the same level when they spoke. The refrigeration unit in the morgue began to stammer, then died. He reached beneath his overalls into his pocket for a cigar and a matchbook. He struck a match and puffed on the cigar until it caught. The smoke helped to disguise the smell of decomposing flesh; in this heat, it wouldn't take long before the room was rank. At one time, he and Apiro had dabbed petroleum jelly beneath their nostrils, but there was none to be found.

"So do you think our victim got these in a Russian jail?" Ramirez asked.

"I can't say for certain." Apiro rooted around in his clothing for his pipe. "But there was a prison camp in the Urals that was well known for the quality of its artists. Prisoners tried to get transferred there just to get tattooed. And these are quite beautiful."

Ramirez nodded and handed Apiro the matchbook. "They could help us find out who he is. We haven't had much luck so far." He brought Apiro up to date.

"The good thing is if these are Russian prison tattoos, they can practically disclose a man's entire history," said Apiro, lighting the tobacco in his pipe and drawing on the stem. He shook the match to extinguish it and returned the matchbook to Ramirez.

"My colleague told me the practice started in World War Two in the prison camps. Russian prisoners were tattooed by other inmates to indicate their rank within the camp hierarchy. But then the Russian mafia adopted them as well, as a kind of secret code."

"I'm not exactly sure who we can find here to interpret them," said Ramirez.

"We'll have to ask around. Perhaps there's someone at the university. Meanwhile, we have a good set of fingerprints. There's nothing in our system, but I've sent them off to Interpol, marked 'urgent.' They promise to email results within twenty-four hours. Of course, that assumes we can receive them." Apiro had no computer of his own, but the technical unit had one with authorized Internet access.

The small man smiled, but Ramirez knew the smile masked frustration. There were several problems with AFIS, Interpol's automated fingerprint system. The database contained fewer than 150,000 prints, and only of convicted criminals, not suspects. And AFIS emailed its results, which was often problematic, given the unreliability of Cuban access to the Internet.

Pipe smoke curled above Apiro's head. "I'm sure we'll have more information about this man in the next twenty-four hours, Ricardo."

Ramirez nodded. But he had the sense, somehow, that they couldn't wait that long.

7

One of Special Agent Dan Yaworsky's two fake passports was tucked in his wallet behind the special licence authorizing him to travel to Havana to attend the trade fair. The other was concealed inside the lining of his suitcase beside his real one.

The special licence would allow him to fly directly to Cuba. Now *that* was the American way, Yaworsky thought. Tighten the rules, expand the loopholes.

The Havana International Trade Fair was Cuba's largest. Quite a few countries maintained good relations with Cuba. Fifty or sixty of them would be there, including France, Canada, China, Russia, Brazil, and more than a thousand exhibitors. They'd be selling everything from toys and cosmetics to pharmaceuticals and leather goods.

But there'd be dozens of American businessmen in Havana too, negotiating the sale to Cuba of food and agricultural products and medicines. These were exceptions to the U.S. trade embargo, so long as the Cuban government paid with cash up front.

It was an American businessman's wet dream. Cuba was a captive market. Once you were in, you were in, with access to the last remaining communist country in the western hemisphere, and, even better, with a monopoly. Your product might not be advertised anywhere, but it would be the only one on the shelves, and that's all that mattered.

All the American exhibitors would have special licences like Yaworsky's; without them, they weren't allowed to spend any money. However, once they had that licence, there was nothing to stop them from spending lots of it, if they chose to. Or making it.

Cubans needed almost everything because of the long-standing U.S. trade embargo. But they were cautious: they didn't put out calls for bids or conduct business the way other countries did. They were more likely to approach sellers individually, check them out first, see how they felt about them.

The decision to take out Raúl Castro was at its heart economic, however the Captain tried to spin it. No one knew what would happen once Fidel died, which had to happen eventually, even if there were some who joked he'd come back like Jesus.

When Fidel had taken sick and transferred power to his brother Raúl, the Cuba Section of the CIA held its collective breath, wondering if he'd loosen the chokehold on his people or clamp down. So far, it looked like a continuation of the status quo, but it was too soon to tell.

A dead Castro, on the other hand, thought Yaworsky, was something the U.S. government could work with. It would force a regime change, and that would be good for business as well as politics, which were usually one and the same thing. Billions of dollars would flow into Havana, almost all of it from the United States. After all, Americans had a long history of trade with Cuba, one that reached back long before the revolution. Even Al Capone had had a deal with Cuban refineries to supply molasses to manufacture rum during Prohibition.

As it was, over the next few days, there'd be close to a billion dollars' worth of deals signed in Havana. Then there'd be the illicit agreements, the ones cemented with handshakes in hotels and bars. They were the ones Yaworsky was interested in, the reason he'd been assigned to Special Ops in the first place.

He leaned back in his seat and went over the details of his cover story one more time. He would be posing as Nathan Wallace, a thirty-two-year-old Pennsylvania dairy farmer.

"You'll be at the trade fair as part of the American delegation," the Captain had said. "I want you there when Castro gets his reward— oops, now there's a Freudian slip," he grinned. "I mean *award*."

"But I don't know anything about cattle," Yaworsky protested. "Anyone who does is going to see that right away. Which one's the heifer, the female or the male? Hell if I know."

"You don't have to know," the Captain said. "These days, the cattle business is all bullshit and jacking off. Any good agent should have lots of experience with those. Now, listen: you'll be meeting the operative at twenty-one hundred hours on the terrace of El Patio, that's a restaurant at the Plaza de la Catedral. If he needs logistical support, it's going to be up to you to provide it."

Yaworsky nodded. He knew the square well. The cathedral had been built by Jesuits and purportedly held Christopher Columbus's ashes until Spain demanded them back. Personally, Yaworsky thought Columbus was delusional. The explorer refused to admit he couldn't find India and had simply renamed the nations he encountered. It was very CIA.

"What's the agent's name?"

The Captain shrugged. "Doesn't matter, does it? It won't be his real one anyway. You see a 'likely' at the meeting place, you say, 'It sure is hot here, isn't it?' If it's him, he'll say, 'Not if you have an umbrella.'"

Yaworsky felt like a character in a John le Carré novel. He wondered how many times the CIA operative had responded to an innocent comment with the same ridiculous non sequitur.

"Make sure you take your camera with you. Remember, we always need to verify the hit. Otherwise, some of our operatives would just take our money and run. But I don't need you to bring back Raúl's head," the Captain smiled. "You just be there; take some photographs of Raúl Castro up on the podium to prove he was there. When he stops showing up at scheduled events, we'll know we got him. By the way, there's some other business I want you to take care of while you're down that way. We have an American who needs to be reined in, hard. Franklin Pearce is going to be presenting that award to Ramón Castro. He's a Florida cracker. He's staying at the Hotel Nacional. Track him down when you get there and give him this."

He handed Yaworsky a sealed brown envelope. Yaworsky imagined that it contained compromising shots of Pearce with a woman, maybe even a man. Hell, Special Ops could have even doctored something up with Pearce and one of his cows. Or heifers. Whatever.

"There's nothing in this that's going to get me hung up at Customs, is there?"

"No worries about that," the Captain smiled. "You tell Mr. Pearce that someone in the government paid you a visit. Once he sees what's in this envelope, he'll know we have eyes."

8

About twenty minutes before they began their descent into José Martí Airport, Yaworsky made his way to the tiny washroom at the back of the plane. He pulled the folding door closed and slid the metal latch. He looked at himself in the mirror and took a deep breath. He was as ready as he would ever be. He tore his briefing notes into Chiclet-sized pieces and ran them under the tiny faucet until the water-soluble paper dissolved.

Once he'd retrieved his luggage from the slow-moving carousel, he joined the line for Customs in the crowded terminal and tried to stay calm. Two soldiers in brown uniforms gripped assault rifles. The agents had always said the hardest thing about the first field assignment wasn't managing your nerves but controlling your excitement, and they were right.

A soldier in olive fatigues had a buff-coloured cocker spaniel on a leash. It sniffed Yaworsky's shoes before moving on to another passenger, its stub of a tail wagging its entire rear end. Yaworsky breathed out, relieved.

The dour man behind the Customs wicket examined the fake passport closely. He compared Yaworsky's face to the black-and-white unsmiling picture several times before he finally handed it back and rubber-stamped Yaworsky's special licence instead.

Yaworsky stopped at a currency exchange counter in the lobby and changed some of his American money into convertible pesos, flinching at the high exchange rate.

Dozens of colourful national flags fluttered from flagpoles in front of the terminal building. A long line of old Chevys awaited passengers as well as a row of *chebis*, official state taxis. He hailed one of them and climbed into the back, keeping his suitcase with him. The taxis were even worse than he'd remembered—rusted-out wrecks barely held together with bits of wire. This one was so decrepit, springs poked through what had once passed for upholstery.

A black Virgin Mary stood on the dashboard, the cheap blue-and-white plastic of her robes faded and cracked, a string of red beads wrapped loosely around her throat. The beads were in homage to Yemayá, mother of fishes.

Yaworsky wondered how his wife would feel about him being in Cuba, what she would think of any of this, for that matter. He couldn't wait to get back home and see her.

The taxi set off at breakneck speed. "It runs very well," the driver said, patting the dashboard. "*Pero come mucho gas.*" But it eats a lot of gas.

Scrawny dogs wandered down the middle of Airport Road. The driver swerved several times to avoid them. A few eager hitchhikers stepped into their path too, forcing him to brake hard.

A man in a yellow jacket waved down passing cars. He was an *amarillo*, with the power to force all private cars, except tourist rentals, to accept Cuban passengers. Luckily, his authority didn't extend to taxis or foreigners; Yaworsky didn't want to lose a single minute.

His cab passed horse-drawn carts and rickshaws; American *carros* dating back to the Second World War; Soviet-era Ladas, Toyotas, and Fiats; bici-taxis; ancient trucks stuffed full of tired Cubans. Wild pigs browsed beneath a giant billboard that hailed the work of the Committee for the Defence of the Revolution—volunteer snitches who ratted out their neighbours in return for promotions and slightly better housing.

The air was thick with diesel fumes. Giant murals all along the route called for the release of the Cuban Five, a group of undercover Cuban agents who had infiltrated the Miami network that funded Luis Posada Cariles. The Cuban undercover agents had tried to help the FBI to prosecute Posada by sharing the information they gathered; instead, they ended up charged and convicted of espionage themselves. Despite the intense heat, Yaworsky was suddenly cold.

The driver turned up the radio. "Material Girl."

"You like Madonna?" the driver said. He turned his head, flashing a bright white smile.

"Love her," Yaworsky lied.

He watched the housing grow denser as they entered the suburbs. Then, finally, they were in downtown Havana, a decaying city with all the elegance of an aging starlet. Facades were all that were left, in some cases, of once-famous structures. Children played on a pile of rubble that marked a *derrumbe*, a collapsed building. Pieces of wood propped up sagging balconies. Laundry hung across the front of apartments that no longer had outside walls. People carried on their business on these open stages as if no one could see them. Those who could, like Yaworsky, averted their eyes.

The Hotel Sevilla was just off the Paseo de Martí, not far from the Museum of the Revolution. It was one of the grand old hotels with a stucco-and-tile exterior and ornate arched windows, Moorish in design.

The taxi stuttered to a stop and Yaworsky paid the cabbie with convertible pesos. He walked up the wide marble stairs holding tightly to his bag. The lobby was guarded by a pair of stone lions: one perpetually bared its teeth; the other licked its front paw. He noted the presence of a burly security guard in a navy blue suit and white shirt. The man had a holstered automatic and a black ear bud.

Yaworsky took a deep breath and strolled as casually as he could past the security guard, and around two giant pots of ferns to the reception desk, where he checked in as Nathan Wallace. He was almost amused when the counter clerk told him his room was on the same floor as Al Capone's; the gangster had been dead for sixty years.

"The rooftop restaurant is very nice for dinner," she said, smiling. "It looks right out at the dome of El Capitolio. You can almost reach out and touch it."

"Thanks. I'll keep that in mind." Yaworsky—Wallace—smiled and handed her the doctored passport, so she could make a copy. In exchange, she gave him a room key. He declined the offer of assistance from the bellhop and carried his bag to the elevator.

Once inside his room, he placed his suitcase on one of the two beds and unzipped it. He removed his few belongings, among them a small travel iron. He retrieved the items he'd tucked behind the lining—the passports, a sheaf of American currency, and the sealed brown envelope. American dollars were useless in Cuba; the currency had been declared illegal by Castro a few years before and wasn't in circulation. But it wouldn't be long, Yaworsky was sure, before all that would change. Very soon, if the Captain had his way.

From his shaving kit, Yaworsky extracted a pair of latex gloves and a tiny flashlight with an ultraviolet bulb. He put the flashlight on top of the bright red bedspread and pulled on the gloves.

He closed the drapes and made a cursory check of the room. He used a small screwdriver on his keychain to unscrew all the electrical plates and switches and check the spaces behind them. The hanging light fixture was too high for him to remove, even standing on one of the double beds, but he doubted anyone could have planted a camera or listening device under the mounting bracket; the fixture was screwed into an ornate plaster medallion that would be easily damaged.

He did the same thing in the bathroom.

When he was satisfied he was alone, he opened the little wall safe in the closet and set the combination. He put a few hundred convertible pesos inside and locked it.

He filled the travel iron with water from the bathroom faucet and plugged it into an outlet. When it was hot, he carefully steamed open the brown envelope.

There were photographs inside of a tall man wearing a cowboy hat. But these weren't pictures of Franklin Pearce with women or with cattle. They were photographs of Pearce with the Castros. In one, Pearce was horseback riding with Ramón Castro. In another, he sat next to Raúl on a bench, both men smoking cigars and laughing. In the third, he was seated in a small airplane beside Fidel, gesturing with his hands while Fidel listened attentively. A stewardess leaned over the men, her face concealed by Pearce's Stetson. A purser stood in the aisle next to her, smiling. The cockpit was visible from the angle of the shot, with the pilot seated behind the controls.

Yaworsky went over each picture with his ultraviolet flashlight, looking for a secret message or embedded code, but found nothing.

He put the photographs back in the envelope and steamed the flap again until the glue became tacky, then resealed it. He pressed the travel iron lightly over the edge, flattening it, until he was satisfied with the results.

He looked for a safe place to store his passports before he finally set his eyes on the air conditioning unit. He removed the metal cover and slid the passports behind the coils. He pulled a wire so it wouldn't work—he didn't want his personal papers ruined by condensation—and replaced the cover.

Then he unscrewed the cover of his electric razor and plugged it in; it wasn't really a shaver but a transmitter. He sent a report to his superiors by tapping out Morse code, letting them know he was safely in Havana. The Captain had always said Morse code was simple but efficient, that it was too bad no one used it anymore.

After he was done, he went up to the rooftop restaurant for dinner. The reception clerk was right. It had a spectacular view of the Capitolio, a slightly smaller scale model of the United States Capitol building. He ordered the filet from the French-themed menu, feeling guilty his wife couldn't be with him to enjoy a nice steak. A blind pianist played background music. Service was typically slow; Yaworsky finished eating just as a five-piece band began to set up for the late dinner service.

He charged the meal to his room and glanced at his watch. It was almost seven. He had two hours to kill before his meeting at the plaza with the operative. He decided to stretch his legs and walk to the Hotel Nacional to carry out his second assignment—scare the hell out of Franklin Pearce.

9

Inspector Ramirez was surprised, but pleased, to find General de Soto in his office on a Sunday evening. He'd assumed the older man would be at home with his family. Although in his early seventies, the general had three young children from a second, or perhaps third, marriage. Divorce in Cuba was easy; just a few pesos to a notary and it was over—there was almost never any property to divide.

Ramirez rapped on the open door and cleared his throat.

The general looked up. "Yes?" He smiled at Ramirez. "What are you doing here at this time of night, Ramirez? Don't you ever spend any time with that beautiful wife of yours?"

Ramirez smiled back. "You're starting to sound just like her. It's my day off. We were planning to spend it together, but there was a shooting on the Malecón this afternoon. The victim was a foreigner, possibly Russian. We're still searching for the gunman."

"Ah, yes," said the general. "A foot patrolman filed a report."

He shuffled through the papers on his desk. "Officer Pacheco. Have you been able to identify the victim?"

Ramirez shook his head. "We've sent his fingerprints to Interpol. He has some distinctive tattoos we're looking into. But I'm having problems getting copies of the surveillance tapes from the cameras along the Malecón. We need them. The officer in charge of video surveillance at Cuban Intelligence, Lieutenant Ortiz, isn't permitted to provide them to us without an authorization from his superiors."

Ramirez knew how things worked. One word from the general to the major in charge of Cuban Intelligence and the Major Crimes Unit would be buried in videotapes.

"I'll see what I can do," said de Soto. "Do you need anything else?"

"Possibly a marriage counsellor," Ramirez grinned. "I had to leave Francesca with my parents."

"My first wife used to prefer spending time with my parents to spending time with me. That's probably why I have a second wife." The general chuckled. "I keep telling myself that if the second marriage is a success, the first one wasn't a failure. I'm only here tonight myself because we have to help Cuban Intelligence organize security for the trade show." He pointed to the pile of papers on his desk. "Thousands of Cubans will line up for hours to see products they can't afford. It's like giving them *yeyo*." Cocaine. "We hook them, but we can't supply them."

"Does that mean security's going to be an issue?"

"No more than usual," said the general. "Except on Tuesday night, when Ramón Castro receives an award from the *americanos*. We have to arrange for all the foreign reporters covering the event to check in an hour or two ahead of time and leave their bags in a room set aside for that purpose. Dogs will be brought in to sniff for explosives. Every camera, purse, and cell phone will be opened and examined."

"That sounds like a big operation." Ramirez wondered what

award Ramón Castro was getting. Ramón had been trained as an engineer but soon moved into agricultural pursuits. Ramirez thought he still worked as an advisor to the Ministry of Sugar, despite his age. He was quiet and stayed out of the spotlight but resembled his brother, with his close-shaved white beard and his omnipresent cigar. He often jokingly referred to himself as a *guajiro*, a hillbilly.

The general shrugged. "Typical of any event when the Castros are involved. They've never forgotten the time our trade pavilion was bombed at the Canadian Expo in 1967. We've had good luck at these trade fairs so far, only a few pickpockets and thefts. But, this year, with more foreign businessmen coming in, the minister wants our presence to be discreet. As few uniformed men as possible, he said." The general sighed and feigned a sad look. "It's hard to deter a thief when you're in shorts. My wife says my legs lack authority. My second wife, that is. My first wife liked my legs; she said I looked like one of El Comandante's bodyguards. It was the rest of me she had problems with."

Ramirez chuckled. Most of the Castro family's bodyguards wore *guayaberas*, white embroidered shirts. Only occasionally were they in camouflage. They stood out not because of their clothing but their size. Most were well over six feet tall, some close to seven.

The general looked at his watch. "You had better go rescue your own wife, Ramirez, before we have another domestic murder to deal with." He grinned. "I'll track down Major Diaz tomorrow and see if I can get you a copy of those tapes."

10

The Malecón pulsed with activity as hundreds of *habaneros* and foreign visitors strolled along the seaway. Children with bright *playeros* and baggy shorts ran and played along the stone wall that separated the roadway from the ocean; some waded among the rocks or dodged waves. Street hustlers hit on tourists for soap and medicine: Yaworsky ignored their entreaties.

A few white police cars were parked beside the sidewalk. Yaworsky saw the usual pieces of broken plastic and rusted metal on the road that marked the site of a car accident. Whatever had happened, the scraps of debris were all that was left of what he imagined was a fairly regular occurrence in a city with almost no road signs and cars dating back to pre-revolutionary days.

Nearby, a few Cuban children chomped on pieces of watermelon rind. The juice left dirty streaks down their chins.

As he got closer to the hotel, Yaworsky silently rehearsed what to say to the American. If his discussion with Pearce lingered on the cattle business too long, Pearce would quickly discover that Nathan Wallace was an imposter. Yaworsky decided it would be best to keep things general, get to the point of his visit quickly.

The Captain had provided Yaworsky with a number of articles about Pearce as part of his briefing. The cattleman was outspoken, constantly railing against the embargo and its effects on the Cuban people. "We're starving elderly people and children," he said in one newspaper interview. "I really don't think that's the American way." In the accompanying photograph, he was seated in a wingchair, one lean cowboy-booted leg crossed over the other, his Stetson tipped back on his head, smoking a Cuban cigar he claimed was a gift from Fidel Castro.

Every year, Pearce took down soccer and baseball equipment for Cuban children. He thought the trade embargo was stupid and made no secret of it. His pro-Castro stance had offended the anti-Castro faction in Miami, a group to which George Bush owed his election.

Now that Franklin Pearce's relationship with the Castros was on the CIA's radar, Yaworsky was almost surprised the Captain hadn't ordered his hit man to take out Pearce too.

Yaworsky asked the counter clerk at the Hotel Nacional to ring Franklin Pearce's room. When there was no answer, he took a chance and followed her directions to the terrace bar.

The panoramic view of Havana was extraordinary. He could see the entire Caleta de San Lorenzo, from the fortress at Morro-Cabana all the way to Pirate's Cove. Streaks of burgundy, orange, and pink rippled across the azure sky, deepening in intensity as the sun lowered itself into the ocean.

He recognized Pearce immediately. The cattleman was sitting in a wicker chair, holding a drink, his Stetson tipped back on his head just as it was in the newspaper story.

"Mr. Pearce?"

The man looked up and smiled. "Yes?"

"My name is Nathan Wallace. I'm a dairy farmer from Pennsylvania. I'm here for the trade show. I was hoping I could talk to you for a few minutes?"

Pearce transferred his drink from one hand to the other and lifted himself up from his chair to shake Yaworsky's hand. "Nathan, did you say?" he asked, sitting back down again. Yaworsky nodded. "I was just enjoying the sunset. So, you know who I am? I'm sorry to say I don't recognize you. Have we met somewhere?"

Yaworsky shook his head and pulled up a chair. He put the envelope on the table. "No, but I've read all about you in the press. It's a beautiful spot, isn't it? I've never been inside this hotel before."

"Are you staying here?"

"No. I'm at the Sevilla."

"First time in Havana?"

"Yes," Yaworsky lied.

"Well, this hotel has quite a history. You should look around the grounds before you go." Pearce gestured expansively with his hands. "This used to be the Santa Clara battery. There are a couple of old cannons right over there in the gardens. This whole area is a UNESCO World Heritage Site. It was a fortification designed first to fend off pirates and privateers, then the English. Even the cliff has tunnels built in it for defence. Sometimes I sit here and realize we're surrounded by ghosts." Pearce smiled apologetically. "I do go on, don't I. Now, what was it you wanted to talk to me about?"

Yaworsky breathed in deeply. He didn't have to pretend to be nervous; he was. "Sir, I have something for you." He slid the envelope across the table. "I was asked to deliver this to you. Personally."

"This is for me?" The rancher tore it open and shook out the photographs. He frowned as he flipped through them. "Where did you get these?"

"Someone from the government. He didn't give me his name,"

Yaworsky said. "He came to my farm last week. He knew I was registered for the fair and told me you were too. He even knew where you'd be staying. He said I should give you this envelope and to tell you they have their eyes on you. Sir, I don't mean to frighten you. But I think the government is conducting some kind of investigation into your affairs."

Yaworsky had learned to keep his lies as close to the truth as possible. It made them easier to remember.

Pearce looked disgusted. "No need to apologize, son. I've been expecting something like this for a while. Well, so what if the U.S. government has pictures of me with the Castros?" He tossed the envelope and photographs on the table as a white-shirted waiter approached. "We're on the wrong side of history on this one, Nathan. Even some of our senators are starting to figure out that what we're doing isn't hurting Cuba, it's hurting the Cuban people. Get me another glass of rum, no ice, *por favor*," he said to the waiter. "And one for my friend." The waiter smiled and turned away.

Pearce watched him go. "These Cubans, they're the best people you'll ever want to work with. They're loyal. Once you're in, you're in. And once the U.S. figures that out, things are going to change faster than anyone at home can even begin to imagine. I can see it already. We could end up moving a hundred thousand head of cattle a year back and forth. Daily cruise ships between Havana and Miami. Charter flights, tourism—this place will explode. It's an investor's dream. There's an educated, hardworking, bilingual population down here, busting to do business with the outside world. We've got to get our heads out of the sand. Right now, we sell Cuba a few tons of apples and peas every year. As soon as that embargo comes down, we'll be able to sell them anything we can think of. The embargo doesn't make any sense economically anymore, if it ever did. You say you're in the dairy business?"

"Still learning the ropes, sir. My uncle died, so I moved to Pennsylvania to take over his farm. I'm hoping to develop some channels here. You know what the economy is like these days. Cash customers aren't easy to find." He stopped, not wanting to reveal too much of his cover story in a single breath.

Pearce nodded. "Well, be sure to drop by the main pavilion on Tuesday night. Ramón Castro will be there; that's Fidel's brother. The Florida Ranchers' Association is giving him an award. I'll introduce you."

"Really?"

"You bet."

The waiter materialized with their drinks. He put a coaster on the table for Yaworsky's glass and placed the bill discreetly face down beside it before he slipped away.

"The fact you're interested in doing business with Cubans—that you're down here at all—makes you okay in my books," Pearce said. "Lots of people think we should just leave these people to fend for themselves until Fidel Castro dies. I think we get further ahead by working with them, the way we used to."

Yaworsky listened carefully as Pearce talked about the cattle trade between Florida and Cuba before the revolution. He was surprised to learn that Florida had a history of ranching that reached back more than five hundred years; that a Florida "cracker" was a cattleman.

"We used to ship cattle back and forth all the time before the revolution shut all that down. But things are starting to pick up again. In 2005, we landed our first shipment of cattle here since the embargo and last year, I shipped thirty heifers. There are some Americans who have been brainwashed into thinking that Cubans are our enemies. But believe me, Nathan, they're not."

Pearce threw back what was left of the rum in his glass. He signed for the drinks, then stood up, straightening the brim of his Stetson.

"Now, don't you forget to drop by on Tuesday night. He's a fine man, Ramón. Warm, generous. If you two hit it off, he'll move heaven and earth to help you get started. You take a good look around while you're visiting. Meet some locals. Try to get invited inside someone's home. Make up your own mind. Don't believe everything you read in the papers." He smiled. "That includes the ones here."

"Aren't you worried about the U.S. government coming after you?" Yaworsky pointed to the photographs, still scattered on the glass table.

"For what? Everything I do here is perfectly legal. To be honest, I'd be more concerned if they'd sent someone from the tax department to talk to me instead of you." Pearce laughed. "But I have damn good lawyers. It's one of the perks of being well-off."

Yaworsky got to his feet. "I'll see you on Tuesday night, then. Thanks very much for the drink, sir. And the advice."

"Tuesday it is," Pearce said. He stooped to pick up the photographs and the torn brown envelope, then strode off, whistling, his boots clicking time on the patio stones.

11

Dan Yaworsky walked back to Old Havana. He found a table on the terrace at El Patio, where he waited for the operative. A small group of musicians was serenading diners under the stars, but Yaworsky only feigned attention. Now he was worried.

The nine o'clock cannon sounded, with no sign of his contact. At ten, the bells of the old baroque church chimed. Another half hour passed without an approach. No one mentioned a word to him about umbrellas. No one paid much attention to him at all, for that matter, except for the waiter who kept refilling his water glass and a Brazilian physician at the next table, who tried unsuccessfully to engage him in a conversation about the sins of capitalism.

Yaworsky waited another ten minutes before giving up. He had no way of reaching the Captain, no way of knowing what had gone wrong. He left a generous tip on the table and walked across the square, confused and a little spooked by the eerie backlight the bright moon cast against the cathedral spire.

He made his way through the maze of back lanes and alleys that led to the Hotel Sevilla, trying to decide what to do next. It was possible the agent had been arrested. He could be in custody right now, being interrogated, maybe even tortured. How far would he go to protect the CIA? Was Yaworsky at risk of having his cover blown? Jesus, he thought, and mentally crossed himself.

He looked over his shoulder, avoiding his blind spot, keeping an eye out for a tail in the crowd. If he was being followed, there would likely be a team of two. A man or woman on the opposite sidewalk would act as the control. The second team member would stay at least fifty feet away. Yaworsky was careful to double back every block or so, pretending to window-shop in the many art galleries, watching for a stranger's reflection to appear behind his own more than once.

He was pretty sure he was alone, but it had become his second nature to be cautious. He remembered his instructor's lecture on surveillance techniques: "All surveillance operators will try to blend in with their environment so they won't look out of place. The clothes they wear will be neutrals—greys, black, navy blue—colours that won't stand out, nothing jarring. Same with cars. They'll be discreet, nondescript, practically invisible."

But in a place like this, it was the person wearing a neutral suit—in fact, any suit—who would stand out. And there was no such thing as a discreet car in a city where all the cars were painted the colours of raucous parrots.

He was indifferent to the charm of the magnificent balconies, the restored buildings, the cobbled streets. He forced himself to slow down, to stay unnoticed, as he walked down Calle Obispo, past the open-walled apothecary with its rows of glass bottles, the array of art galleries, boutiques, and souvenir shops. He passed El Floridita, a hotel supposedly haunted by Hemingway's ghost. Despite the late hour, it was crowded with white, sunburned, overweight foreign men, most of whom seemed to be accompanied by, or looking for, young Cuban women.

He cut through the Parque Ciudad and left Old Havana behind. He turned right onto El Prado, reasonably confident now that he was on his own. People strolled along the tree-lined centre median, with its sentry of eight bronze lions, enjoying the night breeze. Men played dominoes on fold-out tables on the sidewalks under the dim light of ancient wrought-iron street lamps. The sweet cry of a saxophone hung in the night air. Artists were slowly taking down their works from the day's art fair.

Yaworsky was shocked at how many of the beautifully proportioned buildings along the Prado had collapsed. The palace that once housed the national school of ballet was a mere shell, the ground floor littered with debris. Dogs shivered with mange or ran around in circles, crazed with pain.

He cut left on Animas to Blanco and took a deep breath as he approached the portico of a three-storey walk-up near Trocadero, its once-mint-green paint badly peeling, laundry flapping from its rusted iron balconies. He glanced over his shoulder before he dared to pull open the heavy wooden door. A man was hauling a cart with empty bottles along the street—the flower seller packing up his wares—but no one gave him a second glance.

He let the door slowly swing shut behind him, taking a few moments to let his eyes adjust to the dimness. A single light was on in the second-floor hallway. He made his way up the wide stairs, wary of rotten boards, careful not to put weight on the loose bannister.

He knocked twice on the scarred door at the top of the stairs. A paper picture of the evil eye was tacked on the door to ward off bad luck. He rapped again, louder, more insistently. The door opened, revealing an extremely attractive woman. She'd aged since he last saw her, but she was still beautiful.

"*Si?*" she said, peering into the darkness. She put her hand to her mouth when she realized who it was. "Oh my God. Danila?"

Yaworsky placed his hand firmly against the door. He poked his head inside, scanning the cramped room. "Are you alone?"

She nodded. "This late at night? Yes, of course."

He entered the room, pulling the door closed behind him. He pressed his mouth to hers and pushed against her urgently. He walked her backwards to the bed. She unbuttoned his shirt as he pulled down her shorts.

Ten minutes later, Yaworsky lay beside her, stroking her thick dark hair while she snored lightly. Be like the *vorys*, his trainers said in the camps. Have no family, make no friends.

But despite his line of work, that wasn't possible.

12

Long after Fernando Espinoza and Natasha Delgado had finished their shifts and headed home, Inspector Ramirez was still hard at work. When he finally pushed himself away from his desk and glanced at his watch, he was surprised to see it was almost midnight.

He sighed and reached for his jacket; Francesca would be annoyed. He ran down the stairs and out the front door to the parking lot and started his small blue car, then checked the back seat in his rear-view mirror. There was no sign of the murdered man's ghost.

He drove off rapidly, dodging the taxis and *bicis* and carts that still plied the night streets.

He was tired and disappointed at how little he had to show for his long hours. He had not been able to identify the victim from the Malecón, and they had no new leads. Meanwhile, a cold-blooded killer, possibly a professional, roamed the city freely, and that worried him.

He parked his car at the curb in front of the decrepit apartment building where his parents lived and walked up the sagging stairs. He was almost overwhelmed with exhaustion, and the thought of Francesca's anger only made it worse.

He opened the apartment door to find his wife seated on the couch, reading. She put down the book and put her fingers to her lips, letting him know everyone else was asleep. He nodded and took off his jacket. He hung it over the back of an old wooden chair and pulled off his shoes.

There were only two bedrooms in the apartment. One was separated from the living space by an old bed sheet that hung from the ceiling. He pulled the bed sheet aside and peeked inside. His children lay curled like kittens beside his mother and father, their faces slack and peaceful, his father snoring.

Francesca got up from the couch and tiptoed into the kitchen, which amounted to little more than a cooktop, sink, and tiny *frigo*. She took two glasses from a shelf on the wall above the sink and poured a healthy shot of rum in each. She cut a fresh lime and squeezed in some of the juice, then opened the refrigerator and added ice cubes. She walked over to him and handed him his drink. He kissed her cheek, grateful she wasn't angry, and sat on the lumpy couch.

Normally, his sister, her husband, and their two teenage children would be there as well; they lived with his parents while they waited for the government to assign them living quarters. They had been on a waiting list for the entire eighteen years they'd been married. But they were in the countryside this week visiting other relatives—without them, the cramped apartment seemed deserted, almost spacious.

"What happened on the Malecón, Ricardo?" Francesca asked in a low voice as she sat down beside him, the ice in her glass clinking.

He told her what little they knew.

"A man was shot to death?" she said, putting her hand to her mouth. "Here, in Havana? And you don't know why?"

He tried to reassure her. "I suppose the good thing is that if it was a targeted shooting, the gunman has no reason to hurt anyone else."

"That doesn't make me feel very safe," Francesca said. "People can be caught in the middle of something like that. What if the man who got shot wasn't his only target?"

Ramirez nodded. "I agree. We're doing our best. Nothing has turned up at Customs, but there are thousands of foreigners who come to Havana each week. It makes it difficult to track down some- one who has no identification. A witness may have seen something, but we have no way of asking for help, except by knocking on doors." It was government policy not to mention murders in the media, in case it frightened off tourists. "We think the victim was Russian."

"Don't the Russians who come to Havana have to register with their embassy?"

Ramirez looked at Francesca and smiled slightly. "That's a good suggestion. I'll check into it tomorrow." He glanced at his watch and drained his glass. He exhaled, resigned. "I suppose we should wake up the children and take them home to bed."

"It's so late," Francesca said softly, leaning into him. She set her glass on the floor and put her arm around his waist. "We'll end up waking everyone up. Estella will fuss. And Edel has a test tomorrow at school. Let's just stay here. Your parents won't mind. We can sleep on the couch, the way we used to when we were dating. Before we had our own place."

"As I recall, we didn't sleep much whenever you stayed over," Ramirez said. He smiled as he brushed her hair with his lips.

He recalled all too well the many times he and Francesca had sex on the uncomfortable sofa, giggling and trying not to make a sound while his parents pretended to be asleep. But that was the reality of Cuban life. There was no such thing as privacy in a country where several generations of a family, from toddlers to grandparents, were often forced to live together, crammed beneath the same collapsing roof.

He put his glass down on the floor and kissed his wife. As always, her responsiveness excited him. "We have to be careful not to make any noise," he whispered, his fatigue melting away. "The children might wake up. When the time comes, I'd rather tell them about sex than demonstrate it."

Francesca laughed softly. She got off the couch and kneeled in front of him. He felt her warm breath as she undid his fly. He glanced around the room one more time to make sure they were alone, but there were no apparitions and no curious children. "Then you'd better stay very quiet," she whispered. "We don't want to scar them for life."

13

Dmitri Nabokoff sat behind a console of sophisticated recording equipment, listening as tape-recorded voices dissolved into static. A tall, muscular man stood a few feet away, massive arms folded, legs spread apart, balancing his weight on the balls of his feet like the professional athlete he once was.

"Fucking Chinese satellites," Dmitri said. "That's the end of it, Slava. The listeners picked this up yesterday; they've been working on it ever since. It's a transmission from a location a few kilometres outside Washington. They've done everything they can to decipher the rest but have nothing yet. We believe the older man is American CIA. The head of the Special Activities Division of the National Clandestine Services section. They call him the Captain."

Slava Kadun frowned. The CIA section known as Special Ops conducted covert paramilitary action around the world. He put his head close to the speakers, hoping intelligible words might yet magically emerge from the metallic background hum, but the recorded conversation disintegrated. There was nothing that resembled human voices, only a sound like a piece of paper being crumpled. "That's it—that's all we know? There's a CIA plot to assassinate Raúl Castro?"

"We already know more than the Cubans, Slava. That's the problem. We can't just call them up to tell them. There are no secure channels these days; someone's always listening. Nikolai wants you to go to Havana and brief their authorities personally. Apparently Putin doesn't want anything to happen to Raúl Castro; he thinks he will be easier to deal with than his brother. Your orders are to do whatever it takes to stop this from happening. Nikolai has drafted a letter of introduction. It's in Spanish translation. It should be ready shortly."

Nikolai Patrushev was the head of Russian intelligence as well as the FSB, or Federal Security Services, the former KGB.

Dmitri took off his headphones and turned to face his friend. "Lucky you. You get to fly on Scare-o-flot. The ticket's on my desk along with your passport." He nodded towards the battered desk in the corner of the room. "It's a thirteen-hour flight. Assuming the plane doesn't crash, that is." He grinned, revealing a row of bright steel teeth. "But it's eight hours earlier there with the time change, so you'll arrive in Havana late afternoon. Lots of time."

Slava Kadun wrinkled his forehead. "Fuck your mother. How am I supposed to find an undercover CIA operative in less than two days?" He rubbed his bald head with his thick fingers.

"You won't be on your own," Dmitri smiled. "You'll be working with Cuban Intelligence."

Slava snorted. "Cuban Intelligence? You must be joking."

Dmitri chuckled. "I'll contact you through the Russian embassy if we find out anything else. You can call me from there too; let me know how it goes. It's as close as we can get to safe communications."

"Can't the sleeper handle this?" Russia had thousands of agents who lived secretly in foreign countries for years. Some were not even Russian, but they were always ready to deploy.

Dmitri shook his head. "Nikolai says Putin asked for you

himself. I can't believe you don't want to go to Cuba for a few days. Hot women, hot sun, just the place for a hot guy like you. Believe me, Cuban women love a *nastoyashi muzhik*." A real Russian man.

"I had other plans," Slava said simply. "Why can't someone pick up the phone and tell Cuban Intelligence what's going on? So what if the CIA finds out? Raúl Castro cancels his appearance and lives to make a lousy speech some other day."

Dmitri made a face. "The Americans will know we can hear them. We will lose our ability to eavesdrop on their conversations."

Slava nodded reluctantly. It made sense. "What will I take for weapons?"

"Nothing. Your hands. And that hard head of yours. You're on a civilian flight. It's too dangerous to carry guns these days, with all the fucking security, and there's no time to send a throw-down by diplomatic pouch. We don't want you to get tied up at some stinking airport and miss your connection. You'll have the letter of introduction; that's all you need."

Slava frowned. He had been trained in the use of all manner of weaponry, not just guns, but rifles and machine guns as well as knives and grenades. Typically, when he was sent on a mission, he was equipped with either a sniper's rifle or a silenced gun and at least a few hand grenades, although strictly speaking he didn't need them; he was an expert in Wen-Do, judo, and karate. He'd instructed men in camps all over the world on how to make powerful explosives from common household materials. He preferred not to kill if he didn't have to; a former professional boxer, he much preferred punching.

"I can't defend myself with a fucking piece of paper," he said, although he knew he probably could if he had to. Rolled up tightly enough, even a piece of paper could puncture a larynx. "You know what I'm afraid of, Dmitri? A bunch of trigger-happy Cuban security forces. Once they find out about this, I'll be lucky if I don't get shot at that trade fair myself. What about the watch?"

"It's been assigned to someone else."

The last time Slava had been on mission, Dmitri gave him a watch that held a tiny transmitter. The crown acted as an antenna. "I should be able to pick you up even if the sound quality is shit," Dmitri had explained. "Make sure the crown is pushed down if you decide to fuck someone, okay? I don't want to listen to you grunting."

"Who would I screw? Your mother will be here," Slava laughed, as he slid the watch on his thick wrist.

But this time, he wouldn't even have the watch. He raised his heavy black eyebrows. "If this is so important a mission, why aren't you coming with me?"

"I just got back from my last one. Nikolai says Putin wants me undercover in the labour camp where Khodorkovsky is serving his time. He wants to make sure he doesn't get parole." Mikhail Khodorkovsky was an oligarch, imprisoned on trumped-up charges, but the Russian people liked him. Because of this, Putin considered him a threat, even behind bars.

"That's a pretty rough assignment," Slava said. The prison where Khodorkovsky was being held—YaG-14/10—had a reputation in the Soviet era as one that prisoners rarely left alive.

"Don't worry, I'll be careful," said Dmitri. "Getting inside, and then gaining his trust, will be the hardest part, but I think I've worked something out. It's complicated but believable. All I have to do now is figure out how to get arrested. You have the better assignment this time, for sure." He grinned. "Don't forget to pick up vodka in the duty-free shop at the airport, Slava. The vodka in Cuba is shit. It's all from France."

Slava walked over to Dmitri's desk and picked up the Aeroflot ticket. "You know, Dmitri," he said, "it wasn't until I flew on a foreign flight that I found out passenger jets aren't *supposed* to shake." He ran his fingers over his smooth scalp again. "So that's it—I have no say about losing my vacation time?"

Dmitri shrugged. "Not my circus. Not my monkeys."

14

About thirty minutes after her unexpected visitor showed himself out, Yoani Ravela heard a soft tap on the door. She smiled as she went to open it, adjusting her clothing and patting her hair. Maybe Danila had changed his mind and would stay the night after all.

She was a little worried about the Ceperos, her next door neighbours, seeing him come and go. There wasn't much that went on in the building that escaped their attention. They were members of the CDR, the Committee for the Defence of the Revolution, responsible for ensuring loyalty to revolutionary ideals. They would wonder who her guest was but would never ask her directly. Instead, they'd gossip about it for days. Or even report her to the authorities for prostitution.

But this time, Yoani didn't really care. Having sex wasn't illegal; only taking money for it was. And she'd tucked his money under a loose floorboard with the rest of her stash.

She pulled the door open as quietly as she could but saw no one. "Danila?" she whispered.

She made her way cautiously down the hallway, wondering what game he wanted to play. It was pitch black. The light bulb in the hallway had already burned out. So much for the new energy-efficient light bulbs, she thought. A group of Communist Party Youth had come to the building to replace the bulbs in all the fixtures; they'd smashed the ones they'd removed so they couldn't be reused or sold on the black market. But at least the old ones had worked. These were only energy efficient because they were useless.

She stood at the top of the staircase, peering into the darkness. She thought she heard someone move behind her. "Is that you?" She turned, expecting him to come out of hiding and kiss her neck, caress her, sweep her up in a hug.

Instead, the last thing she felt was her neck snap. The last thing she saw was a blinding star explode behind her eyes.

15

The small apartment was in chaos the next morning as they tried to get the children organized. Estella had misplaced her doll, and since she only had one, she refused to go home without it. Ramirez's mother finally found it lying on top of the sheets and the little girl stopped wailing.

"You see?" his mother said to the toddler. "Your dolly was playing a game with us. She was hiding in plain sight. We were looking so hard to find her, we couldn't see her."

Ramirez's neck was stiff from sleeping without a pillow; it cracked when he turned his head. He caught Francesca's eye and winked as he rubbed the back of his neck. She grinned back. We aren't exactly teenagers anymore, he thought, massaging the knot with his fingers.

Breakfast was a fruit salad of mangos and papayas from the *agromercado*, but there was no milk for Estella, which made her cry all over again. Ramirez tried to explain that his parents were too old to get milk in their rations but, at three, she was too young to understand. Despite all that, they somehow managed to get the two children fed and dressed without triggering a complaint to the CDR.

At home, Ramirez took an abbreviated shower. As usual, there was no hot water, and no time to boil any in their battered collection of saucepans; he was running behind.

The ration book allowed his family to share a single tube of toothpaste every four months, but the *bodegas* hadn't had any for months. Toothpaste seemed to have gone the way of plastic bags, hand soap, and pencils. He brushed his teeth with water, then shaved, cursing as he nicked his chin with a disposable razor that was already older than his daughter.

"I have to go now, sweetheart," he said to Francesca, when he was finally dressed and ready to leave for work. "But I'll be home tonight for dinner to make it up to you for running off yesterday, I promise."

He kissed her and the children and drove to the medical towers, manoeuvring smoothly through the traffic. Although it was early, he found a shady spot to park: the morning sun was hot.

He jogged to the front door of the medical towers and nodded to the receptionist as he swung himself down the stairs by the railings, then pushed open the metal swinging doors to the morgue.

"Good morning, Hector. I'm sorry I'm late," he said to Apiro, hanging up his jacket on the hook beside the door. "We ended up staying overnight with my parents. Getting the children rounded up in the morning is a challenge at the best of times. I sometimes think that having two children is a little like having ten; I can't imagine what three would be like."

"*Hola*, Ricardo," said Apiro. The small doctor was standing at the counter, lining up his scalpels by size. He turned to smile at his closest friend. "Yes, I'm sure there's an exponential increase. Not to worry; I was a little late getting here myself. I had a call around ten o'clock last night from the Hospital Provincial de Camaguey.

They wanted me to drop by this morning. A patient died of organ failure yesterday, but they can't identify the cause. It's peculiar, Ricardo. He was in perfect health. You have to be, to be an airline pilot. He had annual checkups. Low blood pressure, no cardiovascular issues, no problems with alcohol. He told his wife he thought something might have stung him at the airport. He developed a high fever a few hours later, but it wasn't an allergic reaction, from what we can tell."

"An airline pilot?" said Ramirez.

"He flew with Aero Caribbean, yes. Captain Nelson Acosta Lopez."

"That's odd. Do you remember Mama Loa from those murders this spring?"

Ramirez had investigated the murder of several prostitutes in March. Two had been Mama Loa's goddaughters.

"Mama Loa. Is that the *houngan*?" said Apiro. "The one who claims to see the future?" Apiro had no use for *houngans*; as an atheist, he thought they were little more than witch doctors. Ramirez had once felt the same way, but now he wasn't so sure.

Ramirez nodded. "She came to see me yesterday. She told me that some of the people who fly in the clouds are going to die." It sounded ridiculous, even to him, to hear it out loud.

Apiro cocked a bright eye at Ramirez and chortled. "Well, that seems like a reasonably safe prediction, given our aging fleet of aircraft."

In 2002, Apiro had been working at a medical clinic in Santa Clara when a Soviet-made Antonov AN-2 crashed. Four British tourists, including a newlywed couple, were among the sixteen passengers and crew on the small plane. Apiro had told him how difficult it was to match the limbs strewn among the trees to what was left of the bodies. Identification had been a challenge; the wedding rings helped.

"It's a little like fortune cookies, isn't it, Ricardo? Maria and I went into Barrio Chino for lunch on Sunday. Hers said, 'You will meet a handsome stranger.'" Apiro laughed, with the sound of a raspy saw. "Then again, so did mine."

The pathologist pulled on a pair of thin latex gloves. He selected one of the razor-sharp scalpels. He clambered up his stepladder by the gurney and adjusted the angle of the gooseneck lamp.

"Well, the pilot's an interesting case," Apiro said. "I use the word *interesting* in the same way the Chinese do when they say, 'May you live in interesting times'—as a curse. It's perplexing." Apiro tipped his large head "His white count soared before he died. There's a poisonous mushroom that can do that—the death cap—*Amanita phalloides*. But we didn't find anything in his system to suggest that's what this was. The major concern, I suppose, is that he might have picked up a new virus, perhaps from a passenger. That's how AIDS spread around the world, you know. Thanks to a rather promiscuous Canadian purser who became infected."

Ramirez shuddered. "So what can you do?"

"The epidemiologists are still working on it. Meanwhile, the body has been quarantined. The family, of course, wants it released, so he can be buried. I'll do an autopsy as soon as the tests are completed, likely in the next couple of days. I really have to."

Ramirez nodded. Where possible, the dead were buried within eight hours. The tropical heat was not kind to corpses and, unlike Apiro's, few morgues had refrigeration units, not even in the hospitals. Even in Apiro's hospital, power shortages and interruptions, although less frequent, were still all too common. Apiro planned his days on the assumption that he could lose power at any time.

Apiro made a Y-shaped incision from below the tattooed man's shoulders to just beneath his navel. He pulled aside the skin and underlying tissues.

"His heart looks good. Normal. Better than normal, actually. Ah, that explains it." Apiro pointed to the grey, fatty liver. "Our man was a drinker. Alcohol reduces cholesterol; it has anti-inflammatory properties. The worst alcoholics have wonderful hearts."

Apiro always chattered away to Ramirez during an autopsy. Ramirez knew the banter was intended to distract him from the unpleasant aspects of Apiro's work, and appreciated it. He pulled over a stool and sat down, then removed a cigar from his pocket and lit it. As well as masking the odours, it gave him something to do with his hands.

After the small pathologist had removed and weighed each organ, he probed the wound in the man's temple with a gloved finger. "See? There's the powder residue in the wound track, and you can see the burning at the edges. A hard contact discharge releases carbon monoxide. It causes the tissues inside the wound to turn bright red."

Ramirez got up to look. The area around the wound was the colour of *granada*, pomegranate seeds.

"But we're lucky, Ricardo. There's no exit wound, which means the bullet is still in there. Normally, I would order an X-ray before proceeding further, in case I dislodged it, but we are low on film. The priority at the moment is the living, not the dead."

Ramirez was always irritated by the constant obstacles Apiro had to navigate in carrying out his duties. He wondered how long it would be before the sheets stuffed in the morgue's laundry bag would be washed: there was no laundry soap in Havana these days either, only lye.

Apiro climbed down his stepladder and exchanged the scalpel for an electric saw with a long, frayed cord. He gingerly plugged it into an outlet near the metal gurney, as if expecting to be electrocuted. The fluorescent lights flickered but stayed on. Apiro looked up at the stained ceiling and grinned. He clambered up the stepladder again, holding the saw. He turned it on and sliced into the victim's skull as neatly and cleanly as if he were cutting the top off a hard-boiled egg.

Ramirez swallowed. He never liked watching Apiro autopsy a brain. He focused instead on the smoke curling lazily from the end of his cigar.

Apiro held the organ closer to the gooseneck lamp, gently turning it from left to right. "The bullet must be lodged somewhere inside the skull." The brain was riddled with worm holes, probably from a ricochet. Jagged white bone fragments stuck out of one side.

Apiro stepped down. He unplugged the saw and placed it on the counter. He retrieved a pair of long metal tweezers, and back in his original position on his stepladder, he peered inside the skull cavity. "Ah, there it is. Good."

A few seconds later, Apiro gripped a spent cartridge in the tweezers. He held it out so Ramirez could see it. The front of the bullet had peeled back, forming five sharp points like flower petals. "Only expanded hollow-point bullets deform quite like this," said Apiro. "I've never seen a bullet like this one, though. I'll take it over to Dr. Garcia at the Academy of Sciences to examine. He's an expert in ballistics as well as weapons. And he has access to the National Ballistics Intelligence Service Database in London if he can't identify it himself."

"Can we be sure it was the bullet that killed our victim, then, and not the crash?" Ramirez said.

Although the answer seemed obvious, Ramirez had to ask. Hollow-point bullets were designed to kill, not wound. Even so, a juridical panel might be persuaded by a clever defence lawyer that the victim was already dead or dying from other causes and acquit an accused of first-degree murder. Defence lawyers in Cuba were required to advance the state's interests, but some members of the law collectives had rather bravely, or perhaps stupidly, decided this meant requiring the state to prove its case.

"I think so, yes," Apiro said. "He suffered a graze to the forehead and a few bruises. But I haven't found anything else yet that would have caused, or even contributed to, his death."

16

As soon as the autopsy was over, Inspector Ramirez headed back to his office. He parked his car in the police parking lot, leaving the windows down. The doors no longer locked, so there was no point in rolling the windows up. There was nothing left inside to steal anyway.

He walked through the wrought-iron gates that surrounded the beautiful multi-turreted building that served as police headquarters. The massive stone structure looked more like a castle than a paramilitary institution. Fragrant wisteria climbed the walls.

Tourists often stopped to snap photographs until foot patrolmen chased them off or, as more often happened, confiscated their cameras. There was a long list of places it was illegal to photograph in Cuba. Military establishments and police stations were on the list; so were aircraft and almost anything that might compromise the security of the Castros.

Ramirez nodded to the guard and walked up the stairs to the

second floor, where the Major Crimes Unit was located. Both Detective Espinoza and Detective Delgado were out, their usually neat desks cluttered with paperwork. He entered his office and seated himself behind his desk, looking ruefully at the piles of paper that had accumulated during his own brief absence.

He started by rifling through the daily stack of missing person reports. No one had reported a male foreigner missing. That wasn't unusual, particularly if the tattooed man had travelled alone. Tourists often left their hotel rooms to take overnight tours; hotel staff usually didn't notice unless their guests missed their checkout time. Even then, since most stays were prepaid, absences were rarely reported.

The rest of the morning was spent on routine paperwork. By noon, Ramirez felt he had achieved some success in organizing shift schedules and payroll matters. He found himself glancing around his office from time to time, half-expecting the ghost of the tattooed man to materialize and silently scold him for not spending more time searching for his killer.

When his stomach started rumbling, he stood up and stretched. He thought he might go outside and look for some street food for lunch instead of going to the subsidized cafeteria in the basement. There, the menu was always rice, black beans, and bread, or, for variation, bread, beans, and rice. He was reaching for his jacket when the phone on his desk interrupted his culinary plans.

"*Hola*, Inspector Ramirez," said Sophia, the night dispatcher. "Detective Delgado is on her police radio; she would like to speak to you."

"*Hola*, Sophia. You're working days?"

"All week. I rearranged my schedule to take my mother to the trade fair. She wants to look at kitchen sinks. She's tired of using an old metal bucket to wash her dishes. Of course, she can't even afford to buy a new bucket, but she likes to dream."

Ramirez smiled. "Don't we all?"

"I'm sorry to disturb you, sir," said Natasha Delgado once she was patched through. "I'm at an accident scene that was called in this morning—a fatality. A woman fell down the stairs in her building and broke her neck. Officer Pacheco—that foot patrolman from the Malecón the other day—was the first responder. He asked Dispatch to send someone from Major Crimes to take a look; Sophia called me. I don't see anything suspicious, but, just in case, I contacted Dr. Apiro. He's here now. He asked if you can drop by to see the scene before he signs off on the death certificate."

"Who's the victim?"

"Yoani Ravela, according to the neighbour who found her body. She's an attendant with Aero Caribbean. The dead woman, I mean. Not the neighbour."

"A stewardess?" said Ramirez. He thought of Mama Loa's prophecy and felt his stomach muscles clench.

"I think they call themselves flight attendants these days," Delgado said, gently correcting him. Like Francesca, she was a strong feminist. Ramirez always suspected she was a lesbian, but felt her sexual orientation was none of his business.

"Where are you?" asked Ramirez. He scrambled through the papers on his desk, looking for his notebook and a pen that still had ink.

"On the main floor of a walk-up on Blanco near Trocadero." Delgado recited the number and Ramirez scribbled down the address. "There's barricade tape across the front door. Officer Pacheco managed to find some. I don't know whether I should leave it there or not." She lowered her voice. "I don't really know what to do, Inspector. He is a little too"—she hesitated—"enthusiastic."

Ramirez understood her concern. The Major Crimes Unit was small and often needed help from Patrol. It was important to keep good relations with the foot soldiers. Natasha Delgado was a woman in a profession still dominated by men, and she hadn't been a detective for long. She didn't have sufficient rank to tell an eager young foot patrolman that he was probably wasting Major Crime's scarce resources by calling them to attend what was most likely the scene of an accident.

That's if it *was* an accident, he thought. For a fleeting second, he wondered if Mama Loa had pushed the woman down the stairs herself to make her prophecy come true. "I'll be there shortly," Ramirez said. He put down the phone, troubled.

17

Dan Yaworsky smiled as he thought about the night before. It was exactly what he'd needed to relieve his tension. The sex made him feel as if all his sacrifices had been worthwhile. He hoped no one saw him slip out of the building and back to his hotel; he couldn't risk having any witnesses.

He wandered around the Plaza de Armas for a while, pulling his mind back to work. He hadn't yet called the Captain to tell him the undercover operative hadn't shown up. Doing that required going to the U.S. Special Interests Section in the Swiss embassy. Almost all the personnel there were CIA; as soon as he walked in the door, he'd blow his cover.

The plaza was a beautiful square that had dozens of booksellers selling thousands of books from their stalls in the shade of the kapok trees. There was a view of the Castillo de la Real Fuerza, one of four forts that guarded the harbour.

La Giraldilla de la Habana stood on top of the Castillo's tower. A bronze figure with long braids, she held a palm frond in one hand and a cross in the other. She was watching the ocean, waiting for her missing husband, the Spanish governor, to come home. But Governor Hernando de Soto had been lost at sea. La Giraldilla replaced him as governor herself, so perhaps she didn't spend all her time simply watching the waves, as the legend had it, but got on with the business of living. Yaworsky thought of his wife, forced to cope without him, and hoped that was so.

He walked past the Palacio de los Capitanes Generales, with its nine arches. It was built as the governor's palace, repurposed as a city hall, and finally recycled as a museum. These plazas had been restored, but Yaworsky knew that most of the buildings around them had sagging walls, mildew, and collapsed balconies.

He found himself heading in the direction of the walk-up on Blanco again, despite the risk. Returning to the scene of the crime, he thought. The smile on his lips faded when he saw yellow tape strung across the front of the building: *Cuidado*, it said. Caution.

He watched a tall Cuban with a straw fedora get out of a small blue car parked by the curb and slam the driver's door. The man pulled aside the barrier tape and entered the building. Although he wasn't uniformed, he looked like a man with authority. Was he Cuban Intelligence or PNR? Yaworsky pushed down his sense of panic. He'd done nothing to expose himself that he could think of. Had there been a theft in the building? Not likely. But something was going on. He'd wiped his prints, he'd been careful; the money he'd left behind was clean.

They can't possibly know who I am or what I was doing there, he thought. Unless they've found the CIA operative and he's turned me in. But he probably doesn't know who I am either. We never met; he doesn't even know what I look like. What am I supposed to do now?

Yaworsky had broken all the rules of his training. He had to keep his cool; he had to stay on track. Damn it. He should never have gone to see her. He'd jeopardized everything. He took a deep breath, turned around as casually as he could, and melted into the crowd.

18

The woman's body lay twisted at the bottom of the long, winding staircase. Her body faced in one direction, her head in the other. Her legs were bent, knees pointing left. A high-heeled shoe dangled from one foot; the other lay several metres away. Hector Apiro was squatting beside the body. A young foot patrolman, wearing the light grey-blue shirt and blue pants of the Cuban Revolutionary Police, stood beside Detective Delgado, making notes.

"Inspector Ramirez, this is Officer Pacheco," Delgado said.

"I hope you don't mind that I called this in," the foot patrolman said. Ramirez guessed he was even younger than Espinoza, barely out of his teens. He picked up a slight country accent.

Thousands of young men from the countryside came to Havana each year to find work; most were unsuccessful. *Habaneros* called the migrants Palestinos, because they were homeless. Most ended up living in squatter settlements on the outskirts of town, in shanties like Mama Loa's. Young Pacheco was either lucky or well connected.

"It doesn't hurt," said Ramirez. "Sometimes homicides can look like accidents. By the way, that partial licence plate you recorded yesterday helped us identify the shooter's car. It was good police work."

Pacheco blushed. "*Gracias*, Inspector Ramirez."

"You say she was a flight attendant?" Ramirez asked, gesturing to the body.

Pacheco nodded. "According to the next-door neighbours, yes. But they thought she might be entertaining men for money too. Señora Cepero, that's the neighbour—she's the block captain for the CDR—heard the sounds of intercourse last night." He shrugged. "The walls are thin."

"Ah, yes," Ramirez said. "Well, you know the saying: 'Love is blind but the neighbours aren't.' So the neighbour thinks she was a *jinetera*?" He looked at the body more closely.

Pacheco shrugged. "She says there was no boyfriend, no husband, no fiancé. "But look at her—she was hot. Believe me, these days, pretty girls don't give it away."

Detective Delgado rolled her eyes but said nothing. Ramirez glanced down at Apiro and was relieved that the pathologist didn't appear offended by the young man's remark.

It was true that planes full of mostly middle-aged foreign men looking for women travelled to Cuba every day of every week. The sex trade in Cuba was active, despite frequent police crackdowns. Prostitution was a venture into capitalism that Castro had first encouraged during the Special Period, then tried to stamp out when it became too successful. All the regular police sweeps did was drive the trade underground; it was far too lucrative to stop.

But many of the women who hooked up with *extranjeros* simply wanted to get into a nightclub that was otherwise closed to them. Others hoped to find a husband who would take them away to a better future. And then there were women like Hector's girlfriend, Maria, who did it because she needed the money.

Ramirez thought of his little Estella and hoped she would never be forced to sleep with men to just get by. But having sex late at night hardly made a woman a prostitute. Delgado was right: this young patrolman was making almost acrobatic leaps of logic. That kind of youthful enthusiasm, if taken too far, could prove dangerous.

"All right, Natasha," Ramirez said, turning to Delgado. "Now that I'm here, you can leave. Get someone on Patrol to give you a lift to the station if you need one. I'm sure Officer Pacheco can stay to lend us a hand."

She nodded, relieved. "Fernando asked if I can help him finish canvassing the hotels. Is that all right with you?"

"Absolutely. It's a big job; he can use the help. I'll catch up with you both later."

———

Inspector Ramirez stood over the body. Pacheco was right about one thing: the woman had been very pretty. She appeared to be in her late twenties, perhaps early thirties. Her dark eyes were frozen in the death stare Ramirez was all too familiar with. The instant the life spark was snuffed out, the dead turned into plastic mannequins. It was hard to explain, but they no longer looked as if they'd ever been alive. Ironically, only their ghosts appeared real.

"If she fell," Officer Pacheco offered, "she should have bumped against all the stairs on the way down and made a big noise. But the neighbours heard nothing. Well, nothing except people having noisy sex around midnight."

Ramirez nodded slowly. He looked up the stairs. A wooden riser was loose, the board split and splintered. He guessed that was where the woman had caught her heel and fallen. "Do we have a time of death, Hector?"

Apiro stood up painfully and snapped off his latex gloves. He adjusted his pants absent-mindedly, pulling up the waistband. "If they heard sounds of intercourse at midnight, I certainly hope it was after that," he said, and chuckled. "Her rectal temperature suggests a range of between nine and twenty hours. Lividity begins to set in after four hours—by ten, it's permanent. When I press on her skin, it still blanches. So I would guess that she died roughly nine or ten hours ago."

Apiro turned his wrist to look at the scarred face of his old metal watch. "That would make it between two and three this morning."

"Should we search her apartment?" Pacheco asked. He was so eager that he was almost bouncing on his toes. Ramirez tried not to smile. Being a foot patrolman was one of the most boring jobs in Havana. It paid relatively well, the equivalent of roughly ten American dollars a month. But on most days, there was nothing to do except stand on busy street corners, hoping to see criminal behaviour while braving the heat. Some officers worked Patrol for years without ever seeing a single major crime, yet, in less than forty-eight hours, this young man had already chased after a car and helped investigate a homicide.

"No," Ramirez said. "Until we have grounds to suspect that a criminal offence has occurred, we have no legal basis to search a private dwelling. But we should probably question the other neighbours about what they may have seen or heard."

Pacheco snapped a crisp salute. Apiro looked up at Ramirez and grinned.

"How long have you been with the PNR?" Inspector Ramirez asked the foot patrolman as they walked up the stairs to the second floor, both careful to step over the broken riser.

"Three months," said Pacheco. "But police work is in my blood. My grandfather was with the Secret Police—I grew up listening to his stories. He was one of the special agents who spoke French and English, in the group that dealt only with tourists."

Before the revolution, the Cuban republic had several distinct police forces. The National Police were uniformed and did the same basic work that Patrol did now. But it was the Secret Police who handled serious investigations involving robberies and homicides and contraband goods. They were an elite group of detectives, trained in medicine and psychology as well as forensics, much like Major Crimes.

The Major Crimes Unit was initially created to deal with crimes involving foreigners, after a policeman shot a Danish tourist to death on the sidewalk and caused a diplomatic war of words with Denmark. Now it dealt with serious crimes, like murder, along with anything else the ministry wanted buried and out of sight.

Pacheco pointed to a scarred door that had a paper evil eye tacked on it with a nail. "This is Señora Ravela's apartment." He pointed to the door beside it. "Señora Cepero, the witness who found the body, lives here. She's with the CDR."

"See what you can find out from the other neighbours on this floor. Ask if they heard an argument, whether she was married, if they know where she was from."

Pacheco nodded and walked down the hall; Ramirez heard him rap sharply on a door. Ramirez turned to the Ceperos' door. So they were CDR; that meant they listened to everything. The citizen watch groups were supposed to encourage the political and moral welfare of their neighbours by promoting the merits of communism but really their members were snitches. Thousands of dissidents arrested after the failed Bay of Pigs invasion were turned in because their names appeared on CDR watch lists.

CDR leaders reported all counter-revolutionary behaviour to the authorities. This could amount to almost anything: someone with too-long hair, a neighbour complaining about the living conditions, a citizen joking about the Communist Party. Even talking to foreigners qualified as a reportable offence. If Yoani Ravela hadn't died, they probably would have reported her to the authorities this morning.

The only reason Apiro and I haven't been turned in, thought Ramirez, was because we *are* the authorities.

Before Ramirez could knock at the Ceperos' door, it swung

open. A woman who looked to be in her seventies peered at him through the gap. He introduced himself, amused by the fact that she had been peeking at him through the rusted keyhole.

"Señora Cepero? Can I ask you a few questions about the incident this morning?"

"Yes," she said, gripping the door frame. "I was on my way to the *bodega* with my *jaba*, and there she was. Lying crumpled at the bottom of the stairs."

"May I come in?" Ramirez asked.

"I'm sorry. I'm still in shock." She pulled the creaky door open all the way, letting him enter. The apartment was very clean, he noticed. Plastic sheets were fixed across the windows in place of curtains. "Can I offer you something to drink? Water?"

"No, but that's very kind of you, *gracias*," Ramirez said, removing his hat and holding it in his hand.

"That's my husband on the couch. And that's my mother-in-law, over there."

An even older woman was seated on a wooden spindle-backed chair beside the tiny stove, crocheting. She looked at him and grunted. There was nowhere else to sit, so Ramirez stood.

Señor Cepero was watching a battered old television that sat on a round wooden table. The television dated back to the Soviet era and had a greenish-hued screen; the top of the set was adorned with religious icons and plastic flowers.

The children's program *Elpidio Valdés* was playing. It featured the adventures of a band of nineteenth-century revolutionaries rebelling against the Spanish. Two small children sat on the floor, leaning against Señor Cepero's knees, completely engaged by the show's rather disconcerting mix of comedy and violence, giggling as a Spanish general was shot in the head. Ramirez thought of the man on the Malecón and frowned.

"May I ask how long you have lived here?" Ramirez asked Señora Cepero.

"Ten years."

"Eleven," her husband offered. "Enrique had just entered the military, remember? He was seventeen." That was the age of compulsory service.

"These little ones are his children," she explained. "Our son and his wife live with us. That young policeman who questioned me asked me to stay at home in case you had more questions, so she's gone to get groceries."

Ramirez pulled out his notebook from his pocket. "How long did Yoani Ravela live here?"

"She was already here when we were assigned to this apartment."

It was funny, thought Ramirez, how people never thought of apartments being assigned to them but the other way around. "Did she live alone?"

"I never saw anyone else, but she kept to herself. It's a big apartment. Maybe she has rich relatives in America. After all, she's light-skinned."

This was a stereotype, but like many it had some truth to it. There was a mass exodus of wealthy middle-class Cubans after the revolution, most of them white or light-skinned. According to the myth, lighter-skinned Cubans got lots of money from their American relatives, while Afro-Cubans had to hustle.

"But she was generous," Señor Cepero hastened to add. "She often had my mother over for lunch."

Ramirez wasn't surprised to hear that. Despite the limited rations, Cubans helped one another out, sometimes trading rations, sometimes simply giving away whatever they didn't need.

"She worked for Aero Caribbean," the husband said. "I would see her wearing her uniform when she headed off in the mornings."

"Did you ever see her with a man?"

"Never," his wife said. "Well, not until last night."

"And we didn't *see* him. We just heard him," her husband said. "Actually, we heard *them*. As loud as cats." He rolled his eyes. "It's a good thing my wife snores."

"Do you know who he was?" Ramirez asked the woman.

"No. He left early," Señora Cepero said, as if that explained everything. "I don't blame her, if that's where she got her money. I might do something like that myself if I wasn't so old."

Her husband snorted. "You? I'd die laughing."

His wife smiled. "I'd kill you first."

The great-grandmother suddenly spoke up. "She was a very nice woman, Yoani," she said to Ramirez. He was almost surprised to discover she could speak. "She had a relative in the United States; that's what she told me. Someone who sent her money. It helped her get by. She always talked to me and listened to what I had to say. I'm sorry she's dead."

"When was it that you discovered the body?" Ramirez asked Señora Cepero.

"Around eight o'clock this morning."

"Closer to seven," the husband corrected her. "*The Dark Side of the Moon* was starting, remember?" It was a popular soap opera with a cast of gay characters.

Señora Cepero shrugged. "All right then, seven."

"Did you move her?"

She shook her head. "I was a nurse; I know better. Move someone with a back injury and you can paralyze them. But she was already dead."

"You say the man who was with her last night left early. Do you know what time?"

"I heard him knock on her door just after eleven. He left around one, a little after."

"How do you know?"

"Because we heard the door close when he was leaving," the husband said. Ramirez noted the use of the word *we*. There wasn't any snoring going on in this apartment last night, he thought—they were listening to everything through the wall.

"Did you ever see him?"

"What, you think we were spying on them?" Señora Cepero said indignantly.

Ramirez tried not to smile. Eavesdropping was apparently acceptable behaviour; watching someone surreptitiously was not. "Did you hear anything out of the ordinary? People arguing?"

"The only thing I heard after that," the old man said, "was when my wife went out to get our rations and started shouting." He smiled at her fondly. "But that's not unusual."

———

Ramirez looked at the light in the hallway as he walked back towards the stairs. It had no glass cover, just a bulb. But the bulb had burned out. It was new, he noticed, one of the energy-efficient ones that was supposed to last for years. He put on a pair of latex gloves and reached up to tighten it; the light flickered back on.

He rapped on the Ceperos' door again, and Señora Cepero opened it. "Excuse me for disturbing you again, Señora. The light in the hallway. Was it working last night?"

Señora Cepero nodded. "Has that bulb burned out already? They took away all the old ones. Yes, it was on when we came home last night from our walk."

"It's working," Ramirez said. "But I'm going to have to take it with me. I'll bring it back as soon as we're done, I promise. Be careful on those steps. We don't want any more accidents."

He removed an exhibit bag from his pocket, unscrewed the light bulb, and placed it carefully inside.

He walked out of the building, past the caution tape, and joined Officer Pacheco on the sidewalk. Hector Apiro was standing there too, smoking his pipe while they waited for the van to take the body to the morgue.

"No one else saw or heard anything," Pacheco said. "They don't know anything about her family. So that's all we have. Nosy neighbours."

"Be grateful for them," Ramirez said. "They often help solve cases. Well, I suppose it could just be a fall. A very bad one. It happens." Too often, thought Ramirez, with stairs in such a dangerous state of disrepair in so many buildings. And with the hallway light out, the corridor would have been dark. But the light had been on before Yoani Ravela died. Had someone deliberately loosened the bulb to darken the hallway? He decided to check it for prints.

"I still think her client killed her," Pacheco said.

"Well," Ramirez said, trying to rein the young man in, "we don't know for sure that he was a client. It could have been a friend. Besides, she died quite a while after he left, according to the neighbours. It was hot last night. She might have stepped out for some fresh air. Maybe they were drinking. She could have been unsteady on her feet and, with the light out, she could have missed the top step."

But, even as he said it, Ramirez knew that theory involved a few too many "could haves." "Was there any sign of drinking in her apartment?" he asked Apiro. "Glasses, an empty bottle?"

"Nothing," Apiro said. "But if she had a client, she could have gone to a bar with him. I'll do an autopsy on this one, Ricardo. Just to be sure. I can run a toxicology screen as well."

Ramirez nodded. He turned to Pacheco. "If Dr. Apiro finds anything unusual, we'll let you know. But, for now, we'll treat it as suspicious. I'm going to head back to headquarters; I'll take Dr. Apiro with me. Perhaps you can wait for the van?"

As he drove Apiro back to the medical towers, Ramirez thought again about Mama Loa's prophecy. The fact that the pilot and the flight attendant worked for the same airline was just a coincidence. It was a big airline, with hundreds, maybe thousands, of employees. They probably didn't even know each other.

But he had never really trusted coincidences.

19

As soon as Inspector Ramirez entered police headquarters, the uniformed guard at the front desk informed him that a Dr. Pedro Garcia was waiting to see him. The guard pointed to a small bespectacled man sitting on the wooden bench in the hall, thumbing through the pages of a book.

It took Ramirez a moment to place him. "Ah, Dr. Garcia," he said. "You must be the ballistics expert Dr. Apiro told me about. I hope you haven't been waiting long."

"No, only a few minutes," Garcia said, getting up to shake Ramirez's hand.

Ramirez escorted the man up the flight of stairs to the Major Crimes Unit. He closed the door to his office and motioned to one of the wooden chairs in front of his desk. "Can I get you a coffee?"

"Oh, no, *gracias*," said Garcia, and lowered himself onto the chair. He leaned forward and placed the book on Ramirez's desk along with a plastic exhibit bag. "I'm afraid I've been spoiled. Dr.

Apiro brought me a full thermos this morning when he dropped off the bullet for analysis."

Ramirez smiled to himself. Delivering a thermos of freshly brewed coffee was Apiro's way of greasing the wheels, of making sure his request for assistance was placed at the top of the pile. Apiro bought fresh coffee beans on the black market almost daily. He was precise about making coffee, and his was always delicious. Rationed coffee, which was all most Cubans had to drink, was cut with chickpea flour and tasted bitter. Only *turistas* had easy access to the rich coffee that Cubans loved.

"As soon as I saw it, I knew exactly what it was," said Dr. Garcia. "The bullet, that is, not the coffee." He smiled, "Although I haven't had such good coffee for a while. I would have come sooner, but it took me a while to find this." He pointed to the book. "I thought it best to see you in person. You never know these days who might be listening."

"Now you've piqued my interest."

"It will take me a little while to explain," said Garcia. "May I smoke?"

"Of course, go ahead," said Ramirez. He reached for his cigar and Garcia pulled a pipe from one of his pockets.

"I will have to give you a bit of a history lesson, Inspector. I hope you don't mind. Are you familiar with the term 'wet work'?"

Garcia gestured as he spoke, the unlit pipe held absent-mindedly in his fingers, its purpose already forgotten.

"I assume you mean murders?" Ramirez struck a match and leaned across his desk to offer it to Garcia. Garcia drew on the pipe several times until the embers in the bowl glowed red. He nodded gratefully. The pungent smell of pipe smoke filled the air.

"State-sanctioned assassinations," Garcia said. He pointed the pipe stem in the air to emphasize his point. "Men who engage in such activities need weapons that can be easily concealed, used, and then discarded. Soviet scientists, in particular, were highly experienced in developing these kinds of weapons. Well, in fairness, so was NATO. After World War Two, they came up with a gun—the Soviets, that is—that looked like a cigarette case. It had three short barrels inside and a trigger, but because of its small size, it couldn't be fitted with a silencer. So the scientists came up with the idea of developing silent ammunition instead.

"Originally, they used round-nosed bullets, but these were easily recognized, which defeated their value for use in clandestine operations. They replaced them with 7.62 mm cartridges, standard ammunition, which were harder to trace. Over time, they developed cartridges that were better at long distances, but they had two-stage telescoping pistons, which meant they couldn't be used in semiautomatic weapons. And so eventually they created what became known as SP-4 ammunition. Instead of a telescoping piston, the bullets have a piston that stays in the case when the bullet is fired."

Garcia reached for the plastic exhibit bag. He opened it and shook the petal-tipped bullet into his palm. He handed it to Ramirez.

"This is an SP-4 bullet. They're made of steel and fitted with brass bands. And there's only one gun in the world that can fire them. It's a six-shot, magazine-fed, semiautomatic pistol. The PSS, or *pistolet sptsialnyj samozaryadnyj*, is a special self-loading pistol. It was originally developed for special personnel of the Soviet KGB. Here, I have a picture of one."

Garcia reached for his book and flipped through the pages until he found it. He tapped on the photograph, then slid the book across the desk. Ramirez examined the image—a small black gun with a short barrel.

"That's consistent with what our primary witness observed at the scene," Ramirez said. "No one heard any shots, although at least two were fired."

Garcia smiled tightly. "That's the reason. These weapons are still used, but mostly by members of the Russian Federal Security Services—the FSB, as you know, replaced the KGB—as well as *spetsnaz*."

"What are *spetsnaz?*"

"Russian Special Forces. Much like the British SAS or the American Delta Force. These days, they're involved in intelligence and antiterrorist squads. If you remember the theatre incident in Moscow, when all the hostages were gassed, the elite commandos they sent in were *spetsnaz.*"

Ramirez remembered the incident well. Armed Chechens had taken eight hundred people hostage in a Moscow movie theatre, demanding that Russia withdraw from Chechnya. Even before the hostage taking was over, the entire incident had been re-enacted on television. Cubans had watched along with the rest of the world, united by their horror.

Nikolai Patrushev, the head of the Russian FSB, offered to let the Chechens live if they spared their hostages. But, before a deal could be struck, Russian Special Forces gassed the theatre. The Chechens had gas masks; their hostages didn't. There were a hundred and twenty-nine casualties, including nine foreigners.

What struck Ramirez at the time was that Russian authorities refused to identify the gas used, not even to the doctors treating the injured.

"Now you know why I wanted to meet you in private," Garcia said. "This bullet came from a deep-concealment weapon. One intended for use outside Russia."

20

Inspector Ramirez escorted Dr. Garcia out of the building. When he returned to the second floor, he found Detective Espinoza working at his desk. Ramirez asked the young detective to step into his office, and told Espinoza what Dr. Garcia had said.

"Why would a Russian *spetsnaz* come all the way to Havana to kill someone?" Espinoza said, eyes wide. "Does that mean our victim was a Chechen terrorist?"

"I don't know," Ramirez admitted. "We have to be careful not to jump to conclusions. But it looks more and more as though our shooter was connected to Russia. Have you had a chance to go to the Russian embassy yet?"

"No. I'm still working my way through the hotels. It's taking longer than I thought, even with Natasha helping. There must be a thousand Russians in the city this week, maybe more, because of the trade show. The Russian pavilion is huge—over thirteen hundred square metres."

"Carry on, then, Fernando. I'll head over to the Russian embassy myself."

Ramirez drove down Quinta Avenida in Miramar. Fifth Avenue was a broad boulevard with huge trees. It served as Havana's embassy row. Most of the mansions had been restored; their beauty marred only by the leaning telephone poles and tangled electrical wires at almost every intersection.

The Russian embassy was easily distinguished from its graceful neighbours by its ugliness. It was an imposing building, part of a compound that sprawled across almost ten acres of land. Its jutting tower had been constructed in the shape of a spark plug. The entire complex looked as if it should be manned by prison guards—Cubans called it the Bunker.

Ramirez parked his car and walked up the path. As he entered the lobby, he noticed that the bust of Lenin was no longer there. A huge framed photograph of Vladimir Putin hung on the wall instead. Its cold, light-blue gaze followed him; he took a step to the left, a step to the right, and then walked right up to the portrait to make sure it was a photograph. The unblinking eyes were unnerving.

"Good afternoon," Ramirez said to the woman sitting behind the reception desk and showed her his badge. "My name is Inspector Ricardo Ramirez. I'm with the Cuban National Revolutionary Police. I would like to speak to someone concerning one of our investigations."

The woman picked up a heavy black telephone and spoke quietly into the mouthpiece. Ramirez didn't understand Russian, but he thought he picked up an undertone of anxiety in her voice.

While he waited, a Cuban woman wearing high heels and a top with a plunging neckline hurriedly exited an office that bore a sign marked Visas. She was clutching a brown envelope. A few minutes later, a stocky man walked briskly out of the same office. He closed the door tightly behind him. He raised his thick eyebrows as he approached Ramirez.

"Inspector Ramirez?" he said with a strong accent. "My name is Anatoly Klopov. I am a Russian consular officer. I will be happy to answer your questions."

He snapped his fingers at the receptionist and said something to her in Russian. She jumped to her feet and ran off to perform whatever task she'd been assigned.

The consular officer escorted Ramirez into an oppressively dark room with wood panelling and no windows. A stack of blank visa forms lay toppled over on the long table. Klopov pushed them aside.

"Now, what can I do for you, Inspector?" He curved his lips into a smile, but Ramirez saw a certain wariness in his eyes. "What kind of investigation is this?"

"A homicide. A man was shot to death on the Malecón yesterday," said Ramirez. "We have reason to think he was Russian."

"I am sorry to hear that," said the diplomat, but Ramirez had the contradictory sense that he was actually relieved. "Who was the victim?"

"We don't know yet."

"He didn't have a passport?"

"Not that we've found. But according to our expert, the ammunition used to kill him came from a weapon issued only to the FSB and Russian Special Forces. It concerns me that someone may have carried out a state-sanctioned operation in Havana without our knowledge."

Klopov frowned. "Well, Inspector Ramirez, as you know, there were Soviet troops in Cuba for decades. Even if your expert is correct, it is always possible some ammunition was left behind."

"Yes, that is a possibility," Ramirez said. "Although the circumstances of the murder suggest that the person who found it also managed to get their hands on the only gun in the world that can use it."

There was a knock on the door. Klopov rose to open it. The receptionist held a black tray with a teapot, two white china cups, and a plate of round cookies rolled in icing sugar. She placed the tray on the table and let herself out, avoiding eye contact.

Klopov pointed to the tray as he sat down again. "Please, try these. The cookies are delicious. The Mexicans call them wedding cakes, but they are actually a traditional Russian dessert." He smiled pleasantly and offered the plate to Ramirez.

Ramirez took a cookie, Klopov another.

"Before I rule anything out," said Ramirez, "I would like to know if anyone serving with Russian Special Forces has been in Havana recently, if not officially, then perhaps on unofficial business. If so, it's always possible that his gun and ammunition were stolen."

The diplomat popped the cookie in his mouth. "If it was official business, I can't tell you. And if it was unofficial business, no one would tell us." He smiled again. "You know what national security matters are like."

Ramirez had the feeling that the only concrete information he would leave with was the Mexican name for the cookies.

"Perhaps you can provide me with some background information, then, Señor Klopov. Who are considered enemies of the Russian state these days?"

The Russian wiped his hands together to dust off the icing sugar. "Chechen terrorists are probably our greatest concern. Particularly the Chechen mafia."

"Tell me about them," Ramirez said. He ate his cookie and dusted off his hands as well. The interview technique was called mirroring. It involved mimicking the action of the person being interrogated, their body language, their stance, to help break down their resistance. Ramirez suddenly realized that he was treating Klopov as a suspect.

"It is very complicated," Klopov said, and shrugged. "Sometimes people call the Chechen mafia, Russian mafia, because they operated in the former Soviet Union. And, of course, almost all Chechens speak Russian." He reached for the teapot and filled Ramirez's cup, then his own. There was no milk, only a small pile of sugar cubes on the platter. Klopov used a pair of tongs to drop one in his cup.

Ramirez did the same. The tea was very black, its bitter taste cut by the sweetness of the sugar.

"The Chechen mafia was already active in Russia when Russia invaded Chechnya, but most of its members left Russia to fight in the Chechen wars. The Chechens are still a big problem for us," Klopov said. "I would never tell you how to do your job, but if I had a Russian-speaking victim of a shooting, I would probably ask myself if the victim was Chechen. Also the shooter."

"I didn't say the victim was Russian speaking," said Ramirez.

"No," said Klopov. He popped another cookie in his mouth and licked the sugar from his fingers. "But you implied it."

Ramirez nodded. He sensed that Havana could easily become a battleground in wars that didn't concern it. An image popped into his mind from his grandmother's stories—giant octopuses wielding deadly blue jellyfish, waving them deep below the ocean's surface like trailing blue scarves. The jellyfish had become weapons in battles that weren't of their making. Ramirez was starting to feel like a jellyfish himself.

"Do you know this man?" Ramirez asked. He removed a photograph of the shooting victim from his jacket pocket and passed it to Klopov. The diplomat glanced at it and shook his head, almost too quickly. "Do Russian citizens have to report to you when they arrive in Cuba?"

Klopov shrugged. "Registration is not a legal requirement, just a suggestion. In case something happens to a family member, for example, and we need to reach them."

Ramirez nodded. "Can I have a copy of the list of all the Russians who have registered with you in the past thirty days?"

The diplomat narrowed his eyes. "I'm afraid I can't give you that." He shrugged. "It's confidential."

"Fair enough," said Ramirez. He knew he'd never be able to get that information if Klopov wouldn't provide it. The diplomatic corps was immune from all legal proceedings, including warrants.

He pushed himself up from the table. He had heard enough to know he was wasting his time. But then, a government that refused to divulge what poisonous gas it had used that sickened innocent theatregoers, including its own citizens, was not likely to cooperate with Cuban authorities regarding the death of an unidentified man. "You will, of course, inform me if you come across any information that could be helpful to our investigation?" Ramirez said, leaving unstated but clear that Klopov had been no help at all.

"Of course," said the diplomat, standing up as well. "Relations between our countries are at an important juncture. It is in our interest to cooperate on sensitive matters."

"*Gracias*," Ramirez said, trying to keep the sarcasm out of his voice. He left the photograph on the boardroom table. "Perhaps you could put this up somewhere, in case someone in the embassy knows him?"

"Of course," Klopov nodded, but Ramirez felt sure the photograph would end up in the wastebasket.

The diplomat opened the door to the hallway. He escorted Ramirez through the lobby, past the frightened-looking receptionist. He pushed the front door open for him, as if to ensure that Ramirez would really leave.

"Thank you for your time," said Ramirez. He stopped. "By the way, Señor, do you know anything about Russian prison tattoos?"

"I'm afraid I don't," Klopov said. He smiled, exposing brown-stained teeth. "Although I have been inside a few Russian prisons."

For the first time since they met, Ramirez believed him.

21

As his flight prepared to land, Slava Kadun wondered why Vladimir Putin wanted him, instead of Dmitri Nabakoff, to go to Cuba. Dmitri often worked security for the Russian president. Putin trusted him.

Dmitri had told Slava about working one time at a reception when Putin stole an American Super Bowl ring from the winning coach, Pat O'Brien. Putin asked O'Brien if he could see the ring, and the coach naively took it off and handed it over.

"I could kill someone with a diamond that big," Putin said, and laughed, although Dmitri later thought he might have said he'd kill someone *for* a diamond that big, which was also possible. Then Putin put the ring in his pocket and walked away, flanked by his bodyguards.

The American was left standing, dumbfounded, as his prized possession disappeared. A few weeks later, when the media asked him about it, he squirmed awkwardly and said it was a gift.

But Dmitri saw it for what it was—open theft. "That's Putin," he said, and shook his head admiringly. "Now that he has power, he can do almost anything and get away with it."

And now, thought Slava, Putin wanted *him* to handle a problem, the same way Putin turned to other Special Forces members and FSB from time to time to do his bidding. Other so-called problems had included the vice chair of a commission that was investigating allegations that Putin was behind the apartment bombings in Moscow. He was gunned down. Another was the editor of an international magazine that reported the story. Shot dead. Journalists Igor Domnikov, Sergey Novikov, Iskandar Khatloni, Sergey Ivanov, Adam Tepsurgayev, and Anna Politkovskaya. All were either murdered or "disappeared."

Anna Politkovskaya was shot to death on Putin's birthday, in the elevator of her apartment building. She had been investigating human-rights abuses and atrocities in Chechnya and high-level corruption in Russia. Some of her stories were sharply critical of Putin, a former KGB spy.

Alexander Litvinenko, another KGB officer, claimed that Putin ordered the hit. Soon after, a retired Russian policeman conveniently confessed. He claimed that Boris Berezovsky, a Russian billionaire who had been Putin's mentor but now criticized Putin openly, had paid a triggerman to kill her.

Litvinenko and Berezovsky both fled to London for asylum. Three months after Litvinenko pointed the finger at Putin for Anna Politkovskaya's murder, he was poisoned to death with polonium-210. Then Scotland Yard got wind that a Russian hit man, identified only as "Vladislav," was on his way to London to kill Berezovsky too. They deported the hit man back to Russia, where no charges were laid. There wasn't enough evidence, Russian authorities told the international media. They'd made sure of it.

It had been Slava's first international assignment. Travelling back from London was the first time he'd ever been on a plane that wasn't Soviet built. He remembered how surprised he was when the seatbacks of the chairs stayed upright when the passengers stood up to exit. The ones on Aeroflot all fell forward like a line of dominoes, as if all the seats had decided to bow, one row at a time.

He sometimes wondered whether he would have gone ahead with the hit if Scotland Yard hadn't intercepted him. He wondered what would happen to him and Dmitri if Putin ever found out who tipped off Scotland Yard.

The airplane began its slow descent into José Martí Airport, circling lazily above dull red tobacco fields. The plane bounced when it landed on the airport's one long runway. On the tarmac, a brand-new Russian TU-204 sat beside a Cubana Airbus. A mural on the outside of the main hangar displayed a khaki-clad revolutionary holding a machine gun, posing with the Russian fleet. But Slava saw no other Aeroflot planes, even though twenty thousand Russian tourists a year came to this island looking for sun, nostalgic for the days when Russia was a Cuban presence. Instead, he saw row after row of Air Europa and Air France and Air Canada planes.

It took Slava an hour to clear Customs, and another before he was able to retrieve his olive-green duffel bag. He changed his rubles for pesos at the exchange wicket and exited the terminal building. He looked at the address on the letter of introduction and asked an English-speaking cabbie to take him to Revolution Square.

"You are here for business, Señor?" the cabbie asked him, looking at his uniform. "First time to Havana?"

"Yeah, first time," Slava said, and climbed into the back of the cab.

"Staying long?"

"Two nights."

"That's not much time to have fun."

Slava smiled. "I will do what I can to make up for it."

He was struck by the number of old Ladas and Soviet-era buses still on the road, leaking smoke and diesel fumes. The taxi driver pointed out the National Botanical Gardens and the Lenin Park Zoo on the way. "There aren't a lot of animals there anymore," he said as they passed the zoo. "During the Special Period, everything disappeared. We used to joke that the government changed the signs from Don't Feed the Animals to Don't Eat the Animals." He laughed. "There is a pilgrimage down this road," he said, gesturing with his hand. "It starts in a few weeks. The road closes so the pilgrims can ask San Lazaro for favours. They walk in their bare feet. Some of them tie rocks to their ankles. Sometimes I think they should ask San Lazaro for shoes, but then, our shoe stores are usually empty."

The ramshackle buildings and rusted cars reminded Slava of other places he'd worked. The Ukrainian countryside was the worst, its poverty stamped into the faces and bodies of its people. Years of beet picking had turned once-strong women into tiny stooped *babushkas* with gnarled hands and crippled backs. He recalled the feudal thatched huts between Dnepropetrovsk and Chernobyl, the people stuffed into carts and wagons on election day dressed in their finest clothes while pigs and goats rode beside them.

Belgrade shared the same dour Russian architecture he observed here—ugly, plain apartment buildings. But it was the women of Cuba that caught Slava's eye as they drove into Havana: they were every shade of olive, brown, and black. The young ones were dressed in tight clothes with low-cut tops and high heels, and all of them, even the older ones, showed their legs.

He saw the taxi driver turn his head from time to time, whistling softly. Cuban men appreciated them, Slava could tell. Through the open car window, he could hear the hoots, the catcalls, the hisses.

He smiled. He loved women too. Russian women could be strong and beautiful, particularly the gymnasts, but they held themselves with reserve. They were suspicious, and cautious, which made them sexy.

He'd always thought the women in Kiev were the most beautiful, with their stylish clothes and flair, the care they took with their makeup and hair. He'd loved Serbian women as well, the confidence they displayed, with their dangling jewellery and bright colours. Picking just one to take home after a night in the bars was like being a bee wandering through a garden, trying to decide which flower to taste.

The Cuban women looked to be just as colourful and comfortable in their skin as the Serbs. They stood in groups, hands on their hips, debating, gossiping, flirting. They swayed through the streets. Some were walking, linked arm-in-arm, with older foreign men, punctuating their words with wide gestures and laughter.

They wore T-shirts and shorts, halters and long skirts, colourful strands of beads, bandannas, sandals with flowers, jewelled shoes. They were lush in a way that fit perfectly with the exotic location, the heat, the intense colours of the landscape. There was no mistaking who they were or what they were—they were alive in a way that stirred the senses. They were sensual and unafraid.

The cabbie saw his reflection in the rear-view mirror and smiled. "Sex is the one thing the government can't ration, Señor. There's lots of it around."

"How old do the girls have to be to have sex here?" Slava asked the cabbie.

"Sixteen." The driver caught his eye and grinned. "You like the little ones? You can have anything you want here, any age, even boys, as long as you have money."

22

As soon as he got back to his office, Inspector Ramirez ran upstairs to see General de Soto. He relayed the contents of Dr. Garcia's expert opinion, then his frustrating conversation with the Russian consular officer.

"Those fucking diplomats," said de Soto. "They have immunity and they know it. They never tell us shit. Well, I'd better contact the Minister of the Interior and see what he wants us to do. The minister won't be happy to find out that there may have been a Russian military operation conducted in Havana without our knowledge." He picked up his phone and made the call, motioning to Ramirez to wait. When he was done, he hung up with a sigh. "He wants a briefing right away," he said. "Go get your reports. I'll meet you there."

———

Ramirez drove quickly to the Plaza de la Revolución. A smiling Fidel Castro looked down from a billboard that said *Vamos Bien*.

We're Doing Well. It was a little like living in a George Orwell novel, Ramirez thought. Only a matter of time before the Ministry of the Interior was renamed the Ministry of Interior Happiness.

The Plaza de la Revolución was a giant square in Vedado known before the revolution as the Plaza de República. The Palace of the Revolution was located there, physically linked to Communist Party headquarters. The seven-storey building housing the Ministry of the Interior, or MININT, as it was widely known, was an ugly concrete block on the north side of the plaza.

MININT was responsible for the Cuban National Revolutionary Police as well as Cuban Intelligence and immigration. A giant steel outline of Che Guevara's head was mounted on the side of the ministry building, with the words "Hasta la Victoria Siempre" written beneath the iconic image.

As always, dozens of yellow and blue tourist buses rimmed the plaza. *Extranjeros* came to Revolution Square by the thousands to see the memorial to José Martí. The four-hundred-foot-tall obelisk was made of marble and had an elevator inside that took tourists up to see the view from the top, the highest point in Havana. At its base was a huge statue of Martí posed like Rodin's *The Thinker*.

It struck Ramirez as ironic that José Martí had once been jailed for treason. But then, so had Castro for leading an uprising against Batista; Castro had quoted Martí in his defence. Clearly, one generation's terrorist was another's hero, he thought, as he found a shady place to park.

Ramirez walked up the cracked concrete sidewalk, glancing around him. The last time he had been summoned to brief the Minister of the Interior, the ghost of a murdered cigar lady accompanied him all the way inside. She had stood in the corridor, examining the photographs that hung on the walls. Only later did he understand she'd been trying to give him clues to help his investigation. He looked around again before he opened the massive door, but he was on his own. He felt the pang of something sharp, a little like homesickness.

He made his way to the minister's office. The minister's clerk was seated behind her desk. Ramirez was usually forced to wait patiently while she gossiped on the phone or took breaks or simply ignored him, but this time she ushered him directly in to see the minister.

The Minister of the Interior paced behind his giant polished mahogany desk. General de Soto was already there. He leaned against a wall, smoking.

Ramirez wasn't sure if he was supposed to sit or stand, but he selected one of the deep, worn leather chairs on the opposite side of the minister's desk and eased himself in. Ensconced in the other chair was Major Marcelo Diaz Fleitas, the director in charge of Cuban Intelligence, wearing green military fatigues and high brown boots of the Ministry of the Interior. Major Diaz was well liked. He was rumoured to be first in the line of succession if both Castros retired.

"Good. You're here, Ramirez. Tell everyone what you've learned," said General de Soto. "And don't leave out any details."

Ramirez outlined the circumstances around the shooting. He summarized the investigation to date, the unusual ammunition recovered from the corpse, and the professional nature of the shooting.

"If there is a Russian antiterrorist squad in Havana, Cuban Intelligence certainly wasn't informed of it," Major Diaz said.

General de Soto nodded. "Neither were we."

"That doesn't mean anything," said the minister. "I wouldn't expect the Russians to warn us if they planned a clandestine operation here, or to admit to it now. Not even if we caught them red-handed. Every nation has operatives working in other countries, ours included. We've had agents in the U.S. State Department for over fifty years. Even James Casson, when he was head of the U.S. Special Interests Section, said we had very good agents. The whole idea behind clandestine operations is secrecy. Only the Americans are so stupid as to think foreign spies should register." The minister snorted.

General de Soto raised his eyebrows.

"We had an undercover agent in Florida, a professor," Major Diaz explained. "Carlos Alvarez. The FBI picked up his communications with us. He'd been spying for us for almost three decades. They sent him to prison because he failed to register with them as a foreign agent."

"Completely trumped-up charges. It's because he's Cuban," the minister said. "Ernest Hemingway worked for the KGB too. Did the Americans ask him to register as a foreign spy? Of course not."

"I should perhaps point out that just because we found SP-4 ammunition doesn't necessarily mean this was a Russian Special Forces operation," said Ramirez, trying to bring the conversation back to the point. "Someone could have stolen a loaded gun or purchased it on the black market."

"From a Russian *spetsnaz*?" Diaz said. "I find that unlikely. They're highly trained commandos—the elite of the elite. We've used them from time to time in the camps to train our own men in hand-to-hand combat."

"Well, we need to keep our eyes open, gentlemen," said the minister. "Something's going on. Before you arrived, Ramirez, Major Diaz was telling us there are Chechentsi in town—Chechen mafia. That Russian consular officer could have been telling you the truth."

This surprised Ramirez. When Anatoly Klopov suggested the victim was Chechen, he'd had the clear sense he was being misdirected. "Why would Chechen mafia be in Havana?"

"Probably for the trade fair," Diaz said. "One of the Russian arms dealers, Rosobornexport, has registered. The Americans won't buy its weapons anymore; they claim it sells arms to Venezuela, as well as Iran and Pakistan. It needs to find new markets. And the Chechens need weapons."

"I don't think Vladimir Putin would like it very much if Russian arms found their way into Chechen hands," said the minister. "Particularly ones purchased in Cuba."

"I'm sure some already have," Diaz said. "There's a middleman for everything if the money is right."

"Who exactly *is* here, Major?" asked General de Soto. "And why weren't we informed?"

"A Chechen warlord named Ruslan Dudayev. He flew into Havana last week. There was nothing to tell you; so far, he's done nothing illegal. He collaborated with the Russian FSB a few years ago to turn in his own gang members in exchange for immunity. The FSB arranged for him to be moved out of Moscow, but he keeps popping up. He's a man with many enemies. And extremely dangerous friends."

"Where is he staying?" asked Ramirez.

"The Hotel Nacional."

The minister narrowed his eyes. "Is he alone?"

"As far as we know, yes," said Diaz. "He hasn't gone far. He seems to be holding all his meetings in his room. We haven't seen him for a couple of days."

The minister's phone rang. "I left instructions that we weren't to be disturbed unless it was important," he said, reaching for it. "My apologies."

He listened for a moment. "Now, that's interesting," he said as he put down the phone. "There's a man waiting in reception for you, Major Diaz. He has an official letter of introduction from Nikolai Patrushev. I think perhaps we should invite him to join us. He may have some insight into what's going on."

"Why would we include a stranger in our meeting?" said General de Soto.

"Because Nikolai Patrushev is the head of Russian Intelligence. And his letter says it's urgent."

23

The minister's clerk escorted a tall, muscular man with a bald head carrying an olive-green duffel bag into the minister's office. For a moment, Ramirez thought she might swoon from the testosterone that practically radiated from him. She finally let herself out, glancing backwards at the Russian as she reluctantly closed the door behind her.

"Is okay to speak English?" the Russian asked.

They all nodded.

"Is good, because my English is probably better than your Russian." He grinned. "I am Commander Slava Kadun. I am senior intelligence officer with Vityaz, with Russian Ministry of Internal Affairs." He produced his identification card and handed it with his letter of introduction to the minister.

The minister glanced at it and passed it to Major Diaz, who examined it carefully. Diaz tipped his head to the minister, satisfied.

"Is okay to talk in this room about top-secret matters?" Kadun asked. He looked around the room, clearly asking if everyone there was cleared for that level of secrecy and if the building was secure.

The minister nodded. "My office is swept for listening devices every day. And these men are my top advisors." He introduced the officials, as well as Ramirez, who was surprised to discover he was now one of the minister's top men. "Now tell us, what brings you to Havana, Commander?"

Kadun shrugged. "Bottom line is this—American CIA plans to kill Raúl Castro tomorrow night at trade fair. I have tape of conversation." He produced a small audiotape from his duffel bag.

The minister picked up the phone, and his clerk raced in a minute later with a silver-coloured tape recorder. She smiled at Commander Kadun as she showed him how to operate it, and peeked at him again as she let herself out.

Kadun inserted the tape in the machine and pushed a button. He adjusted the volume. The group listened intently until the tape ended and Kadun turned the tape recorder off.

"They plan to kill the acting president at the trade show?" said the minister, shocked. "Who are these men? How do you know they're CIA?"

"Voice analysis. Location of transmission is from motel close to Washington, DC. We believe older guy is head of CIA Special Operations. We don't know who is younger guy."

The minister reached for his phone and punched in a number. "I need Major Rodriguez in here *now*," he instructed someone. "Have him picked up in a police car if you have to." He slammed down the phone.

"I need to talk to my colleagues alone for a minute," he said to Ramirez. "You can wait in the reception area with Commander Kadun. We'll call you back in when we're ready."

Ramirez and Slava Kadun sat down on the worn bench in the hallway. A copy of *Granma* rested on the seat; Ramirez picked it up and idly flipped through it. "*Granma* is the Communist Party's newspaper," he explained to Kadun.

"Does it report news?" the Russian asked. "Ours never does."

"Sometimes," Ramirez said. "It occasionally slips through. It's usually unintentional."

"We have joke about our two newspapers, *Pravda* and *Izvestiya*. *Pravda* means 'truth' and *izvestiya* means 'news.' We say there is no news in *Pravda* and no truth in *Izvestiya*. Like story of man in *Izvestiya* last week. Paper said he won one hundred thousand rubles in lottery, then issued correction. We found out it wasn't last week, it was last month, and it wasn't lottery but chess game, and he didn't win one hundred thousand rubles but one thousand rubles, and he didn't actually win chess game, he lost."

Ramirez chuckled.

It wasn't very long before Major Rodriguez arrived. A tall man, with an angry look on his face, he walked briskly past them and thrust open the doors to the minister's inner sanctum.

———

"What's going on?" Major Rodriguez said. "I was in a meeting with Raúl Castro. Your clerk said it was urgent."

"We have a major problem. Actually, two of them. Let's deal with the first one first."

The minister replayed the tape and then summarized what Commander Kadun had said. "You're the security expert. Is this a genuine threat? What can we expect?"

"From the CIA?" Rodriguez said. "Anything. One time, they were going to kill El Jefe with an exploding seashell when he was scuba diving." El Jefe—the Chief—was the name Fidel Castro's bodyguards used to refer to him. "They poisoned his boots once. They even poisoned his cigars."

The minister shook his head, as if horrified at the sacrilege. "That's why Fidel switched to Cohibas, you know," he said, pointing to the humidor on his desk. "Fabian mentions it in his book."

"Fabian told only some of the stories. They tried to infect El Jefe's beard with a fungus, too," said Rodriguez. "They thought if it fell off, no one would respect him. That's how crazy the *americanos* are. But they're dangerous. We found ninety kilograms of plastique in the podium at the Ibero-American Summit in Panama in 2000 before Castro gave his speech. Enough to blow up an armoured car."

"That was Luis Posada," the minister said.

"It was the CIA, Minister," Rodriguez scowled. "Where do you think Posada got the plastique? The Americans say he's not working for them anymore, but that judge in Texas let him go, not even a slap on the wrist. The evidence was so strong. That had to be political pressure."

Posada had been tried in Texas on charges of lying to U.S. immigration officials about how he entered the country, as well as for lying about his involvement in a fatal bombing of a Havana hotel in the late 1990s. Cuba sent expert witnesses to assist the American prosecutors. One was Major Diaz, who took Manuel Flores's place after Flores was arrested. Flores had handled Posada's file for decades.

"It's like I told *Granma*," Diaz said. "Posada was so confident of his acquittal, he slept through the entire trial. His lawyers asked me irrelevant questions on cross-examination, like whether Cubans were really prohibited from entering tourist hotels and why we have so much prostitution. The whole thing was a setup, if you ask me—a sham trial."

"What can we do to stop them?" asked General de Soto.

"What we always do," said Rodriguez. "Exercise extreme caution. El Jefe no longer accepts food that hasn't been tasted by his personal chef. He only drinks water brought to him by his security detail. And it's no different with the acting president. We expect the worst and prepare for everything. We had already planned to

have our men at the trade fair tomorrow night. We'll have a medical team on standby, but our men are instructed to shoot to kill
on sight."

"I think we should use a double for Raúl at the awards cere-
mony," the minister said. "It's too dangerous. We can't take the
chance. Not now, not with Fidel still in the hospital."

Major Rodriguez shook his head vigorously. "Raúl will never
agree to it. El Jefe never did. He might use a double occasionally in
a car, but never for public events. Too many people would know it
wasn't him. He's afraid of losing face."

The minister sighed. "Have you done background checks on the
foreigners who will be with Ramón when he gets that award?"

"Of course," Diaz said. "The man presenting it is a personal
friend of the Castros. An American named Franklin Pearce. He's
been to Ramón's ranch many times. He is completely trustworthy.
And the others are the same—businessmen who have dealt with us
for years despite the trade embargo, at great personal risk. Friends
of Cuba."

"Then we'll need to have enhanced security throughout the entire pavilion," said General de Soto.

"How many people does the main pavilion hold?" asked the
minister.

"Several thousand at any given time," said Rodriguez. "But
thousands more will visit throughout the day. The trade show is
always busy."

The minister let out a low whistle. "How can we possibly police
those kinds of numbers? Wouldn't it be better to cancel the acting
president's appearance?"

"We can't," Diaz said. "We need Raúl Castro to go so we can
identify the CIA operative. Otherwise, he could turn up anywhere,
any time. We have to let events unfold and trust security to do its
job. Major Rodriguez knows what he's doing."

"It's a big risk," said the minister doubtfully.

"It puts civilian lives in danger, too," said General de Soto. "If something goes wrong . . ."

"We can't change course because of threats to the Castros," said Rodriguez. "If we did, no one would ever see them in public again. Believe me, we deal with threats like this all the time."

"Who is going to tell Raúl about this?" the minister asked.

"I will," said Major Rodriguez. "I have to go back and finish going over his schedule with him. Just like El Jefe, he keeps it unpredictable precisely because of threats like these. I'll impress upon him the importance of being vigilant tomorrow. He was a soldier. He knows the risks."

"All right, then," the minister nodded. "Well, we need to discuss who is going to do what. But we have to keep our security arrangements to ourselves. Which brings us to our second problem. Major Rodriguez just confirmed what I have always understood to be the case. Raúl Castro's schedule is never released in advance." The minister leaned back in his chair and furrowed his brow. "Yet, somehow, the CIA not only knew that he was going to be at the trade fair tomorrow night, they knew the exact time. We need to be very careful who we trust, gentlemen. Only a few people have access to that information. There could be another Betancourt."

The men around the table nodded. Lazaro Betancourt Morin had been one of Fidel Castro's bodyguards. He defected to the U.S. while Castro was attending a summit in the Dominican Republic. The minister shook his head. "We may have a mole."

24

"*When did you arrive in Havana,* Commander Kadun?" Inspector Ramirez asked the Russian intelligence officer.

"Please, call me Slava. Three hours ago maybe. Very long flight." Slava mimicked yawning, then yawned for real. He turned to face Ramirez and inclined his head to the minister's closed door. "Lots of big shots inside. But you are police investigator?"

"I'm certainly not a big shot." Ramirez smiled. "I'm a policeman. The head of the Havana Major Crimes Unit. We had a murder in the city yesterday. The victim and the shooter both spoke Russian. It looks like a professional hit. According to Cuban Intelligence, there are members of the Chechen mafia in town. The minister wanted a briefing. That's the only reason I was there; I'm not really sure why they let me stay once you came in."

"Fucking Chechens," Slava spat. "I was in Argun during Chechen wars when suicide bombers attack Russian military and police headquarters. Twenty-five troops killed. Eighty more badly hurt. Mostly men I train for combat in mountain warfare brigades. That's why I join Vityaz."

"What does Vityaz do, exactly?"

"Counterterrorism. Sometimes prison control, riots. Russian prisons are tough, you know? Guys go little bit crazy. Fucking dangerous guys when they get out. Means we have to be even more dangerous."

Slava looked at the minister's clerk and winked. She had stopped typing and was hanging on his every word. "Don't worry," he said to her. "I don't kill nobody if I don't have to. Unless someone tries to hurt you. Then, don't worry, I will kill them."

She stifled a giggle before pretending to work again. Ramirez suspected that if he looked at the page she was typing, it would have nothing but line after line of gibberish.

"Then maybe you can help me with something, Slava. Our shooting victim had tattoos. Roses on his chest. A soldier's epaulette on his shoulder." He cupped a hand to his left shoulder in case Slava didn't understand. "Our pathologist thinks he might have got them in a Russian prison."

Slava nodded. "Probably he is right. I need to see them to be sure. Could mean victim is captain. Very big guy in Russian mafia."

"You mean the Chechen mafia?"

"No," said Slava. "Russian mafia. Chechens got their own."

"Would you be able to look at the body while you're in Havana? It would really help with our investigation."

"Sure. Is no problem. We can go after meeting, if big shots don't need me."

"*Gracias.* How long will you be staying in Cuba?"

"Only until day after tomorrow," Slava said. "Then I have flight to Haifa. Is family anniversary. I was supposed to be on holidays this week." He shook his head.

The phone on the clerk's desk rang. She answered and put her hand in the air to catch their attention. "They only want to see you this time, Inspector Ramirez. Commander Kadun can stay here with me. Don't worry; I'll keep an eye on him." She smiled at Slava warmly. Ramirez was sure that as soon as he was out of sight, she'd not only have both eyes on the good-looking Russian, but both hands too, if she could swing it.

"Raúl Castro is going to be at the event tomorrow night," the minister said as soon as Ramirez pulled the door closed behind him. "Major Rodriguez and his men will handle security inside the venue. The PNR will check all vehicles. Cuban Intelligence will monitor the inside and outside of the main pavilion for explosives, detonators, and weapons. The airport dogs will be fully utilized. We have to be careful to make sure that nothing looks out of the ordinary; we don't want this CIA operative or his handler to know we've uncovered their plans. Only the PNR and the Special Brigade will wear uniforms; everyone else will be in plainclothes."

"We are going to need all the help we can get tomorrow, Inspector Ramirez," said General de Soto. "I want you there. But leave your cell phone at the office. And no police radios. We can't have any transmitters in the building; they could trigger a bomb."

"What about Commander Kadun?" Ramirez asked. "Do we need him for anything? He's here for another day or two."

"I don't think so," Major Diaz said. "He's already told us what little he knows."

"I disagree. He's had more time to think about this than we have," said General de Soto. "He was involved in analyzing that CIA agent's voice. He may see or hear something we miss."

"All right," the minister said. "Bring him to the fair with you tomorrow, then, Ramirez, if he's agreeable. If not, we have no claims on his time."

Ramirez nodded. "What about this evening—do you need either of us?"

Major Rodriguez shook his head. "The sniffing dogs will go through the pavilions tonight. If what's on that tape is accurate, tomorrow will be the big day."

"You can leave now, Ramirez," said the minister. "Be sure to thank Commander Kadun for coming all this way to tell us about this."

"Before Inspector Ramirez goes, Major Diaz," said General de Soto, "there's one more thing. He needs access to some of your surveillance tapes for his investigation. Lieutenant Ortiz is waiting for orders before he'll release them."

"Of course," Diaz said. "Whatever you need, Inspector. I'll let him know."

"*Gracias*," said Ramirez.

"We need to make sure that all boiler rooms, elevators, and switchboards are locked and that only authorized people have access," Ramirez heard Major Rodriguez say to General de Soto as he closed the door behind him. "Even a tiny device can be lethal."

25

After Hector Apiro completed Sera Ravela's autopsy, he returned to his cramped office to think about what he'd discovered.

Señora Ravela's body showed no signs of malnourishment. The Cuban diet was heavily weighted towards carbohydrates and starch, so certain fat-soluble vitamins, like A and D, were not easily absorbed. As a result, B_{12} deficiencies and anemia were present in almost all of Apiro's autopsies of Cubans. But Señora Ravela's levels were normal. From a forensic point of view, this finding was significant.

Even the government itself admitted that the calories supplied by rationing were insufficient to meet basic nutritional needs. The monthly food ration allocated to each citizen was barely enough to last a week, perhaps ten days at the most, regardless of how careful one was. And that was if the food items could even be found at the government-run *bodegas*, the stores that distributed the supplies. Most often, the shelves were empty.

Cubans could buy what they needed at the agricultural markets, or on the black market, and one could purchase milk and yogurt sold surreptitiously outside government bakeries. Then there were the *chopins*. These were dollar stores that originally carried goods for foreigners but were opened up to Cubans after the Special Period ended. In its typically bureaucratic way, the government had renamed them "Stores for Recovering Foreign Currency"—Cubans created their own name for them from the English word *shopping*.

But going to the *chopin* cost money, and no one's salary paid enough. The only people who could afford it either worked in the tourist industry and made tips, or were sent remittances by Cuban relatives who lived outside the country.

Having grown up in an orphanage, Apiro had no relatives either in or outside Cuba to send him money, and the dead had proven to be lousy tippers. He worked three part-time jobs to make ends meet.

Apiro had learned, like most Cubans, to make do: to trade whatever he didn't need for what he did, and to steal what he had to. One might skim meat from the butcher shop, if that's where one worked, or cheese from cafeteria sandwiches. For the police, there was the exhibit room. One didn't think of it as theft, but as *resolver*. Solving one's problems.

Perhaps Yoani Ravela was a *jinetera* after all, he thought. Prostitutes earned a good living, much better than a doctor, even a plastic surgeon. Maria could out-earn Apiro's monthly salary in a night or two. Only the oldest of the professions was at the top of the Cuban economic hierarchy; all the others—doctors, lawyers, engineers, professors—struggled to get by.

That Yoani Ravela had recently had intercourse was certain: the vaginal swabs he took from her body revealed motile sperm under the microscope. This was consistent with what the neighbours heard, and provided Apiro with a reliable source of DNA. If Ramirez could provide him with a second DNA sample from a suspect, Apiro could tell him with a high degree of certainty whether it came from the man she'd had sex with.

But what he really needed to find out was whether she'd had any recent chiropractic treatments. Getting that information could take a little digging. He decided to prepare for what could be a long wait.

He pushed aside a stack of medical articles on his desk to make space for his French press. He picked up his electric kettle and hopped down the hallway to the washroom, where he filled it with water. Back in his office, he plugged the kettle in and spooned a measured amount of fresh coffee into the glass press, careful not to spill any of the precious grounds. Once the water had boiled, he poured it in.

While he waited for the coffee to steep, he called the hospital switchboard. "Good afternoon," he said. "Can you look up the number of the *consultorio* that serves the families living on Blanco near Trocadero for me? Please call me back when you have it, *gracias*."

Cubans received primary health care from family health clinics. A *consultorio* provided services to a hundred or so families, and always in a defined area. Because the physicians and nurses often lived in the same building in which their clinic was located, they usually knew their patients well. If he could find the right *consultorio*, he could probably find some answers.

His phone rang a few minutes later. "I have a number for you, Dr. Apiro," the operator said. "I'll put you through."

"*Hola*," he said to the nurse who answered. "It's Dr. Hector Apiro. I am hoping you can help me concerning a patient of mine. Yoani Ravela."

It was one of Apiro's quirks that he considered the dead to be his patients. A well-known plastic surgeon, he had even been known on occasion to tweak their appearance during an autopsy, making them more beautiful in death than they had been in life. "Can you retrieve Señora Ravela's treatment records? I'm happy to stay on the line while you look."

Apiro played with a bent metal spoon, enjoying the rich smell of coffee, while the nurse went off to forage. Medical records were usually organized by family and kept up to date for the purpose of gathering statistics; a few minutes later, she returned to the phone. "I have her file here, Dr. Apiro, but there's nothing much in it. Only her annual checkup every year."

"No history of neck or spinal injuries, then?" Apiro inquired. "Is there anything that would require chiropractic treatment? It might not be a chiropractor she saw; it could have been a homeopath or a neurologist."

He heard her rustling through papers. "No, nothing like that," she said. "But let me check the charts to see if we made a referral to a *policlinico*." These were specialist clinics. Most *consultorios*, lacking computers, kept large paper charts tacked on their walls to track their referrals; without a referral, a patient couldn't receive treatment.

She returned a minute or two later. "I couldn't find anything. According to her file, she's in very good health. But as I recall," the woman continued, "she's a flight attendant. Like pilots, they need regular medical checkups. If there are any issues at all, they can be grounded."

"May I have the name of her next of kin?"

"She hasn't named one," said the nurse. "I think she was married a long time ago. They must be divorced; she never talked to me about her husband. Which is strange, now that I think about it. Most times, that's all the women talk about after their marriages end. Our role is often as much about counselling as it is about primary care."

Apiro thought for a moment. "Can you check the system to see if there is an address for her ex-husband or any other relatives?"

"I'll do what I can," the nurse said. "But our records aren't computerized. It could take days, maybe longer."

"Whatever you find will be very much appreciated," Apiro said. "We really need to find a family member. As soon as we can."

"May I ask why?" the nurse said.

"My apologies," said Apiro. "I should have explained. Señora Ravela is dead. I wasn't sure until just now, but she was murdered."

26

Inspector Ramirez found Slava Kadun at the minister's clerk's desk. He was showing her how to read the Cyrillic alphabet.

"You've had a long trip," Ramirez said to him. "You must be exhausted. Have you rented a hotel room?"

Slava straightened up and shook his head. "Not yet. Later on, I find hotel. First, I want to see little bit city. After that, I find vodka." He grinned. "I forgot to buy some at duty-free shop."

"I may be able to help you with that," Ramirez said, thinking of the bottle he'd seen in the police exhibit room. "If you're still willing to lend a hand, I can show you some of the sights on our way to the morgue. I just have to call our pathologist, Hector Apiro, to make sure he's going to be there."

Slava nodded and hoisted his duffel bag across his massive shoulders. "Sure."

Ramirez pulled his cell phone from his jacket pocket and dialed the number for Apiro's office. He walked down the corridor, out of earshot.

"*Hola*, Ricardo," Apiro said. "I'm glad you called; I've been trying to reach you. I've completed Señora Ravela's autopsy. I've been following up on her treatment records. I think she died of a stroke."

"So it was an accident after all?"

"No. She had an arterial tear. We sometimes see them after manual rotation, when a chiropractor rapidly turns the patient's head to adjust their spine. It can cause a cerebrovascular injury that can take a day or two to manifest. But she's never had that kind of treatment. Plus, she was wearing high heels, as you'll recall, and that's the first thing a doctor tells a female patient with a back or neck problem to stop doing.

"Then there are her hands. There should have been some bruising, swelling, maybe even a splinter or two, given the condition of the stairs. When someone knows they are falling, they instinctively grab at something to break their fall. One would expect that she'd have put her hands out to stop the fall—but there's nothing. Clearly, she didn't land headfirst; there's no head injury. And there are no scrapes or bruises on her knees."

"Had she been drinking?"

"The toxicology screen was clear. Ricardo, I think someone snapped her neck and carried her downstairs to make it look like an accident. That would explain why the neighbours didn't hear her falling. But breaking someone's neck like that isn't easy. It requires leverage, and if it isn't done properly it can paralyze the victim instead of killing them. The muscles and tendons usually tear long before the break occurs. It takes tremendous force and skill."

"You mean someone trained to kill did this?"

"I think it was a professional, yes."

The news was chilling. If Apiro was right, it was the second execution-style murder in less than two days. And Apiro was rarely wrong when it came to forensic medicine.

"She had a husband, but they were divorced years ago. We need to find a next of kin to let them know she's dead and where to claim the body. Her *consultorio* is checking."

"Okay," said Ramirez. "Well, let me know when you hear from them. The reason I called you is that I'm with someone who knows about Russian prison tattoos. We're going to head over to the morgue now so he can take a look at our victim's."

"I'll meet you there."

Ramirez said goodbye and placed a quick call to Natasha Delgado.

"Dr. Apiro says that Señora Ravela was murdered," he told her. He summarized the call. "I want you to search her apartment right away. And General de Soto has arranged things so that we can access any videotapes we need from Cuban Intelligence. Get hold of Lieutenant Ortiz—he's the person who handles that. We need to get the tapes from the shooting on the Malecón, but let's find out if they have any surveillance cameras on Blanco as well. If we're lucky and they do, they may have captured a picture of Señora Ravela's killer."

The young detective didn't need to know that the authorization he'd received was only for tapes related to the murder on the Malecón. Ortiz didn't know that either.

Slava was saying goodbye to the minister's clerk. She smiled at him coyly and slipped a folded piece of paper into his hand—either her address or a meeting place for a tryst, thought Ramirez. With few exceptions, owning a cell phone was against the rules, and very few Cubans had land lines that worked.

"Nice girl," Slava said, as they walked out of the cool building into the humidity.

Ramirez said nothing. He had never really thought of the minister's clerk as being nice. Or even female, for that matter. When he thought of her at all, he usually envisioned a snarling dog. He realized he didn't even know her first name and probably never would.

Ramirez glanced behind him as he opened his car door. Whenever he'd left the ministry in the past, one of his murder victims had been squeezed into the back seat, but the car was empty.

"You are expecting someone?" said Slava as Ramirez climbed into the driver's seat.

"I guess I was hoping," said Ramirez, checking the side mirror just in case. The rear-view mirror had been missing for years; it was impossible to find a replacement. There was no one else in the car. "But they seem to be gone."

"You know, every Russian tells jokes about President Putin same way you get into car," said Slava. "By first looking over shoulder."

27

Inspector Ramirez pointed out the sights along the way. The Avenida de los Presidentes was lined with statues of all but two Cuban presidents. The statues of Tomás Estrada Palma and José Miguel Gómez had been toppled after the revolution, when they were deemed to be pawns of the American government. Only their shoes were left standing, no legs.

They drove past the memorial to Ethel and Julius Rosenberg, two Americans executed in 1953 for passing nuclear secrets to the Soviets. Then the Museum of Natural Sciences, the University of Havana, and the Hotel Nacional.

"Have you thought about where you would like to stay, Slava? The Hotel Nacional is a beautiful hotel, but it's expensive." Ramirez motioned towards it. "There's an artificial waterfall at the foot of the cliff it's built on, where La Rampa begins. La Rampa is the road into Vedado." Ramirez didn't mention that due to housing shortages the area behind the hotel had become a slum.

"I prefer something little bit cheap," Slava said.

"Then you should probably stay in a *casa*. You would be living with a Cuban family, but you'd have your own room. Some of them are really quite nice. The rooms. Well, also the hosts. They won't be fancy, but they'll be clean." Ramirez laughed. "The rooms, I mean."

"Sure," Slava said, looking out the open car window at the busy streets, the old cars, the scantily dressed women. "Sounds good."

They drove by the massive concrete square at the place where the Malecón met Linea.

"That is the Plaza Anti-Imperialista. It was built because of Elian Gonzales," Ramirez said.

"Who is that?"

"A little boy. Six or seven years ago, the American Coast Guard found him floating in the ocean after his boat sank. His mother had tied him to an inner tube before she drowned. The Americans took him to stay with his relatives in Miami. Castro was furious. He built that plaza and organized protests there against the United States, accusing them of kidnapping Elian. The Special Interests Section of the United States is right there, inside the Swiss embassy." Ramirez pointed it out. "The Americans retaliated by putting up an electronic tickertape along the side of the Swiss embassy to run anti-Castro propaganda."

The tickertape was smuggled into Cuba by diplomatic pouch. That had annoyed Fidel Castro no end. "When the Americans refused to take it down, Castro put billboards up all over Havana depicting George Bush as a vampire and a Nazi. Anyway, that's the reason why there are so many flagpoles in this plaza—one hundred and seventy-five of them. Each one is supposed to represent a victim of American repression. But they're really meant to block the view of the American tickertape."

"What happened to little boy?"

"Eventually, he was returned to his father in Cuba." At gunpoint,

Granma had reported. Armed American security forces physically pulled the screaming child from his Miami relatives' arms.

"What's funny is that I'm told the tickertape makes it too noisy to work inside the building." Ramirez smiled. "It also interferes with the air conditioning. The propaganda wasn't very effective either. The letters they ran didn't have any accents, so whenever the Americans used *año* to mean year, it was written as *ano*. Which means anus."

Slava roared with laughter.

Ramirez wondered what Slava thought of Hector Apiro's shabby morgue, with its stained ceiling and peeling walls. But Slava seemed oblivious to his surroundings; his eyes were trained on the corpse.

The tattooed man lay on the metal gurney, his dull eyes cast upwards. The gaping incision on his chest and abdomen had been closed with a line of Apiro's tidy stitches.

Before Slava got too far, Apiro pointed to the white overalls hanging on metal hooks by the door. Ramirez took what looked to be the biggest pair and handed them to the Russian.

"Commander Kadun, this is Dr. Hector Apiro," Ramirez said in English. "Dr. Apiro is a pathologist; he works part-time with Major Crimes. Hector, Commander Kadun has come from Moscow; he's here on business." Ramirez didn't explain what that business was, or who Slava worked for. His uniform spoke for itself.

"Is good to meet you," Slava said, extending his large hand to Apiro. Like most strangers meeting Apiro for the first time, he seemed a little startled at Apiro's size. "You are the doctor who did autopsy on this guy?"

"That's correct," said Apiro. "If it's easier for you, Commander, I speak Russian."

"Is better maybe for me to speak Russian little bit, Inspector," Slava said to Ramirez. "After long day, I start to making mistakes. Is that okay?"

Ramirez nodded. "Of course. Tell you what. What if I leave you alone while I see about finding you that bottle of vodka?"

———————

Slava walked over to the gurney and adjusted the gooseneck lamp so it shone directly on the shooting victim's head. He tried to keep the shock from his face—the dead man looked much younger than he remembered. Maybe he came to Havana to have plastic surgery, he thought; perhaps he'd had a facelift. "Do you have any of his belongings?" he asked Apiro in Russian.

"Over there," Apiro said and pointed to some plastic bags on the counter.

Slava strode over to take a look. There were a pair of shoes, black socks, a grey suit, a bloodied shirt, a belt, a wallet, and a metal watch.

He examined the watch closely. Then he went back to the corpse and looked at the wound in the man's temple. It was a hard contact wound; he could tell by the contusion ring around it. The outer edges were black with soot; the inner tissue apple red. That meant the gunman had pressed the muzzle tightly against the victim's head when he fired. Point-blank range.

"That ring is the shape of the muzzle," Apiro said. "Combustion gases forced the skin to balloon around the end of the muzzle. That helps us to identify the firearm used; the bruising creates an exact match."

Slava nodded slowly; he'd seen wounds like this before, many times. He looked at the tattoos and wondered how much he should disclose. If he claimed not to know what they were at all, they might realize he was lying. Best to tell the truth, he decided. They didn't know who the victim was, and these tattoos would never tell them.

"*Da*, these are from a Russian prison," he confirmed. "The barbed-wire tattoo around his ankles means he served time in jail. If you count the number of the barbs, they reveal the number of years he was there." He went through the motions of checking each one and counting out loud. "Eleven. The manacle above the barbed wire is broken; that shows he served his entire sentence with nothing off for good behaviour. The stars on his knees mean he never bowed down to prison officials." He smiled slightly. "He was a shit-disturber."

"He has a sailing ship tattooed on his back, too," said Apiro. "What does that mean?"

"That he wanted to be free. Can I see the back of his hands?"

"They're bruised. He was in a car accident before he was shot." Apiro lifted the man's hands up, one at a time.

Slava pointed to the faint blue marks and shook his head. "These aren't bruises. They are letters. The МИР on his left hand means he had killed before. The letters on the right hand spell out KRAB—*klyanus rezat aktivistov i blyadey*. 'I vow to kill all activists and sluts.'"

"I missed that," said Apiro, looking embarrassed. "What does he mean by activists?"

"Probably prisoners who openly collaborate with prison authorities."

"Was he really a killer?"

"Maybe in the beginning," Slava nodded. "But he became much more than that. The epaulette on his shoulder means he was *vory*. A thief-in-law. That's what we call very high-ranking Russian mafia. Most are involved in money laundering and other criminal activities that bring in lots of money. Like drug trafficking. It is not good that someone killed him like this, with a bullet to the head. It sends a bad message to the members of his gang."

"What kind of message?" asked Apiro.

Slava frowned. "To get ready for war."

28

Inspector Ramirez jogged up the stairs to the second floor and past the doors to the Major Crimes Unit, then strode down the hall to the exhibit room. He nodded to Conchita, the exhibit room clerk, and unlocked the metal door to the storage area. He wandered up and down the rows of dusty shelves, looking for the bottle of Grey Goose, but it was gone. He wasn't surprised, only disappointed he hadn't taken it earlier when he'd had the chance.

When he got back to the morgue, he heard Slava and Apiro laughing as he pulled open the door. Inside, Apiro was seated on the lowest rung of his stepladder. Slava was sitting on Ramirez's wooden stool, the way Ramirez usually did after an autopsy, when he and Apiro discussed what they had just seen, or religion or philosophy, or whatever else crossed their minds.

"Good news, Ricardo," Apiro said in English, smiling. "Slava says these are Russian prison tattoos, just as I thought." He briefly summarized Slava's comments. "I'll have a written report for you first thing in the morning."

"So he *was* Russian mafia," Ramirez said. He wondered why Anatoly Klopov had seemed so certain the victim was Chechen.

"Most likely," Slava said. He stood up and removed his overalls. He handed them to Apiro, who put them in the laundry bag by the counter. "They have turf wars, those guys. You have drug problem in Cuba?"

Ramirez shook his head. "No, not for years." In the late 1980s, the third most powerful military leader in the country, General Arnoldo Ochoa, had been executed by firing squad when his links to Colombian drug cartels became known. Ochoa had been popular, a hero of the revolution. Cubans were shocked; the general was one of Castro's stronger supporters and closest friends. But Ramirez couldn't think of anything he'd describe as a drug problem.

"Really?" Slava said. "Must be only country in world."

"The Colombians sometimes enter our waters to drop off drugs for pickup by American traffickers. But the Cuban Coast Guard intercepts the shipments."

But maybe not always, Ramirez thought. The Coast Guard lacked sufficient fuel and equipment to police the twelve-mile limit as effectively as it should. MININT had offered to collaborate with the U.S. Coast Guard to stop the illicit traffic, but their efforts were rebuffed because of the anti-Castro faction in Congress.

Even so, apart from small quantities of recreational drugs that sometimes found their way into Havana, Cuba was hardly a drug destination. In fact, Ramirez couldn't remember the last time he'd arrested a *marimbero*, a drug dealer. There was sometimes crack cocaine circulating in some of the slums, and there was always a foreigner who managed to smuggle in a joint or two, but that was about it. No, this murder couldn't be drug related. It made no sense at all.

"Must be some reason why guy was in Havana," Slava said.

Why would a Russian *mafioso* be here? Ramirez wondered. It

seemed the Chechens wanted weapons—what did the Russian mafia
want? And why was a leading member of the Chechen mafia visiting
Havana at the same time as this man? Did they know each other?
Were the two cases linked? He shook his head: this case was giving
him a headache.

"I have no idea," said Ramirez. "But thank you, Slava, for your
help. About that bottle of vodka. I'm sorry. I thought I knew where
I could find one but I was mistaken."

"Is no problem, Inspector. I prefer to go out anyway; see little bit
of city. Maybe you two will come with me to have drink?" He raised
his thick black eyebrows.

"I'd better not," Ramirez said, glancing at his watch. It was after
six. "I promised my wife I'd be home for dinner. But I can help you
find a *casa*."

"No need, Ricardo. I have already arranged one for him," Apiro
said. He turned to Slava. "I can have a drink with you, once you get
settled, but I can't stay for long. My girlfriend, Maria, works nights.
We usually try to spend a few hours together before she goes off."

Ramirez was surprised that Apiro had accepted the invitation.
Apiro almost never went out socially. He'd always resisted Ramirez's
entreaties to join Ramirez and his family for dinner. That hadn't
changed even after Maria Vasquez moved in with him. Ramirez wondered whose influence was more at play—Maria's or the charismatic
Russian's.

"Tell your girlfriend to join us," said Slava, punching Apiro
lightly on the shoulder. "Tomorrow morning I need to go to Russian embassy to call my office. Don't worry, Inspector, I will take
cab. I will call you after I am finished. I would like to go to trade fair
tomorrow, so I can see what it is like." He said nothing more in front
of Hector Apiro: the ministerial briefing had been top secret.

Ramirez nodded. "Of course. Do you need a ride to your *casa*?"
he asked Slava as they left the morgue. Apiro locked the metal doors
behind them.

"Oh, no, it's fine, Ricardo," said Apiro. "I've booked Slava a room at Lucido's. We can walk; it's not far."

Lucido's was a *casa particular* located on the Malecón. It had a spectacular view of the ocean.

They walked up the stairs to the main floor, past the receptionist, and into the humidity.

"So, I will see you tomorrow, Inspector?" said Slava. He stuck out his hand.

Ramirez shook it and inclined his head. "I look forward to it. Well, enjoy yourselves."

He had an odd feeling as he watched the two men walk down the sidewalk together, Slava with his long strides and Apiro with his awkward hop. It was a moment before he realized it was jealousy.

29

When Inspector Ramirez got to the parking lot, Mama Loa was waiting for him by his Chinese mini-car. She was dressed as she had been before. He marvelled at how she managed to keep her clothing clean, even in this extreme heat, despite her terrible living conditions. He already had rings of perspiration under his arms and beads of sweat running down his back, just from the brief walk from the morgue, but her skin was smooth and dry.

"So," she said, "you believe me now, Ramirez?"

"About people in the sky dying? We haven't had any plane crashes, if that's what you mean."

"I don't worry about the dead much no more," she said, shaking her head. "There are dead people all round us. They can't hurt us; they're just trying to get by. No, I mean about getting your gift back. Eshu is still angry at you; that's why he's making it hard for you to do your job. But it's not too late. You can wear Eshu's colours. Leave him food on the road; he likes that. When he don't get fed enough, people have accidents."

Elegua, or Eshu, as Ramirez's grandmother called him, was the *orisha* responsible for the crossroads. Small and childish, he was the most temperamental and unpredictable of the Santería gods, a trickster. Those who followed him always made sure to dedicate their first bite of food to him; they wore red and black glass beads, Eshu's colours, to show their devotion.

"I'm on my way home now, Mama Loa," he said, and tried not to smile at her suggestions. He didn't want to hurt her feelings. "Can I drop you off on the way?"

"Is your wife going to get mad at you again if you be late? You go on home now. I got nowhere I got to be, and all the time in the world to get there."

"You shouldn't spend so much time worrying about me."

"Someone got to," she said. "Till you get yourself straightened out."

30

Ramirez drove home in the fading light. He weaved his small blue car around potholes and tried to make sense of what he'd learned. Who was this shooting victim, and why was he shot in Havana?

He parked the car and walked up the rickety stairs to his third-floor apartment, careful not to put much weight on the loose hand-rail.

"Thank goodness you don't have to work late again tonight, Ricardo," Francesca said when he opened the door. She was bustling around their small kitchen making *cocido de garbanzos*, chickpea stew. "I was just letting the *congrí* sit."

Boniato con mojo simmered on the stove—sweet potatoes in a lemony garlic sauce. *Congrí*, her special Eastern version with red beans and rice, rested in a covered pot to let the rice absorb the remaining water.

Ramirez leaned against the doorway, watching Francesca work her magic. He loved the way she could make plain ingredients taste special. She had been a social worker before the children were born, but he always thought of her as an alchemist. "I thought I might have to stay late, but there's not much we can do until we have more information."

He didn't mention the assassination plot. She'd find it hard to keep something like that a secret. Information spread quickly through what Cubans called *Radio Bemba*—the radio of lips—as gossip leapt from one person to another. "I spent most of my day running around in circles. I'm getting a little old for the kind of legwork that Fernando and Natasha enjoy so much."

"Oh, you," his wife said. She nudged him with her elbow, still stirring the pot. "You're not old. Because if you were, I'd be old, and I refuse to believe it. Besides, no one wants to hire old people."

With Estella about to start daycare, Francesca was starting to think about going back to work. "I ran around in circles today myself. The water's been shut off again. I had to buy bottled water on the *bolsa negra*." She wiped her hands briskly. "It cost so much money, I almost fainted. And even then, I don't trust it's safe. I've been boiling it all day so we can have *frijoles negros dormidos* tomorrow for dinner." "Sleeping rice" was cooked and left to sit overnight, then served with black beans.

As Francesca bustled around the kitchen, she provided him with updates on a preoccupation she shared with most Cubans—trying to find food.

"I went to the black market looking for bananas. They had tiny yellow ones, the size of Estella's little finger, and some red ones, but they were too expensive. There were green plantains that I didn't really want, but I bought some anyway. Like *pollo por pescado*." Like chicken for fish.

For years, the bodegas had provided an extra portion of chicken instead of the fish people wanted. So many fishermen had defected that the fishing industry had collapsed. There were still fish to be found, but only in tourist restaurants.

"And then, finally, after hours of going from place to place, success—we have bananas! The children are outside playing; we're almost ready to eat. Go get them, will you, Ricky? Tell them we'll have *dulce de leche* with fried bananas for dessert." The rich caramel sauce was one of their favourites.

"Maybe it's not old age that will keep me at home, but your cooking," Ramirez said. He put his arms around her waist and squeezed until she slapped him playfully with the worn piece of fabric she used as a kitchen towel. "Or maybe it's the cook."

"Go on, Ricardo, bring the children in. If they eat well, they'll be tired enough to sleep. Maybe we can get them to go to bed early. You look like a man who could use another neck rub."

Ramirez grinned. He walked outside and into the fading light.

This is my new life, he reflected. No more late nights in Apiro's office, throwing back glasses of rum, laughing about the day's events, decompressing.

And no more ghosts to contend with. That he was involved in a homicide investigation and hadn't seen the murder victim was proof that they were really, truly gone.

For years, they had been a silent, steady presence in his life. The first time one showed up, he recalled, he'd jumped so high his head hit the roof of his car. He'd been newly promoted and thought one of his colleagues must be playing a joke on him. "Is this supposed to be funny?" he demanded of the apparition. "Who sent you?"

The corpse had shrugged, unable to speak; his throat had been slashed. He followed Ramirez around police headquarters all morning like a shadow, vanishing only when Ramirez used the toilet, and again when he entered the morgue.

After Ramirez solved his murder, there were others. A mime from Calle Obispo, beaten to death with his stilts. He was much easier to understand, given his occupation. Then a CDR block captain, his head smashed in with a coconut. And then all the others.

How foolish they must have thought me, Ramirez thought. They were supposed to help me solve their murders, and I spent most of my time trying to pretend they weren't really there, wondering if I was crazy and thinking I was dying.

Maybe Mama Loa was right, he thought, as he looked up and down the street for his children. Maybe the ghosts had been a gift. Without them, he felt empty, bereft.

It was his fault: he'd prayed to the gods to make them go away, and his prayers had been answered. But he had to choose his family. There were other people who could do police work. Only he could be father to his children and husband to his wife. Still, he found it hard to shake the sadness that was slowly settling over him like an early morning fog.

He caught sight of his children and called to them to come inside for dinner.

"Papi! Papi's home," Estella shouted with delight. She ran into his arms and hugged him tightly. Edel followed her, his head down, smiling shyly.

Ramirez walked slowly up the stairs behind them, resting his hands on their small shoulders.

31

After Hector Apiro got Slava checked into Lucido's, and the Russian had changed into a cotton shirt and light-coloured pants, they walked to the local bar.

It was a lovely night to stroll along the Malecón. An evening breeze made the humidity almost bearable. *Neumáticos*, fishermen, stood every few feet along the seawall, bait cans at their feet, lines in the ocean, smoking. Musicians played as tourists snapped photographs of one another leaning against the seawall. Taxis honked; scooters and *bicis* darted between tourist buses and ancient Chevys.

It was the city's living room, thought Apiro. Clusters of Cubans stood all along the seawall, chatting, playing music, drinking rum, flirting, or simply enjoying the cool breeze.

Street hustlers trailed behind tourists, cajoling them for medication, soap, and money; others tried to sell them cheap sex or even cheaper cigars. Some offered to hold their cameras and take pictures of them, then held out their hands for payment. A group of dirt-streaked children ran by, chirping like a flock of birds.

The bar Maria had recommended was located in a basement of a rundown building off one of the numbered *calles*. It wasn't far from their apartment, although Apiro's unit was in an elegant but crumbling old mansion rather than one of the dour Russian apartment buildings this area was better known for. It always surprised Apiro as one of the unexplained laws of physics that the ugliest buildings seemed to last forever. Above the door, a line of bright-coloured laundry swayed on a string hung between two posts that shored up the balcony.

They walked down the stairs and into a venue that few foreigners ever stumbled across. There was no art on the walls in the bar and almost no furniture, only a few round tables and metal chairs. A row of wooden stools stood along the wooden counter, and the men pulled two of them out. Apiro wriggled onto his.

"Can we get something to eat here?" Slava asked, and Apiro realized he probably hadn't eaten all day.

Apiro raised his shoulders apologetically. This was a peso restaurant, which meant that regardless of what was on the menu, it would probably only have pizza.

"Yes. But it won't be the best food around. If you want to try really good cooking, you're better off going to a *paladar*. Maria took me to La Guarida once. It's quite well known. It was featured in a movie, *Fresa y Chocolate*." The movie was about a homosexual affair between a Communist Party member and an artist; it somehow seemed appropriate for his and Maria's first romantic evening together, although she had paid. "They have a nice supply of Spanish and Chilean wine."

That was the night Apiro had realized that Maria had feelings for him. He often thought it was the best night of his life. "I'd offer to bring you home to have dinner with us," he added, "but Maria doesn't cook, so nothing will be ready. And I'm not sure how much you'd enjoy our rations. Although we do have real coffee."

"We used to have that in Russia, too. Rationing, I mean. We almost never had real coffee. There is an old Russian joke. A little boy asks his father, 'Why do we have communism?' His father says, 'Because that way, everyone gets what he needs.' Little boy says, 'But we don't have any meat.' Father says, 'The Communist Party says we don't need meat anymore.'"

Apiro chortled. "When I lived in Moscow, the joke was that Russians used to light their homes with electricity before they started using candles. Of course, no one here would find that very funny. No one here starves to death, but even so, we spend far too much time obsessing over food, how to pay for it, and where to get it."

Slava smiled. "We used to joke about this too. A woman walks into a food store. 'Do you have any meat?' she asks. The shopkeeper says, 'No, we don't.' She says, 'Do you have any milk?' And he says, 'We only sell meat. You have to go to the store across the street to get no milk.'"

Apiro cackled, his laughter the sound of a night gull.

The bar was empty but for a morose-looking bartender wiping glasses with a rag. The only sound came from a black-and-white television in the corner. The flickering screen displayed a soccer game in Europe. It crossed Apiro's mind that, with the different time zones, the game was long over—the victors already celebrating their victory, the losers likely drowning their sorrows.

Slava ordered a shot of vodka for each of them, as well as a pizza. The bartender produced two glasses and poured the vodka. Apiro picked up his and sipped it gingerly.

"No, no, don't drink it like that," Slava said. "Drink like this." He picked up the small glass in his big paw and threw back the shot.

Apiro looked at Slava and took a deep breath, then gulped down the rest of the vodka. He sputtered and almost choked. Slava smiled and clapped him on the back.

Slava pulled his stool closer to the bar. "You know what we say if vodka interferes with the job? Get off the job." He smiled. "Your Russian is very good. How long were you in Moscow?"

"Three years, while I took my post-doctoral studies in plastic surgery. But that was quite a long time ago, before the Soviet Union fell apart. I imagine it's all changed."

Slava frowned. "Everybody is out for themselves these days. You can't trust anyone anymore. Not even your best friend."

"I never found Moscow all that friendly when I lived there," Apiro said, remembering how lonely he had been, the stares. He had graduated from the University of Havana medical school at the top of his class, then taken postgraduate studies in cosmetic and reconstructive surgery in Moscow. Russian literature, Apiro had discovered, was replete with dwarves. His books became a place to hide, to transport himself into a community where he belonged.

Slava nodded. "It would be harder for you, I think. Most Russians are fascinated by little people. Blame it on Tsar Peter. He collected them. And giants, and Siamese twins too. There are skeletons from his collections on display in the Kunstkamera. It's very sad. People should be buried properly so their family can pay their respects." Slava held his empty glass out so the bartender could refill it. "You ever hear of the Ovitzes?"

Apiro nodded. "Of course. They were an Austrian family of seven dwarves."

"The Nazis took them to Auschwitz. Josef Mengele did terrible things to them. He was supposed to be a doctor. Here," he clinked Apiro's glass. "To the health of our families."

Apiro shuddered and drank the toast.

"He poured hot water in their ears," Slava said. "He took their blood every day, even from the little baby, Shimshon. The baby wasn't even a dwarf; Mengele tested him anyway."

"Dwarves can have normal-sized children."

"Yes, I know," said Slava, nodding solemnly. "The story of what he did to that little baby always makes me cry, but I only talk about it when I am drinking." He downed the rest of the vodka in his glass and tapped the glass on the counter to get the bartender's attention.

"How do you know so much about the Ovitzes?" Apiro asked.

"My grandfather was Red Army. One of the soldiers who liberated them. They took them to a refugee camp in Siberia. Mengele let them keep their clothes, and he let the women keep their cosmetics. My grandfather told me how Frieda Ovitz wore red lipstick every day. She wanted to look pretty for Mengele, even when he was torturing her. That's how she stayed alive, my grandfather said. He used to misquote Sartre: 'I do not believe in God, but in the concentration camp I learned to believe in women.' My grandfather loved her."

The bartender refilled Slava's glass. Slava clinked it against Apiro's and toasted. "To our grandmothers. You know, in Russia we say only alcoholics never toast before drinking. We don't stop drinking until the bottle is empty." He put his glass down and turned to face Apiro. "Now to business. Why didn't you tell Inspector Ramirez you knew me?"

"Doctor–patient privilege," Apiro said. "Besides, I didn't recognize you right away. You had hair back then. And we were both a lot younger."

"I shaved it after Chernobyl," Slava said, running his hand across his scalp.

"Were you there when the reactor blew?"

"No. But close enough to become radioactive. I used to set off airport scanners." He laughed, and then he frowned. "But I was never your patient."

"No," Apiro said. "But you consulted me. That's enough to invoke the privilege." He tossed back the rest of his vodka. "Where did you get it done? I don't see any scars."

"Laser surgery," said Slava. "It's all over Moscow. You can get your eyes fixed so you can see long-distance without glasses. They can make your teeth so white they're almost blue. It's not perfect; I still have marks on my chest. But the big one, the one around my neck, is gone." He ran his fingers across his throat as if rearranging a scarf.

"What did the dagger on your neck mean?"

"You have a good memory. It means you are a hired killer. The drops of blood below it show how many men you killed in prison. You knew this, and you weren't afraid to go out for a drink with me?"

"I killed a man once," Apiro said. He signalled the bartender for another shot. "I frightened him to death."

Slava laughed. "You did? Every doctor kills someone eventually. Even the good ones."

Apiro took a deep breath. "Did you shoot the man in my morgue? I suppose that's a stupid question. You wouldn't tell me if you had."

Slava smiled. "I wasn't even in Havana until this afternoon, little man. I got those tattoos because I was working undercover in a prison and I needed to fit in. I didn't want to keep them after the job was done, but I didn't want to be scarred for life either. It's good, though, about the doctor–patient privilege. If you tell someone, that's not so good for me. There were men in those jails I had to kill; others that I betrayed. Fucking dangerous guys."

Shortly after they demolished the pizza, Maria Vasquez stepped lightly down the stairs and into the bar. She was tall, almost six feet in her open-toed stilettos. Even the bartender stopped to look at her. She wore a tight blue dress that accentuated her long, shapely legs. Her sunglasses matched her pink tote bag.

Slava stood up as Apiro introduced them. He took Maria's hand and brushed it with his lips.

"Slava is visiting Havana," Apiro said in English, his way of letting Maria know that the man spoke no Spanish. "He's Russian."

"Let me buy you drink, beautiful lady," Slava said. He waited for Maria to sit before he did the same. He motioned to the bartender. "What do you like? Are you hungry? We just ate pizza."

"Only something cold, *gracias*. It's so hot out today," she said in her husky, whisky voice. "Too hot to eat." She wiped perspiration from her forehead, pushing her thick streaked-blond hair away from her face and tucking it behind her ears. She smiled at the bartender. He looked as if he would melt beneath her gaze.

"I know just the thing," the bartender said. He twisted the top off a fresh bottle of rum and flicked the cap away, pouring a little on the ground for luck. He prepared a *Cuba libre*, adding ice and Mexican cola, a twist of lime as a garnish. He placed it carefully in front of Maria, like an offering to the gods.

Slava raised his glass and toasted her beauty.

Maria smiled. "Thank you, Slava. Where in Russia are you from?"

"I grew up in Odessa. Ukraine. My father was Polish. But I am Russian citizen."

"Hector is trying to teach me Russian," she said, frowning slightly. "I'm not very fluent yet. He reads me Russian poetry sometimes, for vocabulary."

"Ah," said Slava. "I am big lover." He laughed. And then, in Russian: "'With all my many sins, both great and small, I am perhaps of love unworthy. But if you would pretend, you would deceive me.'"

Maria clapped her hands, delighted.

"It's Pushkin," said Apiro. "It's called 'Confession.' Well, we should probably get going, Maria." He tossed a handful of pesos on the bar and slipped off his stool, staggering a little. "I have a shift at the hospital later tonight. I think I'd better go home first and have a nap."

"Keep this," Slava said, and handed him back the money. "I buy drinks. It was my pleasure."

They said their goodbyes and Slava watched the two of them walk out of the room, his eyes narrowed.

"Beautiful girl," said the bartender in English.

"*Da*," Slava nodded, but he'd looked at her thick wrists; seen the Adam's apple bob in her throat.

He'd met women like her before, in prison.

32

"*There are so many Russians in* Havana this week," said Maria Vasquez as she and Apiro walked back to their apartment. She was holding his arm to help steady him; the small man was more than a little drunk. "All the girls are talking about it. There's one telling them he'll give them each ten thousand dollars to go and work for him in Europe."

"Doing what?" Apiro asked.

"I imagine the same thing we do here."

"He's a *chulo*?" Even in his altered state, Apiro realized as soon as the words escaped his lips that he had crossed a sensitive line. A *chulo* was a pimp.

Maria stopped and let go of his arm. "Hector, you know what I do for a living. It's what I've always had to do to survive."

"I'm sorry, Maria. I didn't mean it to come out that way. I just don't like the idea of someone exploiting women."

He didn't seem able to control the words that tumbled out of his mouth: it was as if the vodka had wiped out any filter between his brain and his lips. "How are they supposed to leave Cuba? No one can afford the exit permit, assuming the government would ever let them go."

"He says he has transportation arranged; they're supposed to leave around two on Wednesday morning. And there are lots of wealthy Europeans interested in *quemar petróleo.*" Burning oil—a white person having sex with a black one. "Some of the girls are very serious about leaving. After all, it's not easy." *No es fácil.* "You know the dangers."

They were both always afraid she'd be arrested and sent off for re-education in one of the camps.

"Well, I'd like to see what kind of transportation this man thinks he's going to get," Apiro said. "What about visas and passports? Those take time to process, and they're expensive. Most things that sound too good to be true aren't."

Maria didn't respond to that directly, but then again, Apiro had always told her she was too good to be true as well.

"You can't blame them for wanting to leave, Hector. Ten thousand dollars is more than they will ever make in Havana, even if they work hard their entire lives."

"You sound as if you're tempted."

Apiro was developing a major headache. He realized he was about to experience his first hangover. And now it seemed he and Maria were having their first argument too, and he wasn't sober enough to extricate himself.

That was the problem with drinking: you didn't know you were drunk until it was too late. Then your brain lied to you, because it drunkenly, wrongly, had convinced itself it was sober. "Money isn't everything, Maria," he said, and immediately wished he hadn't.

"No, it isn't," said Maria sharply. "But it makes being miserable easier to handle. Perhaps if we had more, we would think about it less. I have to go now, Hector. I have to go to work now and do things I'd rather not do. To make *money.*"

She strode off, and Apiro was suddenly acutely aware that despite his intelligence and professional training he would never be able to provide for her.

She'd used the word *miserable*. Was she unhappy? With her life? With him?

He'd done his best. They'd met when she was just a child; he'd begged for and borrowed and stolen the supplies he needed for her surgery. He always worried that she was only with him because of gratitude, because he'd made her the woman that she was.

He wondered how much money he could have made if he had stayed in Russia, removing gangster tattoos and scars, wondered if having more money would compensate for his ugliness, for the way people stared when they saw the two of them together.

He stumbled on the curb, his eyes on her as she disappeared down the crowded sidewalk, his chest as empty as if its contents had been scooped out.

He was transported back to the day his parents abandoned him at the orphanage, his disbelief as the big car pulled away, his confusion, the same sense of impending loss. Would the day come when Maria left him too? Was it just a matter of time?

How could he have ever thought someone like her would stay with someone like him? Was love supposed to hurt this much?

33

Inspector Ramirez stood on the cracked sidewalk in front of the police headquarters building while he ate a *pan con queso y guayaba* for breakfast. The bread was covered with guava jam and a slice of white cheese. Ramirez thought he might have a *tamal* wrapped in corn leaves as well, maybe some maize fritters, too.

That was the good thing about street food: it was cheap.

Detective Natasha Delgado stepped out of the building, looking around. For him, he realized, when she raised her hand to catch his eye and jogged past the iron gate towards him.

She was holding her black police notebook open; she was flushed.

Ramirez wiped a crumb from his lip. "You look excited, Natasha. What is it?"

"I just searched Señora Ravela's apartment again, and this time I found a stack of money hidden under a loose floorboard. Over ten thousand American dollars. There's no way of knowing how long it was there. The lab is checking for fingerprints, although I'm not optimistic we'll find any."

Ramirez nodded. Money changed hands often, and paper money was always dirty, covered with oils and grease. It was almost impossible to get prints from it. The first time he'd heard the term "money laundering," he thought it referred to a new police technique to get around that problem.

"That's a lot of money," he said. Ten thousand dollars. It was an unimaginable sum; enough to pay his annual income for the rest of his life.

"I know," she nodded. "And there was nothing on the light bulb. I mean *nothing*. It was wiped completely clean of any prints. There's more," Delgado continued. "Fernando is with Lieutenant Ortiz now, seeing what tapes on the Malecón correspond to the car chase. There are dozens to sort through; it will take them a while. But there were two cameras on Blanco, and one is right across the street from Señora Ravela's building. I watched the videotapes with Lieutenant Ortiz last night, and there *was* someone behaving suspiciously. Ortiz said he was engaging in classic counter-surveillance activities—I saw it myself. He walked up to a store window down the street, stopped, and looked at his reflection. Then he doubled back and did it again. He glanced over his shoulder before he opened the front door to the walk-up on Blanco, as if he was afraid someone might see him. That's why I decided to go back and do a second search. In case I missed something."

"What time was he there?"

Delgado consulted her notes. "He entered the building at 11:32 p.m., but the tape ran out almost an hour later, so we don't know what time he left."

"Could you make out his face?"

"It was dark, and the video is black-and-white and quite grainy, but there was one good shot of his features. Ortiz says he'll send a copy to his colleagues in Germany; they have some kind of face-recognition software. If the suspect has ever been through an EU airport, the Germans can tell us who he is. The United States has a similar program that's more comprehensive, apparently, but obviously we can't use it."

"He wasn't local?" asked Ramirez.

"I don't think so. He didn't look Cuban, and his clothes seemed too new."

Ramirez nodded. There was no real way of expressing it, but foreigners looked different from *habaneros*, even Cuban expats who left the island and came back. Their hair, their clothes, the way they moved—everything about them changed once they were exposed to the outside world.

Ramirez popped the last morsel of bread in his mouth and licked the sweet jam off his fingers. "Good work, Natasha. Get Lieutenant Ortiz to get a picture of the suspect so you can show it to the neighbours in Señora Ravela's building. If she was a *jinetera* and he was one of her clients, he may have been there before. Did Ortiz say how long it will take to get results?"

"We should have them today or tomorrow. He says the Germans are very efficient."

"Excellent," said Ramirez, genuinely pleased. "Let's get copies out to Patrol, too. Including one to Officer Pacheco."

It would be like giving a scent to one of the sniffing dogs, he thought, trying to decide whether Pacheco most resembled the energetic spaniel at the airport or the hyperactive beagle.

"I'm not sure we have enough supplies of glossy paper to make that many copies. Maybe we should raid the trade fair tonight. They probably have lots," Delgado said, and for a moment Ramirez thought she was serious. Then she grinned.

"I think that would be a very bad idea," said Ramirez, returning her smile without explaining why. "I'd stick to the exhibit room for now. Keep me informed, Natasha. I'm going to make a trip to the airport. I want to follow up on a hunch."

34

Dan Yaworsky was worried. Maybe the Captain had given him the wrong time for the meeting with the CIA operative, or maybe he had misheard him. Maybe the meeting was supposed to be at nine a.m., instead of nine p.m.

Or maybe *he* was supposed to approach the "likely" and ask *him* if he had an umbrella. The Captain could have got that backwards.

Because, sure as shit, something was wrong. He'd tapped out a message in Morse code to his superiors and so far, nothing. What did that mean? How was the Captain going to react when he found out Yaworsky's mission might have been compromised?

Fuck, thought Yaworsky. I'm going to have everyone on my ass if this thing goes south. I'll find myself in fucking Siberia.

He walked across the cobblestones to the splendid mansion on the northeast corner that housed the Restaurante La Fuente, where he had waited the night before in vain. It was a few minutes after nine a.m. He checked the building's inner courtyard, just in case.

A dazzling fountain created rainbow arcs. But the courtyard was empty. The only people around were the staff setting up tables for breakfast. He jogged up the stairs to the second level. "The restaurant is closed, Señor," a waiter informed him apologetically. "It will be open for lunch. You can have breakfast downstairs, though."

He found a seat at an empty table outside by the square and ordered a cup of coffee and eggs and toast.

He looked around the square, once known as the Little Swamp, and wondered what the hell to do.

Mulatto women dressed as cigar ladies were arranging themselves on the front steps of the church, holding huge, hand-rolled cigars, waiting for the deluge of tourists who would pay to take pictures of them wearing their traditional dress. A few passersby wore the all-white garb that signified adherence to Santería rituals. At the southwest corner of the plaza, artists were setting up their easels. Havana was awake.

Yaworsky sipped on his coffee and contemplated his situation. He had no way of getting into the walk-up on Blanco with that yellow caution tape across the door—the cops would be watching it. What the fuck was going on?

He knew there was no point in reading the paper. *Granma* never reported crimes; they didn't want to discourage tourists from coming to paradise. But if the police were looking for him, he thought, they sure as hell weren't looking very hard. Neither was Cuban Intelligence. But he had to assume his operative had been compromised, which meant he couldn't just turn around and go back to the U.S. without blowing his cover. He was trapped between the proverbial rock and a hard place, and they were both called the Captain.

He found himself staring across the plaza at the Casa del Conde de Bayona; it housed the Havana Club Bar. Graham Greene had used it as his setting for a meeting between his vacuum-cleaner-salesman-turned-secret-agent, Wormold, and the Cuban police captain Segura in *Our Man in Havana.*

Wormold had invented all the intelligence in the reports he filed with MI6, making up fictitious military technologies as he stared at bits and pieces of discarded vacuum cleaners. With no news to report and no sign of the undercover agent, Yaworsky was tempted to start looking around for a vacuum cleaner himself.

35

The Russian embassy was exactly how Slava Kadun imagined it, drab and uninviting, designed to be unappealing. He paid the cab driver and walked up the cracked path and through the front doors. The lobby of the building reminded him of every other Russian embassy he'd ever been in, utilitarian and unadorned.

A photograph of Vladimir Putin hung on one wall, but it wasn't from the series of widely circulated photographs Putin had commissioned of himself. In those, he sometimes posed with dead Siberian tigers and held assault weapons, or was bare-chested astride a Jet Ski or dangling from a helicopter, which made Slava laugh. Putin was a lot of things, but he wasn't exactly James Bond. In this shot, he wore a grey suit and white shirt, and without the staged machismo he reminded Slava a little of the character in the old Harry Potter movie they'd shown on his flight: an elf named Dobby.

The receptionist smiled at Slava as she scanned his ID. "Weren't you here a few days ago? Your name seems familiar."

"It's my first trip to Havana," Slava said.

"Oh, I'm sorry, Commander. I must have you confused with someone else. What can we do for you?"

"I need a secure line to Moscow."

She nodded and placed a call. A few minutes later, a stocky man exited an office at the back of the corridor and joined them. "Come with me, Commander," he said. "I am Anatoly Klopov. We've been expecting you."

———

"What did the Cubans say when you told them?" Dmitri Nabakoff asked from the other end of the line.

"Are you sure we can speak safely?" Slava asked.

"Yes. The embassy is swept every day. I've used it before."

"I don't know what they think, Dmitri." Slava described the meeting with the Minister of the Interior and the other officials. "There was a policeman there, an inspector. I think he was supposed to keep an eye on me. He was pushing me to stay at the Hotel Nacional. If I had, I'm sure my room would have been bugged, so I found a *casa* instead. But all the big brass were there—the head of Cuban Intelligence, the general in charge of the Havana police, the Minister of the Interior, even the head of Castro's security detail. Have the technicians found anything on that tape?"

"There's nothing else on it."

"That's too bad," said Slava, lowering his voice. "But we have a bigger fucking problem, you and me."

"What's that?" said Dmitri.

"This shadow they put on me, this guy Ramirez. He asked me to help him on a homicide investigation involving a Russian guy who was shot to death on Sunday. He took me to the morgue last night to show me the body. They don't know who he is, but I do. He looks ten years younger, but it's fucking Cheetah."

"Cheetah? What was he doing in Havana?"

"Getting himself killed. Whoever did it knew what they were doing, too. One bullet to the temple, gun pressed tight against the flesh, no propellant tattooing. The way we were taught to do it."

"Shit." Dmitri was silent for a moment. "Did you tell them who he is?"

"Of course not. I said it looked like he was Russian mafia, because of his tattoos, which is true enough. I have to be careful—this Ramirez guy is pretty smart. He works with a pathologist who was trained in Moscow. The pathologist knows me from when I worked undercover in the Urals. I don't want to start lying; it's dangerous enough if we get caught. But maybe they won't find out his real name."

"Let's hope not." Dmitri exhaled. "If we're lucky, they'll bury him in an unmarked grave and that will be the end of it. Because you know what will happen if Putin finds out."

"*Da*. He'll know we were lying when we said he disappeared. But I guess it's good that Cheetah got killed here. There's no media coverage of crimes, nothing in the Communist Party newspaper. Nothing on television last night except a baseball game and a Brazilian soap opera. No news."

Dmitri laughed without humour. "Well, at least we don't have to make him disappear again. Maybe no one will ever know."

It was a moment before Slava answered. "There's only one problem with that, Dmitri. Someone else knows he was alive. The person who killed him."

———

Fucking Cheetah. All he had to do was keep his mouth shut, spend his money, let enough time pass that the Colombians would forget all about him. But he was always hustling, that guy, always looking for the deal that would make him rich. Cheetah had not only embraced capitalism when the Cold War ended, he'd had visions of oligarchy.

Slava had stumbled into his high school friend in the jail in the Urals, when he was working undercover.

"You should have stuck to what you know," Slava told him, lying on his hard prison bunk, his hands folded behind his head.

"This *is* what I know," Cheetah said. He was pacing back and forth in Slava's cell like a caged animal in the narrow space between the wall and the stacked metal beds. "It's all about salesmanship. Every addict starts off clean. You have to persuade them to do that first hit, to try something new, to take a chance. So you tell them that your coke is the purest, the best on the market, value for money. That's how you get the edge on the competition.

"You think it's easy for a man to fuck his first hooker? He's scared soft. He worries about disease, that his wife will find out, that maybe a pimp will roll him and take his money, or maybe the condom will break. You have to make it easy for him. That's why I opened a nightclub. It's dark inside, private; the women are hostesses, escorts; you never use the word *prostitute*. You tell the girls to smile and make the guy think he is Brad fucking Pitt. He's happy; he doesn't care if the product's been cut or if the women are secondhand. I learned this in North America: sales are all about marketing."

"And look how far it's got you. You're in jail, just like me."

"That was the fucking DEA. How was I supposed to know the guy was undercover?" Cheetah slammed his hand against the bars. "Look, a rocket launcher is worth what? A hundred thousand on the black market? How many cruise missiles do you think are lying around getting rusty in Russian stockyards right now? Congo, Venezuela, Colombia, there are markets for all of that stuff. Find a way to move it from one place to another; you'd be as rich as Boris Berezovsky. Believe me, if I could have got my hands on a destroyer, I'd have sold the Colombians one of those, too."

"But you didn't." Slava yawned. "You're never going to be rich. Get used to it."

"Maybe so," said Cheetah, lowering his voice to a whisper, "but I wasn't a complete fucking idiot. I kept the deposit."

———————

The Colombians paid Cheetah sixteen million dollars for a submarine they never got. The Colombian drug lord was rotting in jail and very pissed off about that. It was just another deal, Cheetah explained to Slava in his defence: "Trust me, sometimes you're safer in prison."

But Slava knew even then that the duration of Cheetah's safety could be limited. According to Dmitri, there were electronic whispers that the moment he got out of jail, a hit man would slip a knife between his ribs.

And so the three of them worked out a plan.

In exchange for some of the money, Cheetah would get FSB protection. That meant paying off the tattoo artist to add a few embellishments to his personal history.

Cheetah was promoted to the *vor* and he got a new name.

When Putin told Dmitri he wanted the Chechen warlord Ruslan Dudayev taken care of, Dmitri and Slava had discovered a new sideline. "Disappearing" people didn't have to mean only killing them. They could play God. They had the power of resurrection.

The media reported that Dudayev had been "disappeared" in Moscow. It was a term reporters used when they suspected that Russian security forces had killed someone but had no idea where to find the body. But Slava and Dmitri made him come back to life.

Cheetah assumed his identity. After all, there was no television or radio in a Russian prison, and not much outside news filtered in.

"Yeah," Slava said to someone who saw Cheetah's new tattoos in the shower room. "Fucking guy's a *vory*. Who knew? He was in the United States, handling things for the Chechen mafia."

All Cheetah had to do when he got out was nothing. Slava and Dmitri told him to lie low, stay in a remote part of Ukraine near Chernobyl, where no one wanted to live, not even the wolves.

Eventually, the Colombian warlord would die in a shootout or in some other turf war, and then Cheetah could pick up where he'd left off. An anonymous call to the media, and a reporter would find out where the real Ruslan Dudayev was buried. Once Dudayev was officially dead, Cheetah could start to live again.

Or at least, that was the plan.

But now, Cheetah had been murdered, and even if the Cubans hadn't found out who he was, he had to still be masquerading as Dudayev. That meant there was a chance Putin would find out that "Ruslan Dudayev" had been killed in Havana, and think he hadn't been disappeared after all.

What were they going to do to get out of this mess? Show Putin the body? Which one?

Shit. It was all getting far too complicated. To protect himself and Dmitri, Slava might have to find out who killed Cheetah himself.

———

"I need a list of all the Russians who were in Havana on Sunday," Slava said to Anatoly Klopov. "Including the Chechens. I need an office for the rest of the day and secure access to the Internet."

"That's not a problem, Commander," said Klopov. "Come with me."

As Slava followed him down the hall, he wondered why Dmitri had lied about the watch transmitter being out on assignment, and what the fuck Cheetah was doing wearing it when someone blew out his brains.

36

In one of the many bureaucratic oddities that kept Ramirez amused, the fourth of the four terminals at José Martí International Airport was named Terminal Five. It was Terminal Five that was used by the Cuban airline, Aero Caribbean, and that's where he headed.

He drove to the southeast corner of the airport and parked his small blue car beside the sidewalk, ignoring the No Parking signs.

Whoever murdered the tattooed man, thought Ramirez, he must have flown into Cuba; after all, he rented a car at the airport in the name of William Tattenbaum.

And yet, there was no record of a William Tattenbaum going through Customs. Tattenbaum would have had to present his passport at various stages of the arrival process as well as his driver's licence for the rental. Was the driver's licence a fake? Was he carrying more than one? There was no way to know.

Ramirez approached the woman behind the Aero Caribbean

counter. "*Hola*," he said, producing his badge. "I need to see the person who organizes flight schedules for your pilots."

The manager of operations came out to greet him a few minutes later.

"I'm looking for information concerning Captain Nelson Acosta," Ramirez explained. "I need a record of all his recent flights. It's in connection with a police investigation."

He hoped the manager would comply. He had no warrant and no right to that information. In fact, he had no real reason to believe a crime had occurred involving this man, only his intuition. But over the years, he had learned to ignore his gut instincts at his peril.

"How far back?"

"Maybe six months?"

She nodded. "We were all so sad when we heard the news," she said, as she sat down in front of an old monitor at a nearby desk and pulled up the flight crew schedules on the flickering blue screen. "Captain Acosta was such a good pilot. He left a wife and a small child. He was only thirty-five. It's a terrible tragedy."

She hit *print* and a sheet of paper slowly scrolled off the printer. She handed it to him.

"*Gracias*. Do you have Yoani Ravela's flight schedule as well?"

"Why? Did something happen to her too?" she said with a worried look.

Ramirez didn't answer. He felt bad he couldn't tell her that Señora Ravela was dead. But until they notified her next of kin, he wasn't permitted to disclose that information. He waited until the woman answered.

"Yes, I do," she finally said, "but her schedule won't be up to date. She hasn't come in this week. We're starting to get a little worried; it's not like her to take time off without telling someone."

"Maybe she went for a holiday with her family?"

The woman shook her head. "She doesn't have any family that I know of. I don't think she's ever been married. But you know what it's like . . ." Her voice trailed off as she remembered who she was talking to.

Ramirez understood completely. Thousands of Cubans attempted to make the ninety-mile trek across the Straits of Florida every year. They used pieces of wood, old tires, dinghies, even wrecked cars they converted into clumsy boats. Most were stopped by the U.S. Coast Guard and returned to Cuban shores before they ever set foot on American soil. But many others drowned or were eaten by sharks.

When someone left the island and wasn't heard from again, it was as if they never existed. No one wanted to talk to the authorities in case they started asking how they committed the treasonous act of leaving without the proper paperwork, and who had helped them.

He chose his words carefully, not wanting to give anything away. "Did she and Captain Acosta know each other?"

The operations manager nodded. "*Sí*. They crewed together often. They had such bad luck, that crew." She shook her head, eyes sad. "Antonio, their purser, was in a terrible car accident only yesterday. I just found out today."

"Really? What happened?" Ramirez pulled his notebook from his pocket and rooted in his jacket for a pen. "What is his name?"

"Antonio Palacios Barrago. The police said he was driving along the Avenida de Rancho Boyeros when he lost control of his car and hit a tree. I know he was anxious to get home; I guess he must have been speeding." She handed Ramirez the printout of Yoani Ravela's flights. "Here you go, Inspector. Let's hope that's the end of their bad luck."

———

The Avenida de Rancho Boyeros was also called the Avenida de la Independencia, but it was best known to locals as Airport Road. It was the scene of frequent accidents and, because it was in the municipality of Boyeros, it was the Boyeros precinct that investigated them.

The police station had a pink stucco exterior, with the shield of the Cuban National Revolutionary Police mounted high above the front door.

Ramirez walked inside. An old metal fan rumbled in the corner, moving the sticky air around but not cooling it. Iron bars on the windows made opening them impossible. He felt sorry for the people who worked here in this heat.

He introduced himself to the uniformed officer at the front desk, a sergeant. The man had his blue police beret folded and stuck under one of his epaulettes. His smooth forehead dripped with rivulets of sweat.

"I'm looking for some information about a single vehicle accident on Airport Road yesterday," said Ramirez. "The driver's name was Antonio Palacios Barrago. I'd like to see the *denuncia*." The accident report.

The officer walked over to a battered filing cabinet. "There are always accidents along there," he said, "what with all the stray animals and hitchhikers wandering out into traffic." He opened a drawer and ran his fingers through the tabs of brown folders. He removed one, riffled through it until he found the report, and returned to the counter to hand it to Ramirez.

"He swerved to avoid a dog and lost control; his car collided with a tree. Last I heard, he was in a coma with a serious head injury. The car had no seat belts." The man shrugged: most didn't. "He's not expected to pull through. It's a shame. I had to tell his family. Nice wife. Cute little boy about three."

"Has the car been impounded?"

"Technically, no, but the wife says she doesn't want it back. They can't afford to repair it, and after what happened, she thinks it's bad luck. It's in the compound for now, while we decide what to do with it."

"Can I see it?"

"If you like. The mechanic is on duty today. Until he finds a new windshield, there's not much we can do with it, either."

He let Ramirez behind the counter and escorted him to a door at the rear of the building that led to the vehicle compound. Ramirez found the mechanic bent under the open hood of a car, fiddling with an oil cap that no longer screwed on properly.

"The oil cap has lost its thread," the mechanic explained, when he saw Ramirez watching. "I think I can make it hold if I can find something to wrap around the end. A rubber band would work, if we had any."

Ramirez introduced himself. "Can I see the car that was involved in the accident on Airport Road?"

"Sure," the man said. He wiped his hands on a rag. "It's over there."

He pointed to a white car. The front end of the car was crumpled, the windshield shattered. Ramirez winced at the streaks of blood where he guessed the victim's head had smashed into the glass.

"A 1964 Trabant 601," said the mechanic. "German made. A nice little car. Basic parts. Easy to fix. Except it's hard to find a replacement windshield for it. Or any parts, for that matter. Believe me, I've been trying."

"What I don't understand is why he didn't hit the brakes," Ramirez said.

"I'm sure he did, but they didn't work," said the mechanic. "One of the brake lines was cracked all the way through. In this type of car—well, almost all of them built before the 1970s—a fault in one brake line is enough to shut down the entire system."

"Were they tampered with?"

The mechanic shook his head. "They were badly worn. He probably slammed on the brakes and one snapped. With the salt air, it happens."

"Is it possible to take another look?" Ramirez asked. "Just to be certain?"

"Sure." The mechanic opened the hood. "Why do you ask?"

"Let's just say the timing of this accident is suspicious."

The mechanic fiddled around for a minute. "Well," he said, and scratched his head, "I suppose that line could have been cut. If so, it wasn't cut all the way through, only enough to leave a weak spot. It would hold for normal braking, but give way under pressure." He pointed to the brake line closest to the master cylinder. "That's the one, right there. Take a look for yourself. The break at the top part of the line looks a little jagged; I suppose someone might have sawed through it." He looked for his rag and wiped his hands on it again. "But it isn't obvious."

"If I'm right, it wasn't supposed to be," said Ramirez.

The person who did this was a professional killer, he thought. Someone who knew that Airport Road was busy, and that drivers had to frequently slam on their brakes. Would a foreigner know that?

"Tell me, would a person need access to the underside of the vehicle to cut that line?"

"No. All they'd have to do is pop the hood. On this kind of car, that's easy. But some of the brake fluid would have leaked out. Any driver paying attention to their car would notice the puddle." The mechanic looked worried, afraid he might be in trouble for misdiagnosing a serious crime.

"The driver was on his way home. From the sound of it, he was in a hurry," Ramirez said. "He'd been parked in an airport parking lot, a place where cars come and go all the time. One could easily see a pool of brake fluid and think it was from someone else's vehicle. Don't worry, you didn't do anything wrong. But the forensic technicians will have to take over now and examine this car."

The man exhaled, relieved. "I'll tag it as evidence and lock it. I'll make sure no one goes near it."

"*Gracias*," said Ramirez. "If we don't have a copy of your fingerprints on file, we'll need those, too."

"They have them inside," said the mechanic. "I'm sorry. I shouldn't have assumed. . . ."

"Don't worry; we've caught it now." Ramirez squeezed the mechanic's shoulder. "That's all that matters."

He went back into the police station and arranged to have the file transferred to the Major Crimes Unit. Then he called Hector Apiro and told him to send over his technicians and, if he could find them, a few rubber bands.

37

On his way back to headquarters, Ramirez tried to knit together the strands of the information he had gathered so far.

Yoani Ravela lived alone and had no known boyfriend. But she'd had intercourse on Sunday night with someone who arrived late that evening, someone who took steps to conceal the fact he'd been there. Young Pacheco was right—whoever that was probably killed her.

Then a purser she crewed with from time to time was critically injured in what seemed to be an attempt to kill him, too.

And there was Captain Nelson Lopez Acosta, who'd contracted a mysterious fatal illness on Sunday night, too. Their pilot.

It was as if someone had put a curse on the entire crew.

Clearly, the evil eye that Yoani Ravela had tacked on her door to stave off bad luck hadn't worked.

Ramirez tried to imagine if there were secrets that connected these three, what it was they might have known that could have caused their deaths. Maybe Slava Kadun was right and drugs were coming into the country. Maybe this crew was involved in trafficking. They could have been co-conspirators in some kind of airlift.

Since the odds were against there being two professional hit men in Havana at the same time, it was likely their deaths were connected to the murder on the Malecón. Maybe they flew William Tattenbaum into the country illegally. That would explain why he didn't go through Customs. He could have killed them because they were witnesses. But witnesses to what? Illegal drug shipments? Or was this connected somehow to the threat against Raúl Castro?

Ramirez didn't know. It was chaotic. There was too much going on to make sense of any of it. He sat in his car, wishing one of his ghosts would materialize and give him a clue, a lead of some kind.

He called the police switchboard and had Sophia patch him through to Detective Espinoza. "I'm on my way back to headquarters, Fernando," he said, glancing at his watch. "How did you make out with the tapes of the car chase?"

"I still have probably thirty left to look at. It's going to take a full day at least."

Ramirez told Espinoza what he had learned. "As soon as you have a moment, I want a list of all the flights this crew was on in the last twelve months. Let's hope there are only a few. I want to know who their passengers were as well. Try the airline headquarters in Vedado first. If they don't have the records, go to the airport."

"Without a warrant?"

"You'll have to be creative."

"I'll sign out a car. And Inspector, speaking of lists, I have all the hotel guest lists now. I'll leave them on your desk."

"*Gracias*," said Ramirez. He realized, as he hung up the phone, that if his instincts were right, it wasn't one execution-style murder they were dealing with but four. Was a hit man considered a serial killer?

He knew the one man who could tell him, and help answer his questions.

Ramirez turned his car around and drove to Mazorra.

———————

Mazorra was a mental institution, named for the estate on which the Hospital Psiquiátrico de la Habana was located. It was a huge complex with over thirty buildings and twenty-five hundred patients.

It was the national psychiatric hospital, but also the place where political dissidents and prisoners were housed, including the sane ones. Ramirez tried to stay clear of it. With its emaciated patients and sense of hopelessness, it reminded him of Dante's *Inferno*.

He wasn't sure if Manuel Flores would agree to speak to him. The criminal profiler was dying from an aggressive lung cancer. Flores had conspired with the CIA to steal priceless art from the Museum of National Arts to embarrass the Castro government and raise funds for the CIA's off-book activities. Some of the proceeds would have paid for an experimental treatment for Flores's lung cancer in the United States. But Flores was arrested and sent to Mazorra to await a trial that would never take place. His illness was terminal. Letting him die here was far less messy than a firing squad or, for that matter, a conviction. Raúl Castro had no interest in revealing publicly that another one of his brother's leading supporters and friends had conspired against him.

It was because of Ramirez that Flores was arrested, and because of Ramirez that he would be unable to return to the United States for the only treatment that might have saved his life. But Flores was the one person Ramirez could think of who could help him understand the profile of the man behind these murders.

Ramirez parked his small blue car beside the prison's stone wall and stepped out. A soldier in an olive-green uniform was guarding the front gate. Ramirez nodded to him and flashed his ID; the sentry saluted and let him through.

He walked up the path and pushed open the front door.

"I'm here to see Dr. Manuel Flores," he said to the woman at the reception desk and produced his badge. He knew she would know who Dr. Flores was; he had once been the head of the institution.

"Dr. Flores is resting in the garden," the nurse said. "He doesn't get much company these days. I'm sure he will be happy to see you."

"I somehow doubt that," Ramirez said.

———

Manuel Flores was sitting in a wheelchair beneath the shade of a ceiba tree, his head tilted sideways as if he was listening to music that no one else could hear. He was a tall man, but his body had collapsed into itself like the dry husk of an insect. His cheekbones stood out in stark relief against his hollowed face.

"Dr. Flores," Ramirez said as he approached. He squatted beside the wheelchair, holding his hat in his hands. "How are you? I'd say you look well, but I'm not a very good liar."

Flores smiled. "I can honestly say you are the last person I expected to see here, Ramirez." His voice was shallow; his chest heaved as he struggled to take a breath. "I wish I could say I'm doing fine, but then I'd be lying too. They've moved me into palliative care. It's even more depressing than my former room. Flies on the walls, plastic over the windows. They're starving us, from what I can tell, and I think one of the nurses is selling off our bedding. It's even worse than it was when I ran the place.

"I'm sure they'll be changing my diagnosis to terminal cancer *and* paranoia." He chuckled. "But they let me sit outside from time to time, at least on the days when the foreigners are visiting. There's a team of doctors coming from Canada this afternoon to view the facility; they've arranged a little music as part of the deception that this is a pleasant place to be." He laughed; it made a rattling sound in his chest. "I asked them to put me under a ceiba tree, so I can pray for a good death. Only my skepticism keeps me from becoming an atheist."

Ramirez had almost forgotten how charming Flores could be. The ceiba was called the "tree of life." They were considered sacred, their dangling vines worshipped because they joined together earth and heaven. They bloomed every few years, and only in the evening. The buds were forming now. Ramirez wondered if Flores would live long enough to see the flowers.

"So why are you here, Ramirez?" Flores coughed and covered his mouth. "Given our rather sorry history together."

"I need your professional help," said Ramirez, appealing to the older man's ego. "I need a profile of a serial murderer. He could be Russian or Chechen. But I think he's killed, or tried to kill, four people in the last three days alone. He's used a different method for each one." He described the cases.

Flores leaned forward slightly. "Ah, now that's interesting. You've always known how to appeal to my curiosity. The Russians produce extraordinary killers. Like Andrei Chikalito, the Butcher of Rostov. He stabbed fifty-two women to death so he could achieve orgasm. Well, *women* is a relative term. His first victim was nine. Then he moved on to prostitutes and homeless women, as well as the occasional boy. When he lacked a knife to mutilate them, he used his teeth. It was feral, but then, he was a bedwetter, socially untrained. He gouged out their eyes. He believed the old superstition that the image of a killer is imprinted on his victim's eyes. It was a forensic profiler, one of my mentors, Viktor Burakov, who linked the cases together. He was brilliant. He showed Chikalito his sixty-two-page profile and Chikalito confessed. Of course, some of it was rewritten to better fit Chikalito's biography after he was arrested, but as you know, that's part of the business."

Flores leaned back, his eyes gleaming, and licked his thin lips.

"One of the victims was a Russian mafia leader," said Ramirez. "The others worked for Aero Caribbean. I don't know why they were killed, but I think this man is a professional."

"Chikalito was a professional killer too. Fifty-two murders, sixteen in one year alone. It hardly gave him time to eat, much less work."

"I mean a paid hit man. I need to know what to look for."

Flores tipped his head back and laughed. It made him cough again. Spittle dotted his lips; he wiped his face with the back of his hand.

"Then look around, Ramirez. The Communist Party is full of professional killers. We used to line counter-revolutionaries up against the wall and shoot them. What you really want to know is if this one's insane. It's not a medical definition, of course, but a legal one. I'm not being entirely facetious with that example, by the way."

Flores began hacking. He doubled over with pain. He pulled a handkerchief from his pocket and coughed into it. When he removed the cloth, it was spotted with blood. He continued speaking, but his voice was notably weaker. Ramirez looked around for a nurse. He saw one walking with a patient not too far away and waved his hand in the air to get her attention.

"First of all, a hired killer is not a psychopath, Ramirez. Chikalito was a psychopath. Oh, he was able to plan, all right, and he was intelligent enough to hide his actions, but he killed in a frenzy to meet personal urges. That's the difference. The hired killer is cool, composed. He has found a way to justify what he does, like the Nazi guards at the prisoner-of-war camps. There's the idea of a greater good involved that removes any feelings of guilt. Intellectuals make terrible revolutionaries but good assassins, according to Sartre.

"This man thinks of himself the way the hangman does, or the executioner; he's providing an important service. The professional hit man doesn't kill randomly or in a fit of rage, the way Chikalito did. He kills for a purpose, like any other loyal soldier. Remember, the soldier can be despised or revered, depending on the nature of the war he engages in and the side of the conflict you happen to be on. Look at Luis Posada, for example. From our perspective, he's a terrorist. From that of the CIA and most Cubans in the United

States, he's a hero. They love him, the same way the public adores James Bond."

Flores broke into another fit of coughing. This time Ramirez shouted for the nurse and she started running towards them.

Flores grasped Ramirez's hand tightly, his eyes bulging, his face mottled red.

"Remember what I've told you before," he said, as he gasped for breath. "A profiler looks for things so obvious that others miss them. You've been focusing on the hit man, Ramirez. You should be thinking about who gives him his orders."

38

Officer Pacheco was walking through the Plaza de la Catedral square with an off-duty policeman, when he noticed a foreigner sitting at a table on the terrace of El Patio. The man looked familiar. "Isn't that our suspect on the 'Be on the lookout for' list?" Pacheco asked.

"I don't know. I never read those things when I'm not working," Diego said. He yawned. "Who are we supposed to be looking for?"

"A foreigner who killed a woman on Blanco," Pacheco said. He put the heel of his hand on his holster. "Go talk to him while I call for backup."

"Officer Pacheco brought in the suspect in Yoani Ravela's murder a few minutes ago," Natasha Delgado said to Inspector Ramirez as soon as he walked into the Major Crimes Unit. "He was with an off-duty policeman. Pacheco, that is. Officer Diego. The suspect was sitting at a table at a restaurant in Old Havana when Officer Diego approached him." She handed Ramirez an American passport. Ramirez opened it and scanned through it. The suspect's name was Nathan Wallace.

"Pacheco said Señor Wallace didn't seem surprised when Diego walked over, but he did say something odd. He asked Diego if he had an umbrella. Here, Inspector, I thought you could use these when you go in to question him." She handed him the picture from the surveillance camera of Nathan Wallace entering the walk-up on Blanco and the photographs of Yoani Ravela lying crumpled at the bottom of the stairs. "They didn't tell him why they were bringing him in. I put him in the interrogation room."

"*Gracias.*" Ramirez slid the photographs into his jacket pocket. "Do me a favour and run a tape recorder from this side. I don't want him to know he's a suspect."

Delgado nodded. "I'll set one up," she said. "Good luck."

Ramirez walked down the hall and into the interrogation room. It smelled dank and musty with a single light bulb dangling from a wire in the ceiling. The large glass mirror on one wall was two-way, allowing others to observe from the adjacent room without being seen. He knew Natasha Delgado would be standing there with the tape recorder, a cheap plastic Chinese machine that nonetheless had incredible range.

Ramirez let the heavy metal door slam behind him.

Nathan Wallace was sitting on a red plastic chair, his elbows resting on the scratched Formica table. He jumped when the door clanged shut.

"Señor Wallace?" Ramirez said. "My name is Inspector Ramirez. I am in charge of the Havana Major Crimes Unit of the Cuban National Revolutionary Police. Do you know why you have been brought here?"

It was a tactic Ramirez often used. Sometimes a suspect confessed by acknowledging the offence for which they thought they were being questioned. Occasionally, they would blurt out an unrelated crime. Something like, "Is it because I hit my wife?" or "Is it about that theft from the factory?"

"I have no idea," Yaworsky said, and tried to force a smile. The man across from him was the plainclothes officer he'd seen pushing aside the yellow caution tape as he entered the walk-up on Blanco. "I didn't think it was illegal to have a cup of coffee."

Ramirez curved his lips and pulled over a cracked red plastic chair. He sat down beside Wallace instead of across from him, as if they were about to engage in a collaborative problem-solving exercise. "It isn't, unless you are Cuban. Although sometimes we think what they've done to our coffee ought to be a crime. Would you like me to send for some now?"

"No thanks," Yaworsky said. "I think I've had enough coffee today. I'll probably be awake for days as it is." Even as he said it, he hoped it wouldn't turn out to be true. He had visions of batons, of beatings that didn't leave bruises, of Ramirez blowing smoke in his face while he and his men punched and kicked him.

"Tell me, Señor Wallace, why are you visiting Havana? I see from your passport that you are American. Here, you can have it back." Returning it now would encourage Wallace to let his guard down. They could always retrieve it later, when he was formally arrested.

"Thanks," Yaworsky said, surprised. He put the passport in his pants pocket. "I'm registered for the Havana trade fair."

"Ah," said Ramirez. "What kind of goods do you plan to sell?"

"I'm a dairy farmer."

The hit on Raúl Castro was to take place during the ranchers' association awards. The hairs on the back of Ramirez's neck bristled. He tried not to show his excitement; this man might not only have cold-bloodedly killed Yoani Ravela, he could be his prey, the man who'd been sent to Cuba to murder Raúl Castro. "I know very little about cattle," Ramirez said, and leaned back in his chair. He had to appear relaxed. "We have so little beef in our rations; I sometimes think cows exist only in fiction." He crossed one leg lazily over the other and reached in his pocket for a cigar. "When did you arrive in Havana, Señor Wallace?"

"Sunday afternoon. Around two-thirty."

"Where are you staying?"

"The Hotel Sevilla."

"Very nice. An excellent choice. And what have you been doing since then?"

Yaworsky shrugged. "Seeing the sights. Wandering around. Waiting for the trade fair to open. Today, I was drinking coffee on a pleasant outdoor terrace, watching the passersby, when I was told I was required to come here and talk to the police. Can you tell me why?"

Ramirez avoided answering. "Do you have friends in Havana, Señor?"

"You mean people in town for the trade show? No. I don't really know anyone here. I've never been to Havana before."

He was too detailed in his denials, Ramirez thought. He hadn't asked if Wallace had previously visited Havana. A guilty person trying to boost his credibility often said more than what was required. Wallace had not only not answered the question, he had evaded it.

Ramirez waited for the suspect to volunteer additional information. As the silence deepened, the ploy worked. It usually did.

"I did meet another American delegate for a drink at the Hotel Nacional," Yaworsky offered, "but that was it."

"So you haven't interacted with any Cubans?" *Interacted* was a vague term, which was why Ramirez used it. To a juridical panel, it could mean anything from saying *hola* to having sex.

"You mean in their homes? No."

Ramirez saw Wallace's eyelid twitch. But he may have thought it was still illegal for Cubans to get into lengthy conversations with foreigners. Wallace had probably received a briefing about that before he left the United States. A twitch was not enough for Ramirez to prove guilt, only to suspect it.

"I know it's illegal to talk to Cuban citizens," Yaworsky said. "I assume it's all right to talk to you." He counterfeited a smile.

"Luckily for me, most of our laws don't apply to the police," Ramirez said. "Although people sometimes forget that we are citizens too." He removed the surveillance photograph from his pocket and put it on the table in front of them. He tapped on the photograph. "This is the front door to a walk-up on Blanco, near Trocadero. It was taken on Sunday night from a surveillance camera across the street. It's a very clear shot of you, I think, now that I see you in person."

Yaworsky kept his face as neutral as possible. "I was looking for a *casa* to stay at. Someone suggested I try one at that address. It turned out to be the wrong building."

Ramirez shook his head. "But Señor Wallace, you told me you are already registered at the Hotel Sevilla. Usually our visitors at least give our hotels a chance before they go somewhere else."

"The air conditioning in my room didn't work," Yaworsky said, his mind racing. Obviously they knew who he was. Why was he being interrogated by the police? Did Cuban Intelligence know he'd been taken into custody?

"You were inside the building on Blanco for several hours," Ramirez said, stretching the truth. They had no idea how long he had been there. But if he didn't deny it, that was as good as an admission. "That's a long time for someone to stay at a mistaken address. It's not a large building, Señor Wallace. It would be hard to get lost inside."

"All right," Yaworsky said. He leaned towards Ramirez conspiratorially and lowered his voice. "I'll tell you the truth. I planned to find a hooker once I got here. I sat next to a guy on the flight, and he gave me the address on Blanco. He told me she'd do things to me I couldn't begin to imagine." He grinned, man to man, hoping Ramirez would understand the appeal of a night with a strange woman far from home. "And you know what? He was right."

Ramirez looked at him. Could he be telling the truth? There had been sounds of intercourse through the walls of Yoani Ravela's apartment, and the forensic evidence backed it up. It was always possible that Ramirez had drawn links between deaths that weren't related at all.

"Is this the woman you were with?" Ramirez asked. He put the photograph of Yoani Ravela's twisted body on the table and pushed it towards Wallace with his index finger.

"She's *dead*?" Yaworsky's face flashed shock before he composed himself. "Oh, my God. What happened to her?"

He's not exactly the cold-blooded killer I was expecting, Ramirez thought. Either that or he's a very good liar. "That's what we're trying to find out. With your help."

Ramirez was just about to ask Yaworsky about the umbrella comment he'd made when there was a rap on the door.

"Excuse me, Señor Wallace," Ramirez said. "I'll be back shortly."

"We have a hit from the Germans," Natasha Delgado said excitedly when Ramirez joined her. "They checked their database of passport photos. The suspect flew from Moscow to Washington on a flight ten years ago; he transferred planes in Frankfurt. But he wasn't travelling as Nathan Wallace. He was using the name Danila Yaworsky. And he had a Russian passport."

Ramirez looked at the suspect through the glass. "Keep an eye on him, Natasha. I want to search his room at the Hotel Sevilla. It could take a while."

"Should I keep him in interrogation or move him to a holding cell?"

Ramirez nodded. "Leave him there. He won't know when I'm coming back. That should help unnerve him."

Natasha Delgado looked at the man through the glass. His shoulders were shaking; he looked distraught. "Not to be disrespectful, Inspector, but he looks pretty unnerved already."

The Hotel Sevilla was a few hundred metres from the Malecón, between Trocadero and El Prado. It was only a few blocks from the dead woman's building on Blanco, not far from where the coco-taxi chase started on Sunday afternoon.

Ramirez parked his car in the shade and walked into the Moorish tiled lobby. Live music played in the courtyard.

The Hotel Sevilla had originally been built as a hospital, but it turned out to be too close to Prado's noisy traffic to qualify for the required declaration of quietness, so its owners turned it into a hotel. In the 1930s, it was owned by one of the Havana mafia and quickly became a centre for the heroin trade. Al Capone had stayed there; so had the Italian mobster Santo Trafficante.

Ramirez had been inside the hotel only once or twice. Like all tourist hotels, it was off limits to Cubans unless they worked there. But this was police business, and that changed the rules.

He walked past a pair of stone lions and two gigantic potted palms and approached the receptionist behind a wooden counter. The police were permitted to search a hotel room or any other dwelling without a warrant once they had a reasonable suspicion of criminal activity. With the news of Nathan Wallace's fake identity, Inspector Ramirez had more than enough.

"I need the key to one of your rooms," he said pleasantly, and showed her his badge. "Your guest is registered as Nathan Wallace."

She looked up the name in a register and went into the back. She returned a few minutes later with a flat plastic key. "Here it is," she said. "Room 702. Is there a problem we should know about?"

"*Gracias*," Ramirez said, accepting the key. "I don't know yet."

He took the elevator to the seventh floor and stepped out into an elegant hallway. He rapped on the door of Room 702 in case the suspect wasn't travelling alone. When no one answered, he opened it cautiously.

The room was huge, almost the size of his entire apartment. It had a balcony overlooking Trocadero. Oversized pictures of Havana from the pre-revolutionary period, before the decay and shabbiness, hung on bright yellow walls. Two double beds with red bedspreads were pushed together against a mahogany headboard adorned with blue and yellow tiles. A bentwood chair and footstool sat before a generously proportioned wooden desk.

No one was there.

Ramirez removed a pair of latex gloves from his jacket pocket and slipped them on. He was surprised at how hot and muggy it was inside the room, but then Wallace had said the air conditioning didn't work. He opened the balcony door to let in the breeze, then began to methodically search the room.

He opened the drawer to the desk first. There was a copy of an airline ticket issued to Nathan Wallace as well as a boarding pass stub. He checked the times. Wallace had arrived at José Martí Airport at two-thirty on Sunday afternoon, about two hours before the man on the Malecón was shot. It was a tight time frame but not impossible.

There was also a special licence issued by the United States Treasury Department that authorized Nathan Wallace to attend the Havana trade fair.

The dresser drawers contained nothing out of the ordinary—T-shirts, a pair of jeans, men's briefs, a leather belt, three pairs of socks. Two white shirts and a pair of light cotton pants hung on hangers in the closet. There was a wall safe, but it was locked.

In the bathroom, a small black shaving kit rested on the vanity counter. Inside was a new electric shaver. Ramirez rubbed the stubble on his face, felt the scabs from his old blade, and briefly toyed with the idea of seizing it.

A tiny travel iron with a plug and adaptor stood upright on the vanity counter. There was a small scented bar of soap beside it, along with two tiny plastic bottles containing hand cream and shampoo. He removed the caps and smelled the contents.

Francesca had almost emptied the miniature bottles he'd pilfered from the hotel in Canada he'd stayed at in January. She'd love to have some more real toiletries, instead of the grey bar of sudless soap she lined up for once a month.

He took the shaving kit and carefully emptied it out on one of the beds. There was a plastic comb, nail clippers, roll-on deodorant, but no condoms. That surprised Ramirez. If Señor Wallace was telling the truth about wanting to spend the night with a *jinetera*, why hadn't he brought protection? Condoms were almost impossible to find in Cuba. But perhaps like so many other foreigners, Wallace had underestimated the effect of *el bloqueo*, the embargo, on basic supplies. Or maybe Wallace preferred the feeling of sex without them. Having intercourse with a condom was a bit like swimming with your socks on, from what Ramirez could remember; it had been decades.

Ramirez thought of the piece of paper the minister's clerk had handed Slava Kadun, inviting him to contact her. He checked the wastebasket, but the maids had already emptied it. He looked on the desk and in the drawer but found no piece of paper with the woman's address on Blanco, no marked-up map.

A stranger to the city would surely write down that kind of information, wouldn't he? But then, Wallace could have memorized it or thrown it out. If there had been something like that in Yoani Ravela's apartment, Natasha would have mentioned it.

He lifted the mattresses off the beds and looked beneath them— nothing. He sat down on one of them, deep in thought.

Nathan Wallace had travelled to the United States using a Russian passport issued to Danila Yaworsky. He could either be Russian or the passport could be fake.

Why would a Russian pretend to be American to register for a trade show? Or, if Nathan Wallace was his real name, why would an American pretend to be Russian while travelling through Europe?

Ramirez wiped perspiration from his brow. He looked at the air conditioning unit again. Wallace had mentioned the air conditioning specifically when he first lied about why he was in the building on Blanco. Perhaps subconsciously it held some special significance.

Ramirez pushed the *on* button on the air conditioning unit, but as Wallace had said, it was broken. He picked up the phone beside the bed and dialed the receptionist.

"It's Inspector Ramirez in Room 702. Has anyone reported that the air conditioning in this room isn't working? When I turn it on, nothing happens."

He heard her flip through some paper. "No, but we can send someone up to have it fixed right away, Inspector."

"No need for that, but can you send up a screwdriver?"

"Of course," she said. "A bellhop will be right there."

A few minutes later, there was a knock on the door. The bellhop looked disappointed when he saw a policeman standing on the other side of the door and realized there wouldn't be a tip. He gave Ramirez the screwdriver and left quickly.

Ramirez carefully unscrewed the cover of the air conditioning unit. Inside, wedged behind the coils, were two passports. But neither belonged to William Tattenbaum. One was a Russian passport issued to Danila Yaworsky.

It was the other one that surprised him. The cover was dark blue—it was a *pasaporte* from the República de Cuba.

Ramirez flipped through the pages and found an exit stamp dated June 1998. The photograph inside was of a much younger Nathan Wallace.

Except that in this document, his name was Danila Yaworsky Estevez. And the address was the walk-up on Blanco.

39

When Inspector Ramirez got back to headquarters, he jogged up the stairs to the anteroom to tell Natasha Delgado what he'd found. But she was no longer there. Major Diaz had taken her place and was closely watching the man on the other side of the glass. Which meant that Cuban Intelligence was taking over his investigation.

Wallace—or Yaworsky—seemed to have composed himself. He was sitting up straighter, arms folded, spine pressed firmly against the back of the chair. Whatever emotions he'd displayed before were now contained, and Ramirez knew that his chance to secure any kind of insight into the truth had gone with them.

Diaz turned to face Ramirez. "Ah, Inspector Ramirez. Lieutenant Ortiz called me as soon as he received the report from the Germans about your suspect. What do you have on this man?"

"According to his travel documents, he entered Cuba as Nathan Wallace, an American citizen," said Ramirez. "But he has a Russian passport under a different name, Danila Yaworsky. And he has an old Cuban passport as well. I searched his hotel room and found them hidden inside the air conditioning unit."

He removed the two passports from his jacket pocket and handed them to Diaz.

"I questioned him before I went to the hotel. I'm sure it's his voice on the tape we heard in the minister's office. I think he was sent here by the CIA to handle the hit on Raúl Castro. There was a woman murdered on Sunday at the same address as the one listed as his home address in his Cuban passport. The neighbours thought she was a *jinetera*. The suspect admits he went there on Sunday night for sex, but she could have been a girlfriend or an ex-wife. Either way, I think he killed her to prevent her from identifying him."

"What was her name?"

"Yoani Ravela."

Diaz sighed. "I suppose it's possible he killed her," he said, shaking his head. "If he thought she was sleeping with someone else. You know better than most that most murders are domestic."

"Why would you say that?" Ramirez asked. "Were they family?"

"Yoani was Danila's wife."

"They were married?" Ramirez cursed under his breath, angry at himself for missing the obvious. But Apiro had been told she was divorced. "So the Cuban passport is real? He's Cuban?"

"He will always be a Cuban citizen as far as Cuba is concerned, but he has dual Russian citizenship—Cuban mother, Russian father, originally from Poland. He and Yoani married when they were students at the University of Havana. He went on to graduate school in Moscow; Yoani stayed behind. You know the rules."

Whenever Cubans left for studies or work, spouses and children were required to stay behind. It was the only way the government could make sure they'd come back. And Major Diaz was right; the government wouldn't recognize any other citizenship a Cuban might have. Once a Cuban, always a Cuban.

"He's not here to kill Castro, Inspector. He works for us. In fact, he was already working for us when he left to study in Moscow. We arranged for him to study in the United States; we issued a fake birth certificate from Panama. That made him an American citizen. An American professor sympathetic to our cause arranged for him to get a fellowship in Russian Studies at Johns Hopkins University. Danila applied to the CIA for a job as an analyst when he graduated. Because of his background, and his fluency in Russian, English, and Spanish, he was accepted. He was working in defence research and strategic studies when Ana Belen Montes, another one of our friend's recruits, was arrested for spying for us. Danila took over her position in Strategic Defence Intelligence. A few months later, he was transferred to Special Operations. So, yes, that's his voice on the tape. But he's one of ours." Major Diaz frowned. "I'll take over now, Ramirez. I need to debrief him, and there isn't much time. By taking him into custody, you may have triggered events we can't control."

"But what if he killed his wife?" Ramirez said. "I have an active murder investigation under way. He's the only person who entered the building during the relevant time period; we have him on tape. He's our only suspect."

"I'm afraid we have more pressing concerns at the moment. I need you to release him into my custody immediately. And I need a secure room where I can question him in private." Diaz motioned to the two-way glass. "One that doesn't have mirrors. Or tape record-ers."

Ramirez gave up; the major far outranked him.

"When he leaves here," Diaz told him, "as far as your records are concerned, he was picked up for routine questioning and released. Nothing to do with Yoani. He has had absolutely no contact with Cuban Intelligence. Agreed?"

Ramirez nodded.

He watched through the mirrored glass as Diaz walked into the interrogation room to retrieve the double agent. "I have to be there tonight at the trade show," Yaworsky said as soon as he saw Diaz. "If

I'm not, they'll know something went wrong. I'm supposed to take pictures of Castro on the podium before the hit."

"Don't worry," Diaz assured him. "You'll be there."

———

Major Diaz and Danila Yaworsky sat across a desk from each other in an empty office down the hall from the Major Crimes Unit. "What happened to Yoani?" Yaworsky asked, his voice urgent. "Who killed her? I swear it wasn't me."

"I honestly don't know," said Diaz. "I'm sorry she's dead. But we don't have time for this now. We'll have to discuss Yoani later."

Yaworsky nodded unhappily.

"Now tell me more about this man in the CIA, the one you call the Captain," Major Diaz said. "What do you know about him?"

Yaworsky took a deep breath. "Not much. He hasn't been in Special Operations all that long. He told me he got that nickname because he used to captain a submarine. He bragged once that he transported Luis Posada from Panama by submarine. I think he told me that because he thought I was from Panama too. Believe me, it got my attention."

"Tell me everything he said."

Yaworsky thought for a minute. "He told me Posada was a straight-up guy. I think those were his exact words. That he was reliable. Respectful. Courteous. Always showed up on time. He told me it was a shame when they had to officially cut him loose after they found out he had ties to the Miami mafia.

"'And unofficially?' I inquired.

"The Captain shrugged. 'We trained him in explosives. He liked blowing things up. There was a Cuban airliner that went down in '76; it had his stamp all over it. Then some hotels in Havana were bombed in 1997. There were fatalities, a couple of Italian tourists. He as much as admitted doing it to a reporter for the *New York Times*, then claimed he was misquoted. He and his men got caught trying to blow up Castro in Panama in 2000; we managed to get him out of there and over to Honduras. I don't know what he was up to after that, but he showed up in the U.S. in 2005 with a fake passport, asking for asylum. Cuba wants him back, so does Venezuela, but we won't deport him, because our government is afraid the Venezuelans might torture him.'

"The Captain laughed. 'That's almost funny when you think about what's going on in Gitmo. But that's the thing about our business, Dan. Don't trust anything you hear, anytime, anywhere. Safest rule in Special Ops is to assume whoever's talking to you at any given time is lying.'"

"The Captain said Posada liked to make bombs. We already knew that. That's about all," Yaworsky said to Diaz. "I got sent to Special Ops to keep an eye on him. My former boss thought he might be up to something off-book. That's what that place is like, circles within circles. Everyone's fucking spying on everyone else."

Major Diaz sat back in his chair and stroked his chin with his index finger and thumb. "Does anyone else in Special Ops know about the assassination plot, or has the Captain gone rogue?"

"I don't know," said Yaworsky. "I really don't know what the hell's going on. I was supposed to be spying on *him* and the next thing I knew, we were sitting in this shitty little motel near DC and suddenly he was talking about killing Raúl Castro."

40

The airline headquarters for Aero Caribbean, in Vedado, wouldn't turn over flight records without a warrant. *"No está autorizado,"* said the person Detective Espinoza spoke to. But she also told him that Yoani Ravela usually worked on domestic charter flights, so Espinoza decided to drive to the airport to check it out.

Terminal Three handled international flights to and from Cuba, but Espinoza wasn't sure which terminal was used for domestic charters.

He left his unmarked police car at the curb and walked past the colourful 1950s Chevys and Buicks that were lined up waiting for fares. He entered through the glass doors. The odd-looking terminal had been built in 1998 with the help of the Canadian government. Its roof was angled inwards like a deck of cards in the process of being shuffled.

Half the main floor was overtaken by Cubana Airlines with its bright red counters and painted murals of Russian aircraft. The other half was almost empty. High above, the ceiling was crisscrossed with steel girders and exposed ductwork. Espinoza marvelled at how big the space was, and how clean, with shiny white tile floors. Most government buildings had broken windows and dangling wires; this one still looked new. He approached one of the airport security guards and told her what he needed.

"Oh, you have to go to Terminal Five," she said. "That's where Aero Caribbean runs all its charter flights."

Espinoza considered taking the shuttle bus but decided against it. The buses had to leave airport property and drive through streets clogged with carts, rickshaws, and taxis. Few visitors understood the risks of that particular detour. There had been a shootout at Terminal Two a few months earlier. Three army reservists from Managua tried to hijack a plane to get to Miami by first hijacking a shuttle bus. A hostage was killed before the reservists were shot dead—or, as the official report said, "neutralized"—by the police. It was an interesting way to refer to people whose brains had ended up splattered all over the tarmac, Espinoza thought.

Hijackings were not unusual in Cuba. People hijacked planes to get there; others hijacked planes to get out. The government had gone so far as to limit the amount of fuel on charter flights to try to prevent it, but clearly it hadn't worked. Having never flown himself, Espinoza didn't understand the appeal. But he was sure of one thing—you couldn't fall out of the sky if you weren't up there to begin with.

He got back into his unmarked car and drove to the southeast end of the airport. Once inside Terminal Five, he headed towards a trio of attractive women who were chatting behind the blue Aero Caribbean counter. It was framed with bright red pillars, and behind it, on the wall, were giant photographs of restored Spanish colonial villas and empty white-sand beaches. Government propaganda.

Espinoza approached the youngest of the three women. He was ever mindful that although he was twenty-one, he had yet to find a steady—or even an unsteady—girlfriend. But he had already learned from experience that the younger a woman was, the more likely she was to gossip.

"*Hola,*" he said and smiled. He produced his badge so she would know he was steadily employed, and eyed her appreciatively. She returned his interest with a wide smile.

"I'm looking for Yoani Ravela." He didn't mention that Yoani was dead; the girl's response would indicate if she knew. This was something he had learned from Inspector Ramirez and was still trying to apply: *Keep your cards close to your chest. Make a point of getting more information than you give away.*

The woman's smile faded. "I'm sorry. Yoani died this weekend. It's terrible. I just found out a few hours ago. Our manager went to her apartment to look for her when she didn't come into work again today. One of the neighbours told her."

Espinoza feigned shock. "That's awful! What happened?"

It wasn't a deliberate lie, was it? He had seen an old movie from South Africa at the Cine La Rampa about a bush pygmy who tried to return a pop bottle to the gods after it fell from the sky and almost killed him, which was another reason Espinoza was suspicious of airplanes. In one of the tribes the bushman encountered in his journey to the edge of the world, people nodded their heads up and down when they meant to say no.

"It's tragic. An accident. She fell down a flight of stairs and broke her neck. She was such a lovely person. We're all in shock." Her eyes filled with tears; one rolled down her cheek.

"I didn't mean to upset you. Listen, why don't you let me make it up to you over coffee? What time is your break?"

She looked at the other two women. One nodded slightly; the other one nudged her colleague with her elbow and grinned. The message was clear: Detective Espinoza was a handsome young man, and no one should ever refuse an offer like that, not in an airport, where the coffee they sold to tourists was genuine.

"It looks like I can take it now," she said, and let herself out from behind the counter.

Nina Menoya was the airline clerk's name. She was nineteen years old. She told Detective Espinoza that she had worked at the airline for almost a year.

"How did you meet Yoani?" Espinoza asked.

"We'd chat sometimes when she was waiting for a flight. We found out we both came from Guanabo. She used to tease me about being single; she was always telling me I should get a husband." Nina smiled at Espinoza and wiped her eyes.

"Was she a good flight attendant?"

"Oh, yes, the best. She even worked on a flight with Fidel Castro, and they only let the really good ones fly with him." She lowered her voice. "That was the flight when Castro got sick. I was on my shift when they called for an ambulance. Yoani told me later how terrified she was he was going to die onboard and how hard she tried not to show it. She was a professional."

Espinoza raised his eyebrows. "You saw Fidel Castro being taken to the hospital?"

"Not directly. I was at the counter, handling ticketing. We were told they were going to make an emergency landing." She leaned closer. "Yoani told me El Comandante complained of stomach pains almost as soon as the flight took off. At first they thought it was food poisoning, but no one else had any symptoms. Cuban Intelligence questioned her for hours after they landed; I guess they wanted to make sure she hadn't slipped something into his food or water. But she said he wouldn't eat or drink anything because his personal chef wasn't with them."

"Can I get the passenger list for that flight?" Espinoza asked.

"Don't you need a warrant or something?"

Espinoza shrugged. "If I have to get a warrant, people might think Yoani did something wrong. And from what I can tell so far, she didn't. But since you handled the ticketing"—he touched the back of her hand lightly—"maybe you can help me out."

She glanced around the terminal and shook her head. "I can't get you that, I'm sorry. *No está autorizado*; I'm not senior enough. But I'll tell you what I know." She dropped her voice to a whisper. "There weren't many passengers. Yoani told me that whenever El Comandante flies, the only people permitted onboard are his bodyguards, and sometimes a cabinet minister or a friend. And, of course, the flight crew. Occasionally, his doctor, if the flight is a long one."

"Was this flight a long one?"

"No, just a short charter to Holguin. That's why Yoani was so frightened: there was no doctor with them. I saw myself how worried everyone was when they landed."

"How many bodyguards?"

"Just one. His head of security. Major Rodriguez Castro. The head of Cuban Intelligence was with them too, Major Diaz."

"Who else besides Yoani was working as crew that day?"

"It was only a small crew. My God, I just realized. That crew has had such terrible luck; they must be cursed. Captain Acosta was the pilot. He died on Sunday of some kind of food poisoning. The purser was Antonio Palacios. He was in a terrible car crash; he's still in hospital, but I heard he may not recover. And now Yoani falling down the stairs." Her eyes filled with tears again.

"Is that everyone who was onboard?" Espinoza asked gently. He handed her a paper napkin, and she used it to dab her eyes.

"I think so. Oh, no, wait. There was a passenger too. A friend of the Castros. An American. He had a big cowboy hat; I remember that very clearly." She wrinkled her forehead, thinking, then her eyes brightened. "I think his name was Franklin Pearce."

41

Inspector Ramirez was pacing around Hector Apiro's office, angry that his only suspect in Yoani Ravela's murder was in the hands of Cuban Intelligence.

To hell with national security, he thought. He swore Apiro to secrecy, then told him about the Russian tape, the assassination plot, and the reason Slava Kadun had been sent to Havana in the first place.

"It's Nathan Wallace's—Danila Yaworsky's—voice on that tape, Hector," Ramirez said. "He may be working undercover with the CIA, but that doesn't mean he's immune from our laws. Murder is murder. We have him on tape; he was the only person in that building who could have done this."

"I actually think Major Diaz is right," said Apiro, tamping his pipe thoughtfully. "There is a larger national security issue at stake if there is a CIA operative in Havana with orders to kill the acting president."

"But what if this man killed his own wife?"

"Is it better to punish a death that's already happened or prevent another one from taking place? That's a philosophical discussion best left for another day, my friend. But if it makes you feel better, we don't have any real evidence that he killed her, at least not yet. All we know for sure is that he was in the building a few hours before she died. It makes sense to me that he would want to see her after all this time away, and also that he would take care not to be discovered by his neighbours. Even after all these years, I'm sure he was petrified he might run into someone who knew him and blow his cover."

But that's what love does, thought Apiro, it makes you take risks you'd never take if you were behaving rationally.

"Natasha found over ten thousand American dollars hidden under the floorboards in Yoani Ravela's apartment. It had to come from him. I don't even know how he got it through Customs or why he'd give her money in a currency she couldn't use. The whole thing smells."

"He could have been sending it to her the whole time he's been away. He wouldn't be the first Cuban to send remittances to a family member. And American currency has only been illegal here for a few years. But the fact that she had all that money and concealed it only means that Señora Ravela got it somewhere and hid it. We can't determine its source forensically. I know you're frustrated, Ricardo, but you're the one who always says not to jump to conclusions when we don't have sufficient evidence to back them up."

Ramirez forced himself to put aside his anger at losing his only suspect. It was why he turned to Apiro for counsel whenever he found his emotions getting the better of him. A man of science, Apiro thought objectively, relying on facts, and facts alone. If Ramirez was being illogical, Apiro could be relied on to point it out kindly.

There was a rap on Apiro's door. "Come in," Apiro called out.

One of his technicians opened the door. "*Hola*, Dr. Apiro. I have an email for you from Interpol. They've identified your shooting victim."

"*Gracias.*" Apiro got to his feet and walked out from behind his desk to accept the page from the technician, then thanked her again and closed the door. "Well," he said, after he scanned through the email's contents, "it turns out he's Russian after all. His name is Fedor Petrov. He has a lengthy criminal record from the looks of it. But we already knew that, thanks to Slava."

He handed the piece of paper to Ramirez.

Ramirez read through a long list of entries. "Interesting. Not only did he have convictions for weapons and smuggling, but this says there's an outstanding warrant for him in Canada. In Ottawa. Can I use your phone, Hector? I want to call Chief O'Malley and see if he can tell us anything about it."

"Of course." Apiro reached for the phone and untangled the cord, so it would stretch to Ramirez's chair.

Ramirez called the police switchboard and asked Sophia to place a call to Chief Miles O'Malley in Ottawa. Miles O'Malley was in charge of the Rideau Regional Police Force. Ramirez had worked with him when he'd gone to Canada's capital to pick up a priest charged with possessing child pornography.

A few seconds later, he heard O'Malley's thick Irish brogue.

"Inspector Ramirez," O'Malley exclaimed. "It's good to hear from you. How are things in Cuba? Hot, I imagine, this time of year. My God, I wish we had your problem. We've already got an inch of snow and it's only November. Everyone forgets how to drive as soon as it snows; there are accidents everywhere. At times like this, I can't for the life of me remember why I moved to this godforsaken country." He laughed.

"Things are fine, thank you, Chief O'Malley, but we're busy—much busier than usual, which is why I am calling. I wondered if you could help me with some information concerning a homicide investigation. The victim was a Russian named Fedor Petrov. According to Interpol, there's an arrest warrant out for him in Ottawa, but we don't have any details."

"I'm not familiar with that name offhand, Inspector, but let me get someone to check our system and I'll call you back."

"*Gracias*. I'll be heading back to my office at police headquarters in a few minutes. You can reach me there."

———

About an hour later, Ramirez's phone rang. "I have Detective Ben Ryan with me, Inspector. Detective Ryan used to work in Sex Crimes. Apparently, that's what that warrant is all about. I'm going to put you on speakerphone and let you two chat."

Ramirez wasn't sure what a speakerphone was, but a second later he heard O'Malley say, "There, can you hear me?" and then another male voice said, "Hello, Inspector Ramirez."

O'Malley made the introductions.

"So, Fedor Petrov is dead, is he?" Ryan said. "I can't say I'm surprised. From what I heard from the Mounties, the Colombians were gunning for him. That warrant's been around for years, Chief O'Malley; it predates when you got here, so I'm not surprised you haven't heard of him. But he was a bit of a legend. The CBC did an entire show on him. He's a Russian. He owned a bar in Hull when he first got to town."

"Hull's in Quebec, Inspector, just across the river from us here," O'Malley interjected. "The CBC's our national broadcaster."

"He ran into trouble right away," Ryan said. "He was hanging around the bars in the Byward Market—that's in downtown Ottawa—trying to sign up women for the sex trade in Eastern Europe. Bragged right on TV that he could pay a girl ten thousand dollars to go to work for him and make his money back in a week as soon as she got on her back. He went by the nickname Cheetah. One of the girls told me he had a big tattoo of a cheetah on his forearm."

"Did he have any other tattoos?" Ramirez asked.

"He might have. I don't remember."

"Criminal record?"

"Not here, but I know he did time in Russia, some in the U.S. too. Back in the early nineties, before he graced us with his presence, he had a nightclub in Miami that was a meeting place for Russian gangsters. He got real close to a Colombian cocaine dealer. He arranged to get his buddy a decommissioned Russian submarine, so the Colombians could smuggle cocaine up and down the coast of Central America without being detected. One of the people involved in the purchase was working undercover for the U.S. Drug Enforcement Administration. Before the deal went through, Petrov was arrested. He agreed to plead guilty and testify against his Colombian friend if the DEA would reduce his sentence and deport him back to Moscow to serve his time. The Russian authorities must have cut him loose pretty quickly, because he showed up in Ottawa a year or so later. That's why the Mounties were watching him."

Ramirez heard paper being shuffled. "Anything else, Ben?" he heard O'Malley say.

"Well, he probably wouldn't have ended up on our radar at all, except he pretty much admitted on television to trafficking in women," Ryan said. "We had to obtain a search warrant to get the tape from the TV station. The CBC fought us in court every step of the way. It was all over the media, so by the time we got enough evidence to lay charges, Cheetah was long gone. The RCMP told me later he'd disappeared completely. I've heard rumours his Colombian contact had him killed for ratting him out."

"Well, he was alive until last Sunday," said Ramirez. "He was shot to death here in Havana, on the Malecón. It looks like a professional hit. "

"Interesting," Ryan said. "If you're looking for a suspect, I'd probably put that Colombian drug lord at the top of my list."

But Ramirez wondered where a Colombian hit man would get a gun issued to a *spetsnaz* or, for that matter, learn to speak Russian.

"I appreciate your advice, and thank you for the information, Detective," he said. "One more thing, before I let you go. Chief O'Malley, would it be possible for someone to check your criminal record database for us? As you know, we have to go through Interpol, and their information is limited. The gunman abandoned the rental car he used in the shooting a few blocks away. It was leased to an American named William Tattenbaum. The licence and passport he produced for the rental agency had an address in Shakespeare, New Mexico. I assume these documents are fake, but I need to know for sure."

"We can do that for you," O'Malley said. "No problem."

"Sure," Ryan confirmed. "I can check CPIC and NPIC. I can look into the motor vehicle registrations across Canada and in the U.S. for you, too, but that will take a little while. Can I call you back later? I guess the chief's got your number?"

"He does," said Ramirez. "*Gracias.*"

"As always, it was good talking to you, Inspector," said O'Malley.

"Thanks for updating us on Cheetah," Ryan said. "I'll let the Crown know so the court can cancel the arrest warrant. That's one file I'll be happy to close."

———

Inspector Ramirez called Apiro and told him what he had learned.

"Maybe it wasn't drugs that Señor Petrov came to Cuba for," Apiro said. "Maybe it was women. Maria said something about a Russian man offering *jineteras* a considerable amount of money to go to work for him in Europe. Ten thousand American dollars."

"Mama Loa said something about that as well. One of her goddaughters had been approached. I didn't pay much attention."

Maybe that was why Yoani Ravela had ten thousand dollars hidden in her floorboards, thought Ramirez. Maybe she was a *jinetera* after all and had accepted the Russian's offer. It was one way to get out of the country. She might have thought she could somehow reunite with her husband.

But if that was what she'd planned, Danila Yaworsky had no reason to kill her.

42

"All three of them were crew on Fidel Castro's last flight," Detective Espinoza shouted into his police radio. He was standing outside the airport as a Russian TU-204 taxied down the runway. He had a finger stuck in one ear and his police radio pressed tightly to the other so he could hear Ramirez over the sound of the engines. "The one where he got sick."

He told Ramirez what he'd uncovered. "The woman I spoke to says there was an American on the flight too, named Franklin Pearce. I'm sure I saw his name on the list of guests staying at the Hotel Nacional this week."

"Good work, Fernando." Ramirez tried to remember where he'd heard the name before. Then he recalled that Señor Pearce was the person who was going to make the presentation to Ramón Castro at the trade fair.

He heard a car door shut and the background noise became more subdued.

"That's better," said Espinoza. "Man, those planes are loud."

"Where did you leave the hotel guest lists?"

"I put them on the right-hand corner of your desk."

Ramirez looked. Someone had already put a pile of papers on top of them. "I've got them now, thanks." He flipped through the pages until he found the list of guests staying at the Hotel Nacional. "Ah, here it is. Señor Pearce is in Room 615." Ramirez thought for a moment. "Do you remember if you saw the name Fedor Petrov on any of those lists?"

"I don't think so," said Espinoza. "Who is he?"

"Our shooting victim. Turns out he was a Russian criminal involved in the sex trade and human trafficking." Ramirez scanned through the rest of the names on the list for the Hotel Nacional and stopped at one of them. Ruslan Dudayev. Room 623. That was the Chechen warlord Major Diaz had mentioned.

Some of the dead man's tattoos looked newer than others, Apiro had said. Ruslan Dudayev had held meetings in his hotel, according to Major Diaz, but hadn't been seen leaving it for days.

Ramirez remembered what his mother said to Estella when she lost her doll: the reason they couldn't find her was she was hiding in plain sight.

"Ruslan Dudayev is registered on the same floor as Señor Pearce," Ramirez said to Espinoza. "You know I don't like coincidences."

"The sixth floor is the executive level. Who is Ruslan Dudayev?"

"Major Diaz says he's a Chechen warlord. But I have a feeling his nickname may have been Cheetah."

Ramirez drove up the long circular driveway to the Hotel Nacional and parked by a sign that said *Valet*. A hotel employee quickly ran over to admonish him. Ramirez got out of his car and showed his police ID; the man backed away just as quickly.

Ramirez slammed his car door shut and walked up the front steps of the most famous, or perhaps infamous, hotel in all of Cuba.

He passed by framed black-and-white photographs of famous guests: Frank Sinatra, Nat King Cole, Sir Winston Churchill, and Ava Gardner. The American mafia had frequented the hotel as well; in fact, it had once closed its doors so that Lucky Luciano and Meyer Lansky could host the largest private gathering of American mafiosi in history.

The mobster Santo Trafficante had been a double agent like Nathan Wallace, Ramirez recalled. Fidel Castro threw him out after the revolution, then the CIA enlisted him to kill the Cuban leader. They gave him some poisoned pills and, soon after, the Cuban media reported that Fidel Castro was seriously ill.

But as it turned out, Fidel was only pretending—Trafficante was actually loyal to him. It was Trafficante who had told Fidel about the American plans for the Bay of Pigs, allowing him to ambush the invaders. President Kennedy sent six fighter planes from Nicaragua to lend support, but they were confused by the time change; they arrived an hour too late and were shot down by Cuban forces.

Every single part of Fidel's response to the invasion involved spreading misinformation, although they didn't even call *that* by its own name anymore, thought Ramirez. Now, apparently, it was called "disinformation." He wondered if anything had really changed.

He showed his badge to the receptionist and asked for the key to Room 623.

Ramirez made his way to the elevators and pushed the button for the sixth floor, the hotel's executive level. It had a private lounge and a gorgeous view of Havana Harbor.

He decided to visit Franklin Pearce first, if the American was in. If Ramirez was right about Ruslan Dudayev, his tattooed body was in the morgue; he wasn't going anywhere for a while.

"Where is Room 615?" he asked the concierge, holding out his badge. The man pointed, and Ramirez strode down the hall. When he found Pearce's room, he rapped on the door with his knuckles.

The man who opened it was at least twenty-five years older than Ramirez, and much taller. He looked as if he'd been reading; a pair of spectacles was pushed high on his forehead like a second set of eyes. His hair was white. He was tanned and fit.

"Señor Pearce?" Ramirez asked.

"Yes?"

Ramirez introduced himself. "I'm investigating a homicide. I'm hoping you can assist me by answering a few questions."

"A murder investigation, Inspector Ramirez? Well, I don't know how I can possibly help you, but, sure, come on in." Pearce pushed his fingers through his white hair, knocking his glasses to the floor. He bent down to pick them up. "Christ," he said, "I hate getting old. I need the damn things to find them half the time. Can't see with them; sure as hell can't see without them."

Ramirez smiled. He followed Pearce into his room and removed his hat. He was surprised to see how plainly decorated the room was, given the apparent opulence of the hotel. There was a queen-sized bed with a semicircular headboard, a piecrust table, and two uphol-stered chairs. A bronze sculpture of a cowboy being flung from the back of a bucking bull sat on the table. There was a brass plaque on the platform beneath it inscribed to Ramón Castro.

"May I?" Ramirez inquired, inclining his head towards one of the soft upholstered chairs.

"Yes, of course. I'm sorry. I wasn't expecting anyone, certainly not an inspector with the PNR. Please sit down. Can I get you a drink? I have a pretty well-stocked bar. Or I can call room service if you'd like something to eat?"

Ramirez shook his head. "I don't plan on staying long, Señor Pearce."

"Now, look, call me Frank. I don't sit comfortably with being a 'mister.' Makes me feel like my father, and believe me when I tell you that's not a good thing." Pearce folded his long body into the other chair and crossed one cowboy-booted leg over the other. "Now, you said you were here about a murder. What can I do for you? How can I help?"

"A Cuban flight attendant died this week. She was one of the crew on a charter flight you took with Fidel Castro last year. I wondered if you knew her. Her name was Yoani Ravela."

"Well, I've been on a few of those flights with the Castros," Pearce said. "Never did get to know the crew, other than to say hello when I showed them my boarding pass and maybe order a drink. I was usually having too much fun talking to the president."

"Are you a friend of Fidel Castro's?"

"Well, more of the family. Of Ramón Castro, really. I'll be giving him an award at the trade fair tonight to thank him for all his support. There it is, right there." He pointed to the bronze sculpture. "I'm a cattleman, Inspector. I've been coming to Cuba a lot in the last couple of years. Ramón and I got to know each other and things just clicked. I've been lucky enough to be invited out to his ranch several times. That's why the Florida Ranchers' Association asked me to make the presentation."

"How does your government feel about your involvement with the Castros?"

"I can tell you exactly what they think. Not much." Pearce got up and picked up a brown envelope that was lying on the table. He shook out some photographs and handed them to Ramirez. "They got hold of these somehow. Sent someone over to give them to me, to let me know they're watching me. So I guess you could say they aren't too impressed."

Ramirez flipped through the shots. There was a picture of Pearce and Ramón Castro horseback riding; another of the two men sitting on a bench together, laughing. He stopped when he got to a picture of Franklin Pearce seated on a plane. A female flight attendant leaned over Pearce and Fidel Castro. Her face was hidden by Pearce's cowboy hat. He recognized the man standing behind her from the photograph in the accident report about the crash on Airport Road as the purser, Antonio Barragos. He guessed the pilot seated behind both of them in the cockpit was Captain Nelson Acosta Lopez, and the flight attendant was Yoani Ravela.

"When were these taken?" Ramirez asked, looking up.

"Now, that had to be last June," Pearce said. "It's the last time I saw Fidel Castro. Seems like the last time anyone saw him, at least in public. He was on his way to meet with Hugo Chavez in Holguin and offered me a ride. About twenty minutes into the flight, he started to complain about his stomach. He got worse real fast—we had to make an emergency landing. I thought maybe it was a bleeding ulcer or a burst appendix, but I haven't been able to find out anything since he was taken away by the paramedics. All Ramón will say is that he's getting better and should be back to work soon. I don't suppose you have any idea what's wrong with him?"

"Does Cuban Intelligence know about these?" Ramirez asked, avoiding the question. No one knew what was wrong with Fidel Castro; it was considered a national secret.

When Castro was first hospitalized, Cubans were told he would be back to work soon. No one was really surprised when the recovery took longer than expected; after all, he was getting old. His last public speeches before his surgery had been rambling and tedious. Local party chiefs had waved small Cuban flags above his head to let the audiences know when to clap.

But months passed and Castro wasn't better. In December, he failed to appear at a parade honouring the fiftieth anniversary of his return from exile. Then he missed the May Day parade. When he was absent for the celebrations for Revolution Day for the first time since 1959, speculation about his health turned to anxiety about the future. Some Cubans were afraid that when he died, American money would flood in like a tsunami; others were just as fearful it might not. The country had lived on the edge ever since, not sure what the future would look like once he was gone.

"Look, I didn't even know about those photographs myself until last Sunday," Pearce said. "The guy who dropped them off is registered for the trade fair, too. Some bureaucrat in the U.S. told him to deliver them to me. But I don't like being threatened, especially by my own government."

"Who was the person who brought them to you?"

"His name was Nathan Wallace. He told me the person who gave them to him knew he was coming to Havana. He even told him I'd be staying at this hotel." He shook his head. "As if my government doesn't have better things to do with my tax dollars than track down my whereabouts when I'm looking after my own business."

"May I keep these?" said Ramirez, although he didn't need permission. If Pearce said no, he would take the photographs anyway. It was illegal to take pictures of one of Castro's flights.

"Sure. I don't need them."

"*Gracias*, Señor Pearce." Ramirez picked up his hat and stood. "I hope you enjoy your stay. And that you don't run into any problems with your government when you return home."

"Well, thank you, Inspector, for those good wishes. I'm sorry to hear about that flight attendant. Don't you worry about me. I live in a great country, one that's a lot bigger and more sensible than most of our politicians. All we can do is try to hurry things along."

———

After he left Pearce's room, Inspector Ramirez knocked on the door to Room 623. When no one answered, he used the key to let himself in.

The room had been cleaned by the maids, but it still showed signs of occupation. There were clothes hanging in the closet, a pair of shoes on the floor, toiletries in the bathroom, a package of condoms. On a side table, there was an airplane ticket from Aeroflot in the name of Ruslan Dudayev and a paperback. Ramirez picked the book up; it was an English translation of Émile Zola's novel *Lourdes*. He flipped through it; some of the page numbers had been circled.

Ramirez checked under the drawers, beneath the mattress, behind the curtain valance—in all the hiding places he could think of—but found nothing.

He looked more closely at the framed print on the wall. It was a black-and-white photograph of the Hotel Nacional from the thirties. He took the picture down and examined the back. The paper backing had a small tear in it. Tucked inside was a computer printout with a string of numbers. Ramirez had no idea what they represented, but clearly they were important enough to Fedor Petrov to hide them.

Ramirez placed the printout in a plastic exhibit bag and slipped it into his jacket pocket. He was about to leave the room when he glanced again at the book on the side table. Lourdes was the name of the electronic listening station mentioned in the conversation between Yaworsky and his superior. He put the book in another exhibit bag, then closed and locked the door.

As he walked out the front entrance to retrieve his car, his mind returned to his conversation with Franklin Pearce. It seemed that photographs taken on Fidel Castro's flight had somehow found their way into the hands of the CIA. But how? Pictures like that were illegal. Who took them? Were they taken openly or surreptitiously?

All Ramirez knew for sure was that Danila Yaworsky had delivered them to Pearce, which meant he might have some answers. Ramirez called the Hotel Sevilla and asked for Nathan Wallace, but no one answered. Yaworsky was out.

According to the tape Slava Kadun had played in the minister's office, the Captain instructed Yaworsky to be at the trade fair to watch the award presentation unfold. And Major Diaz had assured Yaworsky he'd be able to carry out his orders.

To avoid tipping off the CIA operative that they were on to the assassination plot, Cuban Intelligence would have to let him wander around unimpeded at the trade fair, so Ramirez decided to track him down there. Cuban Intelligence wouldn't like it, but they'd be unable to do anything to stop him without blowing Yaworsky's cover; they'd be angry but helpless. It was always better to act first, Ramirez had discovered during his twelve years of marriage, and beg for forgiveness later.

His cell phone rang just as he reached the car. It was Slava Kadun.

"I'm on my way to the trade fair now," Ramirez said. "Where are you?"

"At Russian embassy. Can I get ride?"

Ramirez thought for a minute. Slava Kadun was the only person in Havana he could think of who would have had access to the special-issue gun and ammunition that killed Fedor Petrov. He claimed he'd arrived in Havana on Monday, but what if he was lying? What if he'd come earlier? It would be a good idea to keep an eye on him, until he could find out what was going on. As Apiro always said, keep your friends close, your enemies closer.

"I'll pick you up in a few minutes," Ramirez said, and pulled open his car door, giving it a moment to let the heat escape before he climbed in. Even though the window was rolled down, the interior was almost steaming.

He looked up and down the road, wishing a tattooed apparition would materialize from the teeming crowds and give Ramirez a hint as to what was going on and why he'd been murdered.

Then he called headquarters and instructed Natasha Delgado to find out exactly what time Slava Kadun's flight had arrived in Havana and when he'd cleared Customs.

43

Inspector Ramirez found the big Russian standing outside the Russian embassy, on a sidewalk that looked as if it had weathered a small earthquake. Slava climbed in. He was so big, and Ramirez's car so small, he had to bend his knees almost to his chest. Seeing it reminded Ramirez of a dead man he'd once transported around town, an Italian ghost who'd enjoyed riding in Ramirez's car and who'd whistled silently at the women he saw on the street.

Ramirez glanced in his side mirror to see if he had any other passengers, but the back seat was empty. It looked like he was going to be without any supernatural assistance in this investigation, and he realized he didn't much like it.

The Feria Internacional de la Habana was held every year at the ExpoCuba complex in Arroyo Naranjo, about twenty kilometres south of Havana. About twenty-five pavilions housed permanent exhibitions of government programs: farming and geology, agriculture, tourism, and defence. The central pavilion displayed major advances in Cuban economic activity and was usually mind-numbingly boring.

When they pulled into the exhibition complex, Ramirez's car was waved over by a *policía* and directed to a parking lot south of the main pavilion. He squeezed the car into a narrow spot.

He toyed with the idea of taking his cell phone with him, but was mindful of the prohibition against it. He ended up slipping the phone under the driver's seat, hoping the policeman guarding the lot wouldn't steal it. He slammed his car door hard and asked Slava to do the same; the doors were so rusted, that was the only way to close them.

They walked past the amusement park, with its artificial lake. Children squealed with laughter on the slides; the water rippled with a thousand tiny diamonds.

Dozens of flags flapped at the entrance to the main pavilion. Each one represented a country attending. A giant banner in front of one building read, EXPOSICIÓN NACIONAL DE RUSSIA; another, BIEN-VENIDOS A COLOMBIA.

Security was everywhere, but it was discreet, toned down. Militia volunteers in olive uniforms patrolled the perimeter with machine guns. A man walked a beagle on a leash; it looked like one of the airport sniffing dogs. Along the roofline, Ramirez saw shadows: police snipers. Slava Kadun cast his eyes up to the roof as well, shading his eyes with a big hand.

"What do you want to do?" Ramirez asked him. "Where would you like to start?"

"I go to check out Russian pavilion first. I will see you later?"

Ramirez looked at his watch. It was almost two hours until the awards presentation. He wasn't sure what time Danila Yaworsky was likely to arrive, but it would have to be before then. He nodded. "I'll be in front of the stage when they present Ramón Castro's award. I'll look for you there."

44

Hector Apiro was sitting in Dr. Garcia's office in El Capitolio. As always, Apiro was struck by the extravagant beauty of the building, despite its humidity and leaky roof. It was a replica of the Capitol Building in Washington, built to a smaller scale. It held the fifty-foot-high Statue of the Republic, reputedly covered in twenty-two-carat gold. Its front steps ran the entire width of the grand central portico. At their base, they were rimmed with 1956 Chevys and line-ups of tourists, along with the ubiquitous beggars, stray dogs, cigar women, and young boys cadging money. As Ramirez once observed, at El Capitolio, even the dogs begged.

An enormous diamond had once been embedded in the floor of the Capitolio's magnificent entry hall, immediately beneath the giant dome. All distances in Cuba were measured from this spot, called kilometre zero. The real diamond, originally owned by Tsar Nicholas II, had long since been removed and replaced with a replica. Most people believed that Fidel Castro had the original hidden away somewhere.

A battered metal thermos rested on the desk between Garcia and Apiro. A trade was under way—a fresh pot of coffee for information.

"After Inspector Ramirez told me how knowledgeable you were about Russian *spetsnaz*, Dr. Garcia, I wondered if you knew anything about Vityaz," Apiro said. He twisted the cap off the thermos and poured some of the hot liquid into a cracked mug. He handed it to the ballistics expert. "I met someone who works there yesterday. A fascinating man. He's in Havana on business."

Garcia wrinkled his forehead. "I would love to know what kind of business someone with the Russian Ministry of Internal Affairs would be up to in Havana. I wrote my PhD thesis at the University of Moscow on the history of the Russian Special Forces; that's how I became interested in their weaponry and technologies." He sipped the coffee and almost sighed with pleasure, then put the mug down and settled into one of his favourite topics. "Of course, I was never allowed to publish it. My professors said if I did, they'd have to kill me." He smiled.

"*Vityaz* means 'knight,'" Garcia continued. "The group was created in the 1990s, but it has always been seen as a political tool of the Russian president. During the 1993 Russian constitutional crisis, for example, Vityaz officers fired into a crowd of anti-Yeltsin protesters. Afterwards, their commander was proclaimed a hero of the revolution. They hunted major targets during the Chechen wars. They assassinated the most successful Chechen fighter, Amir Khattab, by sending him a poisoned letter.

"And then, of course, there were the 1998 Moscow apartment bombings. Vladimir Putin blamed the Chechens, but there have been persistent allegations ever since that the bombs were planted either by Vityaz or FSB officers to help build support for Putin's plans to invade Chechnya. Of course, sometimes the Chechens work with the FSB too, so it's not always easy to know who's doing what to whom."

Apiro put his mug down. "Why would the Chechens cooperate with the FSB if they themselves then get blamed for FSB atrocities?"

Garcia shrugged. "Money has no nationality. There's a great deal of money in Moscow these days. It's almost unimaginable how much. Men became billionaires overnight, based almost entirely on their connections to the president." He reached for the thermos and topped up his coffee. "And almost anyone who has reported that information to the public, or accused Putin of corruption, has ended up dead."

He shrugged again. "But the KGB were the same. I had just started my studies in Moscow when a Bulgarian dissident, a man named Georgi Markov, was murdered in London. He was jostled by a man holding an umbrella and developed a fever later that night. At first, no one believed him when he claimed he'd been poisoned. He died a few days later. Then a second Bulgarian dissident was bumped into in the Paris Metro and complained he'd been stung. When he developed a fever as well, he told his doctors about Markov's death and his suspicions. They examined him closely and found a ricin pellet buried under his skin. Both men were probably shot by an umbrella outfitted with an air compression chamber capable of firing a pellet the size of a pinhead without making a sound."

"And you think the KGB was responsible? But you say these victims were Bulgarians."

Garcia nodded. "It was definitely KGB technology that killed Markov. Russian scientists have always been creative. Look at Alexander Litvinenko. He was one of Putin's most outspoken critics. He was poisoned to death with radioactive polonium-210. Most of the world's supply is manufactured in Russia. I actually think the CIA got most of its ideas for how to kill Castro from the Russians. They even exchange personnel sometimes. The Russians had an officer from Fort Bragg working in their antiterrorist command centre the last time I was in Moscow. The problem, as I see it, is that the definition of *terrorist* changes, depending on one's perspective."

Apiro shuddered. Politics seemed to be a world of dangerously shifting alliances. Russians pretended to be Chechens; Special

Forces pretended to be terrorists; men sworn to serve their countries committed murders and were hailed as heroes; countries that were engaged in post–Cold War conflict shared personnel.

He had a feeling that the tattooed man who died on the Malecón had been caught in these cross-currents, that Russia and America were playing some kind of dangerous game. The idea flickered at the edge of his thoughts before he let it go. He was a man of science, not conjecture.

"We have reason to believe our shooting victim was a *vory*," Apiro said. "A leader in the Russian mafia. Do you know anything about them?"

"Only that they were at the top of the criminal ladder when the Soviet Union collapsed. They get intelligence and weapons, and sometimes training, from former KGB and FSB officers."

"That's incredible. I can't believe that Russian Special Forces officers would work with the mafia." But he recalled the dagger tattooed on Slava Kadun's neck, and the drops of blood below it, and wondered if Slava's explanation for them was the truth or a lie. "Did they ever find out who was behind Litvinenko's death, Dr. Garcia?"

"The British police identified the killer as a Russian spy, a man named Andrei Lugovoi, but Russia refused to deport him to face charges. And then a few months later, a second hit man was picked up on the cameras at Heathrow Airport on his way to kill Boris Berezovsky. He was identified only as Vladislav. He was intercepted on his way to Berezovsky's hotel and deported to Russia, but he was never charged."

"Why not?"

"Why would you expect the Russians to behave any differently than the CIA, Dr. Apiro? Look at Luis Posada. The Americans won't return him here for prosecution either." Garcia smiled. "Have you read Fabian's book yet?"

Fabian Escalante had been the head of Cuba's Department of State Security. He'd just published a book called *638 Ways to*

Kill Castro. It detailed the CIA's attempts to kill Fidel Castro with, among other things, exploding mollusk shells and poisoned pills and funguses and traitorous mistresses.

Apiro nodded. "I assumed it was fiction. Or at least embellished beyond belief."

"He didn't make up a single word," Garcia said. He reached for the thermos again. "It made me laugh, though, when Fabian described how he intercepted false identity papers sent by the CIA to one of their agents in Havana and got himself a new driver's licence."

45

As soon as Inspector Ramirez passed through the main pavilion's sliding glass doors, a woman handed him a flyer translated into different languages. The English text stated that in its twenty-fourth international fair, Cuba was showcasing the "autistic" qualities of its cultural journey. Ramirez smiled. He wasn't sure it was a typo.

Exhibitors wore blue lanyards with white tags. He recognized some as Cuban Intelligence officers. Special Brigade officers with black berets stood in small groups. Normally, they'd be keeping an eye out for the hustlers and pimps who might try to scam foreign visitors, but now they were on full alert, looking for someone who might be armed.

The hall was filled with hundreds of booths that lined the perimeter and formed rows down the middle. Throngs of Cubans strolled from exhibit to exhibit.

Two adolescent boys stared at a variety of new paintbrushes, saws, and grout spreaders as open-mouthed as if they were ogling teenage girls. A shiny metal ladder rested against a brand-new wheelbarrow. Displays of portable air conditioners were barricaded with yellow caution tape warning people to look but not touch. Guatemalan women chattered like bright parrots, wearing wide-brimmed hats and embroidered peasant blouses, and carrying hand-woven, colourful bags.

Chinese motorcycles, a booth of cosmetics, and boxes of medical supplies were crowded in the same space as a row of shiny new cars. Ramirez felt the way he had in Canada, overwhelmed by the vast display of consumer items.

A young girl sat at a plastic table drinking a soda, gazing off into the distance at products she could only dream of buying. General de Soto was right, Ramirez thought. We might as well be giving them that first euphoric rush of cocaine; they'll never experience quite the same high again.

He was surprised to find Mama Loa examining a display of Seiko watches. "I didn't expect to see you here," he said. He wondered how she'd managed to get to the fair. He couldn't imagine her hitchhiking, and she wasn't likely to have the fare even for one of the crowded but inexpensive buses restricted to Cubans. "I didn't think you'd be the type to be interested in new watches."

"Most of the watches people wear around here are so old, they can't tell time anyway. All they do is tell you what people think of themselves, and how they want other people to see them." She inclined her head to the display. "Maybe that's why people call them 'watches.'"

"Can I buy you a sandwich, Mama Loa? You look like you're wasting away."

She shook her head. "I don't have much of an appetite these days. I'm ninety-four years old. When the gods decide they want us, we have to accept that we don't have much time left."

Ramirez nodded slowly. A woman of Mama Loa's age was heading into her last days. He was fond of her, despite her eccentricities.

He hoped that when the day came, she would die comfortably, in her sleep.

"I was hoping I'd see you, Ramirez. My goddaughter's fixing to leave Cuba early tomorrow morning. I keep having the same dream, that she gets swallowed up by a whale."

"Are they leaving by boat?" That could be dangerous—most boats were old and lacked lifeboats, and the waters between Cuba and Florida were full of sharks.

"I don't know for sure. She say they'll be getting a ride around midnight at La Rampa to take them to their transportation. I know once she goes, I'll never see her again."

"Does she have a visa?"

"She don't even have a passport."

"I'll keep my ears open, Mama Loa. I'll see what I can do." He made a mental note to send a car to check on it later, once the threat to Castro was over.

She nodded, resigned. "Your grandmother come to see me again last night. She say, you tell Ricky to find himself a *babalao*. Maybe it's not too late. Maybe he can get his gift back from the gods. She say the dead is your gift, Ramirez. She say it's the dead that keeps you alive."

46

Inspector Ramirez watched Mama Loa walk away. He was unnerved, as always, by the way she seemed to see right through him. As she disappeared into the throngs of people browsing the stalls, he saw another elderly woman he recognized. She was standing in front of a poster of Cohiba cigars that were lined up like a row of cruise missiles.

"*Hola*, Nassara," said Ramirez, as he approached her. "What are you doing here?"

Nassara turned and smiled. "Remembering what capitalism looks like."

Nassara Nobika had been a Black Panther, one of a group of American revolutionaries that engaged in urban guerrilla warfare in the sixties. She was charged with shooting a policeman in the United States. As soon as she was released on bail, she hijacked a plane to Cuba.

Fidel Castro granted her asylum, as he did all the other leaders of the movement who requested it, but he made her serve two years first in a Cuban jail. Most of the other Black Panthers fled back to the U.S., appalled by the poor living conditions. Forty years later, very few of the original asylum seekers remained.

"You hear the news, Ramirez? The U.S. has increased the award for my capture to a million bucks. That's like, what, a hundred thousand dollars a pound?" She grinned. "I think I'm worth more, pound-for-pound, than *yeyo* is right now." Cocaine.

"I wouldn't say that so loudly," Ramirez cautioned. He held his finger to his lips. "There are people who might turn you in. I'm tempted to do so myself." He grinned. "But now that I see you, can I pick your brain for a few minutes?"

Nassara was more tuned in to international politics than anyone Ramirez knew. Her period of imprisonment had given her a wide array of contacts among dissidents, and her experience in guerrilla warfare made her a valuable resource to the revolutionary government.

She sometimes helped the Liberation Directorate at the training camps in the countryside; interacting with revolutionaries from other countries kept her connected to the outside world.

Another policeman would call her his *chivato*—his snitch—but Ramirez knew she would be offended by that notion. She preferred to think of herself as an elder stateswoman. No money ever changed hands, only street food and drinks: at sixty-eight, Nassara got by on a very small government pension.

"Sure. Let's go somewhere where we can talk a little more freely," she said. "You can buy me a nice cold beer."

There was a patio beside the front entry. A six-foot-high brown plastic Bucanero bottle beckoned them in. They chose a white table under a plastic umbrella. Nassara sat down, and Ramirez bought two beers and carried them to the table. He put them down and pulled over a plastic chair.

Nassara took a swig of hers. "Damn, that tastes good. I'd almost forgotten how good a cold beer is; my fridge has been crap for years. What do you want to know, Ramirez?"

He told her about the shooting on the Malecón. "The victim was Russian. He had a run-in with a Colombian warlord that turned out badly for both of them. There are rumours the Chechen mafia are in town. I wondered if you'd heard anything about that, or about the Russian mafia being here as well. Or maybe you know something about the Colombians that might be connected to this man's death. I see they have a pavilion again this year."

"I haven't heard anything about the Russians or the Chechens." She put the bottle down and lowered her voice again. "But I ran into some of my old friends from the Colombian National Liberation Army today. They said FARC has come up with some new way to move *yeyo*, but they didn't say what it is." FARC was the acronym for the Revolutionary Armed Forces of Colombia, a rebel group funded primarily by drug sales. "Have you been inside the Russian pavilion yet?"

Ramirez shook his head.

"It's not just GAZ vans and Automotriz cars on display, like usual. There are Soyuz rockets and a great big arms display by Rosoboronexport. Maybe FARC is going to trade cocaine for Russian rocket launchers. That would be one way to move *yeyo*, wouldn't it? By rocket launcher?" She laughed. "Honestly, nothing would surprise me. Pretty much all the Russians I've ever met were corrupt, and the rot starts right at the top. Vladimir Putin figured out early on what Black Panthers always knew—that the only way to get power is to take it. Not that any other politician is any different. And as much as I love him, that includes Fidel."

"Meaning?"

"Meaning maybe the shooting was political. Look at all the journalists in Russia who've been murdered or disappeared. Anna Politkovskaya was a pain in Putin's ass. She was shot to death on his birthday, in the elevator in her own apartment. That's quite a birthday gift, don't you think? But every country kills its dissidents if it can get away with it."

Ramirez raised his eyebrows.

"Don't be naive. You're talking to a woman with a bounty on her head." She gave him a look. "People have short memories." She finished her beer and put the empty bottle down. "Now it's your turn to share. What's wrong with Fidel?"

"I don't know, Nassara. I heard he had emergency intestinal surgery late last year. I know there was a Spanish surgeon who flew into Havana in December with some special equipment." Hector Apiro had been at the hospital the night the gastrointestinal specialist arrived.

"There's something awfully strange about all of this," Nassara said. "Sometimes I think he's already dead and the Party doesn't want anyone to know. Can you imagine if he was? The Americans would be here within a week, one way or another. And there'd be a helluva street party in Miami."

Ramirez agreed. According to *Granma*, thousands of ex-pat Cubans had danced in the streets of Miami when they heard Fidel Castro was ill. Their wild partying made even Fidel's strongest critics in Cuba uneasy. When Raúl assumed power, the armed forces and tens of thousands of reservists had been put on standby in case of another U.S. invasion.

"Do you think he'll step aside permanently?" Nassara asked. "Raúl isn't much younger than Fidel. I've heard some people say Major Diaz is next in line for the job. What do you think?"

Ramirez shrugged. "Your guess is as good as mine. I always assumed Raúl would take over for a while. But you're right, he's getting old too. I'm sure the Party is already thinking about who will succeed him."

"It's getting harder and harder to get good information these days," Nassara said. She looked at Ramirez, and frowned. "Your guys have been cracking down on satellite dishes again."

Satellite dishes had always been technically illegal, but the police had ignored them for years. The orders to seize them were issued just after Fidel Castro was hospitalized, now that Ramirez thought of it. Hundreds of them were immediately pulled off rooftops and concealed, tucked under floorboards like the typewriter in the movie he and Francesca had watched.

"I couldn't figure that one out, either," Nassara said. "Most people just watch the soap operas; they could give a shit about international news. Why take the dishes away? Makes you think maybe the Communist Party's afraid we might find something out about Fidel's illness. Something they don't want us to know."

47

Just before six, Inspector Ramirez saw Dan Yaworsky enter the main pavilion. Yaworsky made his way through the crowd and down a row of stalls displaying H. Uppman cigars, Italian pasta, and Pinocho crackers, then stopped before a table stacked with boxes of M&M candies. Ramirez followed him, trying to appear casual, knowing that Cuban Intelligence no doubt had eyes on their man. He sidled up to Yaworsky, keeping his voice low. "I need to talk to you, Señor. Let's be discreet about this, shall we?"

He led Yaworsky to a quiet corner stall, where they both pretended to be intrigued by a display of new kitchen faucets, pipe fittings, and plastic soap dishes.

"You are a very interesting man, Señor Yaworsky. I wanted to hold you on suspicion of murdering your wife. Instead, Major Diaz arranged for your release. You seem to be everywhere. I met with an American named Franklin Pearce today. He says you gave him some photographs, including one of him on a flight with Fidel Castro. I need to know where you got those pictures. Several people who were on the same flight have been murdered. One of them was your wife. Something happened on that flight; I'm trying to find out what it was before someone else is murdered."

Yaworsky blanched. "Yoani flew with Castro?"

"She was his flight attendant. You didn't know?"

"I didn't even know she worked for an airline. But you know I can't talk to you about any of this."

"I already know you work for Cuban Intelligence as well as the CIA, Señor. What I want to know is what you were doing for Major Diaz. I don't care about the espionage or intelligence; I only want to find the man who killed your wife. So far, all you've done is lie to me. Don't you want to find her murderer?"

"Of course I do. But I hadn't seen Yoani in years. I wasn't supposed to contact her. It was safer that way. I sent her money whenever I could." Yaworsky looked around the room. "You tell me exactly what happened to her and I'll tell you what I know."

"Someone broke her neck and staged her body so it looked like she fell down the stairs in her building. Another crew member from the same flight is in hospital in a coma: someone cut one of his car's brake lines. And their pilot died on the weekend of a mysterious illness. I might accept two of these deaths as coincidence, but not all three. Now, tell me, where did you get the photographs you gave Señor Pearce?"

"From the CIA. The head of Special Operations. They call him the Captain," Yaworsky whispered, keeping his eyes fixed on the candies. "He told me to give them to Franklin Pearce when I got to Cuba; I was supposed to let Pearce know the CIA was watching him. What were you doing talking to Pearce?"

Ramirez didn't answer. "I heard a tape yesterday in the minister's office that had your voice on it. You were speaking to another man about assassinating Raúl Castro. I was told that was the Captain too."

"That *was* the Captain. But how in God's name did you hear that?"

"The Russians were eavesdropping on your meeting. They sent an intelligence officer all the way here from Moscow to tell Cuban Intelligence what they overheard. He's already briefed the Minister of the Interior, the head of Cuban Intelligence, and Castro's security chief. I was at the meeting; that's where I heard the tape."

"That's not possible," Yaworsky said. "There were no bugs in that room—I swept it myself."

"Did you search the Captain too?"

"Of course not. He was my superior officer. He was outside while I did the sweep."

"Then he must have brought a transmitter in with him. He's the only person who could have. Unless you missed something."

Yaworsky thought back. The bottle of whisky. The Captain brought it in. It sat on the table between them. "Damn," he said. "But why would he do that?"

Ramirez shook his head. He didn't know. "Does he have any ties to Russia that you know of?"

"He was assigned to some kind of antiterrorist centre in Moscow before he came to Special Ops. Look," Yaworsky said, "I was assigned to Special Ops because the director there thought the Captain was up to something off-book."

"Meaning what?"

"Meaning something the U.S. government doesn't want anyone to know about. Something that isn't documented. Sometimes one part of the CIA does stuff that another part doesn't want to know about. You ever hear of plausible deniability? That's why Special Ops exists. But this time it was Special Ops that picked up chatter with the Colombians about something called Project Beluga. The director thought it might be connected with the drug trade, but it wasn't one of his projects. That was my file, okay? That's what I was supposed to be investigating: what the Captain was up to and who was behind it; if it was another part of the agency or if he'd gone rogue. I didn't know anything about this business with Raúl Castro until the Captain told me to meet him in that motel. I had no idea he'd bugged the room or that the Russians were listening.

"Oh, Christ," Yaworsky said, as the implications of his comments sunk in. "There's no way the Russians could have picked that up unless they knew where to look. That means the Captain isn't only working with the Colombians, he's working with the Russians, too. Jesus." He shook his head. "Listen, I better go before someone sees us talking. Franklin Pearce is supposed to introduce me to Ramón Castro tonight. There's security everywhere; I hope like hell they do their job."

"One more question. You said you sent your wife money. How much?"

"Over the years? I don't know. Thousands, I guess."

"In American dollars?"

"In the beginning, when you could exchange it for *kooks*, sure. But not for years. Why would I give her money she can't spend? Look, I have to go. We never had this discussion."

Yaworsky quickly disappeared into the pressing crowd.

Ramirez glanced at his watch. It was almost seven o'clock. He made his way to the front of the stage and looked around for Slava Kadun.

48

It was past his dinnertime, but Hector Apiro was still working in the lab, processing slides of tissue and fluids, trying to take his mind off Maria.

She hadn't come home the night before, and, while she sometimes stayed out overnight, it wasn't like her not to call. She hadn't returned any of the messages he left on her cell phone, either.

He'd walked down to the area near the Hotel Nacional where she sometimes looked for clients; he'd dropped by her favourite bars. No one had seen her.

Since there was nothing he could do, he tried to focus on his work, but in the back of his mind he worried that she was still angry with him.

He was examining the tissue samples he'd removed during Captain Acosta's autopsy. The external examination had revealed nothing remarkable except a small red lump on the pilot's shoulder that looked like an insect bite. Apiro had almost ignored it, and then thought it might merit further investigation. Captain Acosta had mentioned being stung in the airport. He could have had an extreme allergic reaction to an insect bite without displaying any of the usual clinical symptoms.

During the autopsy, when Apiro excised the lump, he found a tiny black speck. He'd placed it on a slide and protected it with a glass cover. Then he put it with all the other blood and tissue samples for examination later on. It could be a tick, or maybe an insect stinger. Or maybe nothing at all.

Other than that, nothing looked unusual. If the pilot hadn't died, he would have been in extremely good health. This was one of those cases in which there might never be a known cause. If he couldn't find a precise reason for the man's untimely demise, it would be noted on the death certificate as "other." Just as if Acosta had crashed his plane and his body was never recovered. It was code for, "We have absolutely no idea what the hell happened."

But more than a quarter of all major findings associated with causes of death were identified histologically from biopsies. On the other hand, sometimes results made no sense, like the trace amounts of barium sulfide Apiro had found in the carbonized edges of the wound on the tattooed man's temple.

Apiro put the slide with the black speck on the microscope's stage and looked through the eyepiece. He lowered the objective lens to tighten the focus, increasing the magnification until the rack stop prevented him from going any further. He watched the blurry image take shape before his eyes.

It was perfectly spherical, with what appeared to be a waxy coating. There was not a chance this was an insect stinger; whatever this was, it was man-made. For the first time all day, thoughts of Maria and where she'd gone were pushed from Apiro's mind. It was extraordinary.

As he examined the object, turning the slide this way and that, he thought about what Dr. Garcia had said about Georgi Markov.

Then he hopped off his stepladder and ran to the wall-mounted phone. He called Dr. Garcia and was relieved when the expert immediately answered.

"Dr. Garcia, do you know anything about the symptoms of ricin poisoning or how the Bulgarian scientists tested for it when Georgi Markov died?"

"I believe they worked with a British germ-warfare scientist. They injected a pig with ricin and followed the disease progression. It's always the same: an extremely high white blood cell count quickly followed by organ failure. No other poison has that effect, so it looks like a natural disease progression."

"*Gracias*," Apiro said. "That's very helpful."

He hung up the phone, his mind working rapidly.

Captain Acosta had been murdered. He'd been poisoned with a ricin pellet. Given the technology involved, and its links to the KGB, this death could very well be linked to the one on the Malecón.

Apiro's eyes widened as he realized the implications of the other information Garcia had shared with him earlier. He quickly dialed Ramirez's cell phone number, but there was no answer. He contacted the switchboard at police headquarters and asked if the inspector was in.

"I'm sorry, Dr. Apiro. Inspector Ramirez is away from the office. He checked in at the trade fair a few hours ago."

"Does he have his cell phone with him?"

"I think he's turned it off."

"Can you have a patrol car pick me up at the medical towers to take me there, Sophia? Tell them to hurry. It's urgent."

The patrol car dropped Hector Apiro off inside the gates of the ExpoCuba complex just as a convoy of black cars pulled up, powerful cars with ballistic-proof glass, reinforced bumpers, and dual foot controls in case the driver was injured.

Raúl Castro, thought Apiro, as he saw two extremely tall men get out of the lead car carrying briefcases that he guessed were really folding bulletproof shields. One of the bodyguards held a hand in the air, signalling to those inside the car that it was safe.

As soon as one of the bodyguards opened the passenger door, Raúl Castro stepped out. He was immediately flanked by his guards and blocked from Apiro's view. The other security officers pulled back, taking up positions around the line of cars.

Apiro hurried as quickly as his short legs would allow, stumbling as he made his way over the cracked pavement and up the stairs, but a row of security personnel kept him back. He couldn't enter the pavilion until Raúl Castro was safely inside.

As soon as Castro was escorted through the glass doors, Apiro was able to scuttle into the main pavilion. People were crowded shoulder to shoulder, with barely any room to move. Apiro looked for Ramirez, but he was too short to see much. He was hemmed in by people, all of them pushing towards the commander-in-chief. He elbowed his way to the front of the room, apologizing all the way, just as Raúl Castro, the small, Asian-looking brother of Fidel, began his ascent up the steps to the stage.

Apiro looked around anxiously for Ramirez, knowing that this was where he'd likely be. Then he saw him, standing to the left of the stage beside General de Soto. Slava Kadun stood a few feet to the right.

Apiro pushed forward, shouting Ramirez's name, trying desperately to get his attention, but his cries were swallowed up by the crush of people eager to catch a glimpse of the acting president.

Ramirez was standing beside General de Soto, his arms folded, alert, trying to keep an eye on the activity in the room.

He heard wild cheering and applause as Raúl Castro entered the building. He caught a glimpse of the acting president as he made his way towards the stage. He saw Franklin Pearce chatting with the Roman Catholic cardinal and Ramón Castro, then watched Danila Yaworsky approach the three men, holding his camera. He saw Pearce introduce Yaworsky to the group. They all shook hands and laughed while Yaworsky took their pictures. Then Yaworsky handed his camera to Pearce, and Pearce took pictures of Yaworsky with Ramón Castro, Castro's arm wrapped around Yaworsky's shoulders.

Ramirez was surprised when Hector Apiro materialized beside him and tugged on his jacket. "It was a ricin pellet that killed the pilot, Ricardo," Apiro said, shouting to be heard above the clamour.

Ramirez bent over. "It was a what?"

"Ricin. It's a deadly poison made from castor beans. The KGB used it to murder a Bulgarian dissident in the late 1970s. I found the remains of a ricin pellet in Captain Acosta's body. The wax coating hadn't completely dissolved when I looked at it under the microscope." Apiro tried to catch his breath. "Back in the seventies, the KGB adapted an umbrella with a compression chamber to fire ricin pellets, but that was a long time ago."

"An umbrella?" said Ramirez. Something nagged at him, something he should remember.

"The technology would be even better now," Apiro said urgently. "The delivery mechanisms would be even smaller. Dr. Garcia reminded me that a Russian dissident, Alexander Litvinenko, was murdered in London with polonium-210. He said an attempt was made on Boris Berezovsky's life that same year by a Russian hit man named Vladislav. The British thought he was Chechen, but the FSB pose as Chechens all the time. Ricardo, I know there are other names like this as well, but the diminutive of Vladislav is Slava. Someone transporting radioactive materials like polonium-210 is exposed to them. Slava told me he was radioactive; he used to set off airport scanners. He explained it by saying he had been near Chernobyl, but he could have been lying."

"You think Slava was sent here by the CIA to kill Castro? But why?" said Ramirez. Slava Kadun was with the Russian Special Forces, not the CIA—he'd been sent to warn them about the plot.

"I can't tell you what I know because of doctor–patient privilege, but believe me, Slava could be the killer."

Ramirez's breath caught. If Apiro was right, he'd let Slava in the door himself. Like a Trojan horse.

49

Slava Kadun was in a state of hypervigilance, his body tense. Seconds expanded in moments like this; time stopped as the senses quickened with the adrenalin that rushed through his veins.

He could hear each individual heartbeat thump against his chest, could feel the blood pulsing in his arteries, almost hear the tap-tap-tapping of a vein in his forehead. Other sounds were distorted, slowed down.

He saw a man in a cowboy hat introduce Ramón Castro and a Catholic priest to a man holding a camera. He watched the three men shake hands and pose for pictures. Ramón Castro patted the man with the camera on the shoulder and then climbed the stairs to the stage with the man in the cowboy hat; they sat down on a row of metal chairs behind the podium with a group of other businessmen. Resting on a podium in front of them was a small bronze statue of a rodeo rider on a bull; the award, he guessed, that would be presented to Ramón Castro.

He saw the crowd part to make way for the acting president. Raúl Castro inched slowly forward as Castro's bodyguards, flanked by security, cleared a path.

The crowd clapped frantically as Castro ascended the stage with Major Rodriguez and Major Diaz. The acting president raised his hand slightly and waved to the crowd.

The men seated on the stage stood to applaud. One moved his right hand slightly towards his left wrist. He wore a watch, but with the face on the inside of his wrist, the way policemen around the world wear their watches.

Slava knew instinctively that the man was reaching for the watch's crown. It took Slava less than a seventeenth of a second to process that information—the speed measured by Russian scientists when they monitored his reflexes during training—as his synapses fired.

The watch that Dmitri had assigned to Slava for his previous mission had a radio transmitter that was activated by pulling out the crown. Those radio transmissions could be used to trigger explosives.

Slava knew in that instant that the man with the watch was activating a transmitter, although he wouldn't have been able to explain how. It was the sum of years of training to become a killer, of training others to become killers, and the experience and knowledge that came from putting that training into practice.

He lunged through the people in front of him, knocking them sideways like skittles. He leapt onto the stage and launched himself at the man with the watch, pushing Diaz and another man off the platform. All three hit the floor hard. People screamed. Raúl Castro's bodyguards rushed to pull Castro to safety.

There was the sound of a blast and something hit Slava's chest like a jackhammer.

How could the explosives have gone off without a detonator? He felt light-headed, the way he had moments after Alexei Kazakov, the Russian light heavyweight champion, punched him below the kidneys and almost killed him.

He smelled the sharp tang of cordite, and realized he'd been shot. He dipped his chin to look at his chest but saw nothing—no blood, no wound.

His hand slipped from the man's wrists as his arms lost their strength and his fingers turned to ice.

What the fuck? thought Slava. Then everything went black.

50

Two men hustled Raúl Castro off the stage as others shielded Ramón Castro with their bodies. The crowd surged towards the exit, almost knocking Ramirez over. Policemen were shouting, pulling out their batons, trying to regain order. Ramirez wasn't sure who was shot or who had fired their weapon. He pushed through the people in front of him to see Slava Kadun lying on his back on the ground. The foot patrolman Pacheco stood over him, a wisp of smoke trailing from the muzzle of his gun.

"Don't shoot, don't shoot," Ramirez shouted at the dozen or so policemen who had their weapons aimed at Slava Kadun's head. "He's already down."

Officer Pacheco was looking at his right hand—still gripping the gun—as if it belonged to someone else. Ramirez realized he had no recollection of pulling his weapon; he'd unholstered it instinctively. He was holding it so tightly his knuckles were white; he had to use his other hand to pry his fingers free. He slowly put the gun back in his shoulder holster and splayed his fingers to get the blood moving.

Hector Apiro ran forward as another *policía* tried to roll Slava Kadun over to put him in handcuffs.

"Don't do that," he said urgently. "He needs medical attention."

Apiro ripped the Russian's shirt off and unfastened his Kevlar vest. He got down on his knees, punched Kadun's chest as hard as he could with a closed fist, then initiated chest compressions. He kept at it until a team of paramedics managed to press its way through the crowd and took over.

"It's *commotio cordis*," Apiro shouted at them. "We need a defibrillator. He's in cardiac arrest."

Ramirez shook his head, trying to clear his ears of the sound of the shot. His ears were ringing as if someone had placed a metal box over his head.

"Are you all right?" he said to Pacheco. The boy had doubled over as if he was going to throw up. "It's not easy to shoot a man. It's okay to feel sick."

General de Soto joined them. "I'm going to have a patrol car take you to police headquarters, Officer Pacheco," he said, placing his hand firmly on the young man's back. "The attorney general is going to want a written statement. You may not get home until late. Do you want me to call your wife?"

"I'm not married," Pacheco said, trying to catch his breath.

General de Soto motioned to a patrolman and instructed him to take Pacheco to headquarters. "I can't believe he planned to kill the acting president with his bare hands," he said to Ramirez. "And from what I've heard about *spetsnaz*, he could do it. And we're the ones who gave him access."

"But I don't understand," said Ramirez. "Why would the Russians want Raúl Castro dead? Or is Slava some kind of dual agent, working for the CIA as well?"

General de Soto frowned. "We'll have to leave that to Cuban Intelligence to find out. I'm sure Major Diaz is already on the phone to Nikolai Patrushev demanding answers."

"How is Señor Pearce?" Ramirez asked. Pearce had been pushed off the front of the stage in the fracas.

The general smiled. "If Señor Pearce hadn't blocked his way, Kadun might have reached the acting president. I'm sure he'll be fine. A little bruised. I wouldn't be surprised if Raúl names him a hero of the revolution. Pacheco, too. That young man is on his way up the ladder. It won't be long before we'll be reporting to him."

Danila Yaworsky was standing by the stage, stunned. He'd watched a muscular bald man in a Russian uniform leap onto the stage and head directly for Raúl Castro. Two men started wrestling with him and all three fell off the stage, then a young patrolman shot the Russian point-blank in the chest.

And suddenly a dwarf in a white lab coat had appeared out of nowhere and started pounding on the Russian's chest, yelling something about cardiac arrest. What the fuck? It was like watching a bizarre action movie.

"He's a Russian intelligence officer," he overheard the dwarf tell the paramedics. "His name is Slava Kadun."

Yaworsky tried to make sense of what had just happened.

The Russian had to be the Captain's undercover operative, but talk about a frontal attack. Was he really a Russian intelligence officer, or was he just posing as one?

Despite himself, Yaworsky was impressed. It was the kind of thing where you could have all the sniffer dogs and policemen in the world on hand and not be able to prevent it.

But that was the easiest way to launch an attack, wasn't it?

Directly and simply, the way a few men armed with box cutters hijacked a plane and brought the United States to its knees.

Then he remembered his assignment.

As he had throughout the night, he pulled out his digital camera and started taking pictures.

51

There was a meeting place on the Malecón near the Hotel Nacional, just below La Rampa. It was a cruising spot for gay tourists, a safe area for male and transgendered prostitutes to wait for clients.

It was just before midnight. Maria Vasquez was standing in the dark, waiting for the *extranjero* who had booked quality time with her online, when one of the girls beside her, Nevara, squealed, "There's our bus!"

A GAZ van with diplomatic plates pulled onto La Rampa.

"What bus?" Maria said. "Where are you going?"

"We're leaving the island, remember? We're going to Europe to work for that Russian. Tonight's the big night."

"Where are your bags?"

"He said to pack light," Nevara said excitedly. "I don't own anything much anyway, so that part was easy. He said we'll have new shoes, new purses, and new clothing when we arrive. We'll be working in a nightclub. We're going to be escorts and hostesses. We'll be classy ladies."

"Are they taking you to the airport?"

"I think so," the girl frowned.

"Do you have a passport?"

"He told me I didn't need one. He said he would take care of it."

"What about exit permits?" said Maria.

Nevara shook her head.

"Did he at least tell you where you're going?"

"Moscow to start. I went to the embassy yesterday to apply for the visa."

"How can you get a visa without a passport?"

Nevara shrugged. "I don't know. I filled out the forms. What difference does it make? Come with us, Maria. We'll have fun."

"I can't. I have a boyfriend," Maria said, but she was worried. No one could get a legal visa without a passport. Exit permits took months to obtain and cost a lot of money. Hector had been right.

She felt terrible. She'd been annoyed with him because of her stupid sensitivity about what she was and what she did, when he was the only man she'd ever known who didn't care about those things.

"I don't like it, Nevara. You have no idea what you could be getting into. They could be taking you anywhere. You could end up as someone's sex slave."

The driver stepped out with a clipboard and stood in the shadows away from the lamppost, marking off from a list the names of the girls who ran over with their bags.

"You worry too much," Nevara said. "Look at the consular plates on the van. I told you, the Russian embassy is involved. So everything must be legal, right? But you know how much I'll miss you."

Maria walked up to the van with Nevara, her uneasiness mounting. Five other girls were ahead of them; they got on, chatting excitedly. The driver came to the last of the names, looked at Maria, and asked, "Are you Yoani Ravela?"

"I'll get on the van with you, Nevara," Maria whispered to her friend. "But only because I want to make sure you are going to be safe. I'll take a cab home from the airport."

"Yoani Ravela?" the driver said again.

"Yes, that's me," Maria said with a sharp intake of breath, and stepped into the van, swallowing her misgivings.

52

Inspector Ramirez was back in his office, waiting for news. Natasha Delgado had brought him a hot cup of bitter coffee. He felt almost paralyzed with shock. Slava Kadun—someone he liked, someone he'd exchanged jokes with—was an assassin?

His phone rang. It was Apiro. "I'm in Emergency. I thought you'd want to know: Slava's going to be all right."

"Did he have surgery? Did they take out the bullet?"

"There was no bullet, Ricardo. He was wearing a Kevlar vest. It stopped the bullet from penetrating his heart, but it diffused the impact across the precordium, so it was like being hit by a train. The blunt trauma sent an electrical charge to his heart and shut it down. It takes only milliseconds after ventral fibrillation is induced. It's very rare: the impact has to occur at a precise moment in the cardiac cycle when the T wave is ascending and the ventricular myocardium is relaxing, so there's about a one per cent chance of something like this happening. But the heart is more vulnerable when it's strained; that's why this injury is most commonly seen in athletes."

Ramirez thought about the absence of any blood, the bizarre spectacle of seeing Apiro hammering on Slava's broad chest. "Why were you punching him?"

"It was a precordial thump. I was trying to revive his heart. Luckily, the paramedic team was close by; if they hadn't had a defibrillator, he would have died within minutes. *Commotio cordis* is usually fatal."

"They only had a medical team there because of Raúl."

"Well, then, Slava's a lucky man. Well, except for the getting shot part. He suffered what is considered a sudden cardiac death, but no brain damage. The defibrillator essentially brought him back to life. He's sleeping now. When he wakes up, he'll need to be evaluated with an EKG and an echocardiogram. But we don't have a lot of data on recovery from this kind of event, since the vast majority of victims die. I'm supposed to tell the guards when he's awake and well enough to answer questions, and then someone from Cuban Intelligence will come to the hospital to question him. Probably Major Diaz himself."

"Do me a favour, will you? Buy me some time. I need to talk to him first."

"Is that even allowed, Ricardo? He's under arrest."

"I have to see him, Hector. I have to know why he did this and if he was involved with the other murders too. Once Cuban Intelligence gets their hands on him, we'll never see him again. We'll never find out what really happened."

"All right. I'll do what I can." Apiro hesitated. "Ricardo, I'm not sure if this is an appropriate time to raise this, but I'm worried about Maria. I haven't been able to reach her all night. She's not answering her cell phone. We had a fight yesterday; she went off to work angry and didn't come home."

"I'm sure she'll get over it. Francesca and I fight all the time; these things pass quickly."

"But she said tonight is the night some of the girls are leaving the island to go to work for that Russian who offered them all that money. What if she's decided to go with them?"

Ramirez realized he hadn't had a chance to bring Apiro up to date. "I don't think you have anything to worry about, Hector. The man who made those promises was a Russian named Fedor Petrov. He's the tattooed man in your morgue. He's not going anywhere."

Natasha Delgado poked her head through the doorway and waved to catch his attention.

"Listen, Hector, I have to go," Ramirez said, nodding to Delgado. "But call me as soon as you have news about Slava. And don't worry about Maria. I'm sure she'll come home."

"You were right about Slava Kadun, Inspector," Natasha Delgado said. "Customs just got back to me. He lied—it wasn't his first trip to Havana. He arrived here last Friday and returned to Moscow on the Sunday evening flight, then flew back to Havana the following day. Which means he was in Havana when Fedor Petrov was murdered. It's circumstantial, I know, but that makes him our best suspect. Although maybe it doesn't matter, after what happened tonight at the trade fair."

Ramirez shook his head, confused. "I can maybe understand why Slava would kill Fedor Petrov. Apiro says that Russian Special Forces are often ordered to assassinate people who are considered enemies of the state. But I don't understand why he'd try to kill Raúl Castro. In a room full of security? That's a suicide mission."

"He's a soldier," Delgado said. "I'm sure he was acting on orders. There are probably politics at play that we'll never know about. Officer Pacheco did the right thing, Inspector. He saved the acting president's life. Tonight, he's a big hero, although no one will ever read about it in *Granma*. I only wish I'd been there to pull the trigger myself. I could use the promotion." She smiled. "Will Kadun be charged with attempted murder?"

"Possibly. But it's weak. He never got that close to Castro; Franklin Pearce made sure of that. I think the most we have at the moment is assault." Ramirez thought for a moment. "He'll probably end up being deported back to Russia. Unless we can prove he killed Fedor Petrov. Do me a favour, will you, Natasha?" He pointed to the exhibit bag on his desk that contained the book he'd removed from Ruslan Dudayev's room at the Hotel Nacional. "There may be fingerprints on the cover of that. Compare them to the ones we got from Interpol for Petrov. I think Ruslan Dudayev and Fedor Petrov may be one and the same person. Petrov's nickname was Cheetah."

"Happy to, Inspector. That shouldn't take long."

She closed the door, leaving him alone to brood. Natasha might be certain of Slava's guilt, thought Ramirez, but he wasn't convinced. Why would Slava warn Cuban authorities about a CIA assassination plot if he himself was the assassin?

And running at Castro that way. It was as if he was some kind of suicide bomber—a "Black Widow"—but without a bomb strapped to his chest.

What he'd done defied common sense. It was destined to get him killed, and almost had. If Russian scientists were so creative, surely they could have come up with a better weapon than an unarmed man. After all, they'd developed an umbrella to kill a Bulgarian.

That recollection nagged at him, but it slipped through his fingers like sand. He found himself trying to hold back a yawn.

Why would Slava leave Havana only to come back again so quickly?

But maybe he didn't plan to come back. Natasha could be right. Maybe he had no choice; perhaps he was sent to do a job by his superiors.

Then, what job? To tell Cuban authorities about a CIA assassination plot, as he claimed, and as Danila Yaworsky had confirmed, or to kill Raúl Castro and end any possible chance of a rapprochement with Russia?

A few minutes later, Detective Delgado poked her head through the doorway again. She handed him the exhibit bag with the book. "The fingerprints match—you were right. Fedor Petrov and Ruslan Dudayev are the same person. What does that mean?"

"I don't know," said Ramirez. "But I'm going to find out."

"I'm at the end of my shift. It's after midnight. Do you want me to stay a little longer to work on this? I don't mind."

"No need, Natasha," said Ramirez. "Go on home. Get some sleep."

"Well, call me if you need me. You have my number."

He smiled at the detective. "I will. *Gracias.*"

After she left, Ramirez patted his pockets, looking for his cigar, and found the other item he'd bagged in Petrov's hotel room—the piece of paper with the columns of numbers. What were they?

Ramirez took a deep breath and tried to organize his thoughts. He was exhausted, but still too wired from adrenalin to go home. He knew he'd only be awake all night, tossing and turning, thinking about Slava's attack on Castro.

Slava Kadun came to Havana; Slava Kadun flew home. It was like a child's nursery rhyme. And then Slava came back to Havana with a letter of introduction and a tape recording of a conversation that made it virtually certain almost every policeman in Havana would be at the trade fair.

Ramirez sat up straight. What if it wasn't an assassination attempt at all? What if the whole thing was intended as a diversion, a way of focusing police attention on the fair so that another crime could take place somewhere else?

Fedor Petrov had come to Cuba under a false name, pretending to be a member of the Chechen mafia. There was a Russian man in town offering ten thousand dollars to *jineteras* to go to work for him in Europe. It had to be Petrov, thought Ramirez, posing as Dudayev, perhaps so the Colombians wouldn't find him.

Petrov had come to Havana to buy women. But how was he

going to get them off the island? You could put people on a boat and get them as far as Florida, but it was risky. Apart from all the other dangers, Cuban boats were old and unreliable. If they didn't sink by themselves, they were often sunk by the Cuban Coast Guard, even after they made it into international waters.

There had to be a boat capable of taking them farther away—a freighter perhaps, or one of the Russian factory fishing ships.

But even if they made it onboard, the women still needed proper papers if they were going to enter another country, and visas if they were going to work legally, wherever they ended up.

Petrov had owned nightclubs; that's where he sold sexual services. He wasn't the type to lock a woman up in an apartment somewhere as a sex slave: he considered himself a businessman, an entrepreneur.

Ramirez looked again at the columns of numbers, but they still had no content. He knew he was close to something important, to a solution, but it was just beyond his reach.

He glanced at his watch. It was almost one. Francesca was going to be angry whether he came home now or stayed at work all night, but once he told her about the attack on Raúl Castro, she'd understand.

He stood up and pulled on his jacket and put the exhibit bag with the paper in his pocket. He needed some fresh air, so he could think straight.

Then the phone on his desk rang. It was Hector Apiro. Slava Kadun was awake.

53

The thing about a hospital, thought Inspector Ramirez, as he walked through the emergency room doors, was that it didn't matter what time of day or night it was, the atmosphere was always the same.

A police station became quieter at this time of night; it had a reduced staff and few visitors. But at a hospital, nurses and doctors and interns and residents and cleaning staff all bustled about doing their jobs as if it were the middle of the day.

To a bored policeman on night shift, a hospital was the place to go for lunch, which was what policemen all over the world called all their meals, regardless of when they ate them. In a hospital cafeteria, a policeman could have a conversation with someone who was sober and awake and understood what it was like to have to work at two in the morning. If he was lucky, that person might be a pretty nurse or a sympathetic clerk.

Francesca had been a hospital social worker. She and Ramirez had met at the Hospital Hermanos Ameijeiras, when Ramirez brought in a sexual assault victim and asked the emergency doctor to do a rape kit. Afterwards, Francesca was assigned to the patient. She was compassionate but firm, and Ramirez was impressed when she told him she didn't care if he was PNR, he'd have to wait until the patient was ready before he could question her.

"She's been beaten and raped, and then poked and prodded by a nurse and a doctor," she said. "She's been violated in the most intensely personal way you could ever imagine. Right now, she needs a hug and a cup of something nice and hot and a good long cry; she doesn't need to be cross-examined by a policeman, however charming he might be. Your investigation will have to wait, Detective Ramirez."

Ramirez remembered the pointed way she'd said "charming," so that he wasn't sure if he'd been complimented or insulted. And the way she'd said his name.

He'd been intrigued.

Francesca wouldn't approve of him cross-examining a man who'd almost died, either. But Ramirez had questions for Slava Kadun, and he wanted them answered, and he wanted them answered now.

———

Ramirez showed his badge to the uniformed *policía* at the door and walked into the hospital room. Slava Kadun was lying on a metal bed, hooked up to some kind of monitoring equipment. A giant purple bruise sprawled across his broad, muscular chest.

"What?" Slava said, when he saw who it was. He scowled, and sat up, wincing. "You come to finish me off?"

"I want to find out the truth."

Slava looked at him and raised an eyebrow. "Truth? They shot wrong fucking guy. There was guy on stage with detonator; I tried to stop him from blowing up building."

"There were no explosives in the building. The sniffing dogs went through it."

"I know what I saw."

"Which man on the stage?"

Slava shrugged. "I don't know guy's name. He was sitting on chair on stage. Older guy with suit. Check your cameras."

They were all older men on the stage. They were all businessmen, and they were all wearing suits.

"Why did you lie when you said you'd never been to Havana before?" Ramirez said. "We checked with Customs. You flew into Havana on Friday and flew back to Moscow on Sunday night."

Slava shook his head. "Is my first trip to Cuba. Believe me, will be my fucking last. I fly here Monday, first time ever."

Ramirez thought for a minute. What if Natasha's information was wrong? What if the flight data was disinformation and Slava Kadun was telling the truth? What if someone had tried to detonate explosives and Pacheco had shot the wrong man? That was a lot of what ifs, and he didn't like it. But Slava's denial seemed genuine.

He opened his cell phone and dialed the switchboard at police headquarters. "Get hold of Detective Delgado for me, will you, Sophia?" He hoped Natasha had gone straight home. She was single; she could be anywhere.

When Delgado answered, she sounded sleepy. "Inspector Ramirez? ¿Que volá?" What's up?

"Sorry, Natasha. You did say I could call if I needed help, and I do. I want you to call your contact at Customs. If he's not working, wake him up. Tell him it's connected with an attempt on Raúl Castro's life; he'll understand we need the information urgently. I need you to check out the photographs from the surveillance cameras at the airport and make sure that the Slava Kadun who flew out of Havana on Sunday night is the same man who came back on Monday."

"You think he might not be?"

"It's possible." He heard her whisper something to whomever she was sleeping with. "Then I need you to sweet-talk Lieutenant

Ortiz into giving you a copy of the security videotapes from the trade fair, from whichever cameras would have filmed the attack. Tell him Major Diaz says we need them."

"Did he?"

"No. You'll need to be creative."

She sighed. "I'll see what I can do. I have to get dressed. I'll get someone from Patrol to take me to the airport. But you'll owe me."

Ramirez smiled. "I already do." He snapped the cell phone shut.

Slava Kadun looked at him. "So now you believe me?"

"Not yet," Ramirez said. "But I'm trying to keep an open mind. Cuban Intelligence is going to be here soon to question you. If you want me to establish your innocence, you have to help me prove it. That man with the tattoos in the morgue—his real name is Fedor Petrov. There's a Canadian warrant out for his arrest for sex trafficking. We know he was a drug smuggler and a pimp. He was registered at the Hotel Nacional as Ruslan Dudayev, a Chechen warlord. There are rumours all around town that a Russian was in town offering women a lot of money to go to Europe to work for him. I'm assuming it was him. Who was Fedor Petrov really? I need to know the truth. And quickly. We don't have much time."

Slava took a deep breath and sat up straighter in the bed. He winced as the pain shot down his chest.

"Fedor is kid I grew up with in Odessa. He always wanted to be big shot. Guys like that, they did very well when Soviet Union collapsed. If they got sent to jail, they were happy—there were lots of oligarchs to make connections with. He left Russia for U.S. and we lost touch. Then he got arrested by the Americans. The DEA cut deal. They sent him back to Moscow to serve his time in Russian prison. I ran into him when I am working undercover."

Slava thought back to how he'd discovered Fedor was in the jail. He was working out in his cell, doing one-armed push-ups, when he heard someone screaming. He ran down the hall and found two big Russian cons holding Fedor Petrov spread-eagled on his back in one of the tattoo artists' cells.

"You want to have sex with men?" one said. "Then you need to wear a sign on your belly, so everyone know you're a fucking queer. Then you'll get as much sex as you can handle, trust me."

They were going to have the tattoo artist ink eyes on Fedor's stomach, on either side of his penis. That would turn his lower abdomen into a kind of permanent face, the way homosexuals were identified in Russian prisons. Fedor was screaming and fighting to get free. Slava didn't blame him; not only would he be raped by anyone who felt like it once he was tattooed, but even looking another prisoner in the eye could get him shanked.

"You think he's queer?" Slava said, leaning against the bars. "You're fucking crazy. I know him, he's from my hometown. I've been out with him to the nightclubs. We've picked up women together. Believe me, he fucks women; he doesn't fuck men." Slava grinned. "But he's like a fucking cheetah when he climbs on. He goes fast, but not for long."

"He was going to fuck Josef Shokoloff in the showers," said one man, looking up. "He put his hand on Josef's cock."

"Josef tells lies to make himself big," Slava said. "He probably wishes someone would hold his prick. Not even a queer would fuck Josef. He probably gets hard telling you that story."

The other man laughed. Josef Shokoloff was small and old and wizened like a prune. He was a manipulator, serving time for drugs. The men let Fedor go but, after that, he had a new nickname. It was one he didn't like but reluctantly accepted and eventually embraced—Cheetah.

Cheetah started coming to Slava's cell to talk. Slava thought maybe he had some kind of crush on him; since they were kids, he'd known that Cheetah was gay. The first time he came into Slava's cell, Slava told him to keep his fucking hands to himself.

"I know he was arrested for trying to sell a Russian submarine to the Colombians," Ramirez said. "But the Colombians never got it. He testified against his Colombian contact in exchange for a reduced sentence. The Canadian police say the Colombians were out to get him."

Slava nodded. "He was very pissed off, that Colombian guy. That's why Cheetah wanted to serve his sentence in Russia. He thought he would be safer in jail. He was right."

It made sense to Ramirez that Petrov hid out in his Havana hotel, pretending to be a Chechen warlord to avoid detection. The deception might have worked if he hadn't been murdered.

"If you didn't kill him, who did?"

"Maybe Colombians found out he is here. That Colombian guy has motive."

"Why didn't you tell us you knew who he was when you saw him in the morgue?"

Ramirez's cell phone rang before Slava could answer. It was Natasha Delgado.

"I'm at Customs now," she said, yawning. "They've pulled the photographs for me. The Slava Kadun who flew out on Sunday had dark hair and steel teeth and looks totally different from the Slava Kadun who flew in on Monday. What's going on? What do you want me to do with the photographs?"

"I'm not sure yet, but leave them in my office," said Ramirez. "And get me those tapes from the trade fair as soon as you can, will you?"

"I'm on it," she said and disconnected.

Ramirez looked at Kadun, his last question forgotten. "Another man used your name to get through Customs on Friday. I'll have the photographs of him soon. Whoever it was, he probably posed as an American—William Tattenbaum—to rent the car he used the day he killed Petrov. Does that name ring any bells with you?"

Slava shook his head. "Nothing."

Ramirez held out the exhibit bag that contained the paper he'd found in Petrov's room. "I found this in his hotel room. Any idea what it is?"

Slava examined it slowly. "Looks like could be coordinates from radio navigation system called Alpha. Is used for underwater navigation by Russian submarines. But it only works maximum ten thousand kilometres from master station in Russia."

Ramirez thought of the diamond embedded in the centre of El Capitolio, and the distances marked on the floor to places around the world. Havana was nine thousand eight hundred kilometres from Moscow. It was just within the range.

"That audiotape you played in the minister's office. The agent the CIA sent to Havana to verify the hit on Raúl Castro is a man named Danila Yaworsky. He works for Cuban Intelligence. He told me the other man on the tape is known as the Captain because he was a submariner. Somehow, these things are connected."

Slava shrugged. "Maybe Cheetah was trying to buy another submarine."

"Where would he get the money?"

"I don't know. Maybe from CIA. I think we need to talk to this Yaworsky guy to find out what he knows."

"We?" said Ramirez. "Your heart stopped working a few hours ago. You're in police custody, under arrest. There's an armed guard outside your door."

"You take care of that problem; I take care of myself," said Slava. He grimaced as he swung himself out of the hospital bed.

When it came to Slava Kadun, Ramirez knew he'd lost all objectivity. But if he didn't help the Russian, it would be like turning Dreyman and his typewriter over to the Stasi. Ramirez only hoped he wouldn't end up like Wiesler, spending the rest of his police career steaming open envelopes. "Get dressed," he finally said as he made his decision. "Wait here."

Ramirez let himself out of the hospital room. He nodded to the policeman standing guard and looked around for Hector Apiro. The small doctor was pacing back and forth along the stained corridor. "I still can't reach her, Ricardo," he said. "She's not answering her phone. This isn't like her at all."

"She might be in trouble, Hector," Ramirez said, keeping his voice low. "It's a long story, but if we're going to find her, I need to get Slava out of here."

Apiro stopped and widened his eyes. "He shouldn't be moved, Ricardo; he just had a sudden cardiac arrest."

"I know that. But Maria could be in danger. Those women, the *jineteras* who think they're leaving for Eastern Europe, may soon be in the hands of Colombian drug lords. There's no time to explain."

"But where are they, Ricardo? What's going on?"

"I don't know yet. But I think Slava can help us find them and get them back. Tell the guards his condition has taken a turn for the worse and that you have to take him to surgery."

"You're sure about this?"

Ramirez nodded. "Yes."

"Then I'll do my best to buy you a few hours. Luckily, without a central computerized system in this hospital, patients get lost all the time. But I'll need him back. And whatever you do, don't let him overexert himself. He shouldn't be stressed. His heart needs a chance to rest."

———

Hector Apiro told the policeman on guard that he was going inside to check on his patient. When the big man was finished putting his clothes on, Apiro told him to lie down. Then he covered him to the neck with an old faded sheet. "Try not to breathe," he said to Slava. "Keep your eyes closed. I need you to look like you're dying."

Apiro took a deep breath of his own and pulled the door open. He walked into the corridor as calmly as he could. "We need to get this man to surgery immediately," he said firmly to the guard. He turned to Ramirez. "He has a clot; he could die. Inspector Ramirez, help me move the gurney to the elevator. There's no time to wait for nursing staff, it's a Code One emergency."

The *policía* jumped to his feet. "I'll help."

"You'd better stay here," Ramirez told him. "If Major Diaz comes to see the prisoner, someone needs to tell him what's going on. You can't abandon your post. *No está autorizado.*"

The policeman nodded, confused. He watched them race the gurney down the hall to the elevators, a worried look on his face.

54

Slava Kadun climbed into the back seat of Ramirez's small car, and Ramirez drove as quickly as he could to the Hotel Sevilla. "There are cameras everywhere," Ramirez said. "Keep your head down."

They took the stairs to avoid surveillance cameras in the lobby and inched their way quietly down the hall to Danila Yaworsky's hotel room.

Slava stood on one side of the doorway, Ramirez on the other. Ramirez knocked softly on the door.

Yaworsky opened it. He was still dressed, but his shirt was unbuttoned; Ramirez guessed his air conditioner had yet to be repaired. His hair was tousled.

Yaworsky looked surprised when he saw who it was. "Isn't he supposed to be under arrest?" he said, gesturing to Slava Kadun.

Ramirez pushed his way through the door, Slava close behind.

"We don't have much time," Ramirez said. "I think your wife was killed because she knew about a plan to move women out of

Havana for the Eastern European sex trade. I think she may have told the people she crewed with about it. Now they're all dead."

Yaworsky widened his eyes.

Ramirez continued. "You told me the CIA thinks the Captain is doing some kind of side deal with the Colombians. There was a Russian murdered in Havana on the weekend. His name was Fedor Petrov, although he was using the name Ruslan Dudayev. He tried to sell a decommissioned Russian submarine to the Colombians a few years ago. I think he was here to arrange another deal. Is that the kind of thing the Captain could be involved in? Could that be Project Beluga?"

"I don't know," Yaworsky said. "I guess it's possible."

"Beluga is experimental Russian SSA diesel-electric submarine," Slava said. "There was only one that was operational. It was put in dry dock in late 1990s, in shipyard in Murmansk."

Mama Loa had a dream, Ramirez remembered: she saw her god-daughter being swallowed up by a whale. A beluga was a whale.

"That has to be it," Ramirez said. "If I'm right, Fedor Petrov was the middleman in the transaction. I think he worked a deal with the Colombians to use the submarine to get Cuban prostitutes to Eastern Europe. He said he'd pay the women each ten thousand dollars to go with him. Your wife had ten thousand American dollars hidden in her floorboards. I think she planned to be one of them."

"She had ten thousand bucks?" Yaworsky said. "But from where? I never sent her that much. Besides, Yoani would never have prostituted herself."

But even as Yaworsky said it, Ramirez knew he wasn't sure. Life wasn't easy in Cuba. She might have.

"She may have just wanted to get out of Cuba," Ramirez said. "She may have believed she'd get to the U.S. once she was off the island. And find you."

Slava paced around the room, absentmindedly fingering his bruised chest. "Once Colombians have submarine, they can easily run women *and* drugs to Eastern Europe. Is very good way to launder money."

"You said Petrov was killed on the weekend?" Yaworsky asked. "Then whoever killed him probably took over his role in the transaction. Where is the submarine now?"

Ramirez shook his head. "No idea. I heard the women were going to be leaving early this morning. If we're right, it could already be inside the twelve-mile limit now, on its way to pick them up."

Yaworsky exhaled. "That has to be what the Captain was working on. An off-book special op. Something the government wanted to be able to deny if it didn't work out. If he could surreptitiously arrange to get a Russian submarine inside Cuban waters, he could blow the whistle on it himself. Leak it to the press. Tell them the Russians had sent a submarine to Cuba. The American military would go ballistic, not to mention the public. It would be a whole new Cuban missile crisis. And what could Vladimir Putin say when he found out? That one of his subs had been stolen? That the Russian Navy has lost control of its shipyards?"

He paced around the room, rubbing his hands together. "Even better, it would let the Captain link Cuba to the cocaine trade. And Cuba wouldn't even know the submarine was here; it doesn't have any kind of antisubmarine detection program. The U.S. could sit back and let the shit hit the fan. You think about it, it's brilliant."

"What about the hit on Petrov?" Ramirez said. "Could the Captain have been behind that too?"

"I could see him ordering it, if he thought Petrov was getting in the way. And we know that the Captain is running someone here. The guy who was supposed to take out Raúl Castro could have killed him." Yaworsky looked at Slava Kadun. "It wasn't you, was it?"

"Not me."

"I thought so," Yaworsky said. "It didn't make sense. I took pictures that night. I was looking through them before you two showed up. I couldn't see who you went for on the stage; my view was blocked. But it wasn't Raúl Castro."

"You see?" Slava said to Ramirez. "He knows it wasn't me. Smart fucking guy."

"I think that was supposed to be a diversion," said Ramirez. "Something to get everyone at the trade fair. I found this hidden in Petrov's hotel room." He handed Yaworsky the computer printout. "Slava says these look like coordinates for submarine movements, but we don't know how to interpret them. They might tell us where the submarine is going to surface."

Yaworsky looked at the paper and frowned. "I could call someone inside the CIA and ask, but then they'll know about the sub for sure. I'm not sure we want that information getting out, if there's any chance of stopping this."

Slava spoke up. "Is better if I make call to Russia. But I need secure line."

Ramirez handed him his cell phone. "You can use this. It's encrypted; it can't be easily traced."

Slava stepped into the corridor and dialed the long-distance number, hoping that despite the nine-hour time change, Dmitri Nabakoff would still be at work.

"Dmitri, my friend," he said as soon as he heard Dmitri's voice. "What the fuck have you done?"

"We have to think about the implications of this," Yaworsky said, as soon as Slava stepped out. "If a Russian submarine is heading inside Cuban waters, it must have permission from someone in the Cuban government. There's no way they'd take a chance on being detected and maybe getting blown out of the water. Which means someone very high up has told the Coast Guard to leave them alone."

"Like General Ochoa did before, with the Colombians," Ramirez said.

"Yes," Yaworsky said. "But when General Ochoa got caught, there was a whole fleet of ships and planes moving drugs, protected by the ministry's special troops unit. I think he was a scapegoat; that kind of thing goes well beyond any one general. I've seen recent CIA intel that says Colombian cocaine gets flown onto the base in Varadero and escorted out of Cuban waters by the Cuban Coast Guard. Castro used to step in to settle drug disputes, like the one between General Noriega and Colombian drug lords over a cocaine processing plant in Panama. Noriega's men raided it after they got a tip from the American DEA. The Colombians had paid Noriega five million dollars for protection; they wanted their money back as well as the helicopter seized in the raid. Castro worked it out, but I'm sure he took a cut. Now that he's sick, maybe someone else has stepped into the vacuum."

"I can't believe Fidel would get involved in drug trafficking," said Ramirez. "It runs against everything he says about drugs."

Yaworsky shrugged. "I believe he doesn't want Cubans using them, but I don't think he's above closing his eyes as long as Cuba gets a cut of the profits when they're sold in a capitalist country. Besides, Cuba needs the money."

"Here's what I don't understand," said Ramirez. "If the Captain is behind this transaction, why would he take a chance on dealing with the Russian Navy? They could expose all of this."

"Well, the CIA works with the Russians sometimes; they just don't advertise it. There's a new Russian smuggling ring that connects the Russian military directly to organized crime as well as to the diplomats they need to handle the paperwork. They've been shipping weapons to FARC in exchange for cocaine; some of the cargo planes fly out of Ukraine. With the Cold War over, Russia has a surplus of submarines in dry dock. They've been trying to sell them, along with rocket launchers and missiles, to FARC guerrillas."

FARC had a new way to move *yeyo*, Nassara had said. "Then that's who the buyer has to be," said Ramirez. "FARC. They're going to pay for the submarine with cocaine."

"Then we can expect them to bring the drugs onshore to make the trade and pick up the women. The question is where they'll show up. And when."

Ramirez nodded. "We don't have much time."

55

"You came to Havana last weekend," Slava said to Dmitri in Russian. "You used my fucking name on your fake passport. I saw the watch on Cheetah's wrist—I know he was transmitting information to you. There's a stolen Russian submarine on its way to Cuba. People's lives are at risk. What the fuck are you up to? Tell me the truth. Why did you kill Cheetah?"

A lengthy pause while Dmitri considered his options.

"All right, Slava," Dmitri said. "I went to Havana, okay? And yes, I used your name, but that was only so I would have an alibi if the submarine deal fell apart. That way, we could both prove we were in Russia when things went down and blame things on an imposter. I wanted both of us protected if anyone found out. The whole thing was Cheetah's idea. But I didn't kill him, I swear. Why would I kill him? We were partners."

And then he told Slava what happened.

"It was a fucking brilliant idea," Cheetah had said, when he got out of prison and met with Dmitri. The two were in an alley in downtown Moscow, in the shadows. Cheetah was picking up the papers to change his identity from Fedov Petrov to Ruslan Dudayev. "Fucking genius. The Colombian drug smugglers already use semisubmersible submarines to move their drugs. They're better than fastboats, because they swim under the surface, so it's harder for the American Coast Guard to find them. But the problem is that if they get detected, they're not fast enough to get away. I was going to sell them a Russian sub and solve that problem."

"You're crazy," Dmitri laughed. "Where were you going to get one?"

"The Northern Fleet has lots of old submarines. They're laid up at shipyards at Gremikha and Severodvinsk and Zapadnaya Litsa and Murmansk. Almost a hundred have been decommissioned. The navy is supposed to take them apart and sell the metal for scrap, but it's expensive, and they don't have anywhere to put the nuclear waste. The Colombians will pay millions of dollars to get their hands on just one, so it's a very nice solution. Better yet, the Colombians know that if the Americans see a Russian submarine in Central American waters, they won't chase it; they'll assume Russia is carrying on operations in those waters."

"So, this wasn't just another scam?"

"Are you kidding?" said Cheetah. " I would do it again if I could."

Dmitri leaned against the wall and lit a cigarette. "How?"

"It's not difficult," Cheetah shrugged. "The submarines belong to the Russian Navy. They get transferred to shipyards run by the Ministry of Industry for dismantling. The shipyards are supposed to get paid a share of the proceeds from the scrap metal they sell and the navy gets the rest. The supreme commander of the Northern

Fleet doesn't like that arrangement. The shipyards don't have enough trained people to do the work; they manage to take apart only maybe one submarine each year. So, he loses money, when he is required by law to make a profit. All I have to do is find a high-level contact in the military, and offer to take care of his problem. I can get him more money for a working submarine than he will ever get from the scrap metal, and he won't have to pay the shipyards shit."

"Who's going to sail it down to the Colombians?"

"That part's easy. Whenever the navy lays up a submarine, they only need one-third of the crew, so there are lots of submarine guys sitting around with nothing to do. No problem to find a crew willing to take a submarine to Central America if you give them enough money."

Dmitri chuckled. "You're going to bribe the supreme commander of the Northern Fleet?"

Cheetah shrugged. "Sure, why not? He pees standing up like the rest of us. Besides, you can only reap what you risk."

"How would you get the submarine out of the shipyard?"

"No problem. We create a corporation that exists only on paper. The company submits a bid to decommission a submarine for less than the shipyard would charge. We bribe the right people, our bid is accepted. We pay off the shipyard, so they're happy; we pay off the supreme commander, he's happy. We even put in a nice mission statement in our paperwork about industrial cooperation between the Russian Navy and private entrepreneurs, so the government is happy too. The only problem is coming up with the money. The Colombians don't like to pay for things up front; they want to see their product first. Last time, all I could get was the fucking deposit, and then I got busted. But that doesn't mean it's not a brilliant fucking idea. Maybe we can even take it a step further: use the submarine to bring Colombian cocaine back to Russia. If I had a fucking submarine I would fill it up with anything I could think of that would make money. Even women."

"What normally happens to the radioactive waste from the de-commissioned submarines?" Dmitri asked.

"The tritium and polonium-210? They are supposed to drain it and send it to Murmansk. But half of it ends up in the fucking Kara Sea, along with the reactors."

"You get me some of that polonium-210," Dmitri said, tossing his cigarette butt on the ground, "and I'll get you your money."

"So what was going to happen?" Slava said. "The Colombians were going to fill the submarine with drugs and women and take it to Russia? That was the plan?"

"Something like that. Once the sub got to Russia, they could sell the product anywhere in Eastern Europe. It's a big market."

"You greedy fucking idiot. Cheetah got a guy in the CIA involved in the transaction. That guy on that tape. The Captain. Maybe Cheetah wanted to protect himself this time, make sure the DEA wasn't going to bust him. The CIA has its own agenda. You walked right into a fucking trap. You need to get hold of the submarine captain. Tell him to turn the ship around and take it straight back to Russia."

"I can't do that," Dmitri said.

"You have to. Pretty soon, everybody in the world is going to know that a Russian submarine is inside Cuba. What do you think Putin will do to you then? You have to make this whole thing stop. Before you end up in jail, or worse."

"If I tell the commander of the Northern Fleet he won't get his money, he'll have me killed. That's worse than jail."

"That's too bad," said Slava. "But if you don't get that submarine back where it belongs, you're going to start a war between the United States and Russia, maybe Cuba too. How many crew are onboard?"

"Around forty."

"You want to see them blown out of the water? The Cubans

know the submarine is coming. If Castro calls Putin to ask why it's entering Cuban waters without official permission, what will Putin tell him? You think he's going to lie and say he sent it? He's trying to build a good relationship with Castro. He'll tell them it's a rogue captain and to treat it as a threat. They'll blow it up."

There was silence for a moment. "I thought he'd just pretend it was one of ours if it was detected. That he'd like the idea of a Russian submarine doing exercises so close to the United States."

"He might, if the CIA didn't know about it. But because of this guy, the Captain, they do. If it doesn't leave now, the Americans will board it the moment it enters international waters. They'd love to accuse Russia of being involved in transporting drugs as well as women. Can't you see what a fucking mess this is?"

"The crew will never turn around. They know they'll be arrested as soon as they get back to Russia. They'd rather drown."

"Then the Northern Fleet commander will have to send another crew. Or send a second submarine to escort this one. I don't care how you do it. Get that fucking sub out of here."

"Shit," Dmitri said. There was another long pause. "I'm not even sure we have another working submarine that would make it all the way there and back—they all have mechanical problems. But Putin has a warship in Central America on manoeuvres right now; maybe we can use that. What about the Colombians? If they find out they didn't get their submarine because of me, they're going to kill me."

"You mean they'll kill *me*; you used my fucking name. We have to fix this, Dmitri, before it gets out of control." Slava thought for a moment. "Maybe we can divert the submarine before the transfer takes place so it never meets up with the Colombians. How do you communicate with the crew?"

"There's a radio frequency. Fedor had the code."

"What kind of code? Where is it?"

"I don't know where he hid it. It's a simple cipher," said Dmitri. "The submarine captain has a copy of a book called *Lourdes*; the frequency is supposed to be the page numbers that are circled in each book. Fedor has another copy. But I don't know where he keeps it."

"We have to find it. Fuck, there's no time. I need to know where the Colombians are going to be waiting. Where is the submarine supposed to surface?"

"Between Punta Gobernadora and Bahía Honda. Near a lighthouse. It's about forty miles west of Havana."

"What time?"

"Two-thirty your time. In the morning."

Slava looked at his watch. He had less than two hours.

56

"Okay," Slava said, as he re-entered Yaworsky's hotel room and closed the door. He told them what he'd learned without mentioning Dmitri's involvement. "We have to divert submarine before it meets Colombians. There is radio channel to communicate with submarine captain. Frequency is encrypted; code is cipher in book that Cheetah had with him. Maybe book is in his hotel room. We need to find it. Quickly."

"What's it called?" said Ramirez.

"*Lourdes.*"

"It's in my office already. I seized it."

"Good," said Slava. He exhaled. "Someone needs to use code to turn submarine away, make it go somewhere else. But once Colombians realize submarine is not coming, they will be very angry. Maybe hurt women. Maybe kill them."

Ramirez was worried now that Maria might be one of the women, and he knew how devastated Apiro would be if anything happened to her.

"The Cuban Coast Guard can arrest them all before they find out," he said. "I'll call General de Soto and tell him what's going on. He and the Revolutionary Palace can work out where to send the submarine. This is way, way over our heads, Slava."

"There's a problem with getting your superiors involved, Ramirez," said Yaworsky. "We don't know who inside the Cuban government is involved in this, but whoever it is, they're working with the CIA as well as the Russians. If General de Soto talks to the wrong person, the Colombians could be long gone, along with the sub, and maybe the women, too."

Slava shook his head. "Danila is right. Colombian guys are not going to let Coast Guard just take boat without a fight. There will be big shootout. Same thing if police show up. We can take the Colombians ourselves, no problem. All we need is little bit weapons. Assault guns. Rifles. Grenades. Stun guns."

"But we don't have anything like that; we'd have to call in the army." Ramirez looked at Slava. "What are you suggesting? That we can take down a team of FARC guerrillas by ourselves? Are you crazy? That's suicidal."

"Will be four-man crew, I think. One fastboat to bring in drugs, escort women back to submarine. Don't worry, I used to train FARC guerrillas in training camps; those guys rely too much on machine guns. Machine guns only work well at close range. If is only four guys, we can do this." Slava shrugged. "Five, little bit harder, but still not too bad. If we don't have weapons, we can make some. I need soda bottles, tinfoil, coffee, flour. You got toilet bowl cleaner?"

"You have got to be kidding," Yaworsky said. "What are you, some kind of MacGyver?"

"I don't know what MacGyver is," Slava said. "But if you have way to siphon gasoline from car, I can make pretty good bomb. You get military involved, people will get caught in crossfire."

Ramirez found himself slowly nodding. He would never be able to look Hector Apiro in the eye again. How would he react if it was

Francesca whose life was in danger? He made his decision, but he was scared.

"I can get some of those things at police headquarters. I have a half-full gas can in the trunk of my car. But before we go anywhere, I have to call General de Soto. He's my superior officer. I'm not prepared to spend the rest of my life in jail. We can't do this alone."

"We won't be alone. Danila is coming with us. Three men against four is very good odds."

"You want me to go with you?" said Yaworsky. "But I don't even have a weapon. The only place I've ever shot a gun is on the range. And I sucked at it."

"Is no problem," Slava said. "All you have to do is throw a few fucking bottles. Okay, Ramirez. Make call." He looked at his watch. "We waste time talking."

57

"*I thought we were going to* the airport?" one of the women said, when the bus turned west as they left Havana.

"Maybe we're taking a ship to Europe," another said. "What do you think, Maria?"

"Shh . . ." Maria said, holding her finger to her lips. "I'm Yoani, remember? I don't know what to think yet."

The other women chattered excitedly for thirty or forty miles until they entered the province of Artemisia. Then the bus driver pulled onto a dirt road. "I think this is the road to the lighthouse at Governess Tip," Nevara said. "Where are we going?"

The driver parked, then turned around and pointed a small handgun at them. The women stopped talking. Maria's heart plunged.

"Give me your cell phones," the driver said. "All of them."

The women quickly complied.

"Now, get out of the van. Bring your bags. Walk in front of me. We're going to the beach."

Nevara looked at Maria, her eyes wide, her face pale in the moonlight.

The brush was dense; they stumbled over tree roots and stumps and fallen branches, then piles of driftwood and rocks, until they finally emerged onto the shore. Maria slipped her high-heeled shoes off; the stiletto heels were sinking in the sand. "But there's no one here," she said to the driver.

"They're on their way. Now, all of you, sit down and be quiet. If any of you scream, I swear, I'll shoot you."

———

The girls sat in a row on the beach, stunned, huddled together to keep themselves warm. The sand was smooth but damp and cool.

Nevara was shivering, either from the night air or shock, probably both. Maria put her arm around the girl's shoulder and pulled her close. She had no idea if they had hours or only minutes before whatever boat or plane that was going to pick them up arrived, before any chance of escape was gone.

The moon was a hazy glow behind some scattered clouds. Behind them, palm trees rustled in the cool breeze. Maria felt the salty tang of the ocean air on her lips and pressed them together, determined not to cry.

It was dark. The only light was from the moon, and the regular, flashing sweep of the lighthouse, high on the hill behind them.

Nevara wept softly. "Don't worry," Maria whispered. "The lighthouse keeper will see us and call the police. They'll come to rescue us."

But she didn't believe it for a moment. It was more likely the lighthouse keeper had been bribed to look the other way. No one knew where they were. No one was going to find them.

The bus driver flashed a flashlight on and off, then something sliced through the water towards them.

It was a small boat, with its lights off, narrow and cigar-shaped, moving rapidly. When it got within a few hundred feet of shore, the pilot cut its engine, letting the boat drift closer. The bus driver got up and waved the flashlight, signalling where they were. "Be quiet," the driver ordered the women. "If these men hear you crying, believe me, they'll kill you."

———

Two men jumped from the boat into the shallow water and dragged the boat onto the beach. Two others were onboard, each with a short machine gun strapped across his chest. The bus driver waded out to meet them. Maria heard them talking, then saw that both men who had come onshore were holding small machine guns, too.

The two men on the boat began tossing bags, or bundles, wrapped in thick blue plastic to the men on the shore. They were almost as big as the men moving them. They grunted as they lifted them; clearly the bundles were heavy.

"What are they?" Nevera said in a low voice.

"*Yeyo*, I think," Maria whispered back. "They're dropping it off to make room for us."

Maria silently counted seven bundles. She guessed they must weigh at least a hundred pounds each. That meant seven hundred pounds of cocaine, or over three hundred kilograms. She did a quick calculation. The street value would be around eighteen million dollars.

Whatever it was that the Colombians were buying in exchange for all those drugs, that quantity of *yeyo* was worth a lot more than all the girls on the shore put together.

She knew that once they got on that fastboat, they'd never be seen again. It was her worst fear realized—they were going to be sex slaves. But there was no way to fight back. They had only shoes and purses; the men had machine guns.

Maybe we can use rocks, she thought, or driftwood as clubs. But looking at the girls beside her, she knew they'd do what they were told. They wouldn't take a chance on being shot. Neither would she.

What would these men do if they found out she was transgendered? Oh, Hector, she thought and her heart sank even further. What in God's name have I done?

58

Inspector Ramirez raced into the police station, leaving Slava and Ya-worsky in his car. He ran down the stairs to the cafeteria. At this time of night, it was almost completely abandoned, except for the cleaning crew and an Afro-Cuban woman manning the coffee station.

"I need a bag of coffee," he told her. "And some tinfoil."

She looked surprised but handed him a pound of ground coffee, and asked him to sign for it. "We don't have any tinfoil," she said, looking at Ramirez as if he'd lost his mind. "Not for years."

Ramirez hoped Slava could use the foil bag the coffee came in. He strode over to one of the cleaning crew. "Do we have any toilet bowl cleaner?"

The man shook his head. "Only lye."

"I need a bottle. Sign it out in my name; charge it to my unit."

Ramirez grabbed the recycling bin; it was full of glass and plastic bottles. He put the coffee and lye inside and ran up the stairs to

Major Crimes, carrying the supplies. He put the bin down beside his desk, then grabbed the exhibit bag with the cipher book in it and called General de Soto at home.

He heard the general quietly cursing as he answered the phone. "It's late, Ramirez," the general whispered. "My wife is asleep. This had better be important."

"There's a stolen Russian submarine heading for our waters," Ramirez said. "It's on its way to Bahía Honda now, for delivery to the Colombians. We think FARC is dropping off cocaine as payment. There is a group of women with them. They think they're going to Europe to find work, but more likely they're being sold into the European sex trade. We think the submarine is going to take them away."

"A stolen submarine?" the general said. "What the fuck? Are you serious? How do you know this, Ramirez?"

The general listened silently as Ramirez explained. "Who is behind this?" he demanded.

"The Russian who was shot to death on the Malecón on Sunday. His name was Fedor Petrov, but he was posing as Ruslan Dudayev, a Chechen warlord. Petrov did this once before, but he was arrested before the submarine could be delivered to the Colombians. I think whoever shot him may have taken over his role as middleman, but we don't know who he is. All we know is that the submarine is going to surface at two-thirty this morning near the lighthouse at Governess Tip."

"*Coño*," said the general. "If the Americans detect that sub inside our twelve-mile limit, this could turn into another October Crisis."

"I think that was the plan. To be honest, sir, I think this whole thing was all part of a CIA special operation. The man on the CIA tape we heard in the minister's office—the Captain—probably fronted Fedor Petrov the money from CIA funds. I think he planned to wait until the submarine was inside our territorial limits and then expose it to the world. Commander Kadun thinks that the best thing to do is to divert the submarine, so it can't make the rendez-vous. We have the radio code to communicate with the submarine captain. It's in a cipher book called *Lourdes*. I have the book in my hand. There are page numbers circled that give the radio frequency."

"Slava Kadun is with you?" the general exclaimed. "But he tried to kill the acting president! He's supposed to be in the hospital, under armed guard."

"I took him into my custody, General. Officer Pacheco shot the wrong man. Commander Kadun was trying to protect Raúl Castro, not attack him. There was a man onstage who had a detonator. Kadun was trying to stop him from setting off explosives."

"But the room was checked for explosives and there was nothing there. They checked it again after everyone left. Someone had a detonator? Who?"

"He doesn't know. After we get the surveillance tapes from the venue, he can show us. Maybe he was mistaken, but I believe him. Right now, it's the only explanation that makes sense. I think the threat against Raúl Castro was meant to be a diversion, so that this transaction could take place without being noticed. But the submarine is real. We have to deal with it before it becomes a much bigger problem."

"I'll call the Coast Guard. They can board the submarine when it surfaces and arrest the Colombians."

Ramirez hesitated. "If they try, there will almost certainly be a shootout. The women could be caught in the crossfire. We're on our way to the meeting place to check it out. I'll call for backup as soon as we have a better sense of what we're up against."

There was a pause before the general spoke.

"All right. But I'll have to call the minister to tell him what's going on." De Soto swore under his breath. "He'll tell the Castros. They won't be happy. They're already jumpy, after what happened last night."

"They'll be even less happy once they realize that there's no way the Colombians would come inside our waters to do a transfer like this unless they had permission from someone in the government. Someone very high up. It could be like General Ochoa all over again. Except with the CIA pulling the strings this time."

"How the fuck are we supposed to deal with this situation?" de Soto said.

"I'd say, we play the same game," said Ramirez. "Use disinformation. Divert the submarine somewhere else, somewhere safe, where our Coast Guard can board it. Maybe right inside Havana Harbour. Keep the crew there until the Russian government can send an escort to take it back; they have a warship in the area, use that. The acting president can carry on as if he was expecting them the whole time. Let the tourists take pictures of it. Let the foreign journalists onboard to have a good look. Russia and Cuba can both pretend the submarine escorted the warship here. The Americans have no way of proving otherwise without admitting what they've done. They can't fly into our airspace and they can't enter our waters."

"But you said the CIA is involved in this. What if they tell the media the truth?"

"They won't. They can't. Not once they know that we know that they were behind this whole thing. If they don't go along with the deception, Raúl could announce that the CIA collaborated with Colombian drug lords and the Russian mafia to sell cocaine by moving it through Cuba. And that they conspired to steal a Russian submarine to avoid their own surveillance systems. It would be like the Iran-Contra affair all over again. President Bush can't risk it. Now we know they're involved, their options are limited. But we need to get going, sir; we don't have much time. I have the cipher; I'll give you the numbers. Someone has to call that submarine captain and let him know he has no option but to do what we tell him."

"Let me get a pen and some paper." There was a moment's pause. "All right, I'm back. Go ahead."

Ramirez removed the book from the exhibit bag and flipped

through the pages, reading out the circled numbers. "I have to go," he said when he'd finished. "The Colombians are probably at the meeting place already. I'll call you as soon as we get there."

"Try not to get yourself killed, Ramirez," said the general and hung up the phone.

59

It was about forty miles from Havana to Bahía Honda—Deep Bay—
but there was almost no traffic and they made excellent time. Punta
de la Gobernadora—Governess Tip—was about two miles northwest
of the entrance to the bay.

"It's a good choice for a drug drop-off," Ramirez said. "The closest
town is a sleepy little fishing village. The sea is shallow around here,
but it's deeper just west of Bahía Honda. The submarine can wait there
safely while the fastboat unloads its cargo and picks up its passengers."

The coastline was bordered with a dense mangrove forest and a
barrier reef. Bahía Honda was itself easily spotted from the ocean because of a distinctive saddle-shaped hill, a local landmark. Governess Tip had a red-and-white-striped lighthouse that was in service
and would make it even easier to identify the drop spot.

Ramirez turned his small blue car down the dirt road to Governess Tip and caught a glimpse of a white GAZ van hidden in the trees.
It had black consular plates. There appeared to be no one inside.

"That has to be what they used to bring the women here," Ramirez said, as he pulled to a stop.

"You stay in the car. I will take look around," Slava said. "I will be back in couple minutes."

"Be careful."

"Always," Slava grinned.

Slava got out of the car and checked the van first. It was empty. He crept through the dense mangroves, following the sound of the waves until he saw the white-sand beach through the trees. A seven-metre-long fastboat had been pulled into the shallows. A group of women sat huddled together on the sand, some of them sobbing softly.

An armed guard stood over them, holding what looked like an MP5 submachine gun. Two men were standing beside the fastboat.

Instead of looking over their shoulders for police, they were watching the waves, waiting for the submarine to surface.

Yaworsky was right, Slava thought. They had to have permission to be inside Cuban waters; that's why they weren't expecting any kind of trouble. They were bold enough to pull into an area with an active lighthouse, a military installation. He couldn't see if the men beside the fastboat were armed, but had to assume that they were.

On the sand between the boat and the women were seven large blue bundles. Another Colombian with an MP5 stood guard beside them. Cocaine, thought Slava.

Four Colombians. Seven civilians. No sign of the van driver. That worried him.

He turned and ran silently through the woods back to where Ramirez and Yaworsky were waiting beside Ramirez's small blue car.

"They're there, on the beach," he said, and described what he'd seen. "Okay. Here is what we're going to do."

He removed the recycling bin from Ramirez's car and opened the foil bag of coffee. "Where is flour?" he asked, looking through the bin.

"The coffee is full of it," Ramirez said.

Slava poured the coffee into a two-litre plastic bottle and capped it. He tore the foil bag into strips. Then he twisted the top off the bottle of lye and divided it evenly between four of the glass bottles. He pulled some packets of sugar out of his pockets, looked at them, and put them back. "You got extra handcuffs?" he said to Ramirez.

Ramirez nodded. He reached inside the glove compartment of his car and handed a half dozen of the plastic strips to Slava, who slid them into his pocket.

"Everybody got lighter or matches?"

Yaworsky and Ramirez nodded.

"Okay, Inspector, you take three of these glass bottles. Go straight into woods over there." Slava pointed through the trees. He handed Ramirez a few strips of the foil. "Keep to your right. When you see beach, roll pieces of tinfoil into little balls. Put a few inside first bottle, screw on cap, shake bottle hard and lay bottle on ground. Then get out of way fast. You have got three, maybe five, minutes before bottle explodes; there will be shrapnel flying, so don't hang around. Do same thing with second bottle, maybe put it fifteen metres east of first one, closer to boat. Then third one as close as you can get to Colombians. Then run like a crazy man; you will need to get out of way of blasts."

"What do you want me to do?" Yaworsky asked, his hands trembling.

"Most guys can throw baseball at least one hundred metres, so you should be able to throw Molotov cocktail almost as far. Assault rifles and machine guns lose accuracy at same distance. At close range, submachine gun is lethal. At thirty metres, is like little girl throwing fastball. You and Ramirez are going to lead women into forest as soon as bombs go off; I want you to throw these behind you at guys with machine guns so they will stay far back."

Slava poured gasoline into three other glass bottles. He pulled off his shirt and tore it into strips. He stuffed a strip inside each bottle, leaving part of it outside as a wick.

"Light end before you throw it," Slava said. "Be careful. When it hits rock, it will explode; don't be too close when that happens. While you are doing that, I am going to disable boat."

"Before we go in, I'm calling for backup," said Ramirez. He pulled his cell phone out of his pocket.

"Go ahead," said Slava. He grinned. "But by time cops arrive, believe me, it will be all over."

***

They split up and made their way through the woods towards the beach as Slava had instructed. Ramirez's heartbeat thumped in his ears. He had never faced men armed with machine guns before. He had never used his gun once in his career.

He hadn't even called Francesca to tell her he'd be late coming home. If he didn't die in a shootout, she'd kill him herself.

He heard ocean waves pounding the rocks. He peered through the mangroves. A group of women were sitting in a row on the beach; he could hear some of them crying. Even seated, Maria was taller than the others; her blond hair gleamed in the moonlight. She was towards the end of the row, closer to the trees and scrub where he was hidden, her arm around the shoulders of the woman leaning against her.

A Colombian stood close behind them, holding a small submachine gun, facing the ocean.

A fastboat was pulled up onshore. Seven blue bales the size of garbage cans were lined up in two rows. Another Colombian stood guard beside those, his MP5 slung over his shoulder. There were two other men standing beside the boat, their backs to the woods, also watching the waves. Yet, as Slava had reported, there was no sign of the van driver, and that worried Ramirez. Where was he?

As soon as Ramirez was about a hundred and twenty yards away from the two Colombians who had stayed with the fastboat, he put his three bottles down on the ground. Trying to stop his hands from shaking, he rolled the tinfoil strips into balls and attempted to insert a few in the first bottle but dropped them. "*Coño*," he said under his breath, running his fingers along the ground until he found them. He inserted them into the bottle, then screwed the cap on tightly and shook it. He placed it carefully on the forest floor, then ran as quickly as he could about fifty feet to the east, where he did the same with the second bottle, then the third.

He pulled out his gun as he moved between the trees, putting as much distance as he could between himself and the bottles, trying to control his breathing, frightened of being seen, terrified the bombs might blow up too soon and maim him.

But it was exactly as Slava said: another minute or more passed and nothing happened at all. Ramirez began to worry he'd done it wrong.

Then the first bottle exploded. In the stillness of the night it was as shocking as if a rocket had suddenly gone off.

"What the fuck was that?" one of the Colombians shouted. He ran towards the forest, spraying bullets from his MP5, but there was nothing there, only a curl of smoke drifting through the mangrove trees. A second Colombian ran up beside him. The first man turned around and signalled to the men aboard the boat by shrugging his shoulders, dumbfounded.

The second bottle exploded, practically at the first man's feet. It sprayed him with glass shards and burning liquid. He dropped his MP5 and threw his hands over his face, screaming.

"Where is he?" the second man yelled. "Come out, you crazy fuck!" He waved his machine gun wildly left and right, trying to see their attacker in the dark, firing wildly into the trees until he'd emptied his entire magazine. But he was shooting at shadows.

In the confusion, Ramirez called out to Maria from the woods. "Maria! It's Ricardo! Get the girls. Follow me." As the women ran towards Ramirez, Yaworsky lit the Molotov cocktail and threw it as far as he could. It flew over the women's heads and exploded in a fire-ball on the rocks in front of the Colombians, pinning them where they were. "Take that, you fucking bastards," Yaworsky said under his breath. "You killed my wife." Then he ran.

With the Colombians' attention on the area where the bombs had gone off, Slava sprinted out of the woods and across the beach. He dove behind a large piece of driftwood and dropped the bottle of coffee and his lighter on the sand. He grabbed the packets of sugar and one of his bottle bombs, then ran into the waves and waded up to the fastboat. He found the boat's fuel tank cover, quickly un-screwed it, and poured in the packets of sugar. Then he tossed his bottle bomb into the boat and crouched low in the water, cursing silently at the ache in his chest. Don't give up on me now, heart, he thought. I need you a while longer.

The man with the empty machine gun picked up the MP5 his injured friend had dropped. He was bending over his friend, asking if he was all right, when Ramirez's third bomb blew up, driving glass splinters into his face and chest. He screamed and dropped to the ground as if hit by a truck.

Slava took a deep breath, wincing at the pain, and ran back to the driftwood, where he retrieved the bottle of coffee and his lighter. He jogged towards the bundles of cocaine, knowing that the Co-lombians couldn't see him in the dark, their retinas seared with the white light of the explosions.

He rolled behind the bundles of cocaine and flattened himself on the ground. Then he unscrewed the top from the bottle and sprayed its contents in the air as if lobbing a grenade and simultane-ously flicked his lighter.

The stream of coffee and flour ignited, creating a seven-foot-long flame-thrower—within seconds, the first bundle of cocaine caught fire.

The two uninjured Colombians whirled around, gape-mouthed, as eighteen million dollars' worth of cocaine went up in flames. Slava crouched down and ran back to the water. A stabbing pain ran from his right arm to his chest. He lowered himself into the waves and waited, opening and closing his right hand, trying to get blood flowing from his damaged heart.

One Colombian ran towards the burning cocaine, waving his arms as if about to put the fire out with his hands, but he was driven back by the heat. "I'll get the extinguisher!" he shouted, and headed for the boat. The fourth soda bottle bomb exploded almost the second he was onboard. The impact knocked him flat.

Slava pulled himself up over the stern and kicked the Colombian viciously in the head. He dragged the man to the starboard side and pushed him over. Then he let himself down again into the waves, willing his body to cooperate.

The other man ran over to the fastboat. "Pedro? Where the fuck are you?" He clambered into the boat and turned on the ignition, but the engine stuttered and died. "Fuck!"

Slava climbed onboard again silently. He came up behind the Colombian and tapped him on the shoulder. When the man turned around, Slava punched him, hard.

The Colombian collapsed like a felled tree. Slava grabbed the man's MP5 and set it for single bursts, then positioned himself in the fastboat, one leg bent, using his knee to stabilize his shooting arm. He fired at the two men who'd been wounded by Ramirez's bottle bombs. He heard one of them grunt as he hit his target.

"Okay, okay, we surrender," the other man screamed in Spanish, or at least that's what Slava assumed he was screaming. The man tossed his MP5 on the ground, putting his hands in the air.

Slava walked towards him, finger on the trigger, sweeping the trees and the ground with the MP5, making sure no one else was behind or beside him, and kicked the man's weapon out of the way. Then one by one, he cuffed all of them, leaving the two unconscious men lying helplessly on the beach as he half-dragged the two Colombians who could still walk through the trees and back to the GAZ van.

Eight women were standing beside the van with Ramirez and Yaworsky.

"Are you all right?" Ramirez said.

"Water was little bit warm," Slava said, shaking the sand out of his clothes. "Very nice beach. There are two other guys enjoying it now. Probably both need doctor." He looked at the women carefully until he identified the extra one. "Ah, I see you found van driver," he said to Ramirez, and pointed to the receptionist from the Russian embassy.

She burst into tears. "It wasn't my idea—it was Anatoly's. He said we couldn't be arrested because we work for the embassy. He said we have diplomatic immunity."

"You think so?" Slava said to her in Russian. "Wait and see what I do to you when you get back to Russia. You still have the keys? Give them to me. Now."

She nodded, still sobbing, and handed them over.

"I will be happy to drive these beautiful women to police station to give statements, Inspector Ramirez," Slava said. He smiled at them and kissed the back of each one's hand, even the receptionist's, as he helped them climb into the van. Then he dropped slowly to his knees and put his left hand on his chest. "But first, maybe you better call little doctor."

Ramirez rushed over to check Slava's pulse; his heartbeat was shallow and reedy and his skin was white and damp. "Don't you dare move again," he ordered the Russian as he opened his cell phone and called the night dispatcher.

"It's Inspector Ramirez. I called for backup eight or nine minutes ago. I don't need them anymore, but I need an ambulance. Right away. I have a man down. We're at Governess Tip, just off the road to the lighthouse. I have four men in custody." He looked at the Russian receptionist. "And one woman." He glanced at Slava again, and then at the bleeding and battered Colombians. "On second thought, you'd better send two ambulances."

As he snapped the cell phone off, far in the distance he heard the whoop of sirens.

60

General de Soto was waiting in Inspector Ramirez's office in the Major Crimes Unit when Ramirez got back from the hospital. He stood looking out the cracked windows at the empty streets. The building was almost deserted; it was just after three in the morning.

The general was wearing shorts and a rumpled T-shirt. De Soto's wife was right, thought Ramirez—his bare legs did lack authority.

"How is Commander Kadun?" de Soto asked.

"He's going to be fine. His heart rate is back to normal now. He insists on returning to Russia on the next flight. Dr. Apiro recommends it; he says a long flight is the only way to get Slava to stay in one spot long enough to heal."

The general smiled. "Okay. Well, the good news is that the submarine has been diverted to Havana Bay. When it surfaces, a Pauk will be waiting. They don't expect any problems."

Ramirez imagined they wouldn't. The Pauk was a class of

Soviet-built corvettes with two antisubmarine rocket launchers as well as torpedoes.

"The minister has been on the phone with the Kremlin for the last hour, working out a deal," de Soto continued. "The Russians have three navy vessels heading for Venezuela to participate in joint exercises. The destroyer *Admiral Chabanenko* is one; *Peter the Great*, a nuclear-powered cruiser, is another. They plan to announce this morning that their warships will visit Cuba for a five-day visit in early December. They'll say they're coming to develop friendly working relations between our countries. When they leave, they'll take the stolen submarine with them. And, as you suggested, Cubans will be allowed to tour the boats while they're in our harbour. It will give the media a nice photo opportunity."

"What about the Americans? How have they reacted to all of this?"

"Major Diaz has already been in touch with his counterparts. The American State Department will issue a press statement later today saying that they don't consider the manoeuvres to be a threat but will monitor the situation. By the way, Natasha Delgado dropped off the surveillance tapes from the trade fair for you. She said there's nothing on them."

General de Soto pointed to a stack of videotapes on Ramirez's desk. "I played them while I was waiting for you. She's right. They're blank. It's as if they've been wiped clean. Major Diaz is going to conduct an investigation. I'm hoping they just wore out." He shook his head. "The last thing we need after all this is another conspiracy. But the good news for Commander Kadun is it means we have no evidence to lay any charges against him."

"That's good. The only thing that bothers me is that we won't be able to lay charges against Anatoly Klopov for murdering that flight crew and Fedor Petrov because of diplomatic immunity."

De Soto scowled. "You think he's responsible?"

"I'm not sure who else it could be," said Ramirez. "We know he took over Fedor Petrov's role as middleman in the submarine transaction. If he gave Yoani Ravela the money we found in her room, he might have discovered later that she was part of a flight crew that had flown with El Comandante. He could have been afraid she'd let something slip that would find its way back to Castro."

De Soto nodded slowly. "I suppose we'll never know. There's no way to search a diplomatic embassy because of their fucking immunity. But it makes sense. I think you can close those files. One other thing, Ramirez. You'd better call your wife; she's phoned several times since I got here. She's worried to death. I hope that, next time, we can deal with international intrigue during working hours. My wife isn't happy with me being here either. She says we need to go to counselling, because one of us is an inconsiderate prick."

The general laughed and clapped Ramirez on the shoulder. "I'd better get home. I hate those fucking counsellors."

After he was gone, Ramirez called Francesca and told her what had happened.

"Oh, my God, Ricardo. Are you all right?"

"I'm fine. But tired. I'll be home a little later. First, I have to get hold of Hector and let him know that Maria is safe. She's here at the police station, giving a witness statement. And I have to head back to the hospital to accompany Slava Kadun to the airport. He's catching a flight back to Russia in a few hours."

61

The sun was coming up as the ambulance pulled to the curb in front of the terminal building. When Ramirez stepped out of the rear doors, the attendants jumped down themselves. "We'll go find a wheelchair," one of them said. But Slava clambered out before they could find one. "I'm fine," he said, and reached for his duffel bag.

"You should be in a wheelchair. Doctor's orders," one of the paramedics protested.

"I don't think Commander Kadun takes orders from anyone," Ramirez said. "I'll make sure he gets onboard in one piece." He turned to Slava. "If you want to walk in there on your own two feet, then I'm carrying this." He picked up the duffel bag. Slava shrugged as Ramirez swung it over his shoulder. "What's in this, rocks?"

"Good guess," Slava said, but he let Ramirez handle the bag.

"Well, Hector wants you to relax, if that's possible for someone like you. At least check this as baggage, will you?"

"Don't worry. I am going on little bit vacation." He grinned. "Has been very interesting visit to Cuba but not much rest."

"My friend Apiro says that calling something 'interesting' can sometimes be a curse."

Slava laughed. "He may be right. I forget to ask, Inspector. What will happen to Fedor's body?"

"I suppose it will be cremated. There's no one here to claim it."

"Then do me big favour," Slava said. "Send ashes to me in Russia. I will take care of things. Every man should be buried properly."

"I can do that for you, Slava."

"One more thing," Slava said, as they reached the ticket counter and he checked his bag. "Another favour."

"Sure," said Ramirez.

"Tell Dayana I will take her out next time I am in Cuba. Or she can call me if she ever comes to Moscow." He handed Ramirez a folded piece of paper.

Ramirez guessed it had his phone number on it. "Dayana? Who's Dayana?"

Slava smiled. "You know her. Nice girl. Minister of Interior's clerk. Lousy typist."

Ramirez put the folded paper in his pocket. He hadn't even known her name.

"So does that mean you'll be coming back to Havana someday, Slava?"

"You can count on it." Slava grinned as they shook hands, and he walked away, his shoulders square, his back tall.

Ramirez saw him stop to chat with a female flight attendant on the way to the departure gate, then bend to kiss her hand.

62

When Slava got back to Russia after his stop in Haifa, the first thing he did was head to Nikolai Patrushev's office.

"I'm sorry to tell you this, but Dmitri's been arrested," Patrushev said, looking up from his desk. "The commander of the Northern Fleet has accused him of trying to bribe him to sell a decommissioned submarine to the Colombians to move drugs. He claims Dmitri conspired with a number of former navy personnel to steal the submarine from dry dock. Dmitri's being held in prison pending charges."

"Where is he?"

"In Prison YaG-14/10."

Slava nodded slowly as he finally put all the pieces together.

"It was a fucking brilliant idea," Cheetah had told Dmitri, to steal a submarine from the Russians and sell it to the Colombians. Everything that happened after that, Slava now realized, was a setup. He was surprised Patrushev was able to keep a straight face; after all, he and Putin were likely behind all of this, all the paperwork, all the lies.

Dmitri had told Slava he couldn't go to Havana. He'd said Putin wanted him to spy on the oligarch Mikhail Khodorkovsky in the labour camp where Khodorkovsky was serving time.

Prison YaG-14/10.

"I think I've worked something out," Dmitri had told Slava, before Slava left Moscow for Havana. "All I have to do now is figure out how to get arrested."

Now Slava knew what achieving that arrest had involved.

Slava sat across from Dmitri. His friend was wearing prison overalls, but didn't seem terribly unhappy about his circumstances. "It took you fucking long enough to get here, Slava."

"I had to stop in Haifa. Family business."

Slava had rented a car and driven to his grandmother's grave, removed the carved headstone from his duffel bag, and placed it on the ground.

It had been sixty-three years since Josef Mengele killed eleven female dwarves in Auschwitz; December 7 was the anniversary. It was Slava's annual pilgrimage, his personal memorial to the woman who gave birth to his normal-sized father and gave Slava a lifelong appreciation for small women with bright red lipstick.

"I'm fitting in," Dmitri said, and shrugged. "The language is the hardest thing to master, but I think I've got it down now. You know the code of conduct. You can't say *svidetel*—witness—it has to be *ochevidetz*—beholder—or someone will beat the shit out of you, maybe even kill you. I discovered that when someone says, 'I have problems in this life,' it means they're homosexual. That was a little awkward," Dmitri laughed. "But I'm adjusting."

"I could have told you things like that. You should have let me know what you had planned instead of hanging noodles on my ears." Instead of duping me.

Slava sat back and crossed his arms. "So you have prison tattoos now?" he said, pointing to Dmitri's hands and arms.

"You like them?" Dmitri said. He showed off the cat wearing a hat on the back of his right hand, the symbol for thieves-in-law. But it was the eight-pointed star on Dmitri's neck that caught Slava's attention: It meant Dmitri was now a *vory*. Or at least, as Cheetah had done, was pretending to be one.

"I have two cats," Dmitri said, and pointed to his forearm. One cat meant a criminal acted alone; two meant he had a partner. But both of Dmitri's were cheetahs; they circled his arm like a bracelet.

"If that cat's supposed to be me, I wasn't your partner. I had no fucking idea what you were up to." But Slava knew the second cheetah was meant to be his deceased high school friend.

"It had to be that way," Dmitri said. He leaned over and whispered, "You can't catch a fish without a pond. I told you I had to be arrested. This was the only way I could get in here and have any credibility. The Special Forces officer who stole a Russian submarine and almost started a war with the United States? I'm in the cell next to Mikhail Khodorkovsky. Let me tell you, he's pretty impressed with me."

"So, this whole fucking thing was a setup from the beginning."

"Brilliant, don't you think? I told you Putin wanted me in here."

Slava raised his eyebrows. "I still don't understand why you killed Cheetah. The nine-hour time difference? That had me confused. You were able to kill him, make your arrangements, and be back in Moscow on Monday morning. How did you get the gun into Cuba? By diplomatic pouch? Did Klopov do that for you too?"

"I told you, I didn't kill Cheetah," said Dmitri. "Why would I do that? He was always more useful to us alive than dead. That's why we saved him in the first place." He put his face close to Slava's. "I swear to God I didn't do it."

"You're an atheist."

"Okay, I swear on my mother's grave."

"Your mother's alive."

Dmitri shrugged. "I tell you, I didn't fucking kill him. I'm guessing that CIA guy arranged it so he could knock out the middleman and handle things himself. It's too bad about Cheetah, but his murder wasn't my fault."

Slava pushed himself up from the table. He shook his head. "Be careful, Dmitri. There are some dangerous men in here."

"I know. Don't forget, Slava, I trained half of them." He laughed. "And you trained the other half. Don't worry. I'll be fine."

Slava nodded and smiled slightly. "Do you have enough money to get by? You get in trouble, this can be an expensive place to get out of quickly."

"Don't worry about me," Dmitri said. "I'm stinking rich."

He held his hands out, fingers curled to his palms. On one knuckle was a tattoo of the letter *A* within a circle, to show he was an anarchist.

And on the finger next to it was the American Super Bowl ring.

63

Inspector Ramirez was at work, or at least he was supposed to be. He was sitting behind his desk, staring at a mountain of paperwork. It was perhaps the most complicated investigation he'd ever been involved in, and he'd had to do it alone. No ghosts, no clues, no help. He was exhausted. But he'd found a submarine and freed an innocent man. That was worth something, even if Klopov got away with murder.

His phone rang. It was the switchboard. "I have Detective Ben Ryan from Ottawa on the line, Inspector. He wants to speak to you."

"Sorry it took so long to get you that information, Inspector Ramirez," Ryan said after they'd exchanged greetings. "About William Tattenbaum? There was nothing on CPIC or NCIC, and I couldn't find anything on any of the motor vehicle registries either. In fact, the only reference I could find to a William Tattenbaum and Shakespeare, New Mexico, was on Wikipedia, and that guy died over a hundred years ago."

"Wikipedia? What is that?"

"It's a kind of free encyclopedia that people contribute to. On the Internet. But it can't be him. That William Tattenbaum died in 1881."

"What did it say?" asked Ramirez.

"He claimed he was descended from Russian nobility, so they called him Russian Bill, but he was a con man. He got lynched for rustling cattle. Nothing remotely related to your case. Sorry I couldn't be more help."

"I understand," said Ramirez. "Well, thank you for looking this up for me, Detective Ryan. *Gracias.*"

"Believe me, it's my pleasure. I'm happy to close the file on that piece of shit Fedor Petrov. Pardon my French, but he was a dick."

Ramirez thanked Ryan again and slowly put the phone down. He'd forgotten about William Tattentaum and his American passport. How likely was it that Klopov would use a fake American passport and rent a Cuban car? Not very. And Slava had been adamant that the assassin was at the trade fair, on the stage with Raúl Castro, when he'd jumped onto the platform and knocked him down.

He pulled out Fernando Espinoza's report of the shooting and slowly reread the witness statement of the coco-taxi driver, who'd seen only the sharp-toed boots of the man who'd shot his fare. He thought about Franklin Pearce, his cowboy boots, his Stetson.

Ramirez recalled how open and friendly Pearce was when Ramirez showed up unannounced at his hotel room. How many *turistas* had that kind of confidence in a strange country when a policeman knocked on their door?

He leaned back, lacing his fingers behind his head. Franklin Pearce had been seated onstage when Slava Kadun rushed the platform. "He was sitting on chair," Slava had said. "Older guy with suit." Not Klopov; he wasn't there. But maybe Pearce.

Ramirez recreated the scene in his mind. He'd thought at the

time that Pearce was knocked over because he'd tried to block Slava
Kadun from reaching the acting president, but he could have been
Slava's target.

And Pearce was also on the plane when Fidel Castro took ill.

Maybe Yoani Ravela had seen Pearce do something on that
flight; that could be why she was murdered. That was the flight on
which Castro took sick and almost died. Pearce could have poisoned
him, then killed anyone who might have connected him to the attempted assassination.

But there was no evidence to prove it. It was pure speculation.
And Ramirez had forgotten to show Slava the photographs Yaworsky had taken of Pearce with the Castros.

He cursed silently at that mistake; by the time he could get those
photographs to Slava in Russia for verification, the men who had
been sitting on that stage would be long gone. Assuming the photographs still existed.

The tapes from the trade fair had been wiped clean, and the surveillance cameras from the walk-up on Blanco had conveniently run
out of tape not long after Danila Yaworsky entered the building.

The only people with the power to do that were Cuban Intelligence.

If he was right, it explained everything.

Cuban Intelligence didn't want the public to know anything
about Fidel Castro's illness; they'd made it a state secret. They'd
never lay charges against Franklin Pearce, even if he was responsible,
because the Castros would never admit that the CIA had tried to kill
Fidel once again, this time on his flight to Holguin, and had almost
succeeded.

No, thought Ramirez. They'd wait to deal with Pearce. They'd let
him think he was safe, and meanwhile, they'd use him. They'd feed
him disinformation until he was no longer useful. Then they'd arrange to take him out discreetly, perhaps "disappear" him during one
of his many visits to Cuba.

And the CIA wouldn't be able to do anything about it, because, if they did, they'd have to admit that Franklin Pearce was the umbrella man.

Inspector Ramirez closed his folder and stood up from behind his desk. He made his way down the stairs and walked into the bright yellow haze of sunlight. It was time to go home, but he had somewhere to go first, someone he needed to thank.

He started his small blue car and headed towards the shantytown where he and Natasha Delgado had first interviewed Mama Loa back in March.

The one-bedroom shacks had been built as squatter settlements during the Special Period. Most had dirt floors. Open sewers and hand-rigged pipes were made of wood and scraps of material culled from garbage dumps.

From time to time, fines were levied against them but, essentially, the squatters were ignored. The government was even considering providing *consultorios* to the residents, turning the shanties into permanent residences.

Ramirez found the dilapidated shack that was Mama Loa's, but there was no sign of her outside where she usually sat in the sun, fanning herself. Her rocking chair was empty.

He knocked on the rickety door; it swung open. A young woman stood inside, folding clothes into a neat pile. She was perhaps in her early twenties. Her eyes were red and swollen with tears.

Ramirez recognized her right away; Nevara was one of the women from the beach. She was one of Mama Loa's many goddaughters, girls she took in and provided with shelter, warmth, and love.

"Excuse me, Nevara, I'm looking for Mama Loa," Ramirez said. "Do you know where she is?"

"Mama Loa?" Nevara said. She looked up, her eyes sad. "She's dead. She passed away last week. At least the gods were kind. She died in her sleep. I always thought she would live forever, but she was ninety-four. I guess it was her time."

"What do you mean she died last week? What day?" Ramirez said. "I saw her a few days ago at the trade fair and she was fine." Although she wasn't, he thought. She said she'd lost her appetite, and she looked pale, her skin almost translucent.

"That's not possible," Nevara said. "I found her body almost a week ago. On Sunday morning. They took her to the hospital for an autopsy, but that little man, the doctor who does them, he told me she died in her sleep. Mama Loa was like a mother to me," she said, and pinched the bridge of her nose, trying to stem the tears. "She looked after me. I'll really miss her." She looked at Ramirez and wiped her eyes with her fingers. "That's why I wanted to go to Europe to work. Without her, I have no one left. She was the only family I had."

"I'm very sorry for your loss," Ramirez said. "She was special to me too."

Nevara nodded. "*Gracias*. Yes. She was one of a kind."

Ramirez slowly walked back to his car.

The old woman he'd talked to on Sunday afternoon in the police parking lot was already dead when they'd had their conversation. It wasn't Mama Loa who had waited for him, then, or who had come back to see him later in the week, or who had spoken to him at the trade fair. It was her ghost.

Which meant the gods hadn't taken away his gift after all.

Mama Loa's ghost had been helping him throughout his investigation, he just hadn't known it. And like all the other ghosts who'd haunted him, she'd offered him clues. She'd told him about the submarine—the whale, the beluga.

She'd told him about the *jineteras* who were promised work in another country. She had given him clues to the links between the pilot, the flight attendant, and the purser; she'd even hinted at Fidel Castro's illness. And, as so often happened with the spirits who visited him, he'd misunderstood them all.

"Your grandmother sees the dead," she'd said to him. "She even talks to them." She'd told him again and again of her conversations with his grandmother.

He'd assumed she was a little crazy. He hadn't realized that those conversations with his grandmother could only have taken place if Mama Loa was already dead.

She'd told him she wasn't willing to leave him alone until he got himself sorted out. And now that she was gone, he guessed that meant he was.

Oh, Mama Loa, he thought. The fun she and his grandmother must have had, planning all of this, watching him stumble, nudging him closer towards a realization of how important the ghosts were to him, to who he was.

As he opened the door of his car, he found himself laughing until he cried.

EPILOGUE

Franklin Pearce sat back in his seat. It was a pretty comfortable one, he thought, for a Cuban airline. He was on the charter flight back to New York, then Miami. The back of his chair was adjusted all the way down; he had his Stetson tipped over his eyes.

He'd sold a few cattle, some heifers, a couple of bulls, and he'd closed a nice little deal with the Roman Catholic seminary to inseminate some heifers with his prize Brahman semen. All in all, it was a pretty good trip, despite that bit of nastiness at the trade fair.

But there would be other lucrative business opportunities; he'd be back again soon enough.

When that young man, Nathan Wallace, had shown up at the hotel and handed him the envelope full of photographs, Pearce knew exactly what they meant. But the photographs weren't intended as a threat, the way Wallace had assumed. They were Pearce's instructions, his next set of orders.

The Captain might have originally been a cryptologist, but over the years he'd simplified his codes.

"Tell him we have eyes meant to make sure no one saw you." Eliminate all witnesses.

After Nathan Wallace left the hotel, Pearce followed him to see what he was up to, just to be sure Wallace was on the up-and-up. He was surprised to find Wallace going into the same walk-up that Yoani Ravela lived in, but he knew just how small a world it could be. Stumbling across Ruslan Dudayev at the Hotel Nacional had proven that.

He'd heard the concierge address the guest in the room down the hall as Señor Dudayev.

"Is that *Ruslan* Dudayev?" he'd asked the concierge, when Dudayev was out of earshot.

"Why, yes, Señor," the concierge said. "Do you know him?"

"Old friend," Pearce responded. "But don't tell him I asked if it was him. Let's make it our little surprise."

It was as if he'd run into a WANTED: DEAD OR ALIVE poster in the Old West, except, in this case, the Chechens that Dudayev had double-crossed had put up the reward.

There'd been a Chechen contract out on Dudayev for years, after Dudayev turned in his gang to the Russian FSB in exchange for immunity. He was supposed to have "disappeared," but here he was in Cuba, which meant there was money to be had. Yes, a small world indeed.

Still, Pearce made sure to get the Chechen's passport before he shot him, so he could verify the hit. The guy looked a little different, but it had been a few years; he'd probably had plastic surgery. Maybe that explained why he was in Havana.

It was too bad about the flight attendant, Yoani Ravela, of course, but that couldn't be helped. The Captain was right to be cautious.

She might have seen Pearce jostle Fidel Castro when he squeezed in beside him on the charter flight to Holguin, might have heard Castro swear as he slapped at the nonexistent insect that had stung his ankle, might have mentioned it to the other members of her crew. Pearce killed her quickly, a sharp twist to the neck. He might be close to seventy, but it was still a helluva lot easier than wrestling a calf to the ground.

After he posed the body, he called Major Diaz, who was the only person in Havana with a completely secure line. Funny how no one ever asked who was most likely to benefit if Fidel and Raúl Castro died, but then Cuban politics was a funny business.

The head of Cuban Intelligence had been trained by the CIA. The Captain often joked that Diaz had been undercover for so long, he wasn't sure if he even knew whose side he was on anymore.

"I'm not asking you to bring me Fidel's head," the Captain had said, when he told Pearce to take out Fidel Castro. "You just get me some photographs of the two of you together; we'll know when he stops showing up at public events that we got him."

Major Diaz was happy to take the picture while Pearce posed with Castro onboard the charter flight, the same way Diaz grinned when he snapped the pictures of Pearce riding horseback with the Castros, knowing the photographs would end up with his handlers at the CIA. But then, Diaz was the only person who could legally take the photographs; not even the flight crew could pull that one off.

A picture really is worth a thousand words, thought Pearce, although the addresses Diaz had provided Pearce for each of the crew members had proved even more valuable.

Diaz had made sure the surveillance tape from Blanco was erased, so there was no sign Pearce had ever been there; he did the same thing with the tapes at the trade fair. No one would ever see Pearce reaching for the crown on his watch, about to dispense a little ricin pellet from the air compression chamber in the bronze statue before that goddamn Russian knocked him over and pushed him off the stage.

That statue had been an expensive piece of technology; it probably cost the CIA a million bucks or more to construct. It was completely useless, now that the pellet had been discharged from the tip of the bronze cowboy's boot, just like the one Pearce launched from his real boot into Fidel Castro's leg when he brushed past him on the charter flight. A nice symmetry, Pearce thought, but then the Captain had always had a pretty good sense of humour.

The compression chamber in the statue would never be activated again, but still, it was a nice piece of art. It would probably be sitting in Ramón's dining room, where Pearce could admire it the next time he was invited over to the Castro ranch for dinner.

That Russian had come damn close to catching him, thought Pearce, but thankfully, the Cuban police were always a little trigger-happy. It was going to take a while before his bruises healed, but it wasn't much worse than being thrown off a horse. The million bucks in his bank account would more than make up for the pain.

Still, this kind of business was enough to drive an old man to drink. Pearce sat up and ordered a rum and coke from the flight attendant when she came by. He could relax now. The money was in his suitcase, protected by his special licence. Cash up front. It was always a pleasure doing business with the Cubans.

He smiled at the female passenger sitting beside him. "Where you from?"

"London," she smiled back. "England."

Pearce hadn't been to London since 1978, when he worked his first contract for the former KGB. But he'd enjoyed the city, and he'd always liked the quiet little gun they'd given him as a backup in case the ricin pellet failed. His PSS semiautomatic was tucked away inside a secret compartment inside his luggage, sprayed with a barium compound to block the airport scanners.

"So, what did you think of Havana?" he asked. "First time there?"

"Interesting place," she said, and smiled. "But bloody hot, don't you think?"

Pearce looked at her kindly. "It's not too bad if you have an umbrella."

ACKNOWLEDGEMENTS

I had an unlikely source of inspiration for *Umbrella Man*. My Russian character, Slava, is based on a tradesman who did some work at my house a few years ago. He was a hardwood installer, and a very good one at that. Not only was he a former Special Forces *spetsnaz*, but like the fictional Slava, he'd been a boxer. He was funny, handsome, and charming, and I knew as soon as I met him that he'd end up in one of my books. I hope you enjoy him as much as I did; I just wish I needed new hardwood floors again.

As far-fetched as *Umbrella Man* may seem, shortly after I wrote it, the media reported that the U.S. Coast Guard had intercepted a Colombian submersible submarine loaded up with cocaine. (And for those of you who plan to visit Washington, D.C., the International Spy Museum has a poison-tipped umbrella on display.)

I love the folks at Simon & Schuster Canada, and I'm grateful to Chris Bucci for getting me in the door. I am especially indebted to Kevin Hanson, Brendan May, and Rita Silva, who have been an absolute pleasure to work with. Thanks also to my editor, Alex Schultz, for his keen eye. This is the fourth book we've collaborated on; I couldn't do it without him.

As always, a huge shout-out to my external readers: Bill Schaper, Debbie Hantusch, Lorraine Glendenning, Debbie Levy, and Beth McColl. And thanks also to Alexandra Sanchez, who has become my "go-to" source on all things Cuban (and knows an awful lot about Russia, too). Any remaining errors are mine and mine alone.